The Quality of the Light

A Novel in Five Paintings

Robert Fraser

CRANTHORPE
MILLNER

A CIP catalogue record for this title is available from the British Library.

ISBN 978-1-912964-75-8 (Paperback)

www.cranthorpemillner.com

First Published (2021)

Cranthorpe Millner Publishers

BOOK ONE:

A SCENE FROM TERENCE

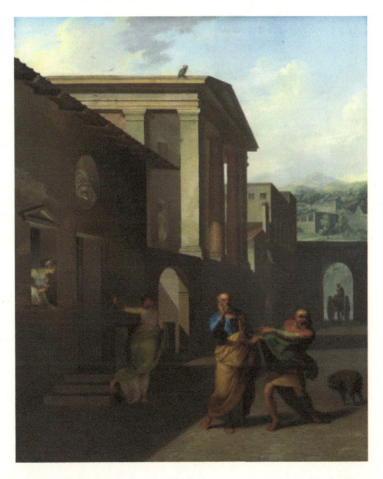

BOOK ONE

"Run now!" yelled the maid. "In God's name, run!"

Once out in the cobbled street, the midwife picked up her skirts and ran, the maid staring from the open window. So little time. Towards her, in the archway at the head of the street, a farm cart clattered. On the roof of the adjacent temple, its ochre walls cut by the late afternoon shade, an owl kept silent vigil. The cicadas droned, the sodden air combed against her, but the midwife dragged on and on. So very little time.

As she approached the temple, she passed two strangers, sauntering. The younger, his hand cupped to his mouth, leaned towards his companion, unctuous, conspiratorial.

"The mother within, sir, seduced by none other than…"

The elder's face cracked wide open, gaping like a gargoyle. At their feet a pariah dog scowled, glowering, mercurial.

From the mantel above the still open window, the obscene face of a god leered from its alcove. On the temple roof, the owl had not moved.

The hours dripped on leadenly towards sundown: *quatuor, quinque*. The dog yawned. In the archway, between the turning wheels, the plebeian still perched behind his horse.

Still the god's face creaked and the hunched midwife struggled to her next appointment, the maid from the window endlessly egging her on, up the narrow street through the cramped arch where the cart still strained, bulging. The strangers continued to grimace. Slowly the light died: *sex, septem*. So little time. In the gateway the cart still lurched onwards down from the olive-clad hill-tops. Still the midwife ran, and the figure before the canvass leaned, leaned and gazed.

I had been watching them both for several minutes.

*****

"Meet me in the Danish Exhibition," he had said. "In the Sunley Room. I shall stand where you can see me quite clearly. You know me by now: the mackintosh, the trilby, same old boots. I'm from the Dark Ages, Benedict," and with that he replaced the receiver. I assumed that he was phoning from a box, though it may have been from the lobby of his hotel.

I was used by now to these sudden summonses, the bleak voice drifting across the telephone wires as if from the Arctic wastes, the halting delivery, and the long draughty silences. It was a form of communication to which 1 had almost accustomed myself, as if to the dialect of a dwindling, though cherished, tribe.

2

There was little seeming pattern to his calls. Sometimes months would pass without a sign or a word. Then maybe a dog-eared postcard from Salford or the Isle of Skye, the conventional coloured view with, on the back, a cryptic message as if in code. Were these messages, I wondered, dangerous? Weeks would go by. There might be another card from somewhere equally distant, though unrelated by any apparent itinerary. Then silence for another age before the pips and the inevitable invitation to the Gallery. Uncle Claud was back in town.

What occurred between these irregular sorties to the city I scarcely dared imagine. The life of a commercial traveller is a long marriage to solitude. It is an immense tangled corridor where one is always an outsider, always the lone man at the single table, spooning food behind the menu and the stainless steel cruet. Sometimes, during one of my occasional estrangements from Andria I too would find myself eating in some empty dining room, and then catching sight of a stranger absorbed behind his paper or else myself sideways in a mirror, and think, "Yes, that is how he must appear, morning after morning, evening after desolate evening, in the drab provinces." The thought would sometimes drive me to such a pitch of sadness that I would lay down my knife and fork and stare into the far distance while my meal grew cold.

But surely, I would think, his passion must in some measure console him? From fragmentary conversations with my father I knew that Claud too had once aspired to be a painter. In the days when the Royal College threw open its door twice a week to talented amateurs he would attend regularly after work, setting out his easel and his paints before life models or collations of flowers and bric-à-brac. I had even seen one of the results, an orthodox still life hanging on the wall of my Aunt Rosie's basement flat alongside her views of Italian cathedrals. There was nothing arresting about the flowers. The china was conventional, the highlights neatly placed, the pages of the book on the table tastefully yellowed and curled. Was it wistfulness that led me to imagine a certain bravura about the colouring, a raffish tilt to the curtains behind, an edginess about the petals that spoke of a spirit trapped in these amateurish constraints and longing to leap out and surprise me?

Yet, whatever his own work may have lacked, he more than made up for in his sensitivity to the work of others. Claud's intense if quirky love of the Masters never ceased to amaze me. And, as once more I stood there in the coldly lit gallery watching his gaunt frame bent in concentration before Abildgaard's *Scene from Terence*, I wondered again at the quality of his concentration.

I do not know at what stage he became conscious of my presence, but after a fragile seeming eternity he addressed me without turning:

"What are they doing I wonder? I've been trying to reconstruct the turn of events."

"Me too."

"Well then, Ben?"

"It's from a play called *The Woman of Andros*. The

4

woman scampering up the street is a midwife. She's just delivered a baby inside the house and is on her way to her next appointment. The parents aren't married, it seems. The child's father just happens to be betrothed to the older man's daughter. The servant to his left has just broken the dreadful news. Hence the old man's displeasure."

"Very good. You're a lot sharper than your old uncle I must say."

"I cheated. I bought the catalogue. Anyway, you can tell it's a play from the way they're gesturing."

His smile had the softness of old parchment. "I knew it had to go something like that," he said. "Somehow one doesn't know if it's quite proper to pry into the murky details. It seems so *impure*. But one cannot help but try."

We'd always begin like that, with the picture. The room might vary, the time, the quality of the light, but never his stance or the intensity of his appreciation. He was a regular man, regular even in his aptitude for extracting pleasure. Perhaps he had never had access to much. Sometimes I thought that it was only in these hallowed and rarefied surroundings, shrouded in paintings like queens, that he ever experienced the keenest joys.

Some might have the impression that my uncle had fallen to the level of his mediocrity. I preferred to believe that he had contrived to combine the best of two worlds. A commercial traveller is one thing, a traveller in fine art quite another. Among the denizens of the road, an attachment to Lawrence Echardt and Sons, Dealers in Reproductions and Fine Prints since 1826, was not I imagined to be disdained. Claud had his own kind of pride, an obstinate loyalty to the firm quite as stalwart in its way as my father's dedication to his more elevated calling. Among the *cognoscenti* of the trade he even, I like to think, passed for something of a connoisseur. To be fair, his tastes were narrow. Though obliged to sell reproductions of all periods, it was to the Dutch school and to the English eighteenth century that he appeared to be especially drawn. For choice he would introduce into his clients' homes a Gainsborough or a Vermeer; he handed over a Turner or a Degas with slight misgiving. He was never an acolyte of the modern school, and a request to carry a Mondrian in his cases would meet, I rather fancy, with a curt refusal. Claud was, if anybody was, a classic.

However did he spend his hours, I used to ask myself, when in London? He was seldom here more than three times a year, when he invariably put up at the same modest guest house in Kilburn. I had never visited him there, nor had he ever invited me. It seemed preposterous that he should retain this degree of isolation when in the vicinity of the family. He would, it is true, visit his firm's offices in the Poultry. And he would usually pay his respects to Rose in her scented den in genteel Maida Vale. But, although I had these irregular courteous invitations to join him among his beloved pictures in the Gallery, between these meetings he was no more apparent than a stoat. I had come to think of him as a kind of bedraggled weasel nibbling through the upper strata of the earth and only occasionally popping out his head for a half hour's social refreshment.

He was a tall man, several inches taller than myself, and, when not bent before a picture, as straight as a drainpipe. He always wore an ancient, soiled Burberry which had seen better days. I had never seen him remove this outer garment, even on the hottest day in July. In its upper left hand pocket could just be seen a neatly ironed pocket handkerchief in the green hunting tartan of our clan, while between its lapels peeped a severely knotted tie in the red of the dress tartan. These two memorials of our family's almost buried past were the only smart aspects of his person. The hat on his head was coming apart at the brim. He carried around with him a slight whiff of old-fashioned shaving soap. His lace-white hands were constantly in movement as if around some imaginary rosary. He had very thin lips which moved slightly in thought, a mop of greying chestnut hair half hidden by the hat, horn-rimmed spectacles, one side of which was secured by Sellotape, and whether as a concession to fashion or out of obliviousness to its passing I could never tell, stout boots double laced. He was, as he often said, a product of the Dark Ages, of what my father would ominously refer to as "before the war".

What the emotional relationship between my uncle and my father was, it would be hard to state. Earlier, before my mother died, they had I think been closer.

There had been family feuds of course - what family is free of them? A quarrel about a gravestone, the proceeds of an estate. On several occasions as a child I remember my father hinting darkly that he had sought Claud out in his London lair, had even tempted him into the saloon bar of a neighbouring pub. There was also, if I am not mistaken, an unusual bond between Claud and my mother. Unusual for, insofar as he indulged in human discourse, Claud was what is customarily referred to as "a man's man". But between my mother and him there was this ephemeral rapport which proceeded beyond Christmas cards and occasional meetings to the infrequent, anxious telephone call. I remember overhearing several of such drowning the music of the wireless as I played round my mother's feet as a toddler. Normally it meant that Claud was in some kind of temporary embarrassment, financial, social, even spiritual. For, as I sincerely believe, in the dusty attic of his heart, Uncle Claud was a truly religious man.

For one in circumstances so reduced he was also given to wild fits of generosity. Many is the time as a young child that I have heard the doorbell ring and my mother answer it to receive a parcel invariably wrapped in dark brown paper and bearing the name "Benedict Henry". When opened it would be found to contain a set of crayons, a sketch pad, even on one memorable occasion my first paint box. To Uncle Claud I must have owed my early interest in water colours. My parents had also felt the benefit of his largesse. Their wedding present had been a set of reproductions of the Dutch masters framed in sombre black wood and hung around the walls of our house in Finchley as reminders of another, gentler age. Many were Rembrandts. As my three year old self dithered with his toys on the immense patterned plain of the Persian carpet, the *Man with the Golden Helmet* looked down in silent reproach. There were also two of the self-portraits, together with a number of domestic interiors by Rembrandt's contemporaries. I especially recall one called *The Music Lesson*. It depicted a lady with her back to me wearing an elegantly waisted bodice of a colour which I would then have called strawberry and playing an instrument which I could not identify. It was in fact a 'cello, or more probably a viola da gamba. Beyond her sat a bonneted matron at the harpsichord while over both stooped the immaculately appointed figure of a flautist, intent on his score. I used to spend hours listening for the notes they were playing. It must be a melody more beautiful, more refined than any I had heard. It was probably a very ordinary trio sonata.

When late in middle age my mother succumbed to a wasting disease, relations with Claud grew cooler. A thin trickle of intercourse was maintained, but more and more it became an affair of little notes scribbled at the base of greeting cards, the very occasional visit. From all of this I was rigorously excluded. For, despite his solicitude for my wellbeing, Claud and I had then never met. The nearest I had ever been permitted to his physical presence was the muffled murmur of voices in the drawing room overhead through the carpeted floor as I lay awake upstairs.

He would never climb up to disturb my imaginings. The painful extremity of his shyness had, by the time I was ten, already won him the status of a legend. As others might say "as timid as a mouse", we would say "as timid as Claud". As far as his living presence was concerned, Uncle Claud led, in my childhood mind, an existence exclusively beneath the floorboards.

Is it any wonder then that as I stood beside him that October morning, I felt obscurely honoured? We are not a clan given to lavish expressions of feeling. Among the Henrys a handshake is treated as an emotional excess, a kiss hardly known. But I will not deny that before the little square of the Abildgaard, with the early lunchtime crowds beginning to mill around us, I felt for my battered, thwarted uncle something very like love.

*****

How shall I explain it to you: the sentimental reluctance of our family? It is something for which more flamboyant members of the species are hardly prepared. Among us there is one inviolable rule: that nothing felt in the passion of the heart should be directly stated. We are not cold-blooded people, but the currents of our feeling flow through seeping, oblique channels. We nudge one another into ardours, steal into fits of anger as others into business contracts, slide imperceptibly into the semblance of a caress. A rap on the table is an orgy of disclosure, the flash of one irascible phrase serves as a conclusive act of revenge.

Not that fervour is foreign to us. Such fastidiousness of self-expression is, if I understand it aright, more usually the product of extreme feeling than its opposite. In our case it was, I always felt, the burden of a contract signalling the peril to which abandonment in the face of implicitly acknowledged feeling might all too easily lead. The channels were clogged with ice, yet they ran deep. During the hours of tense silence that I had been obliged to spend in the company of my father since my mother's decease, the flow of such unspoken passion was as palpable as the tobacco smoke which invariably curled in the air above his armchair. In Claud too, self-containment was I supposed the carapace beneath which seethed sensations of an insistent and sometimes uncomfortable kind. Had I not witnessed him, on one of the few occasions when he condescended to exchange our usual place of meeting for the National Portrait Gallery around the corner, stand entranced before the portrait of Catherine of Braganza, Charles II's devout young bride, where it hung against the blue and white adorning the long gallery on the topmost floor? And had I not from my vantage point near the doorway seen him sink against the matching blue of the seat provided and stare up at those chestnut tresses, those unassuming eyes, those flawless cheeks whose carmine carefully echoed the fading mountain sunset which glowed beyond? Approaching him where he sat enthralled, had I not heard from his lips the simple homage, "Perfect, quite perfect!" To those such as my aunt disposed to view Claud's habitual reticence as a symptom of complacent aridity of heart, I had often had occasion to protest that on the contrary he was, I suspected, the last of the cavaliers.

We talk too glibly of obsessions. If I say that Claud had come to seem to me a man addicted, I do not speak of the cravings which afflict the average mind, but of a devotion to some code of chivalry quite his own.

Not three yards from the portrait of Catherine of Braganza on that earlier afternoon had hung the dissolute likeness of her royal husband in his later years, a cadaverous rake, skin puffy, mouth debauched, tilting his sceptre at a roguish angle while grotesquely displaying his silk-clad legs. Beyond him hung his mistresses: Barbara Palmer, Duchess of Cleveland, Nell Gwyn dressed a shepherdess, Louise-Renée de Kéroualle, Duchess of Portsmouth. To all of these my uncle seemed oblivious, representing as they doubtless did the compromising forces of mere circumstance, of what we in our fixation on historical fact might prefer to call the truth. To truth in this sense of mundane reality my uncle was however perfectly indifferent, contented at such moments with a wisp of a girl in a lace-trimmed dress, her gloves awkwardly twisted in bashful hands, a fragment of melody caught in the wind.

Such dedication to the unsullied sublime had on occasions carried my uncle to absurd and fallacious lengths. On the only other occasion when the Portrait Gallery had supplied our venue, I had rushed up the carpeted stairwell, breathless and a little late, to discover him staring at a small group of panels at the head of the stairs: Henry VIII with three of the wives. Ignoring Katherine Parr and Catherine of Aragon where they hung suspended beneath one another like self-appointed victims, he was apparently reserving his whole attention for Anne Boleyn, before whose pearl-studded bonnet and fur-clad arms he stood transfixed. Did he, I wonder, detect somewhere beneath that pallid forehead, that tight-bridged nose, those cool assessing eyes some figment of innocence lost? Some conviction of vulnerability sufficient to dispel the harsh spectre of Thomas Wyatt's mistress, the six-fingered temptress of popular legend? Or was the mere patina of innocence, the contrived tranquillity of the portraitist's hand, enough? As I stood a little perplexed at his side, I had attempted to give voice to these doubts, but a sharp exhalation of breath had silenced me.

In earlier years there had been times when the temptation to puncture my uncle's dream of feminine calm had grown almost too persistent. Nowadays I was prepared simply to let him be. For, I could not help but think, did not such loyalty to some imagined moral ideal reflect a perverse but undeniable form of honour? However ridiculously such pent-up feelings set my uncle apart from sublunary members of his kind, it at least kept him true - to a mirage of virtue perhaps, a cruelly distanced, but quaintly authentic, refraction of the Good. In his stubborn and intractable way, Claud was a devoted and a tender man.

So it was that afternoon that after a tour of the Danish

paintings my uncle looked at his boots and then said, "I've had a letter from your father."

I said, "I'm afraid I've had several."

"He seems to be enjoying his retirement. He misses your mother dreadfully."

I did not see fit to comment.

"The house must seem rather large for him now. It's an awful pity that they moved."

"Did he say anything else?"

"Not much, but he worries naturally."

"Yes, yes."

"Well, he's fond of you, you know."

My uncle's ability to brush the very end of a nerve was one aspect of his fatal Celtic charm.

*****

So much for the uncle; how then to envisage his nephew standing there, in mixed awe and embarrassment, that bleak October afternoon?

My name, as you will be aware, is Benedict Henry. Henry is a bland enough name, English in resonance, though in fact we are Scottish, descended through the distaff line from the Lovats. That is to say our family is Scottish, though, with the solitary exception of a holiday in Inverness when I was twelve, I have hardly crossed the border. Early in adolescence I was informed by Aunt Rose that, due to some misdemeanour or other at the beginning of the century, our faces would not be welcome in the Highlands. Some amorous escapade, no doubt; we have always veered between phases of asceticism and the most blatant fleshly indulgence. My uncle, you will have inferred, tended towards the austere.

Also we are Catholics. It is as well to get this matter straight at the outset. Scottish Catholics are a hardy and self-conscious breed, as distinct from Protestants as heather is from gorse. Since the time of Mary Queen of Scots, whose portrait hangs above the desk in my father's study, we seem to have been on the run. We now constitute what I suppose would be called a significant minority. I learned to appreciate all of this very early, almost I think before I could speak. My agnostic acquaintance, who vastly outnumber the religious of any persuasion, are not slow to point out that Catholicism is an induced condition. "Give me a child of seven and I will give you a Catholic for life," etc. But once into adulthood it is very difficult to work out what in your make-up is fashioned by education and what by temperament. For me, the matter now seems straightforward: if you are a Catholic, you know it in your bones.

I have not, I might add, been near a church in years. I received my First Communion at the Brompton Oratory at the age of nine, daydreamed my way through six or seven years of Sunday masses, and then ceased religious observance shortly after my sixteenth birthday. It has made little difference: once exposed to those hushed, cool interiors you carry the plainchant and the flickering, hooded lights around with you forever.

Perhaps in reaction against early training many of our family have been drifters: minor poets, third-rate adventurers, professional detritus of every shade of grey. My father was, and is, a lone font of stability. Early in life he was encumbered with the maintenance of an ailing mother; he has continued shouldering various burdens ever since. In his eyes I am the latest of them. For Father is one of nature's infantrymen and carries his pack without flinching. He springs with the purposeful step on one under command, a sort of perennial boy scout. As with the church, I seldom darken his doorstep. Once again, it makes very little odds. His clean, homespun injunctions resound continually inside my head: "Keep to the narrow path, Benedict, and you will seldom stray. Always hitch your wagon to a star." Once you have been scrubbed in spiritual carbolic, it is hard to get clean with anything else.

I wish that I could have continued in deference to his precepts. I wish that I had it within me to be banker, priest, civil servant, or, like him, to adorn the profession of actuary. As it is, I am a freelance artist. I use the term "freelance" reluctantly. It is a word sometimes used to laud the most glorious, freewheeling achievement. Nowadays it more usually means that you are unemployed. Which view I take of myself largely depends on my state of mind at the time. I once overheard Aunty Rose whisper over the teacups: "I rather gather that poor Benedict is finding it difficult to secure a suitable appointment." In sour moods, I find her estimate entirely just.

I live in a two room flat on the outer fringes of North Kensington with my girlfriend Andria whom I met while failing to complete a course in the History of Art at the Slade School. We are, as a mutual friend once said of us, "ideally unsuited". I have no idea whether our arrangement is lasting or even if I want it to be. Nor do I have any idea whether my present condition of life represents a permanent choice. At thirty-one years of age, these matters are usually settled. There is little more desirable in life than mere stability, a condition which for some of us has at times appeared tantalisingly beyond reach.

Sometimes I have flights of fantasy which carry me away with another woman to another city, country, continent, another and invariably more fixed purpose. The practical implementation of these cravings has never amounted to more than the occasional weekend spent at another address, most often alone. Every week or two with an idle eye I look down the 'Situations Vacant' columns of the daily or evening newspaper, hoping that at last my attention wilt alight on the perfect opening, the ideal position, the definite and defining role waiting for me throughout the years of my obstinate vagueness and sullen wavering. As each year passes, I look less concertedly and with less and less real anticipation. When tempted to any drastic step that might change the course of my existence, I invariably defer it, taking refuge in the thought that I am, after all, despite everything, devoted to the art of painting. Sometimes I believe this excuse to be genuine. At others I am even prepared to concede my father's nagging conviction that in me my family's latent fecklessness has once again broken surface. Like them I too am perhaps finally a drifter.

*****

"He worries about you, naturally."

My uncle's voice, lazily insistent, stirred the dull conscience of the afternoon like a dry stick. There had been a silence of some minutes, during which my curiosity as to Claud's intentions forced to remain satisfied with the gentle lapping of his lips. Then he took the folded tartan handkerchief from the pocket of his mackintosh and noisily blew his nose.

"I'm not in London for long this time. Would you give my regards to Rosie?"

I lied: "I so seldom see her now."

"That's very sad. One had hoped … when one sees so little of people one likes to think of them as rubbing along."

We had by now finished with the Danes. Around the Abildgaard there was a little knot of businessmen, crouching, poking their fingers, making guesses of their own. In the cavernous void someone guffawed. A crocodile of schoolchildren dodged past us. Lovers strolled in unison. Somewhere, illicit tobacco smoke curled in the air.

We passed through the Sales Hall out into the great staircase. We stopped amid the brown marble and the potted ferns. My uncle stood underneath the trumpeting statue of Fame. He stared once more at his boots and he said, "Do me a favour, Benedict. Go and see your old dad."

*****

"Did you know that Terence was black?"

"Terence who?"

"Terence the playwright, silly. He had a hard, dusky beauty, so his tutor fell in love with him and sent him to Rome where he started writing plays."

"He'd have done all of that whether he'd been black or green."

"But he'd have done it a different way."

"I really can't see what these tedious biographical details are supposed to do with the quality of someone's work."

"Can't you?"

"Frankly, no. They strike me as exceedingly futile and tedious."

"If it had been Rembrandt you'd have been riveted."

"Andria. Rembrandt was not black."

"How do you know?"

"He painted sixty self-portraits. Don't you think that the fact might have emerged somewhere?"

"Perhaps he was suppressing the information."

"Of what possible use could that have been?"

"The Flemish are very narrow-minded."

"Were. And Rembrandt was Dutch."

"Same thing."

"Isn't."

"Is."

"Andria darling, they are very, very different things."

"Not anymore."

"We were discussing Rembrandt."

"You were discussing Rembrandt."

"Actually I was attempting to paint a portrait of you reading a book."

"Correction. A portrait of me reading a page. I've read this scene five times."

"Well then, turn the page."

"You said I mustn't move."

"You move less when you turn a page than when you yack on at me in this insane, distracting manner."

"I was trying to hold an intelligent conversation."

"And I was trying to paint you."

"You've been trying to paint me for seven years."

"You're a very fugitive beauty."

"Very."

"It doesn't help if you challenge me with your eyes."

"I'm genuinely upset."

"Not upset, Andria. Just bored."

"No, upset. If one persists in being bored one concludes by becoming upset. I am upset."

"That's it. I give up. I resign all remaining responsibility towards this picture."

"Faint-hearted!"

"Andria. It was supposed to be a portrait of a girl reading. Not of a girl upset."

"Well, change it then."

"It is not that simple."

"You only need alter the head."

"Only! Do you have the foggiest notion about the art of portraiture?"

"I'm not a painter."

"You might take an enlightened interest."

"You never display an enlightened interest in what I do."

"What could possibly betray a more dedicated interest than immortalizing you in paint?"

"You just said that you resigned all remaining responsibility."

"Andria. This is the end!"

"Shall we try another separation?"

"We've just tried a separation. It lasted three days. I need your presence, your aura. Besides, you earn more than I do."

"Cupboard love."

"Not love. Not love, Andria. Need."

"You need me like you need a heart attack."

"Andria, we are tied to one another. We agreed on that."

"You agreed on that. I agreed to comply."

"So who sent me a desperate little postcard last week?"

"I did."

"Well then, you're tied too. And people who are tied

keep still. So keep still!"

It was a lank afternoon in early October. Outside all was drab and dullness. There had just been the most almighty rainstorm but this had now cleared leaving the pavements oily with liquid. Round the hearth plates, coffee mugs and stub-filled saucers testified to the drinks and scraps of meals with which we had whiled away the hours. It was three hours since lunch, two before I could decently pour a whisky. There was nothing for it but to work.

Besides I had been offered an exhibition. Or, to be honest, a third share in somebody else's. A one man show had so far eluded my grasp, and might very well always do so. But I had squeaked into this showing by the tuft of a hair, and I was determined that, whatever fits of inertia intermittently assailed me, I would see this thing through. Eleven years previously a lecturer in art history called Jocelyn Enright, once my tutor, had decreed that my *forte* - or should I say my *mezzo piano* - lay in the interpretation of the human form. It brought out, he said, the "cheek" in me, by which I can only suppose he meant a deceitful prying into corners best overlooked, or more simply, scant regard for privacy or pain. I set aside his words then, thinking them the product of a heat-filled brain, but several years later, when my expensively collated collages failed, followed by a disastrous attempt at what, in a fit of affectation, I called my "Green Period", I remembered his words and erected by easel in front of Andria's half-compliant figure.

As a life model, Andria did have her disadvantages. To be frank, she resented the occupation. But then, to be equally frank, she was all that, in default of success, I could afford. There were other considerations. Despite her temperamental unsuitability, she possessed, it had to be admitted, certain plastic potentialities. She was a tall thin girl with knock knees and rather emaciated thighs. In repose or when lying prostrate, she was apt to look simply starved. But then prop her on one elbow, swivel her round, let her hold a vase, and the contortions wrought by the exigencies of the position were capable of wringing from her frame the most unexpected felicities. Hence, her "fugitive beauty".

Often it lasted for less than a minute. Let her drop her arm, scratch her chin, or, most disastrously, burst into speech, and the moment was too easily rent. There was thus in her case the most absolute, the most binding need for stillness, a quality dispensable in other more versatile models, but for her a *sine qua non* of graphic representation. It is not a condition easily enforced, nor one easily explained to one so urgent in her movements, so disregarding of the mere practicalities of my trade. Unfortunately, as I had often protested to her obdurate presence, it was as necessary to the processes of my art as light itself. Sometimes, just sometimes, I thought that I was winning.

She had, as many who saw the results averred; one outstanding gift. Though her skin was unremarkable, beneath it moved, in sundry fluid lights, a multitude, a swarm of little muscles, of tiny conjoining bones which, caught in the firelight, in the glare of a candle or even sometimes in the starkness of dawn, could yield the most satisfying effects. Her thighs, though meagre, had this wonderful plasticity. Her torso too would when one least expected it suddenly ripple as if with a shoal of-submerged, threshing fish. It is, as you might surmise, not an easy quality to capture. One awkward movement, one sharp careless reflex and it was gone. I had often tried to distil these essentially transient instants of beauty on canvas but had so far failed. My only chance, I sometimes thought, was to work from memory, to summon up all those little, fragile moments of casual delight in one final picture which might serve as an act of homage or obituary to our essentially squalid and demeaning relationship. One of these days I would try, but not yet, not yet.

First, I had to get down something solid. And herein lay the difficulty, for about Andria there is very little that partakes of the nature of solidity. Brittleness is the word, and brittleness, whether in art or life, was not what at that moment in time I was searching for. I had too much of it already: I wanted my art, insofar as I required anything of it, to act as a counterweight to my existence. My life was a miasma: my work must have this countervailing quality of steadfastness, of *gravitas*. In the whole of Andria's constitution there is one feature which is capable of expressing this quality: her backbone.

Backbone: the word is deceitful with promise. We speak, do we not, of the backbone of a community, the backbone of a nation? Yet if we examine the anatomy of the part in question, little confirms these expectations. The very word is a misnomer. Instead of a line of tissue running from nape to buttock there is this shifting network of deliquescent interconnections, a dancing hive of bits and pieces. How all these nerves and vertebrae, these channels of information and vessels conveying life contrive to express one single, sublime curve is hard to say. And yet in Andria, storm child though she is, they do so to perfection.

The effect was not so clear when she stood. At attention she resembled a stake of bamboo; one itched to train runner beans all round her. But ask her to bend, to squat, to sit in such a position that her attention was fastened on a window, on a piece of furniture, or better still, a book in which she was engrossed, and the resulting shape has driven me into paroxysms. In that gentle flawless slope, in that miracle of steeped roundness lay, it sometimes seemed, enough serenity and calm to still my restless spirit forever.

*****

It was during one of Andria's infrequent moments of repose that she first attracted me. It was a Sunday evening in February several years previously, and we were both attending a symposium called "Classicism in the Arts: an inter-disciplinary seminar." She was a student at University College then, doing a degree in Greek and Italian. I'd watched her closely all weekend, arguing with her girlfriends, taking thin, bearded men in jerseys to task over obscure points of critical theory. She had not noticed me. I have never thought of myself as the intellectual type: my task is to paint. It is a craft: I don't know how it is done; it just happens. For Andria nothing just happens: it has to be made, and when the process is over, she wants to understand the whys and the wherefores, the ins and the outs. She had been making things happen all weekend, standing in the middle of small hectoring groups, drawing the attention to herself. I was secretly revolted; I hugged my corner and my wine. On such occasions I am my own man. Give me a paintbrush and I can fitfully believe in my usefulness. Without it all I can do is watch. I thought it my consolation and privilege to watch that weekend.

But on the Sunday evening my mood changed slightly, like a veil of cloud shimmying across the sun. There was a chamber concert in the basement of the Bloomsbury institute where our deliberations had occurred. Most of the out-of-town delegates had left, relinquishing only those whose need for conviviality or music could overcome their aversion to dragging themselves out to a last tube. I lived nearby then, and I had my bicycle outside. I stayed on, out of laziness, out of curiosity, to feel the currents of life eddying around me.

A quartet was playing Mozart. There was a brisk opening movement and then during the slow Adagio I looked over the sea of squatting forms in the half-light and there she was, by herself in a little pool of luminosity. She had on a long tweedy dress - it was the age of the "maxiskirt" - and a magenta-coloured Jaeger jumper rolled up at the elbows. I particularly noticed her thin forearms crested with down against the dun heather of her skirt. Her hair was done up in a bow matching her sweater. Her neck was exposed: very slender and lightly pockmarked. She had a mole slightly above the left side of her lip. She had lost all her wild intentness and was for once lost in the music. Her eyelids scarcely flickered: she could have been painted by Caravaggio.

They say that earthly presences mirror heavenly forms, but it is an illusion. Yet the artist is a dealer in illusions and perforce must care for them. I cared for mine that night. At the interval I followed her, dug deep into my threadbare pockets and bought her a drink. She said thank you very nicely and turned to join her crowd. She was immersed in talk about cadences: I dithered at the back of the group, grunting, letting her be. She continued talking. Several pairs of eyes were upon her; my own drifted elsewhere and then back. When she returned to the bar, I begged a moment, but the concert was starting again. Again she said thank you, very nicely.

I do not remember what they played after the break. Afterwards I followed her out on to the pavement where her bicycle was chained next to mine. I tried to explain myself. The intent look came back into her face, but softened slightly. It was three weeks later that for the first time I held her slender wrists across the table-top and wondered what to say.

She let the details of her life out slowly. She was an

orphan: that much I learned almost immediately. She had been brought up by adoptive parents on the South coast, and, her step-father dying early, had been sent to a minor and less than reputable private school where she said she learned very little. She was a most surprising compound of erudition and ungainly ignorance. When I met her, she had not heard of Velasquez. She had no idea who her real parents had been, though why this had been kept from her I did not learn. Much of her life was consumed in a vain attempt to make up for her deprivation. On occasions her daughterly ambitions would fasten themselves on the most unlikely individuals: tutors, librarians, policemen, Roman emperors. Gradually I came to realise that she was eaten up by some kind of hunger for disclosure. She longed to sit at the feet of one into whose lap she could pour her sorrows. Meanwhile I was a sort of stopover, a hitching post on the way to Delphi.

The months passed. She graduated from college; I dropped out of the Slade. We lived in a cramped little studio in Parson's Green. She became a Personnel Manager, why I never could tell, she was utterly unsuited to it. Perhaps her gustiness took them in at the interview. I was making a small name for myself; it was before the collages and the Green.

Then we had a hiccup year. She announced that her Latin was rusty and that she was going back to polish it. She registered at Birkbeck as a part-time postgraduate, working on Silver Age verse, squinting at Loeb editions until the small hours. It took a toll on her office work;

she left and found a two-day job at the Senate House library - easier, she said, on the nerves. I used to see her there sometimes, chatting gaily and stamping things, when I dropped in to consult art books. Even there, bent slightly over the counter, her brows puckered in concentration, there were times when she would not have disgraced Caravaggio.

But insecurity bit into us. I resented her other lives and flung myself into wild, baroque collations: the collages had begun. She announced a doctoral title. I grew desperate: she was getting beyond my reach. The collages grew wilder and more expensive. I needed a little subsidy and one afternoon turned to her.

"Why?" she asked briefly.

"Don't be mean with me, Andria. I am using very good quality sackcloth."

She squinted at me distrustingly. Beneath the quick sands somewhere I recognised a shelf of flint. Her college friends still milled around her. I thought, she is betraying me, but with whom?

Her supervisor praised her. In desperation I took my paint box and produced a canvas, electric and green. She glanced at it disdainfully, noting the change of direction, not deigning to comment. She made herself a cup of coffee and went on reading.

"Don't get lost to me, Andria. We all have our Silver Ages."

Did she resent mine? One of these days, I thought, she is going to desert me and take a turn with Tiberius Caesar.

We needed common ground. Andria bought a cat and christened it Menander.

"Who was she?"

"Don't be dumb, Benedict. He was a Greek poet. He wrote lots of tragedies, which survive just in fragments. I called the moggy Menander because I only see him in snatches."

"How am I supposed to know the sex of cats? I don't go around looking underneath. I don't mind fondling its fur. It's appearances I am interested in."

I toyed with the idea of a cat period, but then dropped it. She wrote an article about somebody called Columella. She even had it published. My canvasses grew darker: I was deeper than ever into the Green. Nobody bought them. The only way I'll get hung, I thought, is to hang myself.

Then the adultery began, if that is what you can call betrayal of nonsacramental union adultery. It is a moot point. I had considered our arrangement a marriage of sorts; how else was I to cope with my catechized soul? She began to stay away at night. I felt hurt, and I wanted to hurt someone back. To be precise I wanted to hurt God. I lashed out at Him in my distress, but my words ricocheted. I left off working and took to roaming the streets. I met an old flame and renewed our intemperate acquaintance. I thought of moving out of our flat to put a stop to this uncertainty forever. But by Christmas Andria was back and I was painting her by the fireside. I would give much for the scraps and leavings of domestic content. Sometimes I would even give the prospect of contentedness itself.

A relationship is a compact against time. Andria and I had increasingly come to feel like survivors clinging to the bobbing surface of a raft, before us the billows and the open sea. At times I was inclined to fill a bottle and send it into the unprepossessing future. My message might read, "My name is Benedict Henry. I am thirty-one years of age. I am tired. I have not yet begun. My love has turned to ashes, my pigments to crumbling powder. The frame is cracking at the corners. Help me." But who would pick the bottle up, and on what looming shore?

When I looked up from my half-finished composition that dreary October afternoon, Andria had vanished. I could hear her in the adjacent kitchenette noisily preparing coffee. I had not yet finished sketching in the outline of her legs. I put down my palette and strolled across to the open doorway. Over the mugs she was sniffing and wiping her nostrils with her sleeve.

I said, "You don't have to stick around if you don't want to." One likes to keep the lines of communication open, even through the rigmarole of despair. I added, "I'm sure you can find someone else who'll let you move about."

She was banging down the jar lid and fretting like a mare. "Why don't you give us both a break for once?" she said. "Why don't you go and see your dear father?"

"I saw him three months ago."

"Benedict, it's not enough," she pleaded, mellowing. "He keeps writing. You are lucky to have a father."

"It's just that he overawes me. I can't compete with a Mock Tudor mansion and all those gilt-edged securities."

"You see your uncle more often."

"That's not strictly true. Besides I'm closer to my uncle."

"Everyone's supposed to feel closer to their uncle. That's if they have one."

"There are uncles and uncles."

"This one sounds so ineffably dreary. Perhaps you were made for one another. He seems about as incapable of love as you are."

I took the mug of coffee which she had made for me, saying gravely, "If only you knew just how false that is." I spooned in the sugar, sending a little eddy into the saucer as I did so.

"You see," I said and then paused. "You see Claud was always a kind of mystery to me. Always, since before I could crawl. The fact of the matter is I don't know him still. You are always closer to the people you don't know. Dad's a known quantity: his opinions, the cut of his mind, the dimensions of his garden. He grows orchids, but refuses to grow himself. What would I gain from spending another weekend at Cheam?"

"Don't you think he may have hidden depths?"

"Probably. But he's long buried them along with the compost. He's dug them in so deep you wouldn't know they were there. If they once sprung roots and burst to the surface, he'd be terrified. He wouldn't recognise himself, and neither to be honest would I."

Winterly she looked at me, quoting:

"Even the dearest that I loved the best

Are strange – nay, rather, stranger than the rest."

"Perhaps. Damn it, at least Claud possesses something approaching mystique. When I was a boy, I used to sit by the firelight some evenings waiting for Dad to return. I knew he'd been to "The Poachers" and I knew he'd taken Claud. You always knew, there was this air of conspiracy. Some family intrigue, money probably. Mum got impatient. She would stomp around slamming doors. I'd squat there for hours pretending to devour the pages, hoping against hope that when they arrived, they'd both come in.

"At long last outside in the porch there'd be a dry scuffle of shoe leather and muffled apologies. Then one lolloping pair of boots would retreat down the pavement out of earshot and Dad would trudge in coughing, wiping his feet in his portentous manner. Once more Claud had been too frightened to come in and pay his respects. I was seventeen before I met him quite by chance at Rosie's. Already he'd become a kind of myth."

"Benedict. He's probably very ordinary."

"Perhaps I'm very ordinary."

"That's all there is to it then. Two very ordinary little men standing in a gallery, gaping at pictures. You needn't make it sound like a romance."

"In a way it is. He's still so clandestine about everything."

"You don't need to be clandestine, Benedict. You've

got a perfectly authentic dad living in the open in Surrey. It's not his fault if he can't abide me. Sometimes I can't abide myself."

"Dad's always tried to push me in the direction of money. I think he'd like me to marry a duchess."

"Perhaps you will, darling. Perhaps he'll fix it up for you. But he won't if you never visit him. Ben, do all of us a big favour. Go and see your poor dad."

*****

So I succumbed and took the train to Cheam. Outside the grimy carriage window the black suburban cutting seemed to stretch on forever. It was like being sucked forward into the grave, or worse the nursery. Beneath my leather waistcoat I could feel the familiar panic rising. I was being dragged into some sort of reconciliation feet first.

When I turned by the plump pillar box at the corner my father was hacking at the hedges, blowing out some sturdy tune. As soon as he caught sight of me, the tune stopped and the briar slid out of his mouth, dribbling. As usual he said nothing. I recognised the quality of that silence. Claud's silences were a shifting mess of mirrors, my father Hamish's a sort of wriggling, hooked accusation.

I did not feel up to his game, so I spoke:

"I got your letter."

He continued snipping, resentment running down the small of his back. He would have liked to have been snipping at me.

I looked at his garden: those stately banks of stakes, the soil neatly turned in toward next spring, the bulbs ready in boxes, the lawn manicured and trim. I looked at the hedge. It scarcely needed trimming.

I remembered the draughty Barber's shop in Seven Sisters to which I had been sent as a child, its snaking sign twisting outside, its interior rank with hair oil. I remembered his monthly admonishment: "There's a shilling Ben, and make sure they give you a decent cut. We can't have you running back there in a fortnight." Later he would feel the back of my neck to see if the hair curled round his thick finger ends. "We don't need the expense Ben." I passed my hand through my clustering locks and remembered. Sometimes I thought that in our house in Finchley love must have been ladled out like porridge.

My abiding impression of the inside of my father's house is one of clocks. "Time hangs heavy": the phrase seems to have been made for him.

In the etiolated gloom of his front room, its latticed windows discretely shaded, its walls a bitter cream, its Axminster carpets hoovered to smoothness, time the arbiter seemed to tread padded. You would have thought there were a hundred clocks in there, and all muffled. In fact there were two: the squat chimer, a gift to Father on his retirement as Church Warden of St Bride's, which, housed in Whitby jet, pressed down on the mantelpiece; and the Grandfather clock which, lugged aloft on the removal van from Finchley, had held dour counsel in the far corner ever since. Next to the great glass-fronted bookcase companion to *Halsbury's Laws of England* it stood like a grim guard's officer, and must it seemed perforce stand there forever unflinching. Would the world shake, would governments rise or fall, stocks burgeon or wane, it would outlast them all, gaunt in majesty, the Grandfather clock. There are some things in this world which are just not worth disputing. As the tables and chairs around it gathered dust and then were polished to sweetness, as the great arched silence of that drawing room lengthened into shadows paced by my father's sighs, as, out in the garage, a solitary tendril broke from the boxed soil each spring and fumbled for air, the clock remained steadfast, counting the score, counting the cost. There had been moments when I fancied I saw it winking.

I looked at it now with its hands reaching and its pendulum alert, and when the minute hand reached the vertical, waited breathless for a chime. Instead there was a dull click. My father sat down, adjusted the heel of his indoor slippers and sighed. He took the silver fob watch from the pocket of his cardigan and checked it. Then he checked the dial of the clock. He snapped the lid of the watch and replaced it in the folds of his cardigan. Prompt to a fault, the jet clock on the mantelpiece droned. My father sniffed, frowned briefly and then rubbed his nose.

"It's hardly worth changing now," he intoned, every inch the widower. "I see people so seldom. Nobody comes near me nowadays."

"Ever since your mother died …" I expected the ritual incantation to continue, but instead again he sighed.

I waited several seconds before he said, "I was wondering when you were going to do me the honour of a visit, Ben. There were one or two things I wanted to speak to you about. I wanted to know how you were getting along. How are you getting along?"

I said, "I survive."

He reached into the pocket of his flannels and pulled out his faithful old pipe, stone-cold now, the white ash falling over his trousers, the bowl clammy.

He blew down it like an oboe-player testing a reed.

"No work I suppose?"

"What do you mean exactly?"

"Well, Ben. One has to keep the wolf from the door."

Briefly I thought I heard the animal growling out in the porch.

"I appreciate you'll have been getting on with your pictures. No harm in that. Your mother would have wished it. But I did just wonder whether you'd managed to obtain any work. You know, paid work."

I noted the habitual equivalence without rancour. I said, "We don't get paid very much in our profession, Dad."

"Then it's all for the love I suppose?"

"Something like that."

There was an adjudicatory pause while he took this in. Down the stem of his pipe the smoke rippled, simmering. Then he leaned forward slightly, his chin searching for the ethical mean. Equity presided between the ill-lit covers.

"Doesn't it ever strike you, Ben, that this manner of life is somehow … unsatisfactory?"

The slight Halifax vowels in the last word grazed against my ear.

He had spent several years in Yorkshire as a child before his own father's health broke, and his mother bustled her brood to London seeking work. It was several years before Claud was born.

I reflected and said, "I get my own kind of satisfaction."

"I know," he insisted, "but you can't live out of tins forever."

In Father's mind the memories of his pinched childhood still rankled, a source of perpetual anxiety. A childhood spent in furnished rooms, haunted by fear of the bailiff and of what he still picturesquely persisted in calling "the workhouse". Was this his mother's phrase, the Victorian bogey inherited in metaphor? Then the long years of study, preparation for a decent calling. "You can't live out of tins forever." My father had grown up half a century before the advent of fast food. And Andria and I had not opened a tin in months.

I said, "As a matter of fact Andria is quite a respectable cook."

He let out steam like a traction engine.

"Ah yes. Andria," he gasped. "That is another subject I wanted to speak to you about."

Andria and Father had only met twice. Neither occasion had been auspicious. He held the Catholic view of matrimony as a literal and life-long union. Sometimes I caught myself wondering whether he had ever, to use a phrase more common in his generation than in mine, been "in love".

It was hard to think of him being gripped by a tormented passion. By the time I came to be able to discriminate, his relationship with my mother had long settled into an affectionate familiarity, like his fondness for his pipe or the chintz armchair in which he now sat cannily sizing me up. But earlier, in early middle age when he had met her, he must have loved in a different way. I imagined a pallid, winnowed warmth, like Autumn sunlight caressing a mossy bank.

There followed a longer pause than any thereto. After some seconds he rose to his feet, walked over to the fireplace and stood against the fender with his legs apart and his hands resolutely behind his back as if defending the hearth. His mouth worked in cogitation. Thoughts seemed to bubble through his eyes. For once I found myself watching him in preference to the clock.

There was a clunk in the grate behind him and then he said, "I've been talking to old Echardt."

Lawrence Echardt was Uncle Claud's employer. He was also an old acquaintance of my father. I had even heard Aunt Rosie imply that it had been Father who had obtained Claud his job, when, my uncle's artistic ambitions fading, some steady means of support, recommending itself to Father's respect for stability, had to be sought. He had worked for Lawrence Echardt & Sons ever since, thirty years of wandering and lonely, mendicant bondage. I did not savour the story, or what it told of either man. Nor had I ever encountered Echardt, who remained one of our gloomier family legends.

My father said, "He's looking a lot older than he was. He must be well into his seventies. There doesn't seem to be anybody he can hand on to. The firm has been passed from father to son for three generations, and Lawrence has only the one daughter."

I was beginning to wonder where all of this was tending. I had briefly attended college with Christina Echardt thirteen years previously. Our acquaintance had been slight and glancing, but I had reason enough to remember it with rancour. I very much doubted if she still remembered me. With her I permanently associated the mordant memory of a girl by a riverbank, a girl glimpsed fleetingly through the serried ranks of a dance hall: all this and a lingering feeling of hurt. I doubted my father would understand.

"I don't know if Claud has ever told you anything of the firm," my father continued. "Of course, he's only on the reproductions side which is running down somewhat. Essentially, they're auctioneers, and that department's never been stronger."

I looked at the De Hooch reproduction hanging over the fireplace above the black clock. It had often surprised me that, as one so intensely aware of the commercial assessment of art, my father had never invested in originals. A few thousand in authenticated canvas would surely have lent the fireplace lustre. As it was, the room was always kept so dark it was hard to make out either of De Hooch's *Two Women in a Courtyard.*

"He is looking for someone with a background in the History of Art to join him and learn the valuation angle. It was a pity that you dropped out of the Slade. But he would be prepared to overlook that."

Like a patched adorable cloak, my sins closed in around me. I held the clasp, feeling its reassuring coldness. There is nothing more to our family's taste than homely recrimination: *mea culpa, mea maxima culpa.* Should I, I wondered, now feel grateful for this offer of redemption? Suddenly, from behind my father's back, the chimes gave out the three-quarters.

I had grown accustomed by now to my family's intermittent bursts of solicitous bounty. During my final year at Camberwell College of Art I had received a slim airmail envelope postmarked Utrecht. Opening it, I had found a letter from my maternal grandfather suggesting that I accept a small position in his wine-importing business. Apparently, I would be useful with the labels. The tone was nicely balanced between concern and urgency, the terms sounded generous, but even then I smelled a rat. Had some eddy of anxiety scurried across the North Sea and the lowland dykes to my mother's hometown carrying news of my imminent joblessness? Had I, still raw and untried in the world, already been weighed in the balance and found wanting? It was not the last of such offers. From that moment on I appeared to be subjected to what I came to see as an orchestrated bilateral campaign to "set Benedict on his feet". Eventually I came to see myself as a cardboard man on a pin table continually buffeted by the balls of chance. No sooner was I wavering or down than rods would be twisted, connections engaged, and no effort spared to put me up straight. Little did they suspect the strength of my inertia, or of my dedication.

My father said, "Well?"

I looked into the glowing coals between his legs. I shifted and stared resolutely into the chrysanthemums. I said, "I'm preparing for an Exhibition."

There was an instant gust of exhaust.

"I know, Benedict," he said, "but it's all very well."

I grasped that last phrase and held on to it. When I suspect a threat to my freedom I look for beacons marking the sandbanks. Few are more trustworthy than the hectoring world. When all those years ago Claud's paint set had loomed from beneath its brown paper wrapping, and evening found me messing with colours on the landing, my father's face had lowered above my small devotion and pronounced, "It's lovely Benedict, but for a growing lad now, it's all very well." When the brochure from the art school appeared on our breakfast table and, torn between it and my cereal I started idly leafing through the pages, his face loured from under the rippling pink sea of *The Financial Times* and warned, "Painting's a fine pastime, Benedict, but as a job you know it's all very well." When, two years after graduation and several months after the Slade fiasco, I arranged to meet my father for lunch at his regular haunt in the City, and in answer to his regular enquiry as to my circumstances I announced the inception of my Green Period, his accusation bit into me once more: "I suppose it serves to keep you occupied, Ben, but time's getting on. At your stage of life, it's all very well."

I coughed and rose to my feet. I said, "Sorry, Father. I can't help you."

Outside the day was dying. Thick layers of inky cloud were smudged across the sky. On the lip of the horizon, glimpsed between the garden hedges, there was a low glimmer fading to extinction. Little patches of mauve chased across the skulking sun.

Suddenly, his anger broke. He shouted, "If you don't take a good hard look at yourself soon, you're going to finish up like Rosie!"

It was the ultimate threat. My sainted aunt had spent the last thirty odd years hiding from the world in a basement flat in Maida Vale. She had been a milliner attached to one of the larger London stores, but business dwindling, Father had single-handedly offered to "establish her for life" in a small boutique in Ealing. She had sniffed at the offer in her characteristic manner, letting it be known that it was beneath her dignity as an "artiste". My father's respect for art, never very high, had dissolved on the spot.

I had the strongest urge to leave there and then. The afternoon was fraying like an old sheet. But between the holes in the fabric his voice broke through once more:

"For years I've warned you that your life is drifting on to the rocks. You would not listen. You persisted with your plan of becoming a painter, but as far as I am aware you are still to sell a single canvas. How old are you? Thirty? You live in mindless squalor with that girl. You've no children. Echardt's daughter is there for the taking. It would be an admirable match. I'm only thinking of your interests. I've seen too many disasters. For my sake, try to put your house in order before it's too late!"

It was one of the longest speeches I could ever remember him delivering. I had a vivid mental picture of myself as a yellowing skeleton walled up in a narrow room resembling a cobwebbed orange box. I was lying propped against one of the walls like an entombed mummy, while against the opposite wall sprawled Andria, equally emaciated, with one bony arm clasping the empty stub of a cigarette. Neither of us spoke, though our exposed jaws were open as if for conversation. I saw us from the side in cross-section. Then I saw us from above.

I shut my eyes very tight. I thought, "I can't possibly stay here tonight." I opened my eyes again. The room had grown marginally darker.

In a quieter voice Father said, "Think about it."

But, for once in my life, all I could think about was Rosie.

*****

I was standing in a dell in the woods. Along the distant thoroughfare, traffic thrummed. Through the thinning trees, where only three weeks before luxuriant foliage had furled, I could now make out the brickwork of Holland House. I filled my chest and thought, bless this clarity, autumn.

Overhead, the sky was almost blackcurrant, sliced by little scurries of grey. There was the slightest of breezes which rattled the embalmed leaves at my feet. Against my right heel I could see a mass of brown fibre. I picked it up and let it wriggle through my fingers. Spent cassette tape, more dead messages.

Against the wall of silence a peacock squarked and then looked blankly at me. There were bundles of rabbits against the bare stalks of the far bushes, and over the crest of the lawn a lone ostrich stretched its neck, lumbering on its bony thighs. I thrust my hands deep into my pockets and again breathed the tart wood smoke in the air. Damn you Sunday, bless you.

Along a corridor of trees to my left a child's voice rang, interceding. On an impulse I called back, but my words were lost in the echo. A gust of wind passed through the branches. Nothing moved.

Against an oak tree to my far right, its umber bark misty with lichen, leant Andria, a solitary figure, still for once as the afternoon.

She was so motionless she could have been an outcrop of the tree. Her arms were twisted round the column of the trunk like creeper. She was wearing her threadbare duffle coat and a pink and white woollen cap which blended with the deepening flush around her. Against the pallor of her cheek the branches threw a shadow cleft like a pitchfork.

I called out "Andria!", and in the lessening distance the child's voice replied.

Suddenly a toddler of a girl in a green anorak appeared in a clearing to one side of the dell. The little girl stopped and, momentarily daunted, placed one gloved hand against her mouth. Then she looked round and immediately swivelled back, regarding me intently. I tried smiling. Out of the corner of my eye, I sensed Andria stir.

I felt as if I had come across a squirrel gathering acorns. I was held by his timid working stillness.

Then a salvo of rockets broke overhead and the girl was running. The season had exploded like a rotten fig. Beneath the crumpled canvass of her anorak her legs toiled backwards and forwards, and her paws were reaching like the squirrel's. I took one step forward, but she ignored me. She was making for the oak. When she reached Andria's feet she stopped, breathing softly.

There was a moment of extraordinary delicacy. I saw Andria reach out an arm to stroke the canvas hood, but then seemed to hold herself back. The toddler was grinning up at her openly. There was a tense, flickering rapport between them, like a cloud of oil creasing on the face of a river, revealing all its lurid, dun colours. Then the cloud dissolved, and the stream of life gushed on. The child clapped both gloved hands together and raced away from us. Mournfully Andria followed the girl with her eyes.

*****

That week, everything about Andria had begun to puzzle me. She would have luminous moments of repose when to trace in her outline or fill in the tints of her flesh was an operation of pure magic. Then with no warning she would stand up, shove her thin hands into the ample pockets of her smock and storm up and down the cramped room shouting at me: "You gawp at me for hours, but I'm convinced you never see me. For all the reality I possess I might as well be a vase. You don't seem to have the faintest notion as to what is going on inside my head. I'm not sure that you even care."

She stopped by the window, and over her shoulder gave me a long look as if to say, "Free me, Benedict. Set me free." I stood rooted with my brush poised not knowing what to say. I had become used to her inexplicable rages, but this mood had a dark undertone to it quite new to me. There was a shrillness to her tone verging on violence.

She stood framed in the windowpane and said "Benedict, look at me."

"I am looking."

"No, not like that. Open your eyes."

She waited a second and then said "Forget it. Why don't you go and clean off your brushes in the kitchen, and do some tidying while you're about it. The draining board's a tip."

Obediently, I walked over and kissed her forehead. Then I dismantled my easel and walked through to the

47

adjoining room where I poured a little white spirit into a jug. The paint was oozy about my fingers. I took a rag, and, dipping it in the spirit, set about my task.

Round the corner, Andria was invisible to me. She seemed to have settled; I could no longer make out the rustle of her tights. I slouched over to the doorway and stuck my head through the curtain. "What were you crying for?" I asked.

"When?"

"In the park just now. You were stifling tears."

"It doesn't matter."

"It matters to me."

"Then I expect you know already," she said.

I was plainly getting nowhere. I retreated into depths of the kitchen and started mournfully dabbing at a patch of Prussian Blue. But her distress was tugging at me. Blindly, as if through the grill of a confessional, I said, "I want to help you."

"You're not using the tea towel!" she replied.

"Stop changing the subject."

"I'm not anybody's subject."

"Oh, yes, you are," I said firmly. "You're mine!"

There was a sneering guffaw. Suddenly my resolve snapped. I stormed through into the other room and glared down at her on the sofa where she had started leafing through a file.

"Andria!" I shouted, as loud as I could.

"I'm working."

"Look at me."

At first, she refused to lift her eyes, but when she did,

I was surprised to see them coated with laughter.

"If you will continue ranting," she taunted, "I shall lose my place. Why don't you go and call on that dotty aunt of yours or something?"

I reached forward and held her softly by the arms. I said, "They don't come a lot dottier than you."

"We're all dotty at heart, Benedict dear. Even you. Just look at you. We're all lost souls. Weeping and gnashing of teeth."

"Gnashing"

"Weeping."

"Weeping"

"Gnashing."

I stooped closer.

"Benedict, you clumsy man," she purred. "If you don't get off me you will positively crush my file. Go and give yourself a treat. Go and pay a visit to your dear Aunt Rosie."

*****

Aunt Rosie lived sunken in her basement flat in Maida Vale, surrounded by a hollow like a moat. She scarcely ever emerged. When asked why she so seldom broke surface she would remark with a wry tilt of the head that she had come down in the world, and there she supposed she must stay. It was a recurrent fantasy of our family that we had once known greater things: a stately home in Morayshire (now appropriately enough a mental hospital), acres of lawn, packs of retainers, an ancient and ghostly pedigree. There was a complementary myth, which Rosie faithfully repeated, of a Cornish great-grandmother, a swarthy nymph with flashing brown eyes who terrorised Penzance with her beauty. Her family, who had inhabited Cornwall since the Conquest, had once owned St Michael's Mount which a rash ancestor gambled away in an evening.

In fact our forebears were landless crofters who settled in the Midlands from Scotland after the clearances sometime in the eighteenth century. This, at least, was my version of events, though I could no more corroborate it than I could hers. We are all trapped in our own legends, and mine I must confess have owed something to a certain matter-of-factness which is one of the few attributes I inherited from my father.

In all probability the truth was stranger than either. I was contented to retain my own myth and allow Rosie her harmless pretentions to aristocratic grandeur. They were virtually all she had left, illusions to which she had been wedded for thirty years, victim to bursts of sudden resentment or compensatory excitement, determined as she was, whatever the incongruity, to "maintain appearances", another deadening family phrase.

As you clatter down her basement steps, your immediate impression is of being hemmed in by shadows. On the far wall of the gulley into which you must descend hangs a bunch of ivy like a storm cloud. In its shadow is the kitchen window, a single frosted pane so cluttered by newspapers and bottles as to permit scarcely any ingress of light. To sue for admittance you must lay siege to the door but first must pick your way through the debris of decades: cardboard boxes, decaying furniture, the remains of a three-piece suite decaying in the rain. There is even a wheel-less tricycle, bequest of a child once befriended and fed before the inevitable rupture, the tears and the parting. If, as you stood on those steps you could survey this detritus with some comprehension of its meaning, a whole inventory of my aunt's spiritual life might lie before you. Instead, in embarrassment you avert your eyes, making for the split, moss green door.

One ring will not suffice. You must wait and ring again. Then a twitching surveillance at the window, and light blooming like a daffodil before the slow approach of slippered feet and, as the many bolts prize open, a stooped, shawled face which peers and tremors before the happy dawning recognition. Once more you feel the bizarre honour of standing here amid these festering lovelorn ruins.

A kiss at the pasty cheek will gain entry but no respite from the litany of refuse. For the hallway is an obstacle course. Here lie the cast-offs of my aunt's successive enthusiasms: the piles of theological journals, the books on heraldry and correspondence with a particular lofty Monsignor. Here are the samplers in frames, the bland refractory icons, the stitched purses, patched gloves, the knitted shawls, the bonnets and the toeless shoes. Between visits the stuff accumulates: a watercolour in an improvised frame, an attempt at a crochet, the hacked disfigured remnant of a stone. Then there are the spoils from her rare, foraging expeditions, her forays into woodland or day-trips to the sea. A heap of shells, a bag of cones, a gaunt dismembered tree branch. At each step through this maze Rosie will mutter her apologies, her rosary of little, tired regrets. This cobwebbed cardboard was once tribute to a Canaletto, this lean volume was lent her by an Earl, that leprous mirror bedecked the dressing room of a long-silent contralto. As she indicates each item, each stark, unbridled piece of bric-à-brac, Rosie's voice turns between pride and shame, sorrow at the muddle and sheer guttural satisfaction at its warped abundance. At moments she will swallow her words in a tiny orgy of self-conceit that make you want to hug her. Only the mascara, the blotched and powdery cheeks restrain you.

As precariously you edge around the planes and angles, creeping inch by inch toward the bead curtain at the other end, your senses are assailed by a complicating element. In your retreat from the kitchen the smells of cooking and potted plants are replaced by a waft of female perfume so strong as to cause you to start. From the first moment of greeting you have been aware of this swell and undertow of scent suffusing all else.

But as you grope toward the lounge the sensation intensifies to such a pitch of piquancy as to make you want to sink to your knees and sing. There is no defining this odour. It has its facets of sentimental rankness, its voluptuary, acrid charms which elude all confinement. If you shut your eyes and concentrate you find yourself drifting through a spectrum of aromas: rose-water and cabbage leaves, tobacco and sweat, musk, eau-de-cologne, burnt toast and lavender, linseed and incense, bird-droppings and candle-grease and civet. It is an ingenuous refinement to be found on no perfumier's stick. It is simply, subtly, and triumphantly Rosie.

Brushing the curtain as you pass, your first impression of the living room is of darkness, a perfumed, resounding void. Only as your eyes adjust to the obscurity do you discern the shapes of objects buried in the gloom. Near the door, containing the draft along the passageway, is a folding prayer screen the colour of brimstone and ashes. As you feel forward seeking a point of gravity, you sense, more by touch than sight, that the near wall is covered by an arrangement of ladies' hats, straw and cloth, relics of my aunt's long-abandoned trade. Gaining in confidence, you venture towards the centre of the room, and your shins encounter wooden presences: a chair-leg, a table, the resistant back of a sofa. It is time to stop and wonder, or rather to remember, since you have been here before, and between each rambling sortie the details have burgeoned and caressed the memory.

Here are the fans and draperies of your recollection, here *The Last Supper*, and Claud's one sad still life; here the early Italian masters, the imitation triptych, the faded, pious panels, the parrot in its cage shouting its *pater noster*. Here too are the stones and twigs in bottles, the louring Bakelite radio, *The Illustrated London News* and *Vogue* for 1959. "In saecula saeculorum" yells the bird and all around it trembles:

the limp and mottled creeper, the plaster cast St Jerome, the owl in its house of glass defying time to move.

Behind the sofa stands a large standard lamp in the shape of a tusk, its surface of copper and beaten brass, its base of ebony. It is, she explains, fingering the pink tasselled shade leaning precariously from its summit like a tipsy durbar umbrella, a gift from Miss Sinclair, lady-in-waiting to the late Lady Howard, cousin to the premier catholic family in England. Lady Howard inherited it from her brother the Brigadier-General; it was her express desire that upon her own decease Rosie should have it. The words "express desire" are clenched between yellowing teeth, parted as if to receive a *petit-four* or communion wafer. The gentility of the vowels, the slight swoop of the y's speak of years spent in faded pre-war Convent schools. The enunciation is exact, the vocabulary unsullied by contemporary usage. Aunt Rosie is a perfectly preserved fossil of respectable Georgian Catholicism.

Like a fossil she stays underground. Against the dingy glass of the far sash windows, their frames flaking and thick with dust, are pasted newspaper sheets of twenty years ago, while, slung across the largest pane, a concession to conventional primness, sags one red velvet curtain. This is Rosie's life dammed against the light, but the light breaks through nonetheless, picking out the contours of chests and boxes, bookshelves caved almost to breaking, and two great pianos. The more imposing of these two, a grand, dominates the centre of the room. It is covered with a tartan rug against falling debris, while from its top extends a single length of copper piping to support the ceiling, lest the world break through and claim her. The plaster, as she carefully explains on each visit, is too fragile to trust. The length of piping has stood office for fifteen years and will so stand 'till the landlord makes repairs or the time comes when Rosie herself must bequeath the copper lampstand.

The smaller piano is an upright, flanked by etchings of the cathedrals of Milan and Ravenna. On its cluttered top, amid the piles of sheet music and almost invisible in the perpetual twilight, is a plain papier mâché frame enclosing a black-and-white print of a gentleman in mustachios and service uniform. I had never dared inquire as to his identity, yet it is emphatically to his austere and noble presence that, as the day outside wanes and the traffic hums overhead, Rosie lowers the one switch illuminating both reading light and lamp stand and, opening up the veneered lid to expose cracked and yellowed keys, croons out in her thin wavering voice:

Caro mio ben
Credimi almen
Senza di te
Languisce il cor.

Her hands float over the notes, her head is with her grief and the music of Giordani, but her eyes are constantly fixed on the picture. It is a rite too solemn to question, too regular to ignore. Like Claud, Rosie is a creature of habit, but all her rituals are bursts of declaration. Her back stiff with pride, her windows sheltered against intrusion, she holds her disappointment aloft like a sacred flame. The photograph, the furnishings feed it:

Il tuo fedel

Sospiro ognor.

Cesa, crudel

Tanto rigor.

Rosie's disappointment is not merely amorous. On the ochre mantel above the sprightly gas fire which bubbles reassuringly all winter sits another tiny frame, silver this time and dented by constant handling. The tints are softer than those which adorn the military gentleman. They are sepia deepening to brown. The photograph depicts a girl of around two, her pigtails tied with ribbon, her smock rumpled by the little hands which hold it, creasing. The smile aimed at the box camera is direct and challenging, the lips defensive and pursed. It is a picture of dainty apprehension, an infant on her guard.

For years I had known that Rosie had once given birth to an illegitimate daughter. It is one more of our family legends, one never expostulated but hinted at, more by omission than by direct reference, during seasonal family gatherings. That Rose is a woman with a "past" had become an integral part of her aura. There are single women who blossom into middle age, alone and defiant, with no sense of incompleteness. With Rose you had always the feeling of a beckoning hand constantly extended to grasp childish fingers which eluded it. The hand would stretch forever, the palm tensed and searching, while somewhere, in the interstices of the universe, was a hand matching its shape, curvature and softness, but smaller, weaker, less needful.

What had happened to the child, or indeed to the military gentleman I had never heard. Rose herself made no reference to these matters. They constituted one of those ingredients in family history which are so much taken for granted as to need no adumbration. For my aunt carried her loss around her as a shawl, an accoutrement never discarded but continually tugged into place as a gesture of belonging. As you stand in that shadowy basement talking to Rosie, the child seemed to stand between you, cooing.

I remember an incident when I was a boy of ten or eleven. There was a large family gathering at our home in Finchley at Michaelmas, shortly before the Feast of All Souls. I had abandoned the adults in the large back dining room in order to fetch from the lounge some gewgaw with which to dispel my boredom: a pipe cleaner, the bellows hanging by the grate, or the *Radio Times* in its limp leather folder. Opposite me at the sumptuously laid table I had half noticed an empty place, but it was not until I entered the front room that I realised who must have vacated the chair. As I tiptoed through the doorway, I saw Rosie, younger than today but already in my eyes a legend, sitting alone at the window seat and staring through the double glazing to the street beyond. The glass was shielded by a lace curtain, across which fell the immense swaying shadow of the lime tree out by the kerbside. Outside there was a sudden flutter of wings, and then a low murmur as if of doves. Rose sat motionless on the window seat, oblivious of my presence, her eyes rapt and distant, following the sound:

"He cometh not," she said;
She said, "I am aweary, aweary,
I would that I were dead!"

One family habit Rose has not inherited. She lives shrouded by hush and the distant drumming of traffic, but there are few pauses in her speech. When she receives the rare visitor her conversation gushes like a Highland brook. Around the tea-cups and the pictures it swirls, eddying across the rugs and the one incongruous curtain. Her subject is history, the family's and her own. To converse with Father is like trudging blindfold through a mist, with Claud, like culling mushrooms from a glade; to listen to Rosie - for she permits little more - is like picking your way across steppingstones. The torrent gushes on:

"The days are getting shorter and one lives alone. If it were not for you Benedict and the occasional card from Claud, I would think that the family had quite forgotten me. I sit by the firelight painting pots. I listen to the wireless sometimes, though all of the stations are different. Now Lady Howard has passed beyond and all my acquaintance drift out of mind, it is as if one had taken the veil really. What did your dear father say? Does he think of me sometimes? He was always so dreadfully solemn, the silly. Still I hold him in my heart and pray for him on Thursdays. I have offered him up to Our Lady of Sorrows often, over there by the cactus. But I had much rather see you than anybody else in the world, Benedict. Between you and myself there has always seemed an affinity. It is a matter of the hair I fancy, and even of the eyebrows. You must promise me to look after yourself. We are all that is left of our strain in the family. You know of course we are descended from Lord Lovat who remained faithful to Prince Charles Edward. He was executed after Culloden. Lady Howard always used to tell me she held his memory dear. We must remember how he stood firm for an honest cause and offer him up at All Souls for his good intentions. There's a monument to him I'm told somewhere in the Highlands. What a pity I have never seen it and dare say will not live to make the trip. It will be as much as I'll do now to struggle once more to Walsingham. I always meant to do it barefoot. How are you getting on over there? Shall I grill you some more toast? Are you quite happy with the Darjeeling? Drink that cup up and I'll make us some fresh. That must be cold by now. I'm afraid there's only the evaporated milk. I used to get it from the dairy but nowadays that mulish milkman just will not climb down the steps. He says my treasure trove bruises his knees. I call it my treasure trove, though I prefer to think of it as a kind of downstairs attic. I could never bear to throw anything away Benedict. It is all too precious. You must know how I feel. We have a great kinship of spirit, you and I. What were you telling me about that lovely girl? Did you tell me she studies the Classics? You are such a clever boy, Benedict, and she sounds such a sweet girl. Don't listen to what your father has to say. His soul is all crabbed like a walnut. We must both pray for him, that he may be happy. But as for this young woman now, when will you bring her to see me?

*****

But Andria would not meet Rosie. Hour after hour she sat scribbling incomprehensible notes in her spindly nervous handwriting, her head bent, her feet occasionally tapping. Notes on the scansion of fragments, on the exact quantities of vowels, notes on the emendations of scholars, and the emendation of emendations of emendations. Andria had her head bowed beneath a heap of erudition and would not turn to answer to me. As I squatted against the Japanese bedspread, sketchbook in hand, I recorded her plangent beauties forever, but my impressions drifted over her head like seaweed.

On the dressing table of our tiny bedroom stood an oval mirror with a cracked mahogany frame. I had often used it for self-portraits, casting sidelong glances into its silvered surface in the hope that it might give back - what? - a definition of myself, a confirmation of my latent sorrows? It was into this mirror that now, raising her head indolently from her work, Andria would peep before her pallid forehead clouded briefly in concern, and, taking up her fountain pen once more, she returned to her page.

I had no idea what this repeated gesture meant. To me Andria's mind was a closed book in a script of which I knew nothing. As times progressed, the covers about the book had grown tighter, the text inside when I was granted a glimpse more convoluted and mysterious. It was the sort of mystery you might live with familiarly, as with an inherited Greek testament, consulted infrequently and in bafflement.

Suddenly the telephone rang out. At first I could not find it and, when I eventually located it beneath the folds of the bedspread and applied the receiver to my ear, I could make out nothing, except a furtive scratching like a mouse nibbling at the skirting.

I said, "Hullo?" and again "Hullo?"

There was a gap of several seconds and then, as if across the Arctic ice-flows, drifted the unmistakeable voice: "Benedict," it said, "do I disturb?"

I was surprised to hear from him again so soon. It had been barely two weeks. Had he left town and immediately doubled back again, or had he sojourned here all the while? Once more the unpredictability of that solitary existence was borne in on me.

But when he resumed speaking, I was struck by something different in his tone. The usual hesitation, the halting progress of the too perfect syntax, was suffused with an unwonted fatigue, a weariness and anxious persistence that lay beneath like a shadow dimly discerned on a doctor's X-ray screen. "I wondered if we might meet on Saturday," he said. "In

Room Twenty-five. By Holbein's *Duchess of Milan*."

Andria called, "Who is it?"

"Claud. He wants to see me in the Gallery." We were lip-reading. "He doesn't sound too well."

"Good," she mimed. "Soon you'll be rid of him."

The voice put it, "It's a personal matter."

My lips gestured, "He needs me. I can't refuse."

Nor did I wish to. Firmly into the receiver I spoke the one word "Holbein", as if offering a password, and then put down the earpiece.

Outside it was now almost dark. Little traces of Monestial Blue were etched against the absorbing blackness. I stared at them transfixed, until, in defiance of my trance, Andria reached over and switched on the table lamp. Immediately the patches of blue were eclipsed by gold.

Squinting back over my shoulder I saw Andria once more consult the oval mirror. Momentarily the light bulb flickered beneath its plastic shade as if a raven's wing had passed across the bald face of the sun. I opened both my eyes full and stared at the black oblongs of the windowpanes.

I remained motionless and silent. Then, glancing round again, I saw Andria's reflection large in the mirror. Anxiously it fingered the corner of its mouth. Then, softly but very distinctly, "I'm pregnant," it said.

BOOK TWO:

THE DUCHESS OF MILAN

BOOK TWO

At first I could not make him out. It was a mild and pleasant Saturday afternoon outside, and Trafalgar Square was thronging with trippers enjoying the unseasonable November air. As I made my way through the choked halls of the gallery, I greeted the more familiar items like friends: Peti's *Marriage at Canaa*, Reni's *Adoration of the Shepherds* and, serene within its gilded frame, Hobbema's *The Avenue Middelharnis* shrouded by its halo of Rembrandts. Room Twenty-five was heaving with tourists, family parties and one motley guided tour. Somehow, I elbowed my way through and searched for the Burberry raincoat.

It was not easy. By time-honoured precedent we had always avoided weekends. Claud's unilateral breach of this convention attested the very urgency of his summons. When in London, it had always been his custom to spend several days resting between one onerous peregrination and the next. If such had been the case on this occasion, his schedule could scarcely have been so pressing as to render a weekday impossible. His choice of a Saturday of all days suggested, contrary to all custom, he had fled the provinces for the weekend only, a recourse which pecuniary and temperamental considerations normally precluded. Even for a weekend, the room was inconveniently full. There was already a cluster of faces around Holbein's *Duchess of Milan,* while at the other end of the room a lecturer intense in red-rimmed glasses was attempting to expound the principle of *anamorphosis* in his double portrait of *The Ambassadors*, pointing to an indistinct blur at the bottom right hand corner, then falling back to reveal its true identity as a Death's Head spelling doom to the worldly pretensions of the emissaries preening themselves above. Some members of the party attempted to follow suit, and one of them – a Texan lady of florid countenance – collided with me. I had just managed to extricate myself from her embraces when I caught sight of Claud, slightly to the left of the group, staring resolutely in the other direction and towards the *Duchess of Milan.*

No death's head was needed to reveal the message written on that face. I had grown used by now to my uncle's air of personal neglect, the unkempt dress, the shelf of stubble which on less circumspect days ran along the contours of his chin. I had always had some difficulty in estimating Claud's age. Since he was younger than my dad by some three years, I took him nowadays to be just a little past seventy. Despite this,

his hair, though often untended, had always lain lush and dark against his temples. Now, as I took my stand beside him, I noticed from furtive side-long glances that the grey, previously confined to his sideburns, was creeping towards the crown of his head. This I might have ignored had it not been for the emaciated appearance of his features, making the nose – in our family resolutely Roman – stand out unnaturally from the face, the sunken aspect of his body, previously inches taller than my own now hunched for warmth within the tatterdemalion lineaments of his coat, for the almost phthisical whiteness of the neck against the lurid crimson of his scarf.

My mind raced back over the few weeks since our last meeting in October. I had grown accustomed over the years to receiving a flow of almost fortnightly postcards, regular as they were cryptic. Over the last month or so, this unrelenting minimal correspondence had been as tardy as my promptness in registering its decline. The reason for this lapse, as for my uncle's intemperate dash southwards, now lay abundantly clear. Even so, nothing could impair the quality of his concentration, every ounce of it now applied to the image before him with the devotional gravity of his posture before the portrait of Catherine of Braganza years previously.

It was some time before with his usual extreme gentleness he said, "She can have only been sixteen."

Before us hung the portrait of a young widow, facing us like an icon. She was clad entirely in black, apart from a crisp lace ruff which peered from beneath her neckline and matching white cuffs at her wrists. The face was haunted by an indefinable blend of modesty and candid entreaty. Around the fourth finger of her left hand she wore a circlet of gold bearing a simple ruby: presumably her wedding ring. On her mourning garb the artist had lavished all his celebrated skill with draperies, the soft lamp black of her cap and belted dress contrasting with the shiny ebony of her fur-edged satin coat. Behind her, the acidic green of the wall was divided by a humped shadow, while a corner fold to the far right betrayed the presence of an adjoining wall to that side. Christina of Denmark, Duchess of Milan appeared to have plucked her eyebrows; her lips too were lightly pencilled with cosmetic. The flawless, wide-cheeked face looked directly towards us, yet gave nothing away. "Do you know the story behind this one, Benedict?" asked my uncle.

Resisting the blandishments of vanity, I laid claim to ignorance.

"Well then, here's something I can tell *you*. Henry was looking for a fourth wife. It was between Jane Seymour's execution and Anne of Cleves. Christina had just lost her first husband the duke. So Henry packed off Holbein to make a sketch, and then to submit a portrait. Henry never married her. He can't have liked what he saw, though I'll be blowed if I know why."

"I think she looks rather sweet. I'll give you that."

"Yes. Fragile. Vulnerable. Millimetres deep, that disdain."

Then my uncle did something which I had never seen before. Turning round, he gave me a thin, watery smile expressive of such sadness and desolation of spirit that my usual attempts to maintain a semblance of conversational flow for once forsook me. "Let's take a walk," he said, and we were out of the room and threading our way through the Rubens collection and on toward the Van Dykes before, taking up his former train of thought, he reduced his pace a little, said, "I wonder…"

"Wonder what, Claud?"

He turned his head and stared back wistfully at the room we had just left. "There is a strong facial resemblance. She's older of course, though the challenge might just suit you. You were at college together weren't you?"

My attitude can only have expressed bewilderment. At college with the Duchess of Milan?

"Echardt's daughter that is. Poor Benedict, I doubt if I'm making too much sense."

"Not a lot."

"Well, sit you down, and I'll try to explain."

We subsided opposite Van Dyke's Charles I, flamboyantly astride his steed. Claud took his time and then, measuring his words, he asked, "Do you have a notion what beauty is?"

"I'm still endeavouring to find out, I'm afraid."

"And all these years I've done nothing but hinder you?"

"No," I protested with total sincerity for once. "You've helped a lot."

"It's the grainy apprehension of perfection. You remember what that Greek fellow said? The philosopher chappy. Plato."

"All life's a shadow of the Good?"

"No. A shadow of a shadow of a shadow. We're nowhere near to it. And I'm not a lot closer than you are."

"At least you've been trying."

"Yes, I have tried. And I'll try again. That's where *you* come in."

"I don't follow."

"Let's put it this way. What's the purest thing you know?"

I thought for a few seconds before gesticulating around me.

"All this…"

"Exactly. And why? Because it's immutable. I'll give you an illustration. You see that Van Dyke over there. Was Charles remotely like that do you think?"

"Not in the least."

"What was he then?"

"A fop, a worldling."

"With occasional flashes of nobility, yes. Do you think it's the foppishness that's preserved? Not a bit. What do we have? Nobility, sovereignty, control: that's what Van Dyke painted."

"Yes."

Then, looking me straight in the eyes, he said: "Give me my dream of nobility. It's all I've got left. It's all I deserve. Let's walk on a bit further."

He took me through a side door and back by degrees towards the front of the gallery and the Early Italians, talking all the way in a torrent of words for him without precedent, an eloquence, bred of the delirium of his sickness: "Do you know how long I've worked for the firm of Echardt? Almost thirty years. Every three months or so I'm here to pick up instructions, fill up my cases, and every week while I'm in London I pay a visit to the company's offices in the Poultry. You've never been there, have you? It's at the top of a spiral staircase and on the landing there's a lobby with comfy chairs and a pile of magazines. Twenty or so years ago it must be, I was sitting reading a Sotheby's catalogue when a silhouette passed across the frosted door that connects with Echardt's office. Then there was a cascade of laughter and the tinkle of a young girl's voice. A few minutes later the door opened and a girl of about sixteen walked out across the lobby, blew a kiss through the still open door, and let herself out."

"Christina?"

"She never even looked at me, and she must have passed across that lobby in front of me dozens of times over the years."

"And always the silhouette? Always the laughter?"

"Not always no. But often enough. I've never even spoken to her, you know."

71

We had almost reached the Quattrocento collection before Claud halted once more and asked, "Tell me, what did Holbein paint?"

"A girl called Christina."

"No. No." His voice was almost strident. "An *ideal* called Christina."

"What the king wanted to see?"

"No. What *he* wanted the king to see. The perfection was in the wanting. Was that subterfuge?"

"A benevolent fraud certainty."

"Is real benevolence ever fraudulent? I wonder. Henry never married the girl. What does it matter? Holbein saw a young woman, chafing at the bit probably, impatient to have done with it, but posing to oblige. Was that what Holbein gave us? No. He gave us perfection, a dream. Can you give me that perfection?

"You want me to be your Holbein?" The enormity of the idea confounded me.

"I'm an old man now, Benedict, and haven't a lot to live for. Flatter an old man's weakness and help yourself into the bargain. What's a painter if he can't paint Truth?"

I thought of the Christina Echardt I'd known all those years ago, a wisp by the canal side, a duplicitous vision seen tormentedly across a dance hall, an apparition in the doorway of my room, dealing out deception, dealing out pain.

"You're asking me to paint a lie," I said.

"No Ben," he said, emphasizing the words. "Painters don't lie. I'm asking you to paint the Truth."

*****

The Willows, Cheam, St Andrew's Day, 1984.

My Dear Benedict,
It was the sweetest surprise to see you earlier in the month. It's such a pity we always seem to fall out. I remember so well how during your mother's lifetime the whole family used to gather together to celebrate the Saint's day, either 30th November itself or the Sunday immediately following. We all seem to live so scattered now.

Enclosed with this letter you will find a slip of paper on which I've written Christina Echardt's address. I got it from her father last week. Apparently the flat's in a largish block overlooking the river in Pimlico. I'm afraid I didn't manage to get her phone number. If you do decide to go, I should drop a line to her first.

Yours affectionately, Father.

*****

One day, while Andria was feeding Menander, my eye drifted up from her hand against the cat's fanged, ravenous mouth to the graceful curve of her backbone, so well-known to me and yet, after her recent announcement, so strange. There was little that I could take for granted in her now. The very stoop of her frame seemed endowed with a kind of wizardry, her wilful moods – for she was still far from reconciled to the prospect of pregnancy – the movement of her wrist as each morning she combed her straggling hair before the oval mirror, the angle of her neck as, again bending, she removed clothes from the apple green chest of drawers which ever so slightly askew stood by our bedside.

She finished feeding the cat, easing her body up into the upright position, and at that very moment an idea took root. I would work on a series of sketches which should stand tribute to this hour. However much she learned to resent it, I would give Andria's unfolding its due.

So it was that, as the date of my exhibition in late May approached, I embarked on a set of studies which I came to think of as its cornerstone. I drew Andria from every angle: lying down whilst poring over her books, playing with Menander, or else gesturing at me: strident, gawky, giving vent to her spleen. In each sketch the position of the spine revealed new and unprecedented possibilities. Soon I possessed a whole portfolio of curves which might be grouped together or else taken singly; as patterns of complementary waves, as horizontal or vertical projections or as segments of an irregular sphere. It was Andria and my child's gift to me.

And yet ever and anon the subject of Claud's bizarre commission tugged at my thoughts. He had left the gallery that afternoon informing me that he wished me to paint the Truth. I had been told before now that artists were truth tellers. My art history tutor Jocelyn used to ramble on about something called *mimesis* in lecture after lecture. You could find it in Titian, you could find it in Vermeer. You couldn't find it in Tiepolo who always seemed to be aiming at something unearthly: he needed the grand scale or all of his dimensions were wrong. The trouble with my uncle was that he wanted majesty to be true *per se*, as if for him Beauty was Truth in a more than fanciful, in an almost philosophical, sense. I itched to take up the gauntlet. But I knew myself unworthy of it. When I look at things or people, I'm always searching for the flaws in the design. For me something is true because it is real, not because it is sublime. I could transmute Andria's spinal column into a thing of grace. Could I dignify into comeliness so worthless, haughty and blemished a subject as Christina Echardt?

My mind went back fifteen years to the summer term of my Foundation year at Art School, and Christina's. She was soon to quit the formal study of art and, taking up the reins of a hastily abandoned academic career, go to read History at Oxford. It was a sultry sort of a June, and the students had taken to drinking outside overlooking the river in little incestuous groups. I had never been one to cultivate cronies, but had temporarily taken refuge from my persistent sense of social unease with a circle of carbuncular jesters who fancied themselves as exponents of a privileged variety of jocular acerbic wisdom. We were of course anything but wise.

The doyen of the party was a lanky Irish lad from Northampton called Jake, a pock-marked youth who invariably dressed in black, wore a St Christopher's medallion round his scrawny neck, and took himself for a weary kind of sophist. Jake was punk before punk, he was grunge before grunge. He was the Sex Pistols ere they fired shot or sperm, he was the one-man embodiment and precursor of every malodorous trend. Jake took himself for a decadent, and his voiced opinions about art and women were of much the same, dingy hue. One Wednesday afternoon, when Jocelyn shared with us a reproduction of Carlo Crivelli's *Annunciation, with Saint Emidius,* which I later got to know better from visits to the Gallery, I was made privy to Jake's inner thoughts. The painting, done in 1486, shows the Virgin Mary of her knees, her head meekly bowed as a beam of light lands on her through her open window. Outside in the street, the archangel and Emidius are deep in conversation, while the saint balances a model of the city that commissioned the work, resting on one holy knee. To Jake, they both looked bored. As for the Madonna, his verdict was emphatic: "Shouldn't she look a bit more exultant? I mean, she is supposed to be having a fuck with the Holy Ghost, for heaven's sake."

I was never quite sure whether comments such as these represented barbed challenges to my recurrent, and occasionally voiced, religious nostalgia, or whether this intemperate young Irishman was attempting to wound something deep within himself. Usually, I said nothing.

Jake and I used to sit in the college bar cutting life classes and passing comments on all who were unfortunate enough to pass before the judgement seat of our table. Few escaped Jake's scorn. He would be fleetingly drawn to a face at another table and then in a desperate reflex of defensiveness turn against the illusion, railing. Some of his less pestilential remarks were spoken out loud, but most disappeared down the foam-streaked top of his beer glass. I recall one occasion when a notorious siren of the period sashayed past, hips swaying, breasts pert beneath her Jaeger jumper. He waited for her to settle at an adjacent table before opening up his notepad and scrawling on a blank sheet which he then tore off and passed across to me. It read: "What, my dear Benedict, do we love in women? We love ourselves."

In the event he was thrown out of the life class for his inability to reproduce in graphic form what the teacher termed "the irreducible otherness of the given."

That afternoon by the riverside, however, such reproof was many months off, and otherness of any description not something to which any of us would have been tempted to give himself, had it not been for the sight of Christina Echardt sitting alone on a low wall. I had witnessed her solitude several times before, most often in the college library, which always seemed pervaded by her fragrance when she left it, a fragrance of languid pulchritude and rose-water. I may have recalled these impressions to Jake, whose enmity to all such sentimental indulgence drove him that afternoon to upbraid me for my wistfulness. It was ten days before the End of Year Ball - an event which under normal circumstances few of us would have contemplated patronizing. But, whether from some distillation of my former impressions, or from her complexion lightly brushed by shade, something drove me to express an interest. And something else about Christina that day – her attitude of self-sufficiency and sovereign reserve, combined no doubt with my own timidly expressed preference – drove Jake to goad me into offering an invitation.

It was the last enterprise on which I would have embarked on my own initiative. I had been a shy and self-effacing student. An only child bred of middle-aged parents, I did not find social overtures of any sort easy, still less overtures to glamourous, self-assured young women. I was also dimly aware of some connection between this eye-catching person and my father and uncle, but for some reason this fact only increased my awe. The notion of introducing myself to one with whom I had not until that moment exchanged more than a word or two filled me with utter dread and foreboding. Nonetheless, two days later at Jake's bidding I dropped the briefest and most apologetic of notes into the pigeon-hole marked 'E' and waited for an answer. None came.

It was principally as a result of my friend's continuing cajolery that I agreed to take the matter further, and found myself the following week standing over her table in the refectory mouthing solicitous words. She looked at me from the depths of her piercing yet oddly remote light brown eyes, nodded slightly as if her mind was on something else and spoke a curt "alright" before I dismissed myself, abashed and disbelieving.

The Tuesday before the dance I was lying in bed finishing off a chocolate bar bought in a mood of idle gluttony from the corner shop on my way back from a Liberal Studies class. There was a sharp rat-a-tat on the door. I called "Come in" and looked round to see Christina framed in the doorway, a black beret on her head, her hands clasped lightly before her in perfect, unapologetic composure. She was saying something about her daddy. Her daddy was sick she said, he wanted her home that weekend, he was a widower and living alone, she must not let him down, she must be excused. Her daddy, she said, her daddy. I could still recall the pout and curl of her lips as she cooed it out. Her daddy. Her daddy. Echardt, I suppose.

I assumed as dignified a posture as I could, and let her go. Then, salvaging as much pride as I could muster, I threw discretion to the winds and invited the next girl who sat beside me in the High Renaissance class. She was, as I recall, far from high, and certainly not Renaissance. Three evenings later I was leaning across her shoulder, during one of the slow numbers played by our college Dixieland jazz band when I happened to peer across the room and saw Christina with her back to me. She had her arms round Jake, who was leaning against the far wall as she pawed at his black shirt while he beamed down at her with lazy, sensuous pleasure.

The long vacation arrived and I was due to travel to Cologne to do some research for my history project. I found myself in a certain area of London needing cash to book my concessionary flight. Recollecting that some months previously I had arranged drawing facilities at a bank in the vicinity, I had mounted the steps into the lobby when I realised that I carried neither cheque book nor means of identification. I was about to leave when, glancing over the counter towards the depths of the building, I caught sight of Christina Echardt fingering through the contents of a filing cabinet. She had clearly secured some kind of clerical employment to defray the expense of her imminent departure for realms beyond my reach, or for that matter of Jake's. Walking over to the counter area, I informed the cashier that I had an arrangement with his branch and that there was someone in the office behind him who could identify me. In response to my request, he walked across to the filing cabinet where 1 could see him whispering into Christina's elegant, upturned ear. She had been staring down at the filed documents with her habitual air of quizzical unseeing possessiveness, but as she lifted her eyes to look in my direction a dull flicker of recognition passed across them followed by a look of the most withering contempt I had ever seen eyes express. Then, just loud enough for me to hear,

she murmured, "Yes. I suppose I do know who he *is*."
An amused shaft of complicity passed between them
before the cashier returned and agreed to fill out a
counter cheque. It was the last time I saw her before
she went up to Oxford. I had heard nothing from her,
from that day to this.

Would she remember me? Were there nights when,
lying awake, across her recollection there drifted the
buffoonish shade of a boy with tousled hair who had
mumbled presumptuous words, then had the temerity
to resent the delayed but inevitable repulse? I sincerely
hoped not. Even if I could bring myself once more to
submit to her clemency, there remained the practical
problem. For obvious reasons I did not wish to insist
upon our previous acquaintance, nor did I wish to give
my father the satisfaction of using the family
connection to gain an entrée into her esteem. There was
just a chance that the very fact of my existence had
passed clean out of her head. Would it not be better to
jettison the past and, employing contrivance for my
uncle's sake, begin entirely afresh?

I reasoned thus. She is now in her mid-thirties. She
has an apartment of her own in one of the more
salubrious parts of London. She works, and, even if she
did not, enjoys a generous allowance. Do I just barge
into this refined and settled existence? Do I ring her
bell, doff my cap - for such I wear in winter - and
plunge in with a sort of fretful abandon: "Madam,
however presumptuous this may seem, of all the
doorbells in London this is the very one which for

many days I have itched to ring. We are unknown to one another. We possess no mutual acquaintance. Our stars have not, as far as I am aware, yet crossed. There is no decent law-abiding reason why I present myself, thus brazen and ashamed, at your door. I have not come to read the metre. I do not represent a political party. Your sewage and water rates are not, as far as I am aware, in arrears. I am not here to fix the curtains, mend the carpet, seal the wiring or insulate the mains, nor do I carry copies of a commercial circular. I stand here merely as a profound if instantaneous admirer, as one who, having caught the merest glimpse of your features, finds himself, in defiance of all reason, enthralled. Madam, may I paint you?" Would I reach the end of such a speech? Would I complete the second sentence?

At length inspiration struck. Whilst in England a man may not with any decency propose admiration of a woman's beauty as sufficient reason for standing unannounced at her door, once admitted on the premises, the case rested somewhat differently. To enter a woman's living room, to turn round in casual scrutiny of the furniture, the décor, the arrangement of her flowers, and then in one seamless conversational progression move to the aesthetic accomplishments of the girl herself, this - especially if elegantly performed - was at least permissible. What I required therefore was not so much a reason as a pretext, something which, if it did not lie easily to hand, might honourably be concocted.

The Christmas season was fast approaching. Garish fabrications were beginning to adorn shop windows. Hoardings emblazoned the December wares. Oxford Street had begun to resemble a greyhound track. The Feast of Walt Disney was nigh, and all along Regent's Street, in endlessly repeated pairs, Micky Mouse and Donald Duck hung suspended like gruesome pagan effigies. Such bustle provided a cloak of anonymity behind which the unscrupulous or desperate might hide. It was the perfect breeding ground of pretexts.

Every November for the previous few years, there had dropped through our peeling letter box in Kensal Rise an envelope containing six conventional greeting cards with a covering letter from an organization calling itself Mouth and Foot Painting Artists. At first I took them for an outpost of the agricultural fraternity, cattle farmers ruined by bovine pestilence and hoping to survive on their secondary skill as Sunday painters. But no: they were, it appeared, unfortunate members of our profession who, having lost the use of their hands, had converted tongue or toe to the execution of the most exquisite draftmanship. Would these unfortunate men and women, to whose needs I had always faithfully subscribed, purchasing full twenty-four cards which then lay wilting and unsigned at the bottom of the apple green chest of drawers for the next twelve months: could they bring themselves to forgive me if, in this my hour of need, and in the interests of our common calling, I made use of their alias? This time, instead of stacking the cards in that dusty lower drawer I would call round and present them to Christina. "Madam, I represent …" Was it too tasteless, too gauche, too crude? It was all that I had.

For days I delayed, fought with myself and practised my lines. I ruined a number of sketches and consumed one whole bottle of whisky. But at length, late one bleak Thursday afternoon, telling Andria that I was paying a visit to my aunt in Maida Vale and, clutching an envelope containing a selection of the MFPA's cards, I made my way to the address inscribed on Father's slip of paper. It was an oleaginous evening infused with the sort of bleached and variegated greys in which the Impressionists had once delighted. "Turpentine gloaming" I used to call such effects, in reference to my futile attempts to imitate Monet or Whistler by loading my brush with a little too much white spirit to thin the pigment to an acceptably suggestive smudge. The more rarefied stretches of the river toward Chelsea have always for me exuded an aura of wealth and opulence quite beyond my station. Father's instructions indicated an apartment in Dolphin Square. As I made my way from the underground station, I felt my pulse rising. I took the lift up to the fourth floor and in due course found myself at Christina's doorway, no longer in tortured fantasy, but about to ring the bell. In my left hand I held the envelope; in my right, I clutched a plastic *portefeuille*. I had left my usual peaked cap at home and could not therefore remove it. I leaned forward, pushed the porcelain bell within its brass surround, and coughed. I coughed again. I placed the envelope in my gloved right hand, moved the *portefeuille* to my left, shuffled in my shoes and paused. I waited some considerable time before next pressing the bell. I was about to ring for a third time when the door slowly edged open.

She was evidently herself on the way out. Around her shoulders she wore a fur-edged cape, generously shaped and reaching almost to the ground. In her tapered, anxious fingers lay a pair of white kid gloves, twisted as if in embarrassment, while on the fourth finger of her left hand, facing outward towards me, was an unpretentious ring bearing a small ruby or garnet. She stood perfectly still looking me straight in the eyes. It was a ridiculously tiny lobby painted the vivid green of corroded copper, and she stood in the corner of it as if guarding a shrine. She was wearing some kind of a cap matching her cloak. A single light source well to her right beyond the rim of the door illuminated her face, while casting an oblique shadow against the containing wall. The mouth was pursed, the nose straight, the eyebrows slightly arched. The eyes appeared apprehensive, but gave absolutely nothing away. All of the carefully prepared words flew out of my head.

What was I to say? Should I, in the face of such austerity and defensiveness, construct another story on the spot? There was no need:

"You're Arnold's friend," she said, archly.

"Arnold," I replied, fumbling. "Yes."

"It's not exactly convenient." Her voice had that

fruity quality of the well-bred English female, rather like a bass flute. "He said tomorrow … Well, come in."

I stepped over the threshold. As I did so, a whole collage of old newsreel shots tumbled through my head: Christina on a summer lawn, Christina pawing at the shirt-front of a long-lost friend called Jake, the smirk in her eyes as she glanced at me from behind a cashier's desk that July. We entered the living room, and for the first time she turned so that I could take the whole impression in. She had changed certainly - a certain fullness around the jaw, an ampleness around the waist - yet the angle of her neck was the same, the reticent lips, the clear brown eyes round whose edges now crept tiny traces of crow's feet which failed nonetheless to detract from their caustic brightness. She had always possessed an air of staring at you without appearing to see you. I searched her face for any flicker of recognition. There was none. For all the familiarity registered by those lofty features I might have been a tradesman. She had mentioned somebody called Arnold. Who in pity's name was he?

"I expected somebody taller," she said. "More on the decorative side. But I suppose you'll have to do. I haven't an awful lot of time."

It was a restrained and orderly room such as one finds featured in the glossier monthly periodicals. Three walls were painted coffee, while a recess was covered in hessian. Metal blinds concealed a set of French windows which presumably led on to some kind of patio. In the middle of the room, on a spotless skin rug, stood a glass-topped table supporting a simple fluted vase holding a flame-red *poinsettia*. The only visible picture was a print of St Mark's Square, Venice in a plain aluminium frame. Next to the door there was a plush Chesterfield sofa, behind which a black-and-white batik print was illuminated by a stainless steel swivel spotlight. In desperation I inspected the ceiling, hoping for mouldings or cornices on which to comment.

"Have you had a lot of experience of this sort of work?" she asked with terse politeness before I had a chance to speak.

We seemed unexpectedly to have come to the point.

"Well," I ventured. "I've been trying … studying the techniques for years. Of course it isn't always easy to capture the essence of what one wants. One usually has to work fairly intensively with the subject over a number of weeks."

There was a slack connective moment before she said: "But surely you only have to stand or sit or something."

"Sometimes," I persisted, dully blundering on, "I like to assess the subject from all possible angles. It's a vital preparation for the selection of a pose: sometimes, remarkably, it's often possible to combine different vantage points from the same perspective. It's rather difficult to explain, but marvellous when it works."

"I wanted a model," she protested, "not a strutting doll."

"I beg your pardon?"

"Didn't Arnold, tell you? It's for a version of *Venus and Adonis*. I was wanting someone to stand in for Adonis. Arnold said you had the appropriate doomed and voluptuous air. He also said you had the thighs."

"The thighs?" My mind inscribed an arabesque.

"I'm sorry if it isn't quite what you were looking for. Perhaps you were expecting to sit in for a profile. If the work doesn't suit you, there's really no problem. Life models are ten a penny, really."

My brain continued to churn on its miserable way. Had I understood her right? Was *she* expecting to paint *me*?

Several years previously, when in the direst straits of penury, when Andria's salary cheque for once had proved insufficient to support us, I had signed on at the Royal College of Art as a model for life-drawing classes. The secretary was not encouraging. The department had its usual people, the academic year was drawing to a close, but if there was anything, they would let me know, or else hand on my name. Several months later, at half past two in the morning, the bakelite phone by our bedside rang. When I picked it up, I heard a male voice, very hoarse and husky. He hoped I didn't mind, but he had been given my number by the college. Could he buy me a drink? We arranged to meet in a pub in Islington. He bought me a drink. His voice grew husky, and he came to the point. He was homosexual and passionate about photography. I fled into the night. I had not heard from the college for many years. Was this Arnold?

I thought fast. I was it seemed the beneficiary of an act of pure chance. In a few minutes the doorbell with the brass surround will ring. She will answer it, and into that cramped copper-green doorway will step a tall and cool individual, doomed, voluptuous, and with appropriate thighs. I must strike while the iron was hot. If I accepted the challenge, I might once and for all upstage him. Christina would leave on the errand for which she was dressed, without knowing the difference.

I said, "I merely called to arrange …"

She gave me one of her traffic light smiles. "Quite," she said sharply. "To get us going, would this Thursday at three be suitable?"

I forgot to give her the cards.

*****

The Willows, Cheam, 6th December, 1984.

Dear Benedict,

When I dropped you a note recently conveying what a great pleasure it had been to see you here last month, I should imagine that I stood accused in your eyes of the direct hypocrisy. I did not expect a reply. Somehow it is always a father's fate to be misconstrued in this manner. There are times when one gets to feel rather like those parental buffoons in the Latin comedies one always seemed to be given to translate at school. It is not a dignified position to occupy. Nevertheless, your visit *was* a pleasure, and such a contrast to the wireless. You still have my loving concern. I was wondering whether you had given any more thought to my suggestion as to your contacting Lawrence Echardt with a view to working for his firm? I saw him quite recently and he was kind enough to ask after you. I came away with the impression that there's still an opening there if you're keen on it. Echardt's not as sharp as he was, but he's a kindly soul, even if his demeanour is occasionally a little gruff. I'm sure in any case that he'd welcome you with open arms. You could do a lot worse, Ben.

Your loving father.

P.S. I have phoned through to you on several occasions but have only ever got Andria. She sounds just a little bit queasy. I know she doesn't take to me, and, as you are aware, I'm afraid that this is mutual.

P.P.S. Did I send you Christina Echardt's address? Dolphin Square. Quite a swish block near the river. E says she lives next door to a queer actor called Thorley Walters. You sometimes see him in films with Terry-Thomas. Saint Trinian's and all that.

*****

I was standing by the glass-topped table.

"Where do I undress?" I asked. She responded with an elegant sweep of the wrist. "Oh dear. I suppose you'd better use the *thingy*. You'll find plenty of pegs. And oh," she added, holding out my trench coat, "you can take this along."

I took the jacket and tiptoed across the passageway to where her bathroom gave out an unfamiliar aroma of queenly sophistication. Above the spotless olive-green bathroom suite her unguents lay in rows: *Opium* by Yves St Laurent, Christian Dior's *Dioressence*, Nina Ricci's *L'Air du Temps*. A plain wood wall cabinet contained preparations from The Body Shop: *Cocoa Butter Hand Lotion*; *Almond and Quince Pomade*. I sneezed and undid my shirt buttons. On the top of an inlaid sandalwood bath stool lay the robe which Christina had given me: a flimsy moss-green mantle that looked as if it wouldn't clothe a scarecrow. I removed my trousers and laid them carefully over a rail spread next to towels which seemed to have been laundered yesterday. I thought of our bathroom in Kensal Rise, its floor a mess of discarded clothes, its linen basket overflowing, its basin a sludge of hair and grime. I took off my vest and out of habit stared at myself in the wall mirror. Then I put on the robe trying to cover as much as possible of the exposed and goose-pimpled flesh. Returning to the drawing room, I stood in the doorway, barefoot, at her command. She was standing over by the metal blinds, one hand on her hip, sipping a cup of coffee. From the kitchen to my right emerged a savour of spice and coffee grounds. She stirred slightly. Then she looked me over from head to foot and said, "You'll do. Now if you'll just perch while I assemble my easel."

I moved across and sat precariously on the edge of the Chesterfield. I was acutely consciousness of my nakedness, my lumpy embarrassed knees, the raw spot at the back of my neck where the material chafed slightly. I had a sharp unwelcome mental picture of myself standing framed in the doorway with Christina, clothed and predatory, poised above me. Then there was a clatter of slats and the vision dissolved, as from the depths of the cupboard she said, "I do hope you're not expecting to participate in a masterpiece. I've only returned to painting comparatively recently. I began studying at Kingston many moons ago but dropped out after the foundation year and went to university instead. I only got the bug seriously again when I was living in Italy. Even then it was mainly an observer's interest. I'm really much more used to sitting than being sat for. Does that sound absurd?"

She re-appeared carrying her equipment. I laughed decorously. The very idea.

"I just thought I'd get going again with a set of mythological themes. I thought of Ishtar and Tammuz at first, but everyone thinks that too obscure. So I've opted for Venus and Adonis. It comes to much the same thing in the end, doesn't it? I'm setting it in a forest glade after the fracas with the boar. He's supposed to be languishing in Venus's arms, but I'll put her in later. Not sure about the boar. Are you alright over there? You're capable of languishing I take it? Are the terms alright? I thought, twice a week perhaps 'til we're through …"

Her voice trailed off. I cleared my throat: "I'll have a bash," I said.

She looked at me appraisingly: "Good. You're not exactly ideal, but never mind. I expected somebody a little more languorous really. But under the circumstances … I think you'll find that rug is perfectly comfortable, unless that is you're frightfully brittle. Now, if you could just sort of *sprawl*."

*****

Kensal Rise, 9th December, 1984

Dear Dad

Thanks for the letter.

No, I don't fancy the leaden chains of commerce.

No, I don't wish to marry Christina Echardt.

Yes, you did give me her address. I have no intention of calling on her.

Yours dutifully

Ben.

P.S. Andria says that, on balance, it's a relief Thatcher escaped that bomb in Brighton. Not sure that I agree with her on that score.

*****

Burton-upon-Trent, Advent Sunday, 1984

I thought you'd appreciate this picture of Derby

Cathedral. It's a bit grim, but then so's everything around here, unless you're smitten with Gothic Revival. What I really wished to know was: any joy with the Sirens?

Claud

P.S. Will try to ring from Leicester.

*****

1 was lying with one knee raised. In my right hand I held an artificial acanthus that I had been asked to clutch to my chest, while my left grasped my waist in a parody of terminal agony. My mantle, several inches too short for me and apparently stitched from a redundant sheet, was beginning to slip over my right shoulder in a provocative and unintentional manner. I was also staring at a fixed point just above the bracket spotlight while endeavouring to maintain this expression of mixed anguish and awe. I was not quite sure that I was succeeding.

I could not see Christina, whose easel lay just beyond my field of vision, and could only guess at her progress by slightly shifting movements I dimly sensed or heard. I had now kept up this humiliating and inconvenient posture for the better part of an hour. Exactly how long it was difficult to tell, since I was unable to consult my wristwatch which lay on the glass-topped table in the middle of the room beyond which Christina worked, absorbed. My left leg, bent at the knee as if supporting my death-throes and gashed with lipstick in imitation of the tragic wound, had grown completely numb, and my back felt as though I had been carrying crates of sculpture up several flights of stairs. I was beginning to feel more than a little absurd.

Moreover, I was tormented by the dazzle. Christina clearly possessed her own ideas as to the quality of light required to illuminate her subject. In an effort to recreate the intermittent shade and glare of a woodland clearing, she had turned off every bulb in the room except one, the stainless steel swivel light which she had trained so that its full brightness fell in the vicinity of my pupils. The purpose was presumably to create some rough-and-ready form of *chiaroscuro,* but as the minutes progressed the solitary beam had assumed the form of a swirling festival of blue-grey blobs which proceeded to spin round in some crazy carolling circle like a funfair wheel. I was just about to protest at this unnecessary multiplication of my discomfort when from the invisible spaces beyond the gloom I heard her say, "It's such fun painting. It's like having an extra finger."

Out of the corner of my eye I could just discern where the tip of her brush, for all the world like some grotesque sixth finger, twirled in silhouette against the distant wall as if executing a monstrous species of hand jive. Then the silhouette vanished. I suspected that she had retreated to the depths of the room where she was summing up the effect of her recent additions to the canvas, but without craning my neck it was impossible to follow her movements. I had to settle for watching the silhouette of her skirt as it swayed beguilingly against the hessian.

"You're pretty wiry you know," she said suddenly from nowhere. "It's really quite satisfying."

"Yes, I suppose it must be."

"But I've made a mess of the shadows. I was trying to get to get the reflection of your torso against the carpet behind you, but the result's far from satisfactory, I'm afraid. Rather murky as a matter of fact. I'm sure my palette's much too dark. Wait a mo. I think I've got an inspiration. If you could just stay still for a minute. I'll see what Burnt Sienna can achieve."

Ah, Burnt Sienna. I had holidayed in Sienna during the Long Vacation immediately following my graduation from Camberwell. It was a humid July and my nerves were in a frayed condition following the failure of my final year show. It was three years since Christina had absconded and, the frump from the High Renaissance class at Kingston long having given me the slip, I had taken up with a wisp of a girl in the Second Year. We'd hired an attic room overlooking the dusty piazza where the palio horse race was annually held. In the event the wisp also stood me up, and I spent the entire fortnight sunbathing on the terracotta tiled roof thinking vengeful thoughts. When the torrid heat of the noontide hours abated, I would walk to the outskirts of the town beyond the medieval walls and ruefully survey the citrous groves and acres of rippling arable land beyond. There was no sign of the famous pigment. I had been told the Sienese possessed the purest vowels in Italy, the most elemental and fructifying sod, but on inspection the soil looked disappointingly like Dorset. As night fell and I returned alone to my lodgings, the shadow of the city walls crept over the surface of the world, covering all in near-darkness. Turpentine dusk again. Burnt Sienna does very well for shadows.

I was considering whether to speak of these things when I gradually became conscious of something happening to the side of my face. It started as a tight patch under my left eye. Then it became a quivering, and bit by bit an uncontrollable nervous twitch. A nerve seemed to have worked itself loose, and despite my best ministrations was now performing a wild dance of liberation beyond the lower rim of my lashes. At first there seemed nothing I could do to allay it, but then I hit on the idea of administering an imperceptible vertical massage. So very carefully I moved the muscles of my left cheek up into the semblance of a smile and then down into a grimace of severe disapproval. Then up again into a half-smile, down into a frown …

"Is there anything wrong? You seem to have *delirium tremens* or something."

"Just my nervous system I'm afraid. Rebels in the camp."

"What a bother. I was just about to start working on your face."

"Sorry."

"Don't be. It's your body. We can't have you expiring for real." She stood back, grimacing. "I'm afraid you're still not quite what you might be. I can't seem to get the shapes right."

"You could start by tilting that spotlight about thirty degrees to the left."

She moved over to correct it: "I'm sorry. It hasn't been burning your retina has it?" She swung the lamp aside so that it described a phosphorescent half-moon against the coffee firmament of the wall.

"Why that's amazing. What did you say your name was again?"

"Henry."

"I can see you a lot more clearly in the gloom. Well. You do have your moments, Henry," she said.

*****

When I returned to Kensal Rise that evening Andria was stretched out on top of the apple-green chest of drawers, her legs twisted in some posture of corybantic cramp, her chin against her chest, her arms pumping. I was slowly growing used to this species of callisthenic contortion, though the configurations never ceased to take me by surprise. Two weeks after her announcement of her condition I had discovered her prostrate in front of the gas fire, reading. When I looked down to inspect the contents of the book I found to my amazement not Catullus but something entitled *Towards Natural Childbirth* published by a feminist press in Peckham. From that moment on, there had been scarcely a spare second which she had not spent either straining against the windowsill or at the foot of the bed, or even incredibly once inside the wardrobe.

The chest-of-drawers however were an innovation. As I entered the bedroom she looked down at me briefly before continuing with this weird species of levitation. Then she said meaningfully, "And how *was* your aunt?"

The question was not one that should have surprised me, for on leaving earlier that afternoon I had felt it necessary to cover up my tracks by informing Andria that I was on my way to pay one of my regular courtesy visits to Maida Vale. The need for this falsehood had been obscure to me even as I had delivered it and was not entirely clear to me even now. There seemed no reason why I should be ashamed of my association with Christina, especially if its eventual outcome might be the chance to include one more portrait, or even set of portraits, in my fast-approaching show. Nor did there appear any reason why I should not let Andria share the intelligence of my compact with Claud. And yet I had contrived to maintain this untruth, justifying my deceit less by any apprehension that Andria might misconstrue my motives than by residual loyalty to my uncle.

There was a delicacy of discretion in Claud's make-up which, if I interpreted him right, he considered incumbent on others, especially those most clearly associated with himself by bonds of kinship. If, as seemed possible, his platonic interest in Christina should prove susceptible of misrepresentation, and if moreover by some contrivance of fate it should come to light, it was, I persuaded myself, my clear and unambiguous duty to protect him against any ignominy which he might then suffer and which I, as an ambivalent accomplice, might share.

So in answer to Andria's inquiry I said, "Rose seems very well. Bit depressed by the weather, but nothing unusual. She seems intrigued by you, incidentally. Every time I leave, she says, 'When will you bring your Andria to see me?'"

Andria abruptly stopped pumping. Then she picked herself up from her position of horizontal self-impalement, climbed back to floor-level and asked, "Didn't you tell me that Rosie once had a baby?"

I said "I've always been led to believe so. It was a girl. She's got a photo of her in the flat."

"Then whatever happened to her?"

"I don't know. It's not a question I ever dared ask. It always seemed a little indelicate. There are some subjects in our family which are just taboo, and that's one of them."

"But somebody must know. Didn't your father ever mention it?"

"Dad's not the most forthcoming of people. Except, that is, when he takes it upon himself to 'speak his mind'. In his eyes certain questions are simply closed. Sometimes you can hardly move for the skeletons in that house."

"You could simply put it to him."

"He would ignore it. Or change the subject. Father is very defensive about the past."

I walked through to the living room and took off my trench coat. Andria's sudden interest in my family was one of the less welcome aspects of her transformation. She had maintained an attitude of indifference for so long, I now took it for granted that she was a part of my life they would never share. Father, Rosie, Claud: in their perfectly preserved isolation, maintained even from one another, seemed to me part of one privacy, Andria of another. It was as if I was surrounded by a set of cloisters from which led off a series of inviolable Trappist cells, the occupants of which were pledged never to speak to one another. I had grown so accustomed to this cut-off, private world that the slightest intrusion from one cell into another represented a sort of threat. I was not sure that I appreciated Andria's curiosity. It was as if her own potential parenthood had healed in her loose threads which, newly spliced, led her in the direction of those she had once shunned. One motherhood beckoned to another. Sooner or later, Andria would ask to meet Rosie. She might even ask to meet Claud.

When I went back to the bedroom she was lying flat out on the carpet with a saucer on her head and her eyes closed. I tip-toed round towards her forehead and looked down into her upturned face. There was not a flicker of movement. I was about to retreat in reverence and respect when her lips opened and she said, "Did you get the cheese?"

Cheese was the last thing that she had asked for before I left the house. It was the latest of a whole series of pre-natal fads. It had not started with food. A week after her announcement that grey November evening she had suddenly discovered the music of Charlie Parker. I had never once before heard her express a partiality for Jazz or anything indeed beyond the severest musical classicism. But one afternoon, on returning from the paint shop, I had discovered on the sideboard a pile of very scratched-looking 78's and an antique wind-up gramophone, dredged from heaven knows what neighbourhood antique shop, parked irrevocably under the window. Beside it was Andria, dressed in patched denim dungarees, peering short-sightedly up at the pick-up and attempting to fit an alloy needle into the slot. Against my better judgement I helped her. For the next few nights my peace was rent by a saxophone that droned on endlessly as if in search of Doomsday. There was no protesting. One intervention, or simple request that the volume be turned down, and she would start to scream, or else rant on interminably about the monotonous insistence of my painting. I learned to bite my tongue.

Then there was the taramasalata. Our second-hand fridge was usually stocked with salad stuffs and a selection of raw vegetables. On occasions, when our means permitted, it held a cheaper cut of meat. We were not adventurous eaters. Brought up on my mother's soups and hotpots I had seldom branched out into more exotic cuisine, and, on the odd occasion on which I had done so, had not appreciated what I had eaten. Andria had always fallen in with my preferences. But one morning, on opening the fridge door to fetch milk for my usual coffee, I had been confronted with row upon row of plastic cartons. On lifting a lid I discovered a nauseating pink substance made, I later learned, from fish roe. For days she would eat nothing else.

After that there was the fudge. Boxes upon boxes of fudge and a carpet littered with sweet papers. On one memorable occasion, the fudge even brushed shoulders with the taramasalata, on one plate. There followed the passion fruit. Passion fruit in every shape and form: in cakes, in mousses, in yoghurts. I had almost lost patience with it when its monopoly of the kitchen table was supplanted by milkshakes in various flavours and hues. When she reached Passion Fruit milkshake, I dreaded a relapse. But onward she swept through blackcurrant and mango, pawpaw and even something called kiwi fruit. Remonstration was useless, jesting fatal. The great experiment progressed.

Now it was the cheese. I am used to the stout burgomaster cheeses of my motherland: Edam, Gouda, cheeses with place names that I recognise. But the latest of Andria's crazes had opened up before me a world that I scarce knew existed: a world riddled with worm rot and twisting blue corridors of fermentation. Cheeses with names like Siberian outposts and rinds like the Great Wall of China. In three days our tiny kitchenette had metamorphosed from an American Milkshake parlour to a continental delicatessen. A meat slicer, one or two drooping salami, and the effect would have been complete.

The names had now grown so extravagant that when, as often, I was despatched to the Polish corner shop at half-past seven in the evening, they had invariably flown out of my head before I reached the counter.

So now I pleaded ignorance and said, "I forget which one you wanted."

She sat up sharply. "I would have thought you could have remembered *Gorgonzola aux fines herbes.*"

"I'm terribly sorry."

"Well then?"

It was now nine o'clock in the evening, but further resistance seemed pointless. I was about to leave the flat when a thought struck me and, poking my head round the door, I said, "Supposing you change your mind before I get back? The fridge is already full of uneaten fudge."

"Then you can just take it along with you to your mysterious auntie, can't you? She's sure to adore it, she's so weird. And even if she doesn't, she can always feed it to her parrot."

I slammed the door.

*****

I watched her as she spooned the coins from the wide pocket of her apron dress into one cupped, manicured hand. Her hands, thin and nervous, had a liquid air of owning everything.

I thought: the magisteriality of wealth.

"I suppose you ought really to count them. It's for the week." As she spilled the mint-new metal into the uplifted palm of my right hand, the soft inside of hers brushed against the mount of Venus. I thought, to touch a stranger's hand.

I looked downwards. There were thirteen coins: two broad fifty pence pieces and eleven pound coins, thick and gross astride my lifeline. I picked up one of the fifties so that it flipped over and jangled dully against the rest. It gave off a tart elixir of perfume.

"Six pounds a session. It's what we agreed. You'll get the rest when we're through. It is sufficient is it? I'm not sure what the going rate is, I'm afraid."

I was scouring the soft place between her eyes just above the bridge of the nose where the double creases were, searching for the fallibility in all this thorough accounting. The eyes themselves were as I remembered them: guarded, curious, hazel verging on brown. There was even an amity of sorts distilled within all the plutocratic dealing. I thought of Claud's assessment of the Holbein: "millimetres deep, that disdain."

"It'll do," I said.

"It doesn't look much does it? Eleven little pounds. Why do they make them so much smaller than the 50p? They're no bigger than those old threepenny bits, the ones with the jagged edges. Pathetic really. Somebody should write and tell them so. Such a paltry number, eleven. In Milan, the lire spill out in thousands. Impressive 'til you realise they're worth zilch. Who was that French courtesan who said you can have me as long as the bank notes on my bedside table burn? She'd have gone broke in Italy. She'd have screwed him all night for tuppence … Well, shall we get on then? There's still quite a lot to do. You're satisfied with the conditions, I take it? I'd hate to feel I was exploiting you."

"I shouldn't lose any sleep over it," I said, mind growing vacant in preparation for a hefty dose of wall-staring. "I adore being exploited."

She looked at me with quizzical affection, a smile hovering around the edges of her mouth:

"You're such a mild little man. You really ought to learn to complain more."

"Not sure I'm capable of it. People nettle me alright, but when I attempt to get really annoyed, I end up all twisted inside."

"Don't you ever wish you could just, well, explode?"

"Oh I detonate inside alright. I've been known to walk the streets all night, fuming and shouting at passing strangers, but by morning I'm feeling contrite and just creep back to my kennel."

"That's perfect for you. It's not so great for the people who might have to share your kennel. I got into trouble at Somerville once for climbing over the wall from Walton Street after midnight when I'd lost my key. One of the English dons usually left her bike leaning against the inside wall, but that night it wasn't there, so I sort of fell with a wail and bruised my knee. The following morning, I was confronted by the formidable Miss Agatha Ramm: immensely tall, clad in tweeds and severe as a German governess. She twisted her arms into a sort of mutual double clasp as I tried to explain. That's what she always did: 'We must always refer to Gladstone as *Mr* Gladstone, you know.' She wrote a book about Gladstone, not that I've read it. All the same, she wasn't what I'd call authentically *angry*. More sort of miffed."

"And were you ever? Authentically angry, that is."

She was adjusting the legs of her easel. "Just the once. We had to go to lectures on 'Gibbon and Macaulay' by that man, Hugh Trevor-Roper. Every week he swept into the room in his black gown and played unrepentantly to the gallery. One week he announced, 'there were two English historians in the nineteenth century called Macaulay and one was ... well, she was what some people call a lady. The celebrated Mrs Catharine Macaulay. She wrote a History of England too, but we'll not trouble ourselves with *her*. I mean, whoever would pay attention to history written by a *Mrs*?' At which *bon mot* all the ridiculous freshmen from Christchurch obligingly guffawed. I left the room. Righty-o, I'd like you in the same crouching position as before."

I walked over to where the metal blinds coldly reflected the glare from the table lamps. Then there was a dull plasticated click and I found myself once more engulfed in tenebrous obscurity through which that cyclopic spotlight pitilessly throbbed.

"If you could just open the top of your mantle a bit more. I need a few inches more chest." I crumbled to the carpet. "Now if you could just raise your head and face me. Right now, a little over to the left. Just above the spotlight. That's it. Now *freeze*."

*****

In nomine patri et filii et spiritui sancto.

The parrot's head, beaked like a scimitar, turned, twisted, jack knifed within its cage. One insane eye held me like a skewer. And on jabbered its meaningless, yacking devotion:

Paternoster qui es in coelis.

Against the bars my aunt's hand fluttered, holding forth temptation in the form of gorgonzola, indulgence for parrot sins.

"There now, Philophilus," but the head wouldn't play. "You'll enjoy it won't you? It's lovely and blue. And just look who's brought it to us? Benedict, yes Ben-e-dict."

Panem nostrum quotidianum da nobis hodie.

"Oh dear," she gasped, her arm dropping, "I do hope he's not taken poorly. He's been refusing his feed all week. What we shall do with him I really don't know. But sit down. Sit down and tell me everything!"

She collapsed into a chair spread with old copies of *The Tablet.* I too sat down, feeling the old springs budge and spill under me. Despite my white lie to Andria, it was a full month since I had sat in the glare of my aunt's gas fire.

"And how is your young lady?" she inquired, rubbing her hands. Her hands, which were much like Claud's, moved with something of the same rosary insistence.

"Pregnant, Auntie, very pregnant."

There was a pause before she showed me her teeth and cried, "Benedict, you never told me!"

Demitte nobis debita nostra sicut et nos dimittimus debitoribus nostris.

"But how wonderful!" she continued, lifting hosanna hands. "Philophilus my dear, did you hear that? Just fancy. Benedict is going to have a baby!"

Et ne nos inducas in tentationem. Have a baby.

My aunt's neck tilted slightly as she took in the theological implications. "Of course," she said darkly, "Father O'Keeffe would have it that marriages are made in heaven. But then it was Father O'Mally's opinion that in performing our devotions each morning we enter the very portals of Paradise each and every day of our lives."

Her eyes went remote with speculation and then squeezed themselves in their sockets into an ecstasy of exquisite Jesuitical contrivance.

"What was it, Benedict? Did you both pray *very* hard? Oh well," she said, suddenly jumping up sharply so that the bob of greying hair bounced slightly against her shawl, "What did the old nun used to say?" Her finger wagged in fervent mimicry. "Faith! Faith!"

Sed libera nos a malo.

"Are you sure that you're not terribly ashamed of us, Auntie?"

"Not in the least," she said, with becoming pedantry. "What on earth is there to be ashamed about?"

Unwillingly my eyes strayed over to where, in its silver frame, the sepia picture of a baby girl stood above the purring gas fire.

When I turned back, our eyes met, and hers lowered. *Amen.*

"Don't look so doleful, Ben," my aunt said, with sudden brightness. "I expect things will turn out all right. After what you've just done, I'd say you deserve a bun!"

*****

It was by now mid-December. As I emerged from the great well of Pimlico station and pursued the well-trodden path towards the river, the sun has already dropped behind the terraces of Regency buildings lining St George's Square. Above the charcoal roofs the sky was transformed to a thrashing shoal of mackerel, their tails futilely struggling against the receding sea of pink. The air had lost its Autumnal smell of wood smoke and now bit keen and hard. I dug my hands deeper within the threadbare pockets of my trench coat, shrank within the folds of my scarf and walked.

But when I followed Christina into her small but sumptuous drawing room I was met by a midwinter conflagration. Every bulb in the place seemed to be ablaze. Two table lamps described glowing highlights on their blue china stands. The ceiling lamp shone in its polished copper shade. Embracing the exigencies of *chiaroscuro,* the steel swivel light has forsworn its penetrating vigilance and now played instead against a flower vase bright with cyclamen that stood atop the glass table. In all of this, there was something of palpable protest against the season.

So matter-of-fact in her habitual opening commands, so insistent in her determination not to waste the hour, Christina seemed for once happy to let things unfold at their own sweet pace. There was a spread of edibles - of cakes, finely-cut sandwiches and dates - on a side table, while from the kitchen moaned the inviting murmur of the kettle.

From the bathroom across the passageway wafted a fragrance of shampoo and expensive soap, perfuming the balmy air. She had clearly not long emerged from her toilette, since her hair smelled of lemon rind and she was wearing a white towelling robe of so flimsy a material it might almost have been summer. From every radiator emanated an intense, spongey warmth as if from a conservatory. From every potted plant and boxed shrub emerged a chlorophyll glaze. There was warmth in her eyes too as with one tapered arm she led me to the food-table saying: "You're somewhat on the early side you know. I wonder if I'm quite ready for you yet. Much too early to think about work."

"I try never to think about work," I said. "If I can help it, that is."

She chewed one finger saying, "Yes, you do look a bit like a lazy sod. Well, we'll just have to think of something to while away the hours won't we? What do you suggest?"

"I'm not sure," I replied. "What pleasures does the establishment afford?"

Instead of replying she shrugged and resumed chewing her finger.

Her arms, which were visible from the elbow, were surprisingly thin and small. She lowered her hand, held her two arms akimbo and, seeming to pause for a moment, suspired with luxurious ease, then reached up and held me round the neck, letting her robe fall slightly off her shoulders as she did so.

"You look quite different this afternoon," I said.

"Oh good. Well it keeps out the grey. In any case, there's no tearing hurry is there? You're not in any great dash to get away? No onerous commitments or anything?"

"Not in the least," I replied, as my mendacious throat grew dry.

She detached herself and, drifting over to the loaded table, picked up a plate of preserved fruit and offered me a fig. I declined but, taking one between her teeth, she spoke through it saying: "Some painters do their people against a backdrop of hills, distant blue and cool. It sets off the expression, so I've heard. I shall always paint you in a forest glade. You're essentially humid, I've decided."

She was steeped in these soap-bubble fancies.

"Whatever gives you that impression? I detest humidity," I said.

"Oh dear Henry. What ails you dear heart? Poor Henry, cool as a cucumber."

She handed me a plate of sandwiches: "Speaking of which…"

She swallowed and then, holding me once more round the neck, proclaimed, "Sandwiches aren't very promising, are they? Are you quite sure Darjeeling's O.K.? You wouldn't prefer wine?"

I frowned thoughtfully and then raised my eyebrows. "No, tea's just the ticket."

I bit hard into the sandwich, tasting the refreshing blandness of the cucumber, the trim pastiness of the bread. I took another bite and then felt the pollen lightness of her lips brush briefly against mine. Her feet were trammelling the carpet with a restless motion. I ate the last of my sandwich and then felt a violent pain in my thigh muscles as her calf caught me sharply round the back of my knee and I found myself against her laughing mouth:

"You should be more on your guard. I took you quite by surprise."

She helped me back on my feet then held me at arm's length, surveying me now with a sort of amorous pity, a conqueror's last-minute compunction. "No," she said, "you'd never do against hills."

She drew her towelling robe back across her shoulders, hugged herself discreetly, and then, turning on her heels, walked the full length of the room. She stopped at the far wall and turned her head.

"There's no problem is there? You're not longing to go?" A momentary ripple passed across her brow. "You do like us like this, don't you? You do like us like this?"

*****

The town hall's the best I can do in Leicester. No pictures that I can find and no phone boxes either, at least none that work. We're back to the Visigoths, Ben. Still, they say that there's a Gainsborough in Loughborough, so *en avant*! How's the portrait?

Claud.

*****

The Willows, Cheam, 11th December, 1984.

Dear Ben,

There's no need to take umbrage about Miss Echardt. I'm no Uncle Pandarus to go round pushing young people together. It's just that, in our generation you know, we always took great pride in paying our respects to family acquaintances. You call yourself an emancipated generation, and yet you all appear to be trammelled with the strangest of inhibitions. Echardt *père* has always taken the kindliest interest in your progress, and I'm sure that the friendship of his daughter, even if it proceeded no further, could prove nothing but beneficial. Think about it.

The evenings are very short now. I potter about in the garden for a few hours, but it's too nippy to do much. What a pleasure it will be to see the snowdrops! I've a Christmas cactus in the hall that's doing well.

Your loving father.

*****

Kensal Rise, 14th December, 1984.

Dear Father,

I feel it my duty to inform you that Andria and I are expecting a child in the late Spring or early Summer. I don't expect you to rejoice or even to condone. I know that you think us monstrously ill-matched, an impression incidentally shared by some of our mutual acquaintance though not normally by ourselves.

I don't want to have to go into tiresome tirades or endless explanations. You are in possession of the essential facts, so there you are. I shall try to bring it up a Catholic if that is any consolation.

Your prodigal son,

Ben.

PS: I should hope that this puts Christina out of the question.

*****

Loughborough, 15th December, 1984.

This is Millais, sentimental tosh. They've apparently moved the Gainsborough, for conservation or something. Here all phone booths stink, and vandalism reigns supreme. How's Hans Holbein the Younger progressing?

From the inclement Midlands,
Claud.

*****

The Willows, Cheam, 16th December 1984.

Dear Benedict,
I received your letter on Thursday.
I'm very lonely now.
The cactus has shown no signs yet.
What a long winter it is going to be!
Much love,
Father
PS You always have my deepest-affection. You know that.

*****

Her right hand was at the nape of my neck, just below the hair-line, playing with the roots. Her fingers discovered the nexus of nerves at the very top of my spine, sending a rippling shiver down my spinal column from the cross-roads of my shoulders to the finest joints of my feet.

"What ails you, my Lord?" she asked. "So crestfallen?" And kissed me nimbly on the tiny crevice at the side of my mouth. Then she lifted her face within five inches of mine so that we were eyeball to eyeball. Within the shaded precincts of her lashes it was early Spring, and jonquils were drooping laggardly with snow. Her iris was a nut-brown plain across which cloud-banks were hurled. There was a sudden downpour outside, the oily insistence of each drop merging with the moody insistent dripping of the distant kitchen tap. The watery percussive duet made a complicit counterpoint with the rhythm of her fingers, the weary tingling of my flesh.

"There's no need to look like a fading flower," she said. "Poor dear Henry. No longer cock of the walk. Have I stolen away your self-possession? I do hope not, or otherwise however shall I forgive myself? I shall set you up upon a catafalque and wail for you. I shall say 'The fields are bare, the running brook dry, the garners empty, the crops despoiled. And then I shall bury you in the ground and lay anemones on your grave. We shall set up your effigy on all the houses. Will that make you feel any better?"

There was a feeling of impending cramp in my right leg so that I wanted to move it, but it lay trapped under hers. When I attempted to turn over, I found myself restrained by one shapely leg. She looked down at me victoriously and then, as if exercising some presumptive *droit du seigneur*, her hand moved back to the nape of the neck, teasing the hairs:

"I do wish I could see any purpose to this," I said.

"I don't see why that need concern us," came the haunted, indolent reply. "Why does everything need to have a point exactly?"

"I mean, will it take either of us anywhere?"

"I shouldn't imagine so. Nowhere in the least. Why should it?"

"It's not as if we even know one another properly."

There was an indulgent smirk at the corner of her mouth: "Well isn't that lovely then?" she said. "Here for a season, gone a season. I rather like this drifting, insouciant existence. Why worry what the future may bring?"

"Have you never worried?"

"Once yes, ever so much. In Italy I seemed to do very little else. What a silly girl I was. In Italy, in the sunshine, and racked with worry all the time. And where did it get me exactly? Here I am in London this afternoon, curling your poor dear hair."

Making one last gargantuan effort, I managed at last to release myself and stretch upwards from the waist, finally releasing my hands.

"I think perhaps I had better get dressed," I said. "Have you any idea where I put my clothes?"

She looked across at me with a sort of affectionate pitying. "Poor dear Henry. Have I detained you so long? The last time I saw them they were in the bathroom."

I rose in an unstable fashion to my feet and, starting towards the hallway, turned round and faced her once more. "I mean you don't even know where I come from. You don't seem in the least concerned."

She flopped over on her front, balancing her chin between her two wrists, surveying me musingly from head to foot:

"Oh, but just think what fun that is. I can make you up as I go along."

*****

Lawrence Echardt & Sons Auctioneers, Valuers and Dealers in Fine Prints since 1826. The Poultry, EC2.
17 December, 1984

Dear Mr Henry,

I have recently been in communication with your father, Mr Hamish Henry, concerning the possibility of your joining our firm for a trial period in the capacity of Valuation Assistant. As you will be aware, such matters are more usually settled by public advertisement and selection through interview. This is the conventional procedure which in many ways I should prefer to adhere to in this instance. But in deference to your father, who has acted for us in a number of ways in the past, and whose constant friendship has been a source of solace to me during much of an in some ways trying existence, I am now writing to let you know that I am prepared to defer the usual technicalities for a limited period in order to allow you a measure of prior consideration. I understand that you possess some knowledge of classical portraiture, and that your regretfully terminated academic studies has nonetheless left you with a certain expertise which would indubitably be of use to us. Your remuneration would be strictly in accord with your age and experience.

If you would like to take up this opportunity which, it is needless to add, will not recur should you refuse it, I would be prepared to leave the position unfilled until the New Year, but no later. Should this overture prove of interest to you, I would appreciate it if you would ring my secretary at the number which you will find opposite the letterhead.

Yours sincerely,

Lawrence Echardt.

*****

"Don't love me."
"Love you."
"Don't love me."
"Do."

Between us the sheet lay rucked like a sand bank. Over the top of the soiled blanket rose Andria's belly, which was beginning to take on the appearance of a minor hillock. Her worn nightgown had collapsed from off her thin freckled shoulders, and now lay in pink nylon folds around the back of the bolster. She was staring morosely at where her nipples sagged slightly towards her abdomen, the aureole showing dark against the surrounding whiteness.

"You might have washed before you got into bed," she said, with familiar mock-distaste. "Your nails are so black you might have been down a coal mine."

I had been painting all afternoon. In an effort to shake off my sense of oppression I had just produced a canvass even blacker than my nails. Mentally, I called it *Fatherhood*. It lay now like a reproach against the far wall sending out a slight whiff of turpentine. Our whole room was compounded of such rankness: milk, linseed, blood.

"Your father rang again," she said, without lifting her eyes. "Why do you never phone him back?"

"He knows where we live," I said. "If he was that desperate, he'd come round and visit." I knew very well that with Father's strict sense of propriety this was a virtual impossibility.

"You wait," she said. "You know him less well than you think. He might just descend on us."

The subject of my father had in fact been tugging at my mind for some time. Over the torpid lagoon of my conscience a sulphurous miasma of guilt would intermittently drift. Soon I learned to ignore it. But like a fog it stayed, drifted and stayed.

"What on earth am I expected to do?" I expostulated. "I'm not responsible for his loneliness. The old choose their isolation."

"Tripe!"

"Yes they do. They barricade themselves behind eight feet of pride, like the inhabitants of a medieval castle. Like the keep down at Arundel. Half the time you can't get within a mile of my family for the moats they throw round themselves."

Andria's eyes drifted over to the collection of dismantled and broken easels which occupied the corner of the room.

"You could always construct a drawbridge. We've no shortage of wood."

It was by now Christmas week. Over by the window leant our apology of a tree, and around the edge of the apple-green chest of drawers stood a shallow fringe of greeting cards. Aunt Rosie had as ever hand-painted hers: a dainty water colour of a lake with swans in whose wake swam an ungainly pair of coots, the white tufts on their foreheads clearly showing ("As bald as a coot," she sometimes said of my father. "As crabbed as a walnut, but as good as gold, Benedict, as fifteen carat gold."). Father too had sent his usual institutional offering, a print of the House of Parliament seen from his side of the river with the whiplash message, "Think about it."

"Think about what?" Andria had asked.

"Think about Christmas," I'd evasively replied. "We'll have to sooner or later."

We had postponed the dreary question of seasonal jollifications about as long as our mutual sense of duty allowed. I for one had never relished Christmases in England. Twenty years ago, when my mother had been in full health, it had all been very different. When at the age of thirty-two she had left her Dutch homeland to marry my father, the two families had reached an understanding. One Christmas in three her people would spend with us in Finchley, the remainder in her hometown of Utrecht, or once, gloriously, mid-way in Amsterdam. Those Dutch Christmases had been life and breath to me. I would lie awake longing for them throughout all the long, tedious months from Michaelmas, tracing patterns in the Morris wallpaper of my bedroom ceiling into the likenesses of step gables, clock gables, windmills and canal boats. Packs of ice would drift across my consciousness, the Zuider Zee once glimpsed frozen over toward Märchen, little trapped wavelets visible like the ripples in cake icing.

Once in 1960 the Dutch canal system had frozen over from end to end, and I still treasured the memory of one bitter, wind-blown January morning when, tumbling down the twisting stairwell of my grandfather's store-cum-house, and emerging through the narrow shop-front, I had been confronted by crowds of other children, whirling along the canal in front of me, spinning, hollering in a little ecstasy of ice-frenzy. It was many years before I was to see a Bruegel, but when my uncle later introduced my twenty-year-old self to one of his winter scenes, I still recall the thrill of recognition. Ever since, Christmas has always been hopelessly associated in my mind with vanished glimpses once snatched from a tiny garret window down to a deserted moonlit canal-side: snowflakes driven slantwise across Herengracht, houseboats with their tight tarpaulins straining under a recent fall, huddles of stationary bicycles, their wheel guards rusty from winter use, their bell hubs powdered with a mantle of early morning frost.

It all belonged to a dead past. Partly due to neglect and partly to my father's obdurate failure to communicate, our connection with Holland had virtually ceased with my mother's demise. Until the early seventies Christmastime had meant thick pea soups, immense savoury pancakes and St Nicholas poking his tousled head through the windows on his separate, incongruous feast-day. One evening in Utrecht, the year before she died, I recalled taking a wrong turning down a side street not far from her father's house and meeting a giant *Sinterklaas* suspended twelve feet above my head, his blotched face swaying in the light chilly breeze, his enormous limbs attached to opposite gables by wires.

But one gruesome morning in February 1972 my mother's coffin had disappeared into a dank little hole in Middelharnis near her grandparents' home in the island of Goeree in the south of Holland. My mother had been buried among her own people, and Father had been led into the drizzle, stifling sobs. With her had disappeared, it now seemed to me, not only Father's last remaining reason for living, but, irrevocably, any possibility of family conviviality. And with that had gone the magic of Christmas, to be replaced by a sullen mutual ache and the tick-toking of Father's clocks as we sat opposite one another in high-backed chairs before his grumbling hearth, year after year.

"I suppose that you'd better go down to Cheam again," conceded Andria reluctantly after a lengthy interval during which the enormity of my obligation had gradually dawned on both of us.

"But I can't leave you in this condition," I replied, looking down to where, between the folds of her mottled flesh, our child lay unformed, unnamed.

"Why ever not? It's not your fault your father can't stand the sight of me. We've managed before and we'll manage again. You don't see him very often."

"Go on," I sneered. "Say it: 'You're lucky to have a father.'"

Andria gave me one of her orphaned looks. "Well, you are."

I looked over to where my painting *Fatherhood* stood on its side, its textures acid with remorse. I sniffed, looked down at Andria's belly and, softly and deliberately, repeated her words: "You're lucky to have a father."

*****

"Tell me," I asked when the picture seemed almost to be finished, "Do you remember a bloke called Jake?" It was the first time I had ever dared broach the subject of our common past.

"Jake," she said dreamily, resting on one arm. "It rings a bell. Was he by any chance up with me at Oxford?"

"I very much doubt it. If so, he'd have certainly read Theology, the better to plead the devil's cause."

Her chin, quaintly dimpled, was resting on two fingers which were propped up like a trestle. "The name's familiar. What made you suddenly ask?"

We were halfway through one of the forty-minute coffee breaks which she had belatedly inaugurated with the intention of relieving the strain on my haunches. I was lying flat on my back while attempting to observe the minute inflections of her profile. She had a conch-shaped ear folded over at the top like a curled up clover leaf. Behind it, there fell the chestnut cascade of her hair.

"A long time ago I used to know a man of that name. He always dressed in black from head to toe and wore a St Christopher medallion around his neck. I think he thought of himself as surly but humorous, like Jacques in the play. I rather took to him at one time."

"Whatever happened?"

"A holocaust or a storm in a teacup, depending on how you look at it. Betrayal of a sort, though of whom I'm not exactly sure. It's just a memory now, but it

126

rankles sometimes. Looking back on it, he was just the weeniest bit sad."

"Sounds as if you were well shot of him," she remarked. Her eyes had drifted across to observe the winter bulbs in the patio beyond her French window.

"I think perhaps everybody was." I reached over and grasped the top of her upright forearm just beneath the shoulder joint. The flesh of her biceps against my thumb was prehensile but soft, the cavity of her arm-pit under the ball of my forefinger dank and crested with light brown hair: "You never know. You might have been attracted to him. Some people were."

"He sounds just a little macabre."

"Morbid certainly, but morbidity's attractive to some people. We desire the quaintest of things. Base things sometimes. And you?"

She thought for a while before saying, "Like most of us, I start off trying to see the best in people, and sometimes end by liking the worst. It's deadly, of course. Miserable creatures that we are." She let her forearm collapse under her and turned nimbly over on her back to observe the far reaches of the ceiling through half-closed eyes.

"So you're attracted to people because they're bad?"

"Not strictly true," she observed. "Like other people, I'm frequently drawn to goodness, but it doesn't always last. Too often, you find what you took for innocence was a mask for something gruesome."

"In that case," I said, taking time over the words, "It might be better to be innocent deep down."

"And wear a mask like a gargoyle?"

"Something like that. Or quite simply to play at wickedness, if you must. Then you can only live to grow better." I lay down on my front beside her, letting my fingers explore the sloping contours of her upper arm. "I've an aunt who would agree with that. She has a saying: 'Innocence, dear child, is something you painfully achieve.'"

She lifted her chin in judicious appraisal. "She's got a point there somewhere."

"And do you? Grow better I mean?"

"If given half a chance," she replied, and I had this abrupt vision of her floating hair borne to me across the packed gyrating couples on a dance floor before she added, "It's hot in here" in reference to the central heating which made little concession to the mildness of the afternoon. Between her breasts, I noticed, hung a relief gold chain bearing a cluster of pearls, above which the letter 'C' was inscribed in gold. She began lazily to play with it, so that the claret of her ring clashed with the white and gold, sending out a confused, dissonant sheen.

"Talking of gruesomeness," she said in a matter-of-fact tone, "I do hope you don't have too far to travel each time. Where is it you hang out exactly?"

"Kensal Rise," I said, making a virtue of proximity.

"Kensal Rise," she repeated, opening her eyelids full for a second. "Isn't that somewhere near the park?" She looked up at me with vague unfocussed eyes as over a filing cabinet so many years ago she'd squinted ("Yes. I *do* know who he is.")

"It all depends on which park you mean. Almost. The other end of Ladbroke Grove. Really much nearer Willesden."

"Willesden."

"Oh, a world away from here."

I reached down and squeezed the slack of her flesh at the base of her neck, letting the moist skin slip gradually between my fingers 'til it lay quite smooth. As I did so, I felt her left hand exploring the hair at the crown of my head, just to the right of the parting.

"So you've a fair distance to come, then?" she inquired.

"A fair old trek yes. I can't say that I mind. It never seems that far."

"Why do you agree to come?" she inquired. I saw her beneath the summer trees, her hair against the gorgeous figment of her neck, holding a faun-like delicious composure in the shade.

"It's pleasant here. Comfortable anyway."

I ran my tongue along the silky roundness of her shoulder, and then slowly across her neck just above the collar of her dress. Her skin smelt like pine needles. I sensed her stir beside me, and, arching her back as thirteen years before she'd arched it for another's pleasing, she drew me to her, saying: "In that case, Mr Model sir. If you've not *too* far to go. Thanking you kindly. Time for a little gruesomeness ere we resume?"

*****

Rugby, 22nd December, 1984.

This is Thomas Arnold. Thought you'd like a portrait of the stern old gent. Am holed up here for a bit. Will meet in London in January. Is Epiphany at all possible? Re: our commission - move with great urgency. Holbein, Ben, Holbein.

Ever anxious,

Claud.

*****

"You're lucky to have a father, you know," said Rosie, "I'm quite sure that Philophilus hasn't."

My aunt leered reprovingly into the cage.

"Isn't that right, Philophilus? Where's your daddy gone then? Lost himself in some tropical rain forest I shouldn't wonder."

Squark. Squark. Libera nos a malo.

Three days to Christmas. A sorry scattering of seeds and breadcrumbs lay beneath the obstinate bird, whose stomach still refused anything beyond liquid sustenance. Its turquoise and red feathers were already looking uncannily bedraggled, and its carcass to my untutored eyes unhealthily meagre.

There's nothing can be done for him, poor bird. I did ring the vet, but what with the Christmas rush it seems they simply can't squeeze parrots in. If this goes on much longer, he'll be able to escape through the bars, and then where will we all be?"

"Perhaps he'll return to his mangrove," I said, enviously contemplating some swampy parrot haven.

Clatter clatter. Blessed art thou among women.

"I've been teaching him the English version," piped Rosie. "He always used to perform his Hail Maries in Latin, but, what with all this refusal to eat, the penances grew rather tiresome. We're a very ecumenical parrot now, aren't we, Philo?"

And the fruit of thy womb, the fruit of thy womb, Eesu.

"He always has a lot of trouble with the last word. I thought at first that he was mispronouncing it out of mistaken reverence. But parrots always have immense difficulty enunciating j's. Where did I read that now? Apparently, it's a well-known fact."

My aunt sat down by the fireside and drew a tartan rug over her knees.

"Your father is a very kind man, Benedict. You must learn to recognise that. He's very steely on the outside, but he's like a tortoise, all mush inside." My aunt's tone had grown sombre: "I remember when I had my misfortune …"

In the growing gloom, my aunt's cheeks momentarily flushed. At first I wondered what she was talking about.

"Benedict. You knew that I had a baby once, didn't you?"

I roused myself from my gas-fire torpor. I had never once heard Rosie refer to her child.

"Yes. It was many years ago. You can scarcely have been six months." There was a pause broken only by the rippling of the gas fire, and then she reached over to the mantelpiece where the silver frame lay in the semi-darkness.

"That's her," she said precisely, and handed the frame over to me.

I peered into the little square of glass. My aunt's flat was inclined to dampness and already there was a little sludge of decomposition on top of the photograph. But, through the dusty glass and the grime, the girl-child looked at me, distrustful, beckoning, across thirty years.

"Whatever happened to her?" I asked, a question which had curled itself around my tongue for as long as I could remember.

"They took her away. Well, I say they. It was a Catholic adoption agency. Maria Assumpta. I had to agree to it. You've grown up in very different times, Benedict, in a new liberal age, but one used to be so under a cloud if … that sort of thing happened."

"You make it sound like an accident," I said.

"Well, it was in a way. Your father wanted me to be allowed to keep her. There was a sort of family conference. They both came round here and wrangled over it for hours. It was like a post-mortem. Horrid. Horrid!"

I looked over to where my aunt sat hunched in her armchair. It was hard to make out her face.

"Who do you mean?" I asked.

"Claud and your father. Hamish was quite willing for me to hang on to her. He knew what she meant to me, you see. He's got very firm principles that one, but they're grounded in a great love and a sort of desperate understanding. It was Claud who insisted."

I placed the picture frame on the coffee table beside my chair. It was now so dark that I could only just about make out my aunt's shawl against the glow of the gas fire.

"It's funny just how different brothers can be," she said. This time, momentarily, even the parrot was silent.

"I can't go and see Dad this year," I said, out of my own pool of darkness. "I can't just leave Andria by herself. You see, Auntie, I'm becoming a father now."

Paternoster. Paternoster.

"Well," said my aunt, with kindly emphasis. "If you can't, then I suppose you just can't.

*****

I was lying once more in a forest glade, my aching thigh dripping with cosmetic blood. The universe had once again shrunk to the two square feet of hessian, all that my gaze encompassed. To prevent my attention wandering I was making strenuous mental efforts to discern individual strands in the wall fabric. Eventually, my head aching, I had to admit defeat. To forestall the creeping numbness in my leg I had evolved a technique of slow imperceptible rocking which enabled me to distribute my weight alternately on my right buttock and on the small of my back. But the base of my neck was beginning to give me trouble, and it was with some difficulty that I maintained the angle of my chin. She seemed to step back from the canvas and then, adopting a pose of mild self-congratulation, intoned, "Do you know, I really think I've almost finished."

"Can I relax then?"

"I think so. Yes, I really think that you can."

I sank to the carpet in a posture of exaggerated exhaustion and abject, thankful release.

Then, arching my arms in a green luxurious sweep and flexing the muscles of my back, I rose gingerly to my feet.

"Got you," she announced, surveying her handiwork with a mixture of pride and judicial reserve. "I really think I've captured you, you know."

"Any chance of sneaking a look?"

She wrinkled one nostril in feigned reluctance. "Oh alright then," she said, and started to mess with her brushes. I made my way round, to the other side of the easel and directed my gaze to where between two wooden clasps leaned her vision of Adonis. It was strangely enough a moment I wished to share, so I took hold of her hand and led her back to join me. I picked up her delicate right wrist, enclosing it in both my hands, massaging the blue black veins at the base of her forearm momentarily before abruptly letting it fall.

"Is anything wrong?" she asked.

Something indeed was wrong. Christina's easel was of a more expensive make than mine, and her style possessed an equivalent brashness. What confronted me was a sort of cruder, updated Poussin, depicted in the deadpan brightness of acrylic. The treatment of the central figure was conventional enough. There I lay with my torso supported on one elbow and the other arm clasped dramatically to my chest, while beneath the hem of my mantle my gored limb oozed synthetic plasma. She had evidently had some difficulty registering the precise timbre of my expression in which pathos strove with embarrassment, terminal agony with plain physical discomfort. True, the glade effect possessed a certain dappled distinction, the shadows encroaching upon the recumbent victim with a sinister opacity which almost, but not quite, concealed the guilty boar slinking within the distant undergrowth, offending tusk glistening in ivory relish.

However, it was not the position of victor and victim, jealous deity and mortal sacrifice, nor the relative gaucheness of the artist's palette, that had caused me to start, but the scene manifestly unfolding to the dying Adonis's right. Christina's earlier notion of depicting the goddess commiserating over her expiring lover had clearly served its purpose and been discarded. If like some lingering pentimento it lay somewhere beneath all those scurrying brush strokes, no sign of it remained. Instead, around the periphery of the forest clearing, a dithyrambic orgy appeared to be in progress. Goatish satyrs roistered on the swathe, some quaffing pitchers of wine, others humorously restraining the odd recalcitrant nymph purporting to struggle in their embrace. Beyond them, within the cover of an oak tree to the extreme left of the composition, stood the magisterial figure of Aphrodite. She was wearing a thin linen robe that seemed recently to have fallen from her shoulders to reveal a necklace carrying a cluster of pearls, above which the initial "C" was inscribed in gold. Her thin arms were bare and extended to embrace a tall cadaverous individual whose back writhed against the tree trunk behind him in fierce, proprietorial pleasure. From head to toe his clothes were all of black. Around his neck, and contrasting nicely with the livid white of Christina's forearms, dangled a St Christopher medallion. His triumphant gaze was directed, not down toward his mistress's secret bestowing eyes, but across to his rival, whose horror-stricken face betrayed how well he understood. This was how things are and must be. What was done was appointed by some unfathomable will, and must be done again. There in that corrupted bower I lay as in a garden, my usurper's garden - broken, tethered - destroyed, humbled, the recurrent cuckold of the gods.

"Who's that to the left?" I inquired, attempting to master my voice.

"Whom do you mean?"

"The rising sun." I pointed to where in vicious luxuriating bliss Jake curled his back against the tree.

"Oh that. A foible of mine. I put it in quite late, after you'd left on Tuesday. I'm quite proud of it, as a matter of fact. I just couldn't see Aphrodite remaining content for long with a lover in his death-throes. Knowing her, her attentions were bound to wander elsewhere, even before he snuffed it. Callous really, but then she was like that, I suppose."

"Yes, I suppose you would think that."

"The guy's not important really. I based him on somebody I knew fleetingly ages ago at art college. It's the recurrent pattern I wanted, the feeling of cruelty and flux."

I was suddenly seized with a white, seething rage. I also had a sensation of impending action, as if I was about not so much to lose control as recover it. My only desire was to leave that tasteful, heartless flat, to walk out of her presence and never to think of returning.

"It seemed more astute than my original conception," she said. "Truer to fact. Not nice facts of course, but then not all facts are, I suppose."

I considered hard. Here I was, a trespasser on my uncle's illusions, here at his urging, conniving in the intended idealisation of this object of his misplaced esteem, as if his plan were a monstrous, hypocritical joke. I had been exhorted to discover virtue. I had uncovered guile. I had made a gesture towards hope, and had my ghastliest expectations confirmed. In one respect alone had I fulfilled the terms of my commission. I had been required to elicit the truth and had despaired of it, only to find truth meeting me shameless at the door. I turned from the easel and began to collect my clothes.

"You're not leaving?" she asked, in what seemed like genuine alarm.

"You implied we were almost through. Anyway our time is up."

"But I did say *almost*. I'm not through with you yet. There are still a few finishing touches …"

"Then finish them off with somebody else."

I was buttoning up my shirt-front, but my fingers had lost their grip.

"But I haven't paid you for the last lot. Have I offended you in some way?"

"It's alright. I'm sure you could use the money. Send it on if you like. I've got to scarper now. Andria's expecting me home."

"Andria?"

"The lady I shack up with. We've been together about seven years. She's expecting a child in April."

"You never told me."

"No, I didn't. Perhaps I should have. I see that now. You said some facts are not nice, but some are a lot nicer than others. You could come over and visit us some time. In Willesden. You'd enjoy meeting her. She'd know all about Adonis. She's got a book on him."

"I do *wish* you'd told me."

"Well, we can't be wise all the time, can we? My fault really."

"No, not your fault. I do wish you wouldn't leave."

I gave her one last despairing, angry, affectionate look. Then she gave me another of her traffic-light smiles and, lifting her hand with the garnet ring on it, blew me a kiss.

"Alright, my Lord" she said. "If I've deserved your scorn. If it's your pleasure, then go you must. But please don't look so sad."

*****

Outside, the night was chill and bitter, with a thin patina of mist. Leaving the complex of Dolphin Square, I crossed the road, and, too agitated to take the tube, began pacing towards Millbank. A couple was cavorting by the portico of the *Villa de Cesari* restaurant, their entwining forms mackintoshed against the wind. I tucked the collar of my trench coat around me and walked. Upstream, across the brackish oily river, Battersea Power Station, newly redundant, lifted up its insolent chimneys through the fog like the spires of some dimly descried Art Deco cathedral. Around them the cloud and mist were so thick and driven that each chimney seemed to drift and plunge like a figure in an expressionist nightmare. I stood in the Public Gardens and watched them sail through the stratosphere, four flung reminders of our certainties, now pensioned off and dumb.

To my left as I continued eastwards the gates of the Tate were closed, closed to me, a right ring of wrought iron exclusion. Avoiding the baroque absurdity of the Electricity Board, I turned sharp right across Lambeth Bridge and then along the Albert Embankment with all its wreathed adamantine dolphins: more, dumb mouths. I felt like a fish mouth too, gaping in the wind, gasping for breath, and I kept to the stern parapet for comfort. That stalwart stone. To my right, downstream, the granite façade of County Hall stretched up like an Italian Fascist monument. On top the number of London's unemployed danced emblazoned in all their grim thousands. I coughed and shrunk further into my coat. At Westminster Bridge I turned left again, and paced the yards towards Whitehall, then onwards towards the Gallery and Trafalgar Square.

Halfway along Whitehall, I saw a tramp humping bundles. You seldom used to see derelicts on the London streets, but over the last few years they seemed to have emerged, as if out of nowhere. He was as drab as the evening and clenched in on himself like an oyster. I looked into his stubble, and his desperate mean face. The eyes were dead and frightened, the hair a mere wash of excrement. His raincoat wrapped around him like a dirty dream, his plastic bags bulging with bottles, he walked straight before him like a somnambulist's assistant. Around him strolled businessmen in Crombie overcoats, shoppers from Weybridge, and international students paired like heraldic lovers. He took no notice, and gave no leeway, but trudged on like the year, solemnly, resolutely, a drear procession into nowhere.

In Trafalgar Square, the Gallery front was darkened. No uncle or misfit encumbered the steps. I descended the underpass towards the underground station, but then doubling back took once more to the pavement. Outside the National Portrait Gallery they were singing carols. I passed them in a cloud of malice: "Oh tidings of comfort and joy, comfort and joy." Along the Charing Cross everyone bore his load. Women huddled in shop doors, chilly schoolgirls dripping with effusions, and, along the side streets toward Soho old men in greatcoats hung their heads. An Iranian protester handed me a leaflet with colour illustrations red with lesions and incinerated toes. A man with a crutch lurched past, then a nun. Amid the turgid swelling music, a tin jangled imploringly: "Do they know it's Christmas?" A punk-faced youth slouched towards me, shouting; a cyclist hit the kerb and abused a passing car. "Rape Crisis" leaped from a hoarding. "Make the night safe for women"; "Electrodes applied to the neck and shoulders"; "Dissidents gagged and held by the hair." I threw the pamphlets in the gutter and staggered on, cursing. Reaching New Oxford Street, I stood with my hands in my pockets, considering my options. Retracing my steps to wait for the bus, I again changed my mind and made for the pubs of Bloomsbury.

*****

"Coo," purred the pigeons, "Coo, coo." It was Boxing Day. Holland Park, recently so garishly Autumnal, was empty and austere. The great trees, once gilded and

141

encrusted with filaments of drying leaves, stood out against the sky like a forest of tensed fists.

We were sitting on one of the benches with our backs to the Orangery, surveying the empty banks of the rose garden. I had dug my hands deep into the pockets of my trench coat against the chill. On the early evening air my exhaled breath curled like incense. It was a little past four o'clock, but already close to nightfall; we had the park virtually to ourselves. There were muffled voices in the distance, and, down towards Kensington High Street, and within the windows of Holland House, lights fizzled and bloomed. Against the hard back of the seat leant Andria, chafing her hands inside their navy blue mittens. It was very, very cold.

"You should really have gone down to Cheam," Andria said. "He's probably feeling desperate by now."

She looked down at me with eyes soft with accusation.

"It would have been a bit of an ordeal, you know."

"You needn't have worried. I'd have coped."

"It wasn't you I was worried about," I said, the truth stealing out in furtive bursts of vapour. "You don't understand. It's not that simple. If I'd have gone down there I'd have come in for all kinds of ghastly pressure."

"What kind of pressure?"

"Oh … things. He wants me to take a job."

Behind me there was an implosion of mirth: "You … a job?"

"It was suggested," I said, endowing my words with as much sarcasm as they would carry, 'that I become a picture valuer."

"Where?"

"In the City. Dad's got contacts there. A man called Lawrence Echardt. He even wrote to me."

"Well, try it then. Why ever not? What have you got to lose? It might take the pressure off us for a while. I can't keep you for ever, you know." She stared down at the swelling beneath her duffle coat with sullen look of appeal. "I certainly can't keep the three of us."

"You're lucky you've got three of us to keep."

"What's that supposed to mean?"

"Aunt Rosie had her child taken away. It went to an orphanage. Or was adopted or something."

"How did you learn that? You told me she never mentioned anything," Andria said, her words coming out in little, steamy tufts.

"She told me when I visited her just before Christmas. Suddenly came out with it. Just like that."

"I wonder why."

"Oh, some elementary need to confess. It's deeply imbued in us Catholics."

The memory of my own first confession drifted up as if from nowhere. It was a stagnant Tuesday afternoon in late July. I was seven. Outside, the heat was stifling. I was in my first suit, and there were patches of sweat under the arms. Within the marbled tomb of the Oratory, the air was motionless. Before me rose the domed canopy of the vestibule. I went inside, drawing the green calico curtain after me. I knelt and put my face close to the metal grill, which gave off a slight stench of saliva, sweat and tobacco. I opened my lips and said, "Bless me, Father, for I have sinned."

*****

"It's your father," said Andria, handing me the black Bakelite mouthpiece. "I think he wants to come over."

It was New Year's Eve. When I applied my ear to the receiver, the voice which emerged was dry, gentle and clear.

"Benedict. How are you?" it said.

There was a lump in my throat. We had just spent the last three hours playing Scrabble, and Andria's Latin tags had defeated me. I was feeling futile, fretful and shamed.

"It's been a long time." His voice was like a missal illuminated by his blatant need.

"Do you want to come across?" Even as I spoke them, the words sounded mean.

"It might be difficult. Transport is not that easy. But I could travel up via Waterloo. If I could bring an overnight bag?"

I realised how much all this must have cost him. Even now his feelings disclosed themselves through many layers. Pride, I said to myself. Why are we both so Goddam proud?

So that is how the three of us spent New Year's Day, in some hideous travesty of Hogmanay: Father in his corner solemnly dragging at an empty pipe, Andria propped on the sofa like a bored child mournfully blowing up balloons, I desultorily sketching - for all the world like a melancholy troupe of clowns. It was not an auspicious beginning to that most auspicious of years. "Beware the Ides of March," they say; "Beware the Hogmanay," say I. None of us spoke. As the hours sagged towards evening, Father's features fell like a silhouette against the small frame of the sky. In the sallow twilight cast by the sash window his tobacco smoke curled like cramped hieroglyphics of pain.

The room was almost black before Andria looked up from the sofa and said, "Hadn't we better switch on a light?"

"Why?" Father asked from his corner. "It's not dark, is it?"

In the coffined gloom, neither of us replied.

BOOK THREE:

THE AVENUE, MIDDELHARNIS

BOOK THREE

I can still recall the first stirrings of my interest in art. Above my bed in the childhood nursery in Finchley hung a small reproduction of *Die Allee von Middelharnis* by Meyndert Hobbema, held in a simple blackwood frame, in imitation of Dutch imperial ebony. It was from Middelharnis, in the isle of Goeree in the Catholic south of Holland, that my maternal grandparents came. It was in Middelharnis that my mother had spent the formative years of her early childhood, prior to her parents' removal to Utrecht. It was in Middelharnis that she would eventually be laid to rest. The reproduction, common enough, represented for my mother a particular kind of memento.

I remember with some vividness staring up at it for hour after hour before sleep stole on me on summer evenings. The painting depicts a double line of immature poplars between which runs a plain, rutted track. Along this road in the middle distance walks a man in buff clothing, caught in mid-stride. On either side of the avenue run narrow irrigation canals, beyond which stretch polders and domestic allotments, in one of which the proprietor stands absorbedly pruning a sapling. The satisfaction of the painting lies partly in the expanse of the sky (a motif Hobbema seems to have learned from his master Jacob van Ruisdael in whose studio he worked while young), and partly in its observation of the nicer demands of symmetry. There were occasions during my childhood when, gazing up at it, I seemed to lose any sense of time, and to it I owe my first experience of disinterested aesthetic delight.

No delight, however, is entirely disinterested. Even if such detachment were possible, a child's mind would be the last place to expect it. Below the eaves of our semi-detached in North London there seemed always to hang the district if rarely voiced conviction that childhood is the locality of sin, or more properly of self-absorption. Innocence, as my aunt once sagely proclaimed, is something you gradually learn. To have been completely innocent or, as Claud might have put it, "pure", my enjoyment would have needed to have entailed the loss, not simply of a sense of time, but also of myself, of my private capacity for anticipatory excitement. It is only latterly, sometime after the events I am describing, that this kind of detachment has become possible for me. On those far-off evenings below the Hobbema reproduction I was if I am honest preoccupied partly by the picture's sentimental associations (since I had visited Middleharnis at least once, if not twice), but also with working out what the man walking towards me would do next. He was like a person in a film momentarily caught in a single frame. In an effort to induce the film to roll, I would try shutting first one eye, then the other in the vain hope that when I again opened them I would surprise him in the process of advancing by one furtive step. It was to my not inconsiderable chagrin that time after time I would discover him still resolutely fixed in his former position, striding determinedly toward me. Where, I used to wonder, was he going? And what was he carrying across his shoulders? The scale of the reproduction was so tiny that it was just about possible for me to believe that the contraption propped on his left shoulder blade was none other than a fishing rod such as I had become familiar with on our infrequent Saturday afternoon jaunts toward Richmond. But in that case where was the river? Did it occupy the unseen portion of the foreground? Did I, the viewer, lie implicitly soaking in the rushes of some gently flowing, carp-infested stream? The track itself, beginning as a mere dot on the horizon, seemed to widen so fast and so alarmingly as to threaten to engulf the whole of the foreground, river or no. Were there fish then in the narrow knife straight channels I perceived to either side of the picture?

The relentless widening of the track towards the bottom of the picture frame was, I later learned, the result of something called "perspective", and the narrowing towards the far end was productive of something else called a "double vanishing point". It was about the time I made these terms part of my vocabulary that I first found myself, a gangling adolescent, before the original of *The Avenue* on one of my earliest visits to the National Gallery. The size of the picture was, to my amazement, many times larger than I had supposed. Its sheer scale and its position central to a wall in Room Twenty-Seven rendered it susceptible to a perusal sufficiently detailed to clear up a number of my childhood anxieties. The setting was no expanse of open country but an island in the estuary of the River Maas, some seventy miles to the South West of my mother's birthplace. Behind a distant line of trees to the right of the picture lay a thin row of specks, too small to make out in the reproduction, now revealed as the masts of ships anchored out in the sound. The solitary walker advancing steadily towards me carried, not fishing tackle, but a gun. The huddle of houses on the horizon, once enlarged, took on the aspect of a rural hamlet crouching round its onion-steepled church. The tints of the sky and the tossing, unfurling trees suggested a benign but blustery afternoon in latish spring. Swallows gathered above the trees to the left: the reproduction had showed me four; on closer inspection there now appeared to be six. Drawn by the mildness of the day, knots of townsfolk could be seen deep in conversation on the outskirts of the village. In this seventeenth century idyll all was calm, ordered, decorous. The slender poplars nodded to one another, as if in neighbourly greeting. The villagers, doffing their caps, indulged in polite discourse. The man with the rifle continued on his untroubled way. Trade peered in the distance but war, discord or passion were nowhere to be seen. Here if anywhere was a home, a sanctuary, a place where all drifting, all uncertainty might cease.

When several years later I began to be summoned by my vagrant uncle to one of our arbitrary rendezvous, it was here that my sojourn would invariably begin, with a lone preparatory pilgrimage to the room where the Hobbema hung in discreet majesty. It a way of quietening my nerves. I used often to wonder why in Finchley my father had banished this of all pictures to the nursery. Was it a way of conveying some kind of oblique blessing on a restless, easily distracted boy? He had never as far as I was aware given it wall space in the drawing room, though much later he was to suspend it above the sideboard of his largely unused dining room in Cheam. Why had he not paid it more attention, this distillation of restraint, this least insistent of masterpieces which from my earliest years spoke to me, and continues to speak, of a condition which craving exhausts itself, where bustle and heartache end, where a man might live at peace, take tea with his neighbours, exchange the minutiae of civil life, might tend his humble homestead and his paved back yard? Sometimes I used to think I would give much for just such sheltered, substantial tranquillity.

So when, six days after our mournful New Year vigil, my uncle phoned from Colchester to announce the imminence of his next visit and to fix a room and - more tentatively – a time for our next meeting, I did not as had once been my wont solicit some blessed plot of his own choosing, but said straight into the mouthpiece, "We'll meet in Room Twenty-Seven, the one with *The Avenue, Middelharnis* and all those Rembrandts. I'll see you there at four." I replaced the receiver and thought, for once let him come at my bidding. The Hobbema was, after all, my discovery. Even if, as Mother had once intimated, the print from which I had first made its acquaintance had arrived as one of a set on their wedding day three years before my birth, Uncle Claud had not directly introduced me to it. I thought, damn it, he can meet me on my ground.

Self-assured as I felt myself to be, I did not however trust myself to confront his presence without the customary preparation, and it was thus that promptly at three-fifty I took up my position among the Rembrandt likenesses so dear to my mind and heart. There they hung, those late offerings, each in its allotted place: the late stricken self-portrait, the studies of Jacob Trip and his wife Margaretha, and that complimentary evocation of spry old age: *An Elderly Man as Saint Paul*. Should I have been shamed to linger in such company? Dreadful to relate, nothing appeared to shame me that afternoon, full for once of an obscene sort of puppy-like assurance. I had given myself the advantage of prior arrival, and would not be cowed, would not be moved. Thus it was that once more I positioned myself before the great expanse of the Hobbema, and, losing myself beneath those spreading, dipping poplars, drunk my fill of its gigantic calm and repose.

At ten past four I looked down at my wristwatch. For the first time in fifteen years of such meetings Claud was palpably late. It was with an unaccustomed sense of proprietary advantage that I glanced at the room's few fellow occupants. A thick-set girl with a prominent fringe had set up her easel in front of Rembrandt's *Franciscan Friar* and was working at what appeared to be a pedestrian copy, squinting myopically at the original before dabbing at the hardboard before her in little blocks of misjudged colour. Even from several feet away, it was clear she had made the shading much too loud, reducing the sitter's expression of resigned melancholy to gloating religious surliness. I was just recovering from the sense of discomfiture caused by her incompetence when I heard a discreet cough behind me and turned to find Claud standing there, his raincoat grubby about him, his hand extended in greeting.

He was visibly weaker than before, and as I took the offered palm I felt it grasp mine with an ardour than seemed born of his sickness. There was no denying now the baneful progress of whatever ate him from within. All my anger and discomfort drained out of me as he held my hand longer than courtesy required and in a voice of unusual warmth said, "Ben" and again, "Ben".

There was no possible reply, so I insisted on precedent and said, "It's much too early to talk. Let's just look at the picture."

We were silent for several minutes. He had seldom forced upon me the urgencies of personal confidence, and to insist now on the priority of what lay but four feet before our eyes seemed not only natural but fitting. Up and down that rough-rutted track our two pairs of eyes sauntered until the very ripples in its texture were like the eddying of a tranquil pool. It was without any intrusion of mood or awkwardness of address that at length I heard him say, "It's always been a favourite of yours, hasn't it? I know."

"Yes."

"You had it on the wall of your bedroom in Finchley right over the foot of your bed, didn't you?"

"How did you know that?" I was certain my uncle had never crossed the frontier into that vanished, childhood kingdom.

"Your mother described its position to me in some detail," he said. "She was very fond of it too, you know. I think in a way it used to remind her of Holland. More than the interiors even, more even than all of these Rembrandts. It seemed to convey some unchanging quality in the landscape itself. I think it was the comeliness and even flatness of it all which she missed."

Missing the Netherlands. How much had she really missed them I still wondered, and how much of that desolation had she bestowed upon me? I had been as used to the muted gutturals of her voice as to the marks on my own skin; yet beneath them bubbled springs I had lost hope every of tapping and, despite our regular Christmas visits and the occasional injunction arriving postmarked Utrecht, my motherland had always remained for me both stately and forbidden. Mother had only had recourse to her own vernacular in what Father like to call one of her "tizzies", when unaccountably she would take wing for some mental region beyond the reach of either of us. My father had only a smattering of Dutch, and my own linguistic shortcomings have always been a source of personal mortification. But, whenever the pressures of the household grew more than usually burdensome, when she suspected some slight, or when the predominant male stuffiness of the family caused her to take offence, she would sit by the stove, hug her chest and rock back and forward in the armchair like a demented gipsy. Sometimes when the fit had left her, she would take solace in song. Was it a lullaby that she crooned, this strange savage and soothing lament? Father and I would stand and stare, contemplating the enormity of our ignorance.

"She was right of course," my uncle continued, deflecting the course of my reflection. "There is something quintessentially Dutch about it. It's always the minor painters that seem to get the national character right. Rembrandt is so marvellous because he's himself, and so unrepeatable. What do we know about Hobbema, or care really? They even say that after a while he gave painting up, and got a job testing wines. Somehow his individuality matters not a jot.

"I think we probably like him just because he's so typical, and in one sense undistinguished. Somehow his ego wasn't caught up in the thing. It's not a great painting of course, but one can tire of greatness. Genius straining at the leash. Too much effort, too much perfection. The famous can never forget who they are. They've got something to defend, you see. Hobbema had nothing. Not even a reputation."

"Mediocre?"

"No, not that. Mediocrity is what happens when the incompetent have a go at greatness. I don't think Hobbema was mediocre, do you? Perhaps modest."

Then he drew breath, and with the subtlest of modulations continued: "Ours was a modest little enterprise, didn't you think? Pleasing an old man's fancy. How is the commission faring?"

And so we were there at last. His preamble was meant to smooth the path, but at the cross-roads self-accusation loomed. He had called our conspiracy modest. Modest in scope it was, yet even in this I had faltered. Was I the mediocrity? For days now, ever since that last phone call and my earlier disruption with Christina, I had anticipated this moment in some hushed inner courtroom of my mind. At times I had stood in for the accused, usher, foreman of the jury, counsel for the prosecution and for the defence. Increasingly the mantle which had fallen around my shoulders had been that of judge. My self-possession earlier that afternoon had been the bravura of one who discovers his own righteously bewigged face staring down at him. "Guilty my Lord!" boomed the foreman, and justice loured from the bench.

I chose my words carefully and replied, "It's a little behind schedule I'm afraid. She's not what you took her for."

He thought for a moment and then said, "You knew that before you took it on. Didn't you?"

He was right of course. This was no valid plea, so I tried again: "I can't make the lady any better than she is."

"Can't you, Ben. How come?"

"I can only paint what I see."

"And what did you see?"

"Something a wee bit distasteful I'm afraid."

There was a momentary pause.

"Then you couldn't have seen so very far," he said softly.

He rested awhile and his eyes drifted around the room - the Rembrandts, a still life near the door, then aloft to the sky-engulfed landscapes of the fens by Hobbema's teacher Ruisdael - before settling on the sober rectangle of *A Bearded Man in a Cap*, Rembrandt's subdued study of the 1650's nestling beside the avenue, and to the careless eye eclipsed.

"Have you ever thought what light is?" he asked quietly, and inconsequentially it seemed at first.

"Naturally."

"Why naturally, Ben?"

"It's my trade."

"Ah!" The expelled syllable was as light as a puffball. Then he gazed intently at the Rembrandt and asked, "But at least you made a start. On the portrait I mean."

"Not exactly."

"But you did some sketches, a *modello* of some sort?"

"Not even that I'm afraid."

"Ah!" he reiterated in whisper, as if half expecting my appeal. "I thought that was how things stood maybe."

His prescience disturbed me and I started to stammer, apologies tumbling out of me. "It was a bit awkward. I tried at first to gain her confidence by finding out if we had anything in common, whether she still painted and so on. As luck would have it, she still did. Nothing professional, but she seemed keen to show what she could do. I knew you'd be anxious for me to get on with our plan but somehow it seemed churlish to persist.

"So as a way of smoothing things over, as a preliminary to the main exercise, just to earn us a bit more time … I agreed that she should paint *me*."

"*She* painted *you*," he said, measuring out the words. "But isn't that just what you wanted?"

"What I wanted? I was trying to please you."

He gave a forbearing smile. "If the case had rested simply on that Ben, I'd hardly have pressed it. You must have found it gratifying at least."

"No, not actually."

"Well," he replied, palliation soothing his lips. "At least you learned that."

Then he looked once more at the Rembrandt and took his time before asking, "About this question of the light. Does light ever see itself do you think?"

"Of course it doesn't."

"What would happen if it did?"

160

"It would curdle, I shouldn't wonder. Like badly mixed pigment."

He smiled across at me, a cherished warmth glowing through the exposed cheek bones. "Is that how you felt, Ben?"

"Curdled? Well, perhaps. Distinctly uneasy anyway."

"I see what you mean. Seeing yourself can be a shaming business. Did she show you the result?"

"Ghastly, I'm afraid."

"A pity. There's no need for all that discomfort. Have you ever watched a light beam pouring through a church window and then reassembling itself on the nave floor? I was watching it just last week at Ely. Or playing on a vase in a museum? Why do we call the light pure? Because it exists for the sake of the objects it illumines, and doesn't serve itself or reflect on its own nature. Why does the light feel no shame? Because it is not conscious of itself. Why isn't it conscious of itself? Because it fulfils its purposes by giving itself away." He pointed to the Rembrandt to our left. "Look at that portrait now. You wouldn't think the artist was striving for a light effect now would you, and yet you know the whole composition depends upon it."

I stared at an old man of wrinkled visage and slightly Semitic cast of feature, his eyes downcast, his simple cloak drawn slightly off the right shoulder. A study for, say, Simeon? The backdrop was walnut, the shading of the clothes undistinguished, the outer edges of the picture almost dull. No flourish of colour or of treatment embellished the setting. All was condensed in that weary radiant face, transfused with a sort of resigned exultant truth. The mouth was open and drooping slightly, the eponymous cap quite without zest, and yet and yet...

"It doesn't insist, you see. Where's the light source? To the left I should say, but were you conscious of it before I asked?"

"Not that I can recall."

"Why not?"

"We're not supposed to notice."

"That's it. Did I say modest? Not everyone can manage it. Just look at that monstrous 'still life' over there." He gestured toward a garish collocation of assembled bric-à-brac by Gerret Willemsz Heda to the right of the door. "Look at that wine glass now. Doesn't it say 'Admire my treatment. See how luminous I am. 'What does it take itself for I wonder? A study for the Holy Ghost?" He brought his hand down flat against the fabric of his coat. "Even in Claude, even in Turner - and they are great ones - the light pontificates and says, 'Look at me. Here I am. Look how cleverly I disport myself.' Vulgar. Vulgar."

He stooped, the agitation leaving his features, washed now with a shy patina of fatigue. He took the plaid handkerchief from the recesses of his upper pocket, deep within his raincoat. He stood beneath the canopy of Ruisdael's *Extensive Landscape with a Ruined Castle and a Ruined Church*, parading its storm-cloud effects across empyrean skies. He mopped his brow and let his own storm-cloud of conviction subside.

"There's nothing further I can do is there?" he asked at length.

"No."

"Don't be discouraged, Ben. I doubt if I'd have fared any better with the lady myself. Worth another try?" he asked, lifting his eyes to mine and then as rapidly letting them fall.

"Worth another try."

It was a fatal response perhaps, blurted out in some unease, yet he took courage at it.

"My dream of beauty can wait if you like," he said. "But don't yield to all this murkiness, don't stop at all this contradiction. Like all good things it should be easy, shouldn't it, and yet it isn't. Just lay hold of this and use it: the light toils not, neither does it spin."

I smiled across to him, affection battling with resentment. "I'll remember."

"Do your worst my boy. Confound me if you can."

Among the sheepish visitors, the somnolent attendant, the solitary student, his injunction sounded forth:

"To her again, Ben. To her again."

*****

"You never told me you were a painter. How was I supposed know?"

"I never dared."

"Never dared? I'm not that terrifying surely?"

163

Her eyes took me in, trench coat, bewilderment and all. "I don't know," she said wearily. "I really don't know what's to be done with you Henry."

"And my name's not Henry."

"Not Henry. But you told me …"

"No, you got it wrong. My surname's Henry. My Christian name's Benedict. Benedict Henry."

Her eyes dilated slowly. "Benedict Henry. Is that what you call yourself?"

"You haven't heard of me by any chance?"

"Hardly. Is there any reason why I should? There was some student at Kingston College of Art when I was there called Benedict somebody-or-other, but he was the most fearful weed. You're not him, are you?"

"I shouldn't think so."

"Thank goodness for that. Well at least this clears things up a little. There's something to be said for knowing who you've almost been to bed with I suppose."

"Not exactly bed."

"No, not really. More carpet. Bit unkind on the skin as a matter of fact. Perhaps, all things considered, we'd better desist."

"Aspire to higher things?"

"Something like that. Besides, one can't go around sleeping with somebody one is having a relationship with. Or vice versa I suppose."

"Quite."

"Far too compromising for all concerned."

"I do so utterly agree," I said and then taking my courage in both hands added, "you could always let me paint you instead."

She looked momentarily nonplussed, and then, pouncing on one exposed fingernail, begun devouring it with tiny nibbling bites. "Do you think that's wise?"

"I should say so. It might even prove to be rather fun. Seeing as I know all about Burnt Sienna and things, and you seem so anxious to learn …"

She looked attentively at her fingernail for a second before asking, "But am I worth it, do you think?"

"Eminently."

"You couldn't pay me I suppose."

"Not really. I'm a little hard up."

"Yes, I thought as much. You did seem rather glad of my six poundses I must say."

"I'm really much better at painting than at sitting. You could give a chance just to prove my good intentions. Just one little study?"

"Study sounds a bit ponderous. Too much like a life-time commitment. A bit of sketching to begin with perhaps."

She made draftsmanship sound like foreplay. I said, "Alright."

"Thursdays again?"

"Thursdays."

*****

I had not heard from Father for some weeks. The morning after our incongruous New Year celebration he disappeared as inexplicably as he had come, making a curt bow at the threshold and departing with nothing more than a brief promise to "keep in touch". It had always been a favourite phrase of his: "We'll get in touch in a day or two", he was fond of remarking. "I'll get in touch at the weekend. In due course. We'll get in touch with one another just as soon as we can." For one so wary of physical contact, it was a garish form of words. Father was emotion's stenographer: he had a shorthand for all his needs. The merest rise in the pitch of his voice, a slight tightening of the muscles around his mouth, and you knew you awaited an appeal, or else a homily.

But at New Year he had neither appealed nor preached, nor dropped the slightest note of insinuation. He had just sat in his corner drawing at his near-empty pipe until the persistent draught through the white-ashed bole threatened to drive me out of the room. For once, even his silences had seemed no indictment. Instead, there was this tame sort of supplication about them which tore at the entrails more effectively than any reprimand or plea.

But on the Wednesday after the resumption of my visits to Dolphin Square, at half past five in the afternoon, the phone on our bedside table rang sullenly twice, and then abruptly stopped. Half an hour later it pealed again: three plaintive peeps and then silence. The pattern was repeated the following night and every evening for the next five days. I had no evidence that the caller was an acquaintance of mine as opposed to Andria's, let alone that it was Father. It could have been any diseased soul who had picked our number at random from out of the book. But then the coincidences of timing, the methodical persistence of the calls, something about the curt supplication of the bell as it resounded hollow through the flat all brought Father irresistibly to mind: standing by the Mock Tudor bay window perhaps, his silhouette hunched against the early winter twilight, bald head gleaming, his pipe hanging, futilely drawing, ash dropping grey onto his cardigan, thinking, "Should I or shouldn't I? Shall I risk a call before my evening stroll?" And then the reaching for the receiver, the tentative dialling before the final loss of nerve. I knew little enough of solitude, but from the dreary years I had passed immediately before meeting with Andria I knew there was sufficient power in loneliness to unhinge the most balanced of minds.

Then, the Saturday following, arrived this:

The Willows, Cheam, Tuesday, 12th January, 1985.

Dear Benedict

It was a saving grace to see you shortly after Christmas and I am grateful for it. I have been a little under the weather lately - a little "browned off" as your mother would have put it - how I miss even her dourer moods - and to see people I find eases the mind considerably. Would you be so kind as to convey my sincere gratitude to Andria? It cannot have been easy, having an elderly person descend on one's household - especially someone whom one knows so scantily - and to lay claim to one's hospitality in so untoward and abrupt manner.

This letter has one principal purpose: to inform you that I have recently been giving some thought to the subject of my will. It is never easy to decide these things, and one's moods do have a tendency to seesaw, particularly in unseasonable weather, but after a preliminary word with my solicitors I feel at last somewhat clearer in my mind as to the provisions I should stipulate. I've made Lawrence Echardt sole executor - he's a decent old boy, if occasionally crochety, and will make sure that everything is done decently and with proper discretion. I see no need to have a public reading and will convey as much in a covering letter. However, all things considering, I though it only fair to you to let you know something of the probable contents in advance so that you will have some idea of what awaits you when you've no longer me to worry about (if you do worry, but that's another story).

Your letter of 14th ultimo announcing the arrival of a child to you and Andria this Spring has left your old dad in a bit of a quandary. As you are more than aware, I am a man of sturdy principles, and though in the past I am sure that you have frequently seen cause to find me inflexible, it is a little late in the day to mend one's ways. I'm of the old school, Benedict, like Claud, I dare say, but as there are so few of us left we may as well stick to our guns. So, when they break open the seal on that thick buff envelope, I'm afraid that you will discover I've fired something of a broadside. One salvo for the old dispensation I'd say, though I'm sure you'll interpret it as ill-tempered crossfire.

I have decided to leave the lion's share of my estate in trust for your child, the remainder to be divided equally between Rosie, Claud and yourself. I like to look forward to the future in my myopic sort of way, and to invest in the coming generation strikes me as the most prudent way of so doing. However, there is a sub-clause which I intend to attach to this specific provision. Should you and Andria choose to wed, the trust clause will of course stand. But should you personally take it into your head to get together with Christina Echardt, two thirds of the sum entrusted will revert to you, on condition that the two of you marry as Catholics, take custody of the child, and bring it up Catholically as the fruit of that union. Such a codicil will appear inexplicable to you at this juncture, but I have long desired that my family and Echardt's should draw closer and have already made arrangements that, should such an eventuality arise, you will be amply acquainted with the reasons. I will say no more at this stage.

You may well detect in these conditions the aberrations of impending dotage, but old men as you know love to lay down the law, to interfere where they are least welcome. I suppose it is the only way left us to influence the way in which the world runs. Nonetheless I am satisfied that I have acted reasonably according to my own lights, and, however peevish you may regard the proposals concerning yourself, you will at least acknowledge that in this manner your child will not suffer, but will on the contrary be amply provided for.

Please let me know what you feel about all of this. I have been ringing the flat for some evenings past but have so far failed to elicit a response.

Once again, my sincere thanks to Andria.

Your ever loving father.

The more eccentric aspects of its fourth paragraph notwithstanding, this letter did not altogether strike out of the blue. I had been expecting Father to perform some kind of gesture for some time, and though the careful inveiglement of our child-to-be constituted an added turn of the screw, there was little in the communication to cause me personal disquiet. It was entirely typical of Father thus to mingle largesse with meanness, far-sightedness with caution, to step a primrose path between family obligation and the severities of moral judgement. Besides, he had clearly gone off his head. After sleeping on it for a few days I could almost bring myself to feel grateful to the old man for making my own position so clear. I have never been mercenary, and while a little luxury after all the penury might not have come amiss, Andria and I had scraped by for years on our own resources and might happily continue to do so. Whatever form our relationship in future took, however onerously I elected to treat the unlooked-for responsibilities of fatherhood, I would neither starve nor fester romantically in a garret. I had not, after all, been cut off without a penny, and to share a widow's mite with Rosie and Claud was even in a way an honour. There would be no influencing me. I had chosen my lot, and I would stick to it.

Nor did the re-emergence of Father's Echardt obsession take me aback nearly as much as he had evidently expected. I was used to this kind of monomaniac nagging, and, if he now cared to give form to his lunatic whims in legal parlance, who was I to spoil his little pleasure? It made absolutely no difference to my situation. Echardt's offer of employment still lay under a muddle of jam jars somewhere on my worktable; I had given little thought to the question of how, or even whether, to answer it. In any case, I assumed that the contents of the codicil had no bearing on Echardt's overture, the terms of which had long expired. As for my increasingly ambivalent relationship to the man's daughter, I considered this a bizarre coincidence that in no way reflected on my willingness or otherwise to comply with Father's more far-flung wishes.

Rosie had of course been right. There was in my father's makeup a scrupulous delicacy which transcended even his occasional sense of pique. He had in no way compromised himself. I would not deny that in his own footling manner he had even been fair. He had given me a chance to comply with his outlandish requests, nor did his displeasure at my present circumstances extend as far as placing them under any embargo. He had simply confronted me with a choice either to fall in with his obsessions or else continue with my modest style of life, cushioned by the reassurance that in so doing I was in no way harming our child.

Andria too had not been without her moment of insight. There were depths and motives in my father's character which I would probably never fathom. Why he had taken it into his noddle to stage-manage my life from the wings I could hardly think. Was this his last most lavish initiative to ensure my future respectability, to "set me up in life" as he always had it? The fact that one half of me craves the very peace and substance he seemed determined to procure on my behalf lent his blandishments even greater piquancy, without in the least tempting me to comply with them. Echardt or no Echardt, Christina or no Christina, I would carry on my way regardless.

*****

And, now that the mischief was over, now the misunderstandings were past, at first I sat her on a window seat and settled her head to look slantwise over her balcony-towards the roofs of Pimlico and the sempiternal river. After so much vexation and stress it seemed wisest to draw her simply, and hence I found myself rejecting all the drapes and bijoux she so lavishly poured forth from her cupboards and chose instead to clothe her in a plain linen blouse with a red and turquoise scarf providing colour at the neck. At the beginning of our second session she inquired, "How do you want me?"

"Want you?"

"Want to paint me? In what position? For painting, naturally."

I looked at her hard and said, "Yes."

"Well?"

Nervous pause. Interval for cogitation, for consideration. Procrastination certainly. Almost for despair.

There was a book, a paperback, lying on the coffee table with Hokusai's *The Wave* on the cover. I said, "Stay sitting. Now open up that book." Vocal mood: quasi-imperious; pseudo-masterful, feigned attitude of one feebly attempting to pretend (pretending to attempt?) he knows what he is doing.

Obediently she opened the paperback where she had turned the page down. "Alright," she said. "Satisfied?"

"Right. Now stand up."

"Stand up reading?"

"No, drop the book. Not on the floor." She placed it back on the coffee table. Then I asked, "Have you got another prop: a mop, a broom or something?"

She gave me a looked of strained and infinite patience, then said with marked emphasis "I don't do brooms."

"Vacuum cleaner?"

"Honestly!" (Not "Honestly?" Exclamation with demonstrative expulsion of breath: "Honestly!"). With protesting weariness she fetched a vacuum cleaner from a cupboard in the hall. It was a Hoover: one of those tubular standing jobs with a fabric bag that puffs in and out. They don't make anymore. She plonked it on the carpet, placed her hands on her hips and said, "You don't actually intend to paint me cleaning."

I painted her cleaning. I painted her reading her book, which was called *The Sea, The Sea*. I did both of these things, side by side, on the same canvass. Let me explain to you, as I explained to her.

To the left of the hallway in our Finsbury house as I was growing up, downstairs from the Hobbema, there were two reproductions of Dutch interiors, hanging side by side and identical in size, each within its identical blackwood frame. They had, I was told, been a wedding present to my parents from Claud, in lieu of his attending the ceremony. Perhaps he had intended them as a compliment to my mother's motherland. In both of them, the room depicted appeared to be the same: a downstairs living room with beams and twin mullioned windows. Both featured a pair of paintings hung side by side, on the left-hand wall just as they themselves were, and in identical blackwood frames. And in each painting, and in each room, a mirror, also in a blackwood frame, was suspended between the windows on the far wall. The paintings in our hallway, furthermore, seemed to have been done from much the same position, and with much the same perspective, but there were tell-tale differences between them, profoundly perplexing to the infant mind. In the painting to the left, the floor was made of scrubbed boards; in that to the right, it was tiled in a double rectangular pattern (that is, with one rectangle inside another). To the left, the upper panes of the mullioned windows came down lower than they did to the right, and the lower panes were correspondingly smaller. In the left-hand painting, moreover, the windows gave onto the street, so that the houses opposite could be glimpsed through the glass. In the right-hand one, they gave onto autumnal trees. In the right-hand painting, the mirror on the far wall was further down, and a third picture, also within its blackwood frame, hung above it. In the left-hand painting, as I carefully observed, this third picture wasn't there. That it was the same room was nonetheless clear from the hump-backed chest, its lid covered with the same blanket of heavy moss-green velvet, that lay against the right hand wall in each, next to the window, with the same leather-seated stool parked at the end nearer to the viewer. (The adult painter in me suspects these were props moved from room to room. At six, I was more trusting.)

There was one human figure in each painting, and in both she was the same person: an elderly woman, I suppose in her sixties, wearing a white bonnet, a long black dress and a waisted gown. In the left-hand painting she was seated, absorbedly reading a book. In the right-hand one she was mopping the chequered floor, and half her pallid face was reflected in the mirror. In the left-hand picture, she seemed to have cast off her leather clogs, which lay higgledy-piggledy behind her, just above the lower frame. (Mother to me: "Don't leave your shoes higgledy-piggledy on the floor!") Despite this, the reading lady appeared to be shod. In the right hand painting no shoes were to be seen, since as she swept the woman's feet were concealed behind the modest hem of her skirt. By the age of seven I was already an accomplished up-skirt fantasist.

Commonplace explanations do not appeal to the growing mind; at least they did not to mine. As a child, I preferred mystery, perhaps I still do. So, was it the same woman, and why and when had she moved? Was it the same afternoon in the same room, in the same house? In that case, why the discrepancies? Individually the paintings did not pose a problem. It was their juxtaposition that rendered them mysterious. Together they schooled me in an insight which I have never quite lost sight of: that life is very strange and very elusive, that people and things are forever different, and forever the same, that they move and that, in the process, they stay still.

And thus it was that I said to Christina: "I would like you both sitting down and standing up, with your face towards me, and yet averted. Intellectual and menial. Intent and distracted. Busy and quiet. If possible, I would like to do you doing and being all of these things at the same time. But you can't, and so I can't. I'll do you and you, different facets of you, side by side.

*****

Claud had told my parents that his wedding present pictures were by Pieter de Hooch, one of the best-known painters of the Dutch school. My mother carried this belief to her death bed, and so in time did Claud. I too believed it for twelve years or more, until over lunch in the snack bar in Kingston, when I was nineteen, Jocelyn put me right. They were now thought to be by the less acclaimed artist Pieter Janssens Elinga, a pupil of de Hooch's so obscure he had often been confused with his teacher. The picture with the old woman reading is in Munich; the one with her sweeping (known as *La Balayeuse*) is in Paris (there is a different version in Saint Petersburg). I don't know if they have ever been exhibited side-by-side, except in our house. When I next met Claud, I informed him of the new attribution; he refused to change his mind. I even informed Dad, who sniffed. So I told Jocelyn that they had proved unpersuadable, and he laughed politely. The next week he brought into college a mock-up of a Perspective Box by Elinga which is kept in the Hague. It sits on a desk and shows a room rather similar to the one in our pictures enclosed by three walls, in one of which is a peep-hole. We had a lot of fun with this. Even Jake did. It taught me a lot about the various ways in which things and people are seen.

Different and yet the same, the same and yet different.

With Christina I alternated the sessions, so as to ease the strain for her of having to sit or stand for a long time in the same position. So, half an hour doing her reading her book. Coffee break. Half an hour doing her with the hoover. Between these sessions I subtly re-arranged the furniture in the room, so that it was the same room, and yet a different room. No kissing now. Chatting, yes: not post-coital or post-amorous, more inter-pictorial. I asked her if she found it as difficult to maintain either of these postures as I had found it keeping mine.

She pondered for a moment, seeming to nibble at the thought and then let it drop. She went into a kind of absorbed silence as she sipped at her cup and then, flexing her shoulders slightly said, "I do hope I'm still enough. Probably not. You know how difficult it is."

"I do. But you're managing wonderfully."

"Stillness is something I'm always trying to achieve, but somehow something always seems to distract me. I remember when I was a young girl on holiday in Dorset standing quite motionless in a field and saying, 'I won't move. I won't. I'll stay rooted here like that oak tree forever.' But after a minute a stubborn itching started up in my nostril, so I wriggled it and losing concentration found all my efforts at stillness to be in vain. I stood on a hump-backed bridge over a running stream one perfect Summer afternoon. In the fields on the far ridge, cattle were grazing and a light breeze blew across the rows of wheat at the river's edge catching the stalks in a leaning immutable frenzy. I looked down at the river beneath my feet and tried to imagine it fixed in a still but unstaying flux of permanent motion, but somehow the sensation always escaped me. I remembered that moment years later, as a bored sixth-former at school. The teacher was expounding Heraclitus and there was this thin, spinsterish voice travestying the wisdom of the ancients, 'Everything flows. Its imperfect because it flows.' And suddenly I thought, 'he's right, you know. Things are always running away from you,' and felt desolate, empty and alone."

"Would you want it otherwise?"

"Oh yes, I think we all would. But you can't have what you want. If people can't accept that, there must be something wrong with them. You can't will into being what's not there, however desirable you might think it. It's like trying to rope a gale, or the sea - pointless. Or like trying to be virtuous. When I was little my dad would say, 'You're a bad little girl. You've disappointed me and you've disappointed your mummy in Heaven and if she was here, she'd give you a good hiding. So go to bed now and say your prayers. Or stand in the comer with your hands on top of your head until you hear the tea kettle whistle.' And so I'd stand in the comer, shut my eyes, grit my jaws and I'd say, 'I'm a good little girl. I'm a good little girl. Everything I do is good. He'll like me. I'll force him to like me. I'll do it by being good.'

"Apparently they called me Christina in the womb. They used to cuddle up to one another, he'd put his hand on her stomach and say, 'Look, there's Christina heaving.' I lost my mother when I was about two, before I could retain any visual impression of her really. All I can recall is a feeling of gentleness sometimes and somebody who used to sit down at the window like this looking fraught. But every so often, just after I had tucked myself up in bed after the nightly story, I'd have this recurring image of her standing at the foot of the bed smiling down at me saying, 'I'm watching you. I'm always watching you. You'll never let me down, will you?'

"Of course, I did so continually. They made a fearful mistake in calling me Christina, I'm a kind of pagan really. At least all of my senses are pagan."

"Nobody's a real pagan," I protested. "If you were a real pagan you wouldn't be sitting there right now. You're the living disproof of paganism."

"How so?" She had turned her face towards me.

"Well, somebody had to create you."

"I don't see why. Mummy I suppose, but I have no memory of her. There's always Daddy."

"Well, somebody had to create *them*."

"I'm not so sure about that. I sometimes think that Daddy must have been there for ever, like the Parthenon."

"Everyone's created somewhere along the line. You're too striking to have emerged from chaos."

She looked startled: "You talk like a child's book of saints."

I smiled indulgently. "I'm just trying to ingratiate you so that you'll let me sketch you again,"

"Stop changing the subject."

"It's quite simple. If you're pretty, you must exist, mustn't you?"

"So?"

"Then somebody must have caused to you exist."

"Supposing I was ugly?"

"That's irrelevant. Besides this painting disproves it."

"Let's take a peek then."

"I'm not sure if I ought to let you. It might just go straight to your gorgeous pagan head."

*****

"When are you bringing her to see me?"

My aunt's parting injunction concerning Andria had over the previous couple of months turned into a ritual incantation. At the end of each visit when, half reluctant to intrude my presence any longer, and half held by the hoped-for prospect of another albeit often repeated tale, I stood by a dexterous lowering of the head to communicate my decision to leave, her question would come sweeping back over me like a high tide against a harbour wall. One of these afternoons I knew that the tide would rise too high and my resolve to keep these two women as separate cells in my life would be inundated. Already one or two stones were loosened in the masonry, and little scurries of sea water had appeared along the well-trodden promenade.

Why, I now ask myself with the sort of hindsight the contrite delight in, was I so reluctant to perform the introduction? In a perverse sort of a way I suppose I had come to consider my aunt's basement flat as a sort of private treasure house the riches of which were out-of-bounds to all but myself. I had always been something of hoarder, and my aunt even more so. It was scarcely my responsibility if at this particular moment in time I was the sole human being in her collection. In my eyes we owned one another, and I was damned if I'd relinquish the exclusiveness of our afternoons. Rose's seclusion was the guarantee of this prerogative. She had been my personal discovery just as surely as had been the Hobbema earlier. Besides, who else would have appreciated the lob-sided lamp shade, the shabby covers, plaster saints and piles of outdated reading matter?

But as January dragged into February and a chill East wind cut through the streets of West London, Andria unaccountably lent her voice to the petition. She had now exhausted the extent of her fads and had taken to sitting for hour after hour before the misty windowpanes of our all-purpose living room staring out into the open street, every passing week a little squatter, a little more contented, a little more the stranger. She seemed temporarily to have lost all interest in her research. Round about the constantly glowing electric fire her well-thumbed Loeb editions -

red for Latin and Green for Greek - lay undisturbed, and her notebooks took on a wan appearance of disuse. I did not seek to probe her as to the reason for this neglect, contented that her dedication had, temporarily at least, abated. Besides, it gave my own dedication to the task in hand all the freer rein. My series of studies of her burgeoning form were progressing better than I expected. An inertness turned to tranquillity, and a faraway look of calm settled on her features, I grasped the proffered prize and devoured her figure with little nibbles of charcoal or paint, filling sketchpad after sketchpad with impressions, battening on this unsought-for state of mute maternal preparedness.

But one afternoon from out of this pool of uncanny serenity she unexpectedly said, "When are you going to take me to meet that aunt of yours?" and the die was cast.

"I can't remember promising anything."

She considered this for a while and then said, "You can't keep us all in purdah, you know."

"Maybe I shouldn't. But all the same I think I'm still inclined to."

"That's typically selfish if I may say so. Whatever do you want her all to yourself for?"

"Maybe I consider she's not fit to be seen."

"That goes for two of us."

"Is this supposed to be some subtle form of moral blackmail?" I asked. "And what makes my aunt so irresistible all of a sudden?"

Nonetheless, two hours later we stood staring at the narrow strip of debris which fronted my aunt's front door amid the first pattering of a rainstorm. It was one of those days, so common in the shifting season betwixt Christmas and Easter, when the very sky seems to hide its face, shrouding the invisible sun with great blankets of indigo mixed with grey. Andria inspected each piece of detritus in turn - the boxes, bottles and each decaying settee - attempting, as I had done so many times before her, to discern its hidden history. The rusting tricycle lay on its side, its hub leaning over as if in mourning for a lost wheel. The succession of winter downpours had reduced the pile of cardboard boxes to a solid, dripping mass, and weeds grew up unhindered from the cracks between the flag stones, their leaves pitted and slimy with rainwater.

I leant over and, tapping once more at the moss-green door, called out twice. There was no response. A third tap yielded no better result, and I had just taken Andria's arm to lead her away, when a timid light pawed at the kitchen window before the familiar fumbling at the bolts.

She appeared to have been doing what - in respect of the relative lack of untidiness in the hallway - could only be called a spot of spring cleaning. As we groped our way along the dimly lit corridor, I noticed that the mountains of bric-à-brac had been edged slightly to one side to provide an erratic and uncertain pathway through which one person of average width might slide. It was an operation which in the old days I had found next to impossible; now it was Andria alone who needed helping. After a time, she gave up trying to find her own way and consented to being led, her fingers trailing over the assorted surfaces like a blind woman reading the lips of a sighted companion. When we reached the door of the living room, she dropped my hand and strained her eyes in an attempt to accustom herself to the lack of luminosity. Then, as the gloom subsided a little and the edges of the objects in my aunt's room gradually made themselves plain, she leant forward before trusting herself to drop into the depths of a worn velvet armchair.

"I feel as if I'm swimming," she said in an undertone, when my aunt parted briefly for the kitchen.

"I know. It is a bit like an aquarium. Your eyes get used to it after a while."

"Why doesn't she open the curtains?"

"They are open."

"I'd hate to see it when they're closed!"

"They're covered over with newspapers. Circa 1959."

"Oh God!"

Despite my best endeavours to prepare Andria en route, I could see that her expedition into the world of my aunt's basement had left her fairly dumbfounded. At length she stood up and started peering blearily at a used copy of *The Tablet* which had been lying on one of the least rickety of the coffee-tables. As she stood there, unconscious momentarily of her surroundings, lost in her effort to distinguish the print, something about her posture brought to mind one of my favourite paintings in the Rijksmuseum, which I had visited as a child on our family jaunts to Amsterdam: a small, oblong Vermeer depicting a young wife perusing a letter from her absent husband, her hands cupped around the script above the big dome of her pregnant belly. In deference to the spinsterish ambiance of my aunt's flat, Andria has caught up her mousey tresses into a bun beneath which the thin down at her nape caught the few flecks of aquamarine light in the etiolated gloom of the room. She was wearing a smock of sea-green, deepened by the semi-darkness almost to turquoise. With her sleeves rolled up to the elbow to reveal her still slender wrists, staring at the journal before with a sort of puzzled candour, she looked for all the world like the girl I'd first set eyes on so many years before, held by a curling phrase of Mozart.

Such idylls of abstraction do not last. Presently my aunt appeared in the doorway laden with a tray. "I'm afraid the biscuits will be a little stale. And as usual I've burned the toast. I hope Andria won't mind hers scraped. Now if you'll just move aside those Encyclicals…"

Rosie's repasts, however frugal, contrived always to assume the aspect of feast, even when the contents constituted no more than the warmed up contents of her bread bin. Andria and I helped ourselves greedily - we had not eaten for hours; since I'd been so absorbed in my work that as usual I'd quite forgotten to go out and fetch any provisions spreading sheaves of margarine on to the thick, tasteless toast, gulping down mouthfuls of strong, acidic tea. It was some time before Andria, unused to this ritual of silence, inquired, "How long have you lived here?"

"Well, that's a question," said Rosie. "I'm not sure if even Benedict knows the answer to that one."

"Before the war anyway," I said. I'd honestly no idea.

"Not quite."

"Before I was born at any rate."

"Do you really want me to tell you, or shall I bore both of you terribly?"

It was Andria who replied, "No, please tell us."

"Well, it all goes back to the air raids. The blitzkrieg you know, always shortened to blitz. Such a skimpy little syllable for so atrocious an event. It was a very dark period and I was terribly alone. I was living in an attic over by Tufnell Park at the time, working at my hats. It wasn't exactly the best time for milliners as you can imagine. Hats. If only you could knit tin ones.

"Claud had been posted abroad somewhere, and Hamish had been allotted civilian duties, after which he spent most nights firewatching in the city. He used to say he'd make sure they missed St Paul's if he had to take the brunt himself. When every so often he turned up to see me, I used to tell him he'd be better occupied defending St Bride's: at least he'd a stake in the place. And then one night the house in which I was staying took the blast from a neighbouring street. Two streets down to be precise, but the force took away our frontage. At first, I was sure I must be dead. There was a rumbling that seemed to go on for ever, like a landslide down a cliff face. Then I looked up from beneath my blankets and there was Virgo as clear as anything through a gap in the bedroom wall, just over what had been the washbasin. I was rescued by wardens, but the landlady was killed outright. When they lowered me down on to the pavement I looked up to the vicinity of her sitting room and there were a pair of combinations fluttering next to the Milky Way. Ten days later I moved in here, and I've been here ever since. Benedict's father came over to see it and said, 'Well, you've found yourself a nice little burrow I must say.'"

"It is," confirmed Andria, able at last to take in everything around her.

The fruit of thy womb, the fruit of thy womb, yelled Philophilus, inconsequential in his cage.

Andria's eyes had drifted to where, over the gas-fire, the oval frame lay perched with its cherished, fading contents.

"Who is that?" she asked. I had almost anticipated the question.

"My daughter."

"Yes, Benedict told me," said Andria, and then on an impulse added, "do you mind if I could look at her?"

"Not at all."

Rosie reached over and handed her the silver frame, which she held close to her face, looking at it intently.

"She's very lovely," she said.

*****

188

On our way back to Kensal Rise we both at first maintained a thoughtful silence. Loping by my side in an attempt to keep up with my jaunty unconcerned steps, there was a ruminative process at work in Andria which initially I failed to place. It was not until we turned the corner of Queen's Park into Millman Road that she suddenly slowed down to a crawl and said, "You know, that woman could almost be my mother."

"I suppose it's possible," I said without slackening my pace, slogging resolutely onwards towards Keslake Road. I was by now so familiar with these flashes of telepathic revelations that placation had come to seem the wisest policy. The only fresh element on this occasion was the sex of the putative parent. Andria had spent the better part of our relationship attaching herself to a series of surrogate fathers - military chiefs of staff, Readers in Classics, Bishops of the Church of England - that to discover her hankering after a mere mother was a minor if welcome variation.

By now she was scampering after me. "She could you know." Her voice was a minor third higher.

"And what made you suddenly think of that?"

"The photograph, I think."

"You're not telling me that could be you."

"Well, it could almost."

"You don't look in the least like that little girl."

"She was only a toddler when it was taken."

"Andria!"

"And there was something else too. Something about your aunt's attitude."

"You're not going to tell me the military type in the moustache was your father."

"I don't see why not."

"There's no reason in the world why not. All I'm looking for is a single decent reason why."

"I suppose you're right. I'm the right age anyway."

"Have you any idea how many little girls were born in 1953? And how many of those went astray or were adopted? A few hundred at a conservative estimate."

"It was just a hunch."

"A pretty feeble old hunch."

We had turned into Peploe Road and I had taken out my bunch of keys to open the outside door. Andria said, "It's just that it would be nice to feel that this kid was going to belong somewhere."

"It does," I shouted, turning into our narrow pathway that ran between the handkerchief-sized gardens at the front of our house. "It belongs here. Number sixteen."

I placed the key in the lock and turned. Passing in front of me her face wore an expression which reminded me of her crying fit in the park the previous November. Then she stopped and stared morosely at the threadbare stair carpet.

"Lucky old it," she said.

*****

Newington, Edinburgh, 21ˢᵗ February, 1985.

Dear Ben,

Caledonia at last! This guest house has a mynah bird like Rosie's parrot which the mistress - a former memsahib - has trained to abuse one in Urdu. Walked up to the Mound yesterday to view Playfair's National Gallery: for all the world like some noble Athenian stoa. Quite a decent bunch of Turners, and even one solitary Hobbema would you believe! Is exhibition fever rising? Are you working hard?

Patriotically yours,

Claud.

*****

It was the coffee break on our third day. We were seated side-by-side on the thick-piled carpet. Above us on the hessian-covered wall hung the reproduction of one of Canaletto's many vistas of San Marco I had noticed on my first visit. It was one of those from the extreme West end of the piazza, with a full-on view of the Basilica's ornamented façade and thin stratus cloud filled with impending rain curling behind the green cupolas of the roof and behind the tall campanile. I remarked, "You never told me what you were doing in Italy."

She sipped at her expresso and began, "Au pairing at first. Learning the language, then…"

Silence. Her forearms were covered in a down of tiny brown hairs. Sometimes as we sat relaxing side by side she would extract a hair-brush from her leather handbag and with the very tip begin stroking the hair ends: backwards and forwards, forwards and backwards until in the end they were all arranged at the same angle like a row of miniature palisades pointing up towards me. I found this subtly arousing. Then gradually she would set about brushing them in the opposite direction so that they all faced back towards her. Sometimes as she did so she would talk idly about herself, in so disconnected a fashion that it was almost as if I wasn't there. At other times she would hold her peace for minutes on end, leaving me to coax the confidences out of her as I squatted on the hearth rug watching her manipulate those lines of hair with an almost macabre tenderness.

"Then I was married."

I said "So? Are you still married?"

"No, not still married."

There was a tense, inquisitorial silence that trembled on the brink of embarrassment. Then she resumed again with the hairbrush, this time teasing the hairs in the opposite direction away from me.

"Tell me about your husband."

"There's not a lot to tell. He was an art collector several years older than me, a business contact of my dad's. We lived in an apartment block near the centre of Milan, not far from the Duomo. Cold marble floors, slatted blinds, a maid *en suite* and all round the walls a procession of very minor masters. I used to sit on a tubular steel chair in front of the floor-to-ceiling window listening to the sound of the traffic. I can still tell you when a Fiat changes gear. He was out all day at working, he insisted I stay at home. Well. Sometimes he would go across to the Uffizi in Florence or down to the Pinacoteca in Bologna, so I was on my own for days with only the maid to talk to: "*Scusi, signora. Per favore, signora. Vorrei una tazza di te?*" She was a widow, a close-fisted pugnacious woman from the Tuscan hills, tight-mouthed, capable, and then every so often she would fly off the handle and rant at me meaninglessly for hours on end in fluent, peevish Italian. The shops, the food, the government, *il signor*."

Look, I was saying to myself. This explains quite a lot, doesn't it, or does it? Father's request and will, Echardt's apparent eagerness, maybe Claud's compliance, not to speak of his bizarre commission. Christina is in her mid-thirties. One marriage seems to have failed. She is an only daughter. Echardt is anxious for a grandchild, someone to whom he may one day bequeath the firm. After all, it is an old firm, according to Claud. At the very least he wants this young woman to be happy. It did not strike me that she was happy.

"Did you love him?"

"At first. In the early days he would often come home for an early lunch and a nap, and we'd sit opposite one another over this rather formal square-topped table while he told me about prices, contacts, deals staring all the while at his rather podgy little hands clasped on the place mat before him. He was a vain, rather weak man I think; certainly he had no gift for closeness.

193

Every few weeks he'd invite some colleagues round for dinner and we'd all sit round in these fake leather seats on the cold marble floor while he opened the wine and put on his cassette of Vivaldi. *La Stravaganza; I Solisti di Venezia*. It tinkled all the way through my marriage, that tape. *Bene. Bene. Dolcissime.* There was little I could do on such occasions except preside. The cooking was all done for me. I can tell you the names of every pasta in the book, but do you know I can't make one of them. Not even starting from a packet. Not even spaghetti ragù Pathetic when you think about it."

"So?"

"We were trying for children. Mario was a Catholic of the official variety - weddings and funerals - we were married in Torino - but he had an ingrained horror of contraception. I'm still not quite sure how it's done. That sort of thing was simply not talked about. He wanted a brown-eyed bambino to dangle on his knee and show off to his mother. We tried for two years. The third Easter he wrote to Daddy saying he thought I was probably infertile but he'd keep me because he still loved me in his upright, slightly astringent way. It never seemed to occur to him that he might be sterile. I was trapped you see, like a princess in a tower."

"And then?"

"The next February I packed my bags and flew off for a few weeks with father. Dear Father. I told him all my troubles, and when it was time for me to catch the flight back from Heathrow, I was still telling him. Postcards. Letters. Telegrams. *Mama mia. Mama mia.* He ran all the way over to Torino to weep in her billowing, capacious skirts. I never went back. A year later he started making noises about an annulment. Divorce of course was out of the question. It wasn't necessary in any case. Early last year he was clinching a purchase in Mantua when he grasped his associate by the hand, turned on his heels, send out a sort of strangulated squeak and fell flat on his face on the Persian rug. He was fifty-two."

She had now given up on her forearms and was practising a bizarre routine with her left hand which she was in the process of sending on a sort of wobbly sentry promenade along the tabletop towards me.

The index and forefingers were pacing the polished surface like a guardsman on parade, prancing before my very eyes like a couple of stout little stilts. When they got within half an inch of the edge, they'd swivel round and just as determinedly, just as precariously stomp back in the opposite direction,

"Do you ever miss him?" I asked, after a decent interval.

"No, not really. There wasn't a lot left to miss. It's better to be alone than with somebody you half care for. I can never quite work out where I stand with anybody. I'm quite a self-contained person."

"So I'd noticed."

"I think," she said, "Italy basically put me off men for a while. Nowadays they feature as shadows flickering around my brain. Sometimes I just can't cope with them. I'm happier here than anywhere."

"So sorry to disturb."

"Don't worry," she said, recommencing her finger-stomping routine. "It's strange. It's as if we'd met a long, long time ago. Almost as if we had been children together. I should add that I'm not in the least attracted to you anymore."

"Were you ever?"

"A bit." She looked up. "Should you be asking that question? I thought you were married or living in sin or something."

"In a way."

"In a way. What do you mean? You don't seem very sure. You said she was having a baby."

"Yes that's right. In about two months the specialist thinks."

"Well shouldn't you be back home looking after her in Willesden or wherever?"

I cleared my throat: "Yes, I suppose I should."

She took her hand from the tabletop and, looking less at me than at some abstract point in the mid-distance, murmured, "I've given ever so much thought to that, you know. How lovely to have a child."

*****

Claud was right of course. It was about time I was working. So far I'd merely been ticking over, preparing sketches, piling up the odd completed item at the top of the stairwell, hoping against hope that at the last minute by some remarkable contrivance of fate the selection would be completed and miraculously perfect. Our living room faced North-West, one of the worst bearings for a studio, but, with the onset of March I would spend longer and longer hours by the narrow window attempting to capture the last few dregs of light as they were deflected off the buildings opposite, grimy with all the dirt of the city. The date of the Opening was fixed for the third week of May. There was additional news, especially welcome under the circumstances. In a letter from a gallery in Bentink Street setting out the arrangements, the director had sprung the surprise that a certain 'anonymous benefactor' had undertaken to make two thousand pounds' worth of purchases, though whether from the exhibition as a whole or from one of the two contributors he did not say. My co-exhibitor, a former teacher who now held the Chair of Painting in the North, was notoriously prolific; my principal fear was that my contribution would be dwarfed in consequence. After all, I was piggy-backing on his reputation. I would never, under any circumstances, have been offered an exhibition of my own. But here too had come re-assurance. The same letter that told me of the prior commitment to purchase had also disclosed that, owing to the generosity of the unidentified benefactor, my share of the exhibition was to be expanded from two walls to an entire room.

It was one morning during the second week of April that my partner phoned me to say that he was coming down to the metropolis the following weekend and would welcome the opportunity of meeting to discuss prior arrangements.

I should, of course, have told you all about my fellow exhibitor by now. Put my reluctance on this score down to false modesty, jealousy or idle pique. I can postpone this chastening task no longer. Now, then, is the time for me to introduce the vexed subject of DOIG, or as I must call him nowadays Doig Evans RA, or more accurately Sir Doig Evans RA (1942-2011). Nowadays, if you need the biographical details, you can go his Wikipedia entry where you will also find a mugshot of that deceased and grandiloquent git looking suave and complacent. Already by that time he was a celebrity in the making. Doig, in a word, was a success, and was destined to be even more of one, whereas I by nature am - and was always bound to be - a failure, more-or-less contented to be so. With that in mind, you had better take everything I say from now on with a pinch of sea-salt, cynical knowingness or just plain, indulgent, human understanding. And therein lies a second problem. In order to comprehend - or even properly to place - Doig, and in order maybe to position me in my lower sphere, you will need to know something about that cellophane-wrapped, that colour-supplement-covered, topic: the Politics of Art, sometimes also known as the Battle of the Styles.

When I started learning my craft at Kingston in the late 1960s, followed by Camberwell, followed briefly by the Slade - back then, I say, painting was still more-or-less king, and figurative art was, if not regal, at least well respected. Not, of course, as supremely so as in ages past, but still basically OK. At Kingston we had a weekly life-drawing class, and in his history lectures Jocelyn, whom I've mentioned already, made no secret of his admiration for the great representational artists of the past: Velasquez, Rubens, Rembrandt. It was at Camberwell, where Jocelyn had moved to teach the year after I registered as a student there, that I had first encountered, and briefly been bowled over by, Doig. But I had also benefitted from the advice of a number of part-time tutors who were practising artists of some promise, later of mild distinction. Ron Kitaj (1932-2007), then in his thirties, I remember trekking in on his motor bike, or else the number 12 bus, from Dulwich. And, of course, the great Guyanese artist Frank Bowling (1934 -), still mercifully with us.

Ron was an eccentric and colourful portraitist, and Bowling was then in his early figurative phase. Both of these men revered paint, and they both venerated the human form. Once I'd got over Doig, these two became my true masters, the mentors to whom I looked, and I had seen little reason in the interval to change my mind. The world, however, was changing fast, and the tide was turning against us. This was the year of the second competition for the Turner Prize; the previous Autumn had witnessed its inauguration. Gilbert and George, as I recall, were on the short list, but the palm had eventually gone to Malcolm Morley (1931-2018). Morley was a Camberwell graduate, but by then he was living in the States, where he had progressed from

Abstract Expressionism to photorealism. He got the award for a large grid-like installation featuring zebras and other mythical beasts. Meanwhile Jocelyn, with whom I had kept up, looked on warily from the wings. At least, he probably believed, Morley was depicting recognisable life and limb. But if Jocelyn believed the tide was turning back towards figurative painting, he was in for a rude awakening. The following year the Turner went to Howard Hodgkin for a piece purely abstract. By the time Damien Hurst won it for his formaldehyde shark, and Tracey Emin for her unmade bed, poor Jocelyn was to be plunged in quiet despair, or so Andria later told me. But that is to jump forwards in time.

Jocelyn, though, is an historian rather than an artist (to be honest, I don't think he's painted a picture in his life), still less a controversialist or a propagandist. Where contemporary art is concerned, he has always kept his opinion to himself. In practice, therefore, Doig at this period was able to operate under the grandiose illusion that Jocelyn was one of his admirers. Already, I knew better. Privately, as I had long been aware, Jocelyn regarded everything that emerged from Doig's studio as the product of the devil incarnate, though naturally he was far too polite to say so. They had been colleagues, and this is England (or was). After a couple of drinks, Jocelyn was wont to speak his mind. His whisky-fuelled estimate, since repeated to me, was that Doig was suffering from a disease he diagnosed as "Conceptualitis Tremens". The more successful Doig became, the more extreme grew these privately voiced opinions. Doig's renown, he came eventually to assert – at least in secret - was less the fruit of "Art Seen" than of the "Art Scene". Of which, more later.

But, back then, Doig trusted Jocelyn, or at least he trusted his discretion. Besides, Jocelyn wrote smoothly, and he had a reputation for impartiality. It was Doig's plan that Jocelyn should write the catalogue for our impending show.

I have never been quite clear about Doig's motivation in all of this. He knew that he could rely on Jocelyn's innate civility and decorum, and the catalogue entries were sure to point up a contrast between our two styles. It was as a result of a helpful intervention from Jocelyn, indeed, that Doig had agreed to share. Whatever the catalogue said, perhaps he predicted that beside mine his work would appear to some advantage (he was right in this, at least so far as the newspapers were concerned). Maybe Jocelyn dreamed, even hoped, that the opposite might be the case.

I am rather conscious that in what follows Doig may come to appear as a satanic figure, and Jocelyn as some sort of angel. To be frank, this is pretty unfair to both of them, since in practice Jocelyn has done me a lot more harm than Doig ever did. So, why do I react like this? Suffice it to say that I have always liked Jocelyn, and have for the most part distrusted - do I mean resented? - Doig in a way only the disillusioned can manage. This, I confess, has far more to do with me than with either of them.

Be that as it may, Doig, who wanted Jocelyn to have a chance of inspecting his recent work more closely, had agreed to transport several of his canvases to Jocelyn's loft space in advance of the show. In the late seventies Jocelyn had moved to a two-bedroom flat, just round the corner from the college, in Camberwell Grove, a street decidedly on the up. His was an apartment on the top floor of a three-storey converted building, and it enjoyed this dry and airy attic. We agreed to meet there three and a half weeks prior to the opening.

I had visited Jocelyn's flat before on a few occasions. As soon as you entered it, you saw and knew that his décor matched his temperament. The walls were painted light grey throughout, and the antique furniture was sparse, choice, and well maintained. Jocelyn has always been well behind – that is well in advance of - fashion. He's always cultivated a liking for Dutch interiors, defending them against all comers (Doig tended to dismiss them as coy). At that time, he had newly contracted a passion for the work of the neglected, and quite obscure, Danish painter Vilhelm Hammershoi (1864-1916), most of whose pictures are of the austerely beautiful apartment he shared with his wife in Copenhagen. Hammershoi's paintings, which draw a lot on the Dutch masters of the so-called "Golden Age", were then largely unknown in England, and would remain so until a major retrospective at the Royal Academy in 2008. But the poet Rilke had been warm in their praise, and the Japanese predictably have always adored them. Jocelyn had made a couple of expeditions to Copenhagen to see them, and he'd since hung two or three Hammershoi reproductions well down on the walls of his flat. As I entered that Tuesday afternoon, he was showing Doig the copy of *Interior: With Piano and Woman in Black, Standgade 30* that enjoyed pride of place on the north-facing wall of his living room above a polished folding table, again very low down. In his precise and pedantic manner, he was explaining how indebted Hammershoi had been to Vermeer and Elinga. Doig was looking signally unimpressed.

Jocelyn, who has this characteristic posture of leaning back on his heels while looking sceptical and benign, was clad in a three-piece suit made of herring-bone tweed, and he wore hushpuppies on his feet. You could tell that he had ordered the suit off-the-peg in the seventies because it had bell bottoms and wide lapels. At that date he still sported a George Harrison-style moustache which he has long since shaved off. Doig meanwhile was dressed in a garish garb that somehow contrived to combine smartness with an impression of almost throw-away ease. It was the latest in a whole series of metamorphoses I had been privileged to observe over the years. In the sixties he'd worn tight shiny suits and tiny floral ties. Then, as the decade had turned degenerate, he'd adopted a kind of Hippy guise until his paunch and greying temples threatened to make him look ridiculous. Now in his early forties, he seemed to have settled for a sort of suave bohemian decrepitude. The guiding principle appeared to be that you could wear anything provided it looked like a cast-off and conflicted did-not conflict with everything else you'd thrown on. As I grasped his proffered hand and, overcome with an old bashfulness, lowered my eyes towards the carpet, I noticed he was wearing unmatching socks.

Doig's art had always been as motley as his dress. I had known him for fifteen years and could already recall dozens of his crazes. When I was newly a student and at my most impressionable, each successive phase had deluged me like an advancing billow from which eventually I righted myself, only to be thrown completely by the next incoming wave. Nor had there been any apparent let-up in his zig-zagging stylistic progress. The more successful he had become, the less he had needed to sell his work in order to survive. He now had a full Professorial salary to fall back on, and this comparative affluence had led him to flights of creative rashness at which his younger self might just have blushed. When exhibiting two years previously, he'd demonstrated a preoccupation with elephants, the result of an expensive Safari to East Africa taken during the Long Vacation. It was entirely typical of him that he should have claimed in a newspaper interview that the luxury of six weeks in Tanzania had simply revived in him a passion which had lain dormant since his seventh year, when a succession of visits to Regent's Park Zoo in the company of a maiden aunt had inspired a passion latterly stifled by more mundane considerations, only to be re-awakened now that a half-a-lifetime of accumulated technique enabled him to give full rein to his obsession. The result had been a series entitled 'Pachyderms' which he explained as the result of the influence of Norman Adams, then Professor of Painting at the Royal Academy Schools. I could not see the resemblance myself, though it is true that Adams had done a sequence of wildebeests.

Jocelyn made me a coffee and then led us across to the folding ladder that led to his loft. As we climbed, Doig was explaining to us how his attentions had lately been grabbed by the compositions of Gustav Mahler whose symphonies, elephantine as the products of his own previous painterly phase, had sparked him off in an entirely fresh direction. Fortunately, though my acquaintance with the musical classics is not what it might be, Mahler is not completely unfamiliar to me. Andria had experienced a passing infatuation with his Resurrection Symphony a few months previously after we'd attended a performance of it in the Barbican Hall with the London Symphony Orchestra and Chorus conducted by Richard Hickox (1948-2008), an impresario almost as swollen-headed in his sphere as Doig in his. I also knew enough to be aware that, despite the composer's earlier neglect, he had long since been embraced enthusiastically by the musical establishment. It was a fact that appeared to have passed Doig by. For Doig, forgetful perhaps of Ken Russell's film about the composer ten years before,

Gustav Mahler was news, and the news was about to break over an astonished London.

The loft took up a whole floor, and his canvases were stacked around the walls. "I call this one 'sermon of the Fishes'," Doig said. He had developed this irritating way of pausing between sentences and inserting into each pause a humming noise that served at one and the same time as an affirmation and an interrogation. He pointing to a particularly crowded creation while taking a large dose of snuff (a variation on an earlier theme; in the sixties he'd chewed tobacco). "It's based on the Scherzo in the Second Symphony. You know, do you, there's a tune in that movement based on an earlier setting by Gustav of a poem describing St Anthony of Padua preaching to the fishes? I didn't. But I do now, and there it is. Mmm? And speaking of fishes…"

Jocelyn, I noticed, was wearing his sceptical expression, and smoothing his moustache. He stood behind Doig and looked across his shoulder (Jocelyn is the slightly taller man) as Doig walked us across to a row of canvases leaning against the blank east wall. "These," he announced, "are what I'm calling my Scaline Studies. Mmmm?" He paused a bit longer as if to say "fish scales, musical scales. Get it?"

Before us were a collection of piscine bones running in different directions as they squirmed across the view. Some swooped as if diving; some looped in lavish turns; others simply turned on their sides and ran downwards. I looked deep into a frantic aquarium of fishtails, bones, fins, flippers, lobster claws, above which coursed a running vine of crochets and quavers, which at one point looped to accommodate a chrome yellow crucifix. It was a scherzo in its way I suppose, a sort of graphic joke. I'd reached the punch line some time before Doig added, "The frieze at the top of the picture introduces the leitmotif of the exhibition: scales. It's a pun linking all of the items together. You'll find it in some form or other on every canvas. Like a continuous logo. Mmm?"

I followed these oblique lines of marching semiquavers from picture. Then I looked across at Jocelyn who gave me a slight wink: he was tweaking his moustaches ever more sceptically as if silently cogitating the banality of this clunking visual double-entendre. "There's every manner of scale here," Doig continued. "Major, Minor, Pentatonic. Gustav loved fluctuating between them: it's an important ingredient of his style. Mmm?"

All this time I was thinking, "Does he actually know which scale is which?" as he leant across to me, humming for my approval.

Doig pointed to a large canvas, throbbing with Jack-boots: "That one's based on Gustav's funeral marches: he has one in virtually every symphony. Mmm?" He passed on to a triptych called "Sixth Death and Resurrection", then a set of six "Songs of the Earth" before resting in front of something called "Finale". "The mystic Ohm. Mmm?"

As Doig recited his litany of titles, something took me back fifteen years to the Spring Term of my first year. I was carried back to a Victorian lecture theatre, its ugly desks spattered with aging stains, its too-high windows, its curt impossible light. Opinions then had seemed to ooze out of him like magenta out of a tube, unguent, compelling. It was that term that Doig discovered Zen. Suddenly he'd seen Zen in everything: Zen in brooks and stones and trees, Zen in Titian and Raphael, Zen in Monet's little finger. We were all growing just a little tired of this obsession when mercifully just before Easter he'd happened upon a Pocket Jung. Suddenly everything was transformed into a psychic archetype.

I would not have been surprised if he had a Pelican History of Music sequestered about his person that afternoon. Mahler lay on his tongue that day, Mahler seeped through his nostrils and lay like a potter's glaze across his eyes. "Damn it, the very word Mahler means painter!" he insisted, stamping the pinewood floor in his excitement, his wispy grey hair bouncing over his ears. "Artists in different spheres have got to be prepared to learn from one another. It's all one great creative mart and exchange. Mmm? Sometimes it amazes me that I've had to wait until my forty-second year before recognizing the essential interchangeability of art." (A strategic word. In the sixties, he'd pronounced it with a kind of proletarian snarl. Nowadays, it rhymed sloanishly with "wort".)

He took us right around the loft again, talking unstoppably as he did so: North Wall, West Wall (the East was covered by the Scales), and every inch of the way he gesticulated and orated. He had developed an annoying way of jumping from one foot to the other in mid-sentence as if delivering a Googly. Down swerved the ball and the lecture swivelled on: "It's an entirely fresh approach Ben, no less than a revolution in taste. I want to teach people to perceive the world in a holistic manner. Synaesthesia in two dimensions, Mmm? I want nothing less than for them to start seeing with their ears."

Having delivered this paradox, Doig mumbled an excuse and dashed downstairs for the John. He had not asked about my own contributions once.

While he was away, Jocelyn brought me up another mug of coffee. We were silent for a while before he leaned back on his heels, tweaked at his moustache, and said "Hmm." Not "Mmm?" but "Hmm." It was the difference between the two men: stylistic arm-twisting versus quizzical restraint.

"They're all right," I said, noncommittally into the silence. "There's something new in them anyway. They've got, er, well verve."

"Verve," Jocelyn repeated slowly. "I might need to use that word."

*****

When I wrote "I can still recall the first stirrings of my interest in art", I should perhaps have refined my phrasing. What I meant back there was "my love of looking at art." The love of making art, of doing the thing, arrived a little later. Following the sort of childish dabbling we are most of us encouraged to do at school, a mild mania for practical business struck when I was around fourteen. Watercolouring, aquatint, I had indulged in desultorily for several years, mostly wishy-washy landscapes en plein air. I had a fondness for depicting the Thames near Kew, though I could never get the water quite right. But for the Christmas of my fifteenth year Claud sent me (of course, he never turned up for the celebration itself) a set of student range Windsor & Newton oil paints, together with an elementary easel and a palette. No manual, of course: he wanted me to work out the basics of technique for myself. Which I did, slowly.

Thenceforth, every Saturday afternoon, with homework evaded or done, I would set up my easel in the back bedroom and remove the lid from the paint box and savour the contents as if I was undressing a girl (not that I had ever had a chance of doing any such thing). How I loved the sight of those tubes of pigment arranged side by side in rows, each with its differently coloured label wrapped round it! And the names of them too, exotic and adult: Burnt Sienna, Cobalt Blue, Cadmium Yellow, Flake White; Titanium White.

Once I had set up and started work, there were two sensations that I recall. The first was grossly physical:

the smell and scent of the medium: linseed oil with its treacherous, musky odour, which in my erotic daydreams mingled with fantasy-led anticipation of the secret parts of the female body: sweat-glands, arm-pits, cunt. Of course, I then had no experience of these delights. Then the brisk, workaday, astringent stench of turps, with which later I cleaned my hands. The other sensation that I can recall (though it might be truer to call it an absence of sensation) was of an absorption in my task so complete as to cause me completely to lose any sense of the passage of time – which is as much as to say, any sense of the passage of oneself, of myself. My initial subjects were still lives assembled from objects in the hallway or around my bedroom: a bi-metallic Victorian dinner gong suspended from its brass frame with a striker held in clasps in front; a set of concentric wooden eggs in contrasted colours that fitted inside one another like a Chinese puzzle (I varied the outer shell from picture to picture but preferred the blue one so that I could show off my "cadmium blue" from the box), some fruit held in one of my mother's glazed bowls in glazed *Delfts blauw* as she called it (Delft blue), that conspire so well with my favoured blue-painted egg. Though I have lost most of these early paintings, I had never forgotten the joy of creating them, a feeling restored every time I picked up a loaded paint brush.

Nor have I ever quite lost that sense of absolute absorption, the delightful abandonment of self-consciousness as you address or undress the otherness of the real. It is as close as I get nowadays to meditation or to praying. I stopped praying as such shortly after I went to the Oratory School, when I recognised that the being I was feverishly invoking in private always turned out to be my pitiful and wretched self. Thenceforth painting took the place of prayer because it enabled one to escape the trap of selfhood and concentrate on something that was by definition not oneself: a gong, a painted egg, some Delft china. Oddly, this turned out to be the case even when doing self-portraits, with which I was much taken at the time.

Which leaves open the question of the connection between painting pictures and looking at them. In certain respects, as I explained to Christina when we were resting, these activities are closely related. (She mocked me for saying this.) Making and seeing are connected because you make what you see, and you see what you make. There was even a sense when as I was a child that I was inventing that Hobbema avenue as I gazed adoringly up at it. Basically I treated it as a story book. That man striding towards me between those rows of poplars, who was he, and where was he going? Sometimes he was Uncle Claud, say, coming to meet me (a daydream enabled by the fact that at that stage we had hardly met). Sometimes it was I that was striding along the avenue towards him, or towards other unknown adventures. So it was too with those two enigmatic interiors by de Hooch/Elinga. I made up all sorts of fairy tales around the reading or sweeping lady, some of them frankly erotic. In one of them, I had her across my knee.

I told Christina quite a lot of this (though not, I confess the last bit) when we were having coffee, either between our forty-minute sessions or after we had finished for the afternoon. After a while we invented what we came to call our "picture games". Thus, after a session of her hoovering (which she preferred to do first, because it was the more boring task of the two), I would say to her, "Close your eyes. Tighter now. Tighter. Now tell me what you can see."

"I'm a woman in a painting."

"What kind?"

"A portrait in a gilt frame. I'm standing in a plain black dress and facing outwards. The picture's hanging in a crowded gallery and beyond the glass a ring of men has gathered to stare up at me. They're wearing mackintoshes and trilby hats, like men in a thirties newsreel. They're all very quiet, subdued almost, glaring up at me with their hands in their pockets. Some of them are smoking Woodbines: they're minor clerks or else out of work. They don't cheer or laugh. They do not move, encourage or egg me on. But gradually the veil between us is reinforced by bars. I am a woman behind bars, powerful, trapped and exulting. Now one of the taller men in the front row seems to have sprung to life. He's raising his right hand and in it there's a torn-off paper like a tote ticket. His lips are open but silent. He's shouting something to the rest of them, not one word of which can I hear. His words can't penetrate my cage. I'm alone, caught in a prison of silence and bars. All that I possess is my power."

"Yes?"

When she opened her eyes, there was a look of horror in them.

Then, later when she had finished her stint reading (*The Sea, The Sea* at first, but she had finished that by the end, and was on to *The Glass Bead-Game*), I'd say, "Try again. Close your eyes."

"I'm a little girl in a polka-dot dress in a summer garden. It is about four o'clock in the afternoon, and I know it must be either late spring or very early summer because the trees are only just flecked with green and I can still see the trace of branches through the bursting buds. In front of me is a thick shrubbery with rhododendrons and azaleas in full bloom. Birdcalls are echoing through the trees: I can make out the repeated high-pitched scraping of the chaffinch, the coruscating arpeggios of the starling. Then above the other voices there's a softer call. It's a woman's voice, tender but tight with concern: it's my mother calling to tea. I stand up and paddle downwards toward the wall of shrubs and parting the first row of leaf-stalks with my hands begin fumbling my way through. The call persists and I try to respond. I know it is my mother beckoning me from behind the greenwood. But the more I struggle the harder it gets, there are branches and creepers in my path, I can't break through though I'm trying, I'm trying ever so hard. And I say to myself, 'I'm a good little girl, a loving little girl, I love my mother, I love my mother, she's calling me to tea,' but as I cry out the voice recedes; it's distant now and dissolving beyond the trees, beyond the houses, beyond everything, and I'm a lost little girl, alone in a wood, caught in this purple blur of love..."

"Yes?"

She opened her eyelids, and the lashes were wet with tears.

"I can't even remember her face," she said.

*****

The Elms, Cheam, March 15, 1985

My dearest Benedict

Thank God Spring seems almost here at last! The house seems so stale after this interminable winter and all the beds need airing. I've made yours up in the spare room just in case you pay me the honour of a visit some time. Time was we'd have made up the cot, but I think you'll find you've outgrown it. Heaven knows why we brought it over with us from Finchley, but it might come in useful now. If you two want to borrow it, do just drop me a line. It's held a few generations in its time, if only it could tell us.

I've taken the fuchsias out of their pots and planted them along the borders. They do wonders in Cornwall I'm told and Sissinghurst has acres of them, but they're somehow dicey in London. By all accounts too we're in for a wet old summer.

Write when you've time.
Your ever affectionate father.

*****

"Close your eyes," said Christina.

"They're closed already," I said.

"Then tell me what you see."

"I'm walking down an avenue of trees towards the distant horizon. Overhead the sky is a perfect cerulean blue, draped at points in fluffy white nimbus cloud. On my right I can hear a chorus of birds practising in a beech copse. On the other side of the path, a couple of women are in conversation while a little further on a man in a green knee-length coat is pruning hops. He's tall and thin and must be somewhat short-sighted because he's holding his face close to the upright stems as he plies them with his secateurs. Further on towards the rim of the horizon everything seems shrouded in haze and all the shapes are indecipherable. The haze is like a lace curtain on which figures sway, merge and then part. There's a pair of silhouettes drifting on curtain, and as I look, they embrace like lovers and then turn aside, joined only by the tips of their fingers. As they notice my approach they seem to shift uneasily and the curtain moves against the sill. It's as if they've been expecting me from a very long time ago. At times, the haze thickens so that the lace almost covers them and I lose sight of them completely. I lumber onwards between lines of trees thinking the road is unending, but still the horizon recedes and the lace curtain is swinging in the light breeze. It is evening and the light is beginning to fail, but the walking has quickened my blood. Inside my buff coat I am starting to perspire. A little rill of perspiration is running down my spine. I look towards the horizon again, hoping that the distance has shortened, but the silhouetted couple are still where they were, huddled round one another in fear now like children, their eyes apprehensive, her finger pointing ..."

Opening my eyes, I discovered Christina's face looming above me.

"Did you see it too?" I asked.

*****

Middlesbrough, March 18, 1985.

Dearest Ben

I think this must be the most artless city in Europe. The skies are steel grey and so are most of the buildings. Funny guest house, but I've made friends with a sparrow who comes calling at my window. Chirps very merrily when I feed him and tells me he's an expert on Titian. How goes the exhibition? Is our commission included? Would love to lend my support, but fear that I'm posted to Wigan.

Yours provincially, Claud.

*****

The next couple of weeks are something of a blank. There are periods when work takes its place alongside everything else as part of the overall design. There are others, in my case I regret to say too frequent, in which it dwindles to a mere row of stitches around the hem. At rare moments - and those few weeks were to me very special - work swells to absorb everything else. When I think back to the month immediately preceding my exhibition, I retain two dominant mental images: of a vast mass of raincloud moving in solemn procession over a louring sky, or alternatively of a single ray of light shining against a surface with all the intensity of a laser beam. Sometimes the two images combine to form a single sheaf of light shining out of a mass of cloud; but in either case I can only view them as symptomatic of an intensity of absorption I have rarely experienced before or since.

Looking back at that period now, I wonder at the source of my concentration. Did I really think I was about to take London by storm? I was as much of an artist as I was ever going to be, and I had existed for long enough on the perimeter of the art world to develop a healthy distrust both of the critics and of the antics of the market. In any case, what little impact I made was bound to be swallowed up in Doig's. Tant pis, say I.

What I've called the Battle of the Styles, moreover, was coming to a boil. For the last year or so I had become dimly aware of the subversive activities of an underground arts collective calling themselves "The Grey Organisation" (G.O.). They'd issued a Manifesto on light grey paper with their initials emblazoned on either side of a black shield, protesting, so it said, at "the prevailing Thatcherite free market consumer culture." Below this message ran their motto: "Alive & Awake". Insofar as I understood their programme of action, they were taking aim at the capitalisation, the consumerisation, the conceptualisation, what you might call the Doigification of art. The G.O. were decidedly not traditionalists, but they were certainly objecting the current zeitgeist. In that purpose I respected them, somewhat grudgingly, as I gathered did Jocelyn, not least when it came to the grey. Neither of us, of course, could endorse the tactics of this bunch of skinheads, which were loutish and delinquent. In January they'd smuggled one of their pictures into the International Arts Fair at Olympia. Since then they'd made a number of rumbling threats. There was no saying what they might do next.

At some subterranean level I suppose I thought I was staging a much milder protest by more civilised means. My weapons were realism and figurative fidelity to what I saw: principally, let us face it, to what I saw in certain women, however disfigured by tension and desire. In a way I was also engaged in an act of self-definition and self-justification. As I choose to see things now, over those weeks of hectic effort I was engaged in a protracted argument with myself. It was as if I would never be able to take myself seriously until

I saw those few square yards of canvas: mounted against a whitewash wall, discovered the light of appraisal in my audience's eyes and overheard the comments as one by one they fingered the catalogue.

But there was something else too, something I would never have dared admit to myself at the time. I was trying to please my father. At the conscious level, I had no awareness of this. After all I had neglected him for months, ignored his calls, treated his letters with less than common courtesy and procrastinated my next visit for so long he must have wondered if he would ever again set eyes on me. To be honest I am not sure that, after the sequence of phone calls in March ceased, I spared his existence so much as a passing thought. It is only in the light of subsequent developments that I have the courage to recognise this truth: that at the root of my steadfast application over those uncharacteristic weeks was a plea for self-justification. For years I had flown in the face of Father's counsels and brushed aside my family's concern over my future, thus forfeiting his respect and, at one level, my own. If I could make a success of this one venture, then all the years of obduracy, petulance and near-starvation might just possibly have been worthwhile. Father was not likely to be there to witness the vindication of my ambitions: that in itself mattered little. But I now believe that I would unconsciously have sacrificed everything I had, even the chance of worldly recognition itself, to have received from him alone the simplest, most grudging acknowledgement.

I spent ever longer periods at Dolphin Square. The set of Vertebrate Studies was now almost completed in Kensal Rise, and Andria seemed to have tired both of them and myself. On an impulse I phoned Jocelyn and asked him to call round and take a look at them so he could cover them in his script. I gave him our address but forgot what he said about his availability. As it transpired, he arrived in my absence and was entertained by Andria, who seemed to like him a lot. I thus considered myself at liberty to devote my attentions elsewhere. I had made much progress with Christina's double portrait, but much still remained to be done. By dint of constant and repeated hoovering, her carpet was now indecently clean. As far as her reading self was concerned, she had long since finished with *The Glass Bead Game* and was halfway through *The Tin Drum*. She reckoned to have read the whole of it by the time we were through. If I failed to apprise Andria of my whereabouts there was not in my mind at the time any conscious desire to deceive. I was careful to give her the impression that I was visiting my aunt; yet even this mendacity featured in my consciousness as no more than a professional contingency. Insofar as I spared a thought for the nature of my evolving connection with Christina, it seemed to me at the time as if our feelings had been through a slow process of withdrawal, like a courtship in reverse. We now appeared to be no more than what the French call *copins*: buddies, at the most comrades in a conspiracy against an unsuspecting public.

Do I protest too much? How hard it is at any one time to assess the level of one's sincerity. Insofar as I can recall the nature of my feelings at the time, it must have appeared to me as if the professional sphere had entirely eclipsed the personal. We were certainly not lovers in any conventional sense. Instead our relationship, if such a term applies, had converted itself into an amicable set of charades, an intellectual-cum-emotional power-game. If the friction of mind on mind, of nerve on nerve, served occasionally to throw light on the one culminating canvass in which I was now trying to summon her fractious, magisterial presence, that was all the gratification which at the time I was conscious of wanting or of seeking.

It is like this: unless a painter devotes himself to each of his subjects entirely, he had better quit the profession. People happen to be my subjects. To ask me to spare a thought for the reactions of one sitter while all of my energies are temporarily channelled toward a second, would be like asking me to paint one picture with my right hand and another with my left. I simply did not view Andria and Christina in relation to one another. In my eyes they belonged to different compositions, therefore different worlds.

This probably all sounds like prevarication: the miscreant wriggling on the end of the moralist's pin. I prefer to think of it as being a kind of painterly subterfuge, the tactful conspiracy of art. All artists are conspirators: against the public, against their subjects, the medium, needless to add against themselves. The painter's occupation is possessed of a bitter lonely integrity - like seasoned varnish or dark chocolate - but its proper attitude towards the world of mundane reality is one of lese-majesty. My instincts are one with my profession. Acting as I did, I was simply following my nose. To put it in other words, I was like a celibate who steals the ink in order to inscribe the most delicate and intricate monkish illumination. Do we question the ethical drives of those who composed the Book of Kells?

So when, ten days or so before the show, the secretary of the gallery phoned me up to say that they would be sending round the van in a week's time to collect my wares, I did not scruple to give her Christina's address in preference to Andria's. I reasoned thus: the Vertebrate Studies were light and easy to transport. I could easily remove them from Kensal Rise by hand, telling Andria I was taking them round to Bentink Street. Instead I would take them over to Pimlico, where the van could pick them at the same time as the larger portrait. I had already arranged that on the Wednesday before I would call round at Christina's flat to decide on the final line-up of items. Time was running short, and besides I trusted her judgement. What would be simpler than to hump across the smaller sketches with me before sitting down to the task of selection over many mugs of steaming coffee? The day proved dull and squally. It was one of those days when Spring can't seem to make up its mind whether it has arrived or not. Splotches of cloud spun across an ashen sky through which the sun peered out momentarily to be followed by a moody gust of rain. When Christina opened the door into that virulent green doorway, she was dressed in a thick woollen dressing gown and stifling a sneeze. Diseases always seem to strike when they are least expected. You get chilblains at Easter and the common cold in June. For weeks now there'd been talk of an influenza epidemic as if the winter's microbes were mounting their last onslaught before allowing us all to enjoy a little pale sunshine.

Carrying my bundle of sketches under one arm I staggered through the lobby into the lounge where I deposited them in a graceless heap on the sofa. Then I turned round and looked at Christina. Her slight indisposition seemed to have relaxed her. We sat down on either side of the pile of drawings and talked; she bunched her knees together and held her handkerchief cupped in front of her like a child. She'd been indoors for days, hadn't even gone to the shops. On an impulse she'd abandoned her part-time job and seemed almost at a loss. For the first time since the inception of my visits the previous November she seemed positively pleased to see me. A warm current passed between us, quite unlike the pleasing tension that had preceded it. Did I mind if she didn't exert herself? Could I possibly filter the coffee? For the first time in my life it seemed I was free to consider her flat my own.

After I had sorted the drawings into more manageable piles, we got down to the prolonged task of selection. Squatting there by her side, and fingering through the sketches and the Vertebrate studies, it suddenly dawned on me that until that moment she cannot have had a clue as to what Andria looked like. True, the drawings could only have given her a very incomplete impression even now. Earlier there had been a couple of profiles I rejected in favour of studies in which the details of skin and expression were subsumed into some purer abstraction. How odd though it must have been for her to attempt to piece together these fleeting impressions of one whose sad, gentle presence she must have sensed lingering on the very margin of her existence, this shade of my albeit unstable affections. As for the Christina diptych, now complete, it lay propped against her easel, which for this purpose I had purloined. To depict her as I had known her and yet remain faithful to Claud's assignment had been no simple matter. Heavenly truth is not the same as earthly, nor is the hermit's pillar- wrought ecstasy that on which lesser mortals feed. The strength of my desire to please my obsessive and celibate uncle had not assisted me make of Christina other than she was. Here was a bookish Christina and a workaday Christina, side by side. Each was true in its way. When I showed it her, she said nothing. I could not read her silence.

At half past nine the phone went. It was her father. After the usual guilty civilities, the tone of the conversation altered and I realised with a shock of recognition that they were discussing the exhibition. Did he then know about it? My father for one would scarcely I thought have mentioned it, and, if so, in so derogatory a manner it could hardly have served to arouse Echardt's interest. Or did he owe the information to Christina? I had no inkling of their consulting about me, assuming, perhaps naively, that these two strands in my life had run parallel for months with no possibility of meeting.

She had put the receiver down and said, "That was Dad."

"The celebrated art dealer?"

"You know jolly well who he is," she said. "Why do you never answer his letters?"

"What letters?"

"Well, letter."

"How do you know about that?"

She didn't answer. "He may be coming to the Opening," she said. "Do you want him to?"

"It makes no difference to me," I said, assuming an air of false nonchalance. I had been rocking backwards and forwards on my heels for some minutes, when, recalling suddenly the source of the movement, I abruptly stopped. Outside there was a distant rumble from across the river. We were apparently in for a storm. She gave me a look of thin, mocking compassion, as once again I asked, "But how do you know about the letter?"

*****

As far as I am concerned, the purpose of painting is to concentrate on something or someone other than oneself. You are supposed to lose yourself in it, or perhaps find yourself by losing yourself, or whatever. I am not even sure it's necessary to say anything, make statements etc. etc. All of that business I happily leave to Jocelyn and his kind: he's very good at it, which is probably why Doig got him to write our catalogue. Did I, I sometimes wondered, have a position or message to convey? Unless, that is, this in itself represented a position. Art, for me, is about attention rather than protest.

Which is why I was a little disconcerted when, rounding the corner into Bentink Street late on the afternoon on Tuesday May 21st, I saw a knot of people gathered outside the gallery. There was a policeman and a policewoman, some nondescript folk in jeans, a TV crew, a number of journalists scribbling in their notepads, and a police car parked on the other side of the street. When I got closer, I saw that the entire front vitrine of the ground floor was smeared in an eccentric coat of light grey paint. It made a strident and aleatoric pattern along the glass: quite a pretty pattern actually with swirls and blotches, and almost certainly the product of chance or impulse rather than of design. Since the police seemed preoccupied, I asked one of the bystanders what was going on. She shrugged. Then her chap mumbled the words "Art Terrorism." Terrorism? I thought. Art? I had always taken these two to be opposites.

I was momentarily worried that the gallery might be closed and our carefully prepared opening cancelled or postponed, but was relieved to find, on trying the glass door, which had apparently escaped the rampage, that it gave easily. I walked through to the office, where I discovered the Gallery Director on the phone. He was giving out addresses and directions and seemed quite agitated beneath an air of professional calm. When he put the receiver down, I asked him what was up.

"We're not the only ones," the Director remarked with languid regret. "The Robert Fraser Gallery in Cork Street has been attacked. One or two others as well. It's the Grey Organization, of course. The scum! What a bleeding mess! They claim they disapprove of the commercialisation of Art. They say they disapprove of *us*."

"They've certainly left their mark," I said.

Then, averting his eyes, he added, "It's a point of view in a way…"

I recalled this conversation when, two hours later, I was standing five foot seven and a half inches in my shoes and staring at a tie pin. The pin was encrusted with onyx and a material that could have been either glass or plastic. It was attached to a spotted silk tie with a clasp of fake gold. Above it, florid and pontificating, loomed a face.

"It's got to be his chef-d'oeuvre," drawled the pin. "Always knew he'd pull it off eventually. Doig's been clammed up for years now. Those elephant things were no good. This Mahler motif seems to have acted as a release."

A tray of glasses skimmed past just below eye-level.

"Would you care for a dip, sir? Smoked salmon sandwich, a sausage, a quiche?"

"Champagne's over there, old man," remarked the tie pin. "Do you know what I think?" it breathed, blowing wine-fumes in my face as it leant over me whilst fingering its tie, "I think a few of these might just be worth a spree. Buying yourself, are you?"

The room was still half-empty, though filling up fast. The invitations, luridly illustrated with one of Doig's Funeral Marches, had specified half-past six, but, "Wine and Canapes" serving as an incentive, the hounds had turned up sooner than expected. In one corner *Scherzo* had its bevy of admirers, while, around the facing wall, raucous dissent had been provoked by *The Mystic Ohm*. My own contributions had so far largely been ignored. In the room set apart for them, a solitary waitress stood sentry, conspicuous with her long legs and tray of dips. So far, nobody seemed to have identified me as the artist, including, I gathered, my interlocutor.

"It's always worth staying with a man while he matures. A few years ago I wouldn't have given three-halfpence for any of Doig's stuff. But one keeps one's feelers out, you know. It's a waiting game. From the look of things, he's about ripe for picking wouldn't you say?"

Out of the corner I could see Jocelyn chatting to an animated-looking Andria. He was leaning back on his heels and wearing a dove-grey lounge suit. Fleetingly I entertained the notion that this sartorial choice conveyed some understated sympathy with the protests of the G.O., then instantly dismissed the thought. Andria was looking up at him in evident admiration and enjoyment of their conversation, while twisting one ear-lobe between two tapered fingers. She was wearing a maternity gown in turquoise-coloured taffeta that was generous enough to disguise her bump. Beyond them, Doig stood amidst a crowd of toadies. He was dressed in a three-piece green leather suit, his ample stomach swelling beneath the well-cut waistcoat, and smoking a cigar.

The exhibition space had been arranged equitably 50:50. The room to the back of us was Doig's, the room in front was mine. In between lay the lobby in which we stood, its walls equally divided between his fishy creations to the right and my Vertebrate sequence to the left. Bone to bone they stared at one another across the intervening space, jammed now with keen-looking journalistic types and the odd rapacious dealer. Along the right wall devoted to the fishes, like poppies crowding a shoreline, acquisitive red dots were beginning to bloom. I looked at the nearest; it edged a placard that read four thousand pounds. Forlornly I looked back to where in my room the solitary waitress kept vigil, just in front of Christina's double portrait that commanded the far end. Not a poppy was there to be seen.

By now the movement around the walls was beginning to assume a clockwise momentum. The space in the lobby was so crowded that we were having to shuffle sideways to avoid the crush. Already I had taken too much champagne, and the din of so much concentrated effusion was beginning to hurt my ears. Behind me, Doig was shouting louder. All too dreadfully in his element, he was holding forth unstoppably on affinities, tendencies, themes. "Frontiers of the senses," I heard him shout, and "orality of paint. Mmm?" Some of the audience were nodding sagely; others were peeling off towards the walls. Somewhere a voice was raised in amazement, a strident guffaw broke through, a gasp. I seemed to have absolutely no connection to any of it.

At that moment, a commotion behind us announced the fact that Doig's entourage was moving. Struck no doubt with some obscure pangs of conscience, he had decided to lead them in the direction of my room. Catalogues were retrieved, glasses refilled; the ghastly cavalcade was decamping. Swept up in their train, and feeling obscurely honoured, I followed them, managing as I did so to lose the tie pin, whose face however duly appeared at Doig's side, plying him with questions about this new phenomenon on the art scene to whom, unbeknown to himself, he had been talking for the last twenty minutes. As we passed through the doorway, others squeezed in for an obsequious word, all of whom Doig parried with a banter of insincere compliments and bad jokes about my being the backbone of the New Movement etc; the punning habit seemed to have stuck. But Doig was King of the Night and unchallengeable. Prescriptions poured out of him like newly uncorked champagne. My work was "trenchant"; I was "robust". With a wave of the hand he indicated the double portrait, the sketches, the Vertebrae, in none of which till that moment had he betrayed the slightest interest, sweeping them up into the maw of his halting but inexhaustible rhetoric. I stood at the back of the group feeling resentment. It did not dawn on me that Doig was simply trying to be kind. Quizzically his entourage listened - retainers at court - while attempting to steer him back to his own collection and the intervening lobby.

I turned away and there at my side, unannounced, stood Andria. Following her conversation with Jocelyn she had been priming the Director, and, though she seemed to have failed to extract anything encouraging beyond the mysterious pledged purchase - the source of which was still a complete enigma to both of us - I clung to her like a drowning man. "What are you doing all by yourself?" she asked. "Shouldn't you be showing influential people around or something?"

"Yes," I replied vaguely. "I suppose I should."

"Why don't you say something? Make a speech or something?"

"Yes, I suppose I should," I said then realised, with a rising tide of panic, that I might have to.

Andria cleared her throat. "Hey everybody," she shrieked against the din. "This man is about to make a speech…"

The din carried on regardless.

"Well," she said, "I tried".

Next to us slouched a couple of fresh-faced individuals whom I took to be Doig's students. The boy wore voluminous pantaloons like a Pierrot's: the left leg was white and the right leg black. His girlfriend sported ribbons, a khaki combat jacket and, in her ears, mother-of-pearl buttons. They were knocking back glasses of wine at an impressive rate while dropping a mixture of cultish argot and assorted adolescent cynicism. I was just getting absorbed in this piquant combination, so redolent of times gone by, when from out of the corner of my eye my attention was arrested by an extraordinary spectacle that was beginning to unfold at the far end of the gallery, glimpsed through the open doorway which led through from the lobby into Doig's enclave. Next to one of Doig's s taller canvasses - a Funeral March with sprouting trumpets and pulsating green Gammadions - stood a strikingly erect middle-aged man of modest stature dressed in a faded pinstripe suit. His white hair curled around his temples, and he sported a regimental tie. Beside him, close pent in conspiracy, stood Claud. He was holding a catalogue in one hand and plucking at his companion's sleeve with the other. As he rolled from side to side, he appeared to be edging his interlocutor further and further to the left until eventually they disappeared beyond my field of vision. I had more or less given them up for lost when they suddenly reappeared on the other side of the doorway and made emphatically in our direction, still hugger-mugger in conference, my uncle still seemingly remonstrating with the figure who strode before him. From their manner of conversation one might have thought them at the culmination of a lifetime's confidence.

As they threaded their way through the jostling crowd away from us, I suddenly caught sight of Christina standing not six feet away. She was clad in an elegantly waisted black satin suit with well-tailored culottes that showed her legs and rear to advantage. I made a welcoming gesture in her direction but she moved off, passing as she did so before Doig's field of vision. As she glided callipygously past, I thought I saw him furtively licking his lips.

Doig's entourage now moved off in the same direction, so that I now stood in a pool of relative emptiness. Within a compass of a few feet were three people with whom my life had somehow got inextricably intertwined. Still engrossed in his altercation with the man in pinstripes, Claud had now reappeared to our right, though such was the hubbub coming through from the lobby that it was hard to catch a word of what they were saying. Gone was my uncle's timid reserve, gone were his winnowed gentleness, his air of world's end calm. Agitation enveloped his features, forthrightness and assertiveness, as if some dam of inner compunction had finally broken, flooding the banks of his customary self-control. He was just reading the pitch of his candid peroration, the burden of which was manifestly not lost on his companion, when to my amazement Christina suddenly stepped out of the crowd and, grabbing the man in pinstripes by the arm, rescued him from my uncle's homily and propelled him with something approaching main force back into the lobby. Claud must have seen this as clearly as I did. For a second or two Christina was in front of him, but he had betrayed not the slightest sign of recognizing the object of his obsession. True she was dressed that in so stylish a manner that evening that he could be forgiven for not connecting her with the girl of whom he dreamed. The fact, though, as I realised then fully for the first time, was that my uncle only had cognisance of an idea called Christina. The flesh-and-blood woman was closed off to him, in body and in mind.

Andria and I now had Claud to ourselves. "Who was that gentleman you were talking to, Claud?" I inquired as soon as there was a chance of making myself heard.

"A character in a comedy of intrigue, masquerading as a company director."

"Not Echardt?"

"Right first time. Valuers and Auctioneers since 1827. Sixth generation they tell me."

"Well I'll be damned. I thought he was mythological."

"No, he's real alright. Only too real. Kept my nose to the grindstone for decades, if the truth were known. Good job us Henrys have tough noses." His face, seldom in repose for long, broke into a grin. "I've just told him a few home truths. Didn't take to them frightfully."

"He did seem a bit huffy."

"True. Still what can he do now? Things come home to roost if only you will let them. And who is this young lady? Come on Ben, do your duty."

"Sorry, Claud. This is Andria. Andria, this is my uncle Claud."

"Your young lady? Hamish told me something about it."

"Dad's not too pleased."

"No. Well he might not be." There was a second or two of mock disapproval before he uncharacteristically struck me across the elbow with his catalogue. "Don't take it so hard, Ben. He may come round in the end. Well then, my lad, finished the picture?"

I lead him through the throng to the East end of the room where Christina's double likeness hung centrally on its wall. For what may have been a minute we stood abreast, Claud in the centre, Andria and I flanking him. My fear was that he would be disappointed, find the textures overworked, the angles forced, the conception artificial. But for all an endless fragment of time he evinced no symptom of perturbation, looking it appeared not so much at the composition as through it, and towards something unfailing. Then out of the depths of some grateful weariness he spoke:

"She's very beautiful, Ben, I'll give you that. De Hooch, of course".

"Elinga," I retorted.

"De Hooch," he returned. "Don't like the Hoover. Prefer her reading. What is she reading?"

I lied. "Thomas à Kempis." I dared not say, "Gunter

Grass." Besides, I was quite sure he'd never have heard of Grass.

"Are there one room or two rooms?" he asked. "I see no division."

"I made no division," I explained. "That is the point. You're supposed to wonder."

"I'm wondering," said Claud.

"So am I," said Andria, who had fallen strangely silent.

"Tell me, Ben, have you ever been hurt?' Claud asked after a pause. "Really hurt?"

"Yes. Yes."

"Hurt so that you could fold up and die?"

"Yes."

"Me too, long ago. Expectations thwarted, love disregarded, solicitude set at nought. It happens. And afterwards, after all the pain and confusions have subsided, what is it do you think that lasts?"

"Irritation?"

"Annoyance? Possibly. What else?"

"Curiosity?"

"Wanting to dredge up the crux of it all? Maybe. But even that palls in time. There's something which survives a great deal longer. I ask you: why's Rembrandt so good? Why and Titian and Velasquez so good? It wasn't technique. Lots of others had that."

"Then I can't tell you."

He waited a while before with a kind of contained exhortation continuing: "Everything turns to dust and ashes, but the light alone forgives. Everything else makes for hurt and destruction, but the light resolves and blends all together. Even your lovely and bewildered friend. Reading or cleaning. Do I make much sense?"

"You're beginning to."

"There's only one way in which you will destroy what the light has resolved and that is to seek to own it. Never seek to own beauty, Benedict, never seek to tie it down. Paint it if you must but seek to entrap it and you'll call a winged vengeance down on your head. Only the light will forgive you then."

They were almost the last words I heard him say. A moment later to my intense annoyance a rise in the volume behind us announced the return of Doig and his retinue. I was enthusiastic to pursue Claud's train of thought, but the influx of people swept ever thing else aside as a palm landed on my shoulder and a well-known voice said:

"Well my boy you're a success. The place is crawling and half of them seem to be after you."

"Jocelyn, meet the wisest man I know."

But, looking round, I discovered that Claud was nowhere to be seen. He had dissolved into the perfume- and sweat-drenched evening like some evanescent will-o'-the-wisp.

"He's gone. Sorry, Jocelyn. My uncle's a leprechaun."

"Best people are like that." He slapped me bodily on the back.

"Go on, Benedict, enjoy yourself. Why, you're Prince

of the Evening."

I suppose I must have looked rigid with worry. In this respect, Jocelyn's antennae were infallible. Though all the scrabble and excitement of the occasion, some anxiety had got me by the throat and would not let me rest. With his empathic skill in the diagnosis of such states, Jocelyn had put his finger on the trouble. I could still hear him twelve years ago peering over my shoulder during one of our in-class exercises. "Don't look so peaky, Benedict. You'll give yourself a fright, man."

But now he placed his right hand on Andria's bare arm. She was still very silent. "Look after this one won't you, Ben," he said almost too softly to be heard. "You're a lucky man. Look after both of them." Then they melted together into the crowd.

I was alone now and feeling the effect of too much drink. With some difficulty I made my way back through the lobby and into the further room. As I reached it, I caught sight of Doig standing erect and looking pleased with himself. Then something very odd and very upsetting happened. Christina in her well-made culottes was loitering to his left with one or two people standing between them. Then the other people cleared. I was about to approach her when suddenly, like a pouncing animal, Doig grabbed hold of her, raised her off the ground and smothered her face in kisses. He did this with a kind of lazy proprietorial possessiveness, a lascivious entitlement that seemed to say "You pretty woman. Me successful man. Yield!"

For some time they were snogging mouth to mouth. I was very sure that he had not previously spoken to her, nor she to him. Probably he did not even know her name. When, twenty-five years later, and on his third marriage, Doig died unexpectedly of an aneurism while on a promotional tour in Aberdeen, I cheered and cheered.

He let her go at length. As he did so, I fell backwards into the lobby and found a chair. I was still sitting there when Jocelyn found me and told me about Andria.

*****

We rushed her into a cab and then to University College Hospital at the top of Gower Street. Jocelyn wanted me to stay: "It's your show, after all." I did not stay, but I cannot say that I was a great deal of use. As soon as we were out of the Gallery, Jocelyn took charge and guided us through the crowd as if from an art historian he had mysteriously been demoted - or perhaps promoted - to a medical orderly. A taxi proved difficult to find. Once we were away Jocelyn once again assumed control, shouting directions to the driver through the glass partition whilst supporting Andria to one side and stroking her hand with a sort of gluttonous uxorious concern.

The journey was infernal. Not only did Jocelyn insist on Andria leaning on his shoulder while he poured out commiseration and incisive practical advice, but just to the East of Upper Regent Street we met one of the worst traffic jams I'd ever experienced. Jocelyn to his credit kept on talking. We must relax, take it easy, the doctors would cope. And all the time the lights kept changing and we were still where we were, honking in the queue.

By the time we were free of it I was convinced I'd see my offspring delivered in the back of the taxi with the aid of a Professor of Art History and a pair of improvised forceps. When eventually we parked in Gower Street, it was only to find that the maternity wing was several blocks away round the corner in Huntley Street, so off we went again with Jocelyn in charge, until we were able at long last to help Andria off the slippery pavement and into the gargantuan brickwork of the hospital. As soon as the orderlies caught sight of her, she was whisked away on a trolly, leaving Jocelyn and myself staring at one another under a red and white notice which read 'Child Psychology'. Even now, I am not clear who was the child.

Do I sound ungrateful? To be honest, Jocelyn was splendid, insisted on taking me up Huntley Street to the Jeremy Bentham Tavern where he plied me with drinks telling the whole bar, to my intense embarrassment, that these were the nerves of a prospective father, "and about time too." We parted in University Street, and when he'd gone, I walked sharply up to the Tottenham Court Road, then turned left. In a doorway a couple gyrated and kissed. Pedestrians stood gazing covetously into shop windows full of microcomputers and procreation on video. A drunk lurched past, missing me by inches. Three blocks down, a burglar alarm droned futilely into the night. Near Goodge Street a fire engine was parked. While three firemen probed a nearby door, their colleagues leant against the chassis and laughed: a false alarm evidently. The firemen looked well-fed and jocular. One of them had removed his helmet and was tugging desultorily at the strap. Suddenly everybody seemed to have too much time. As I stood next to Paperchase with my hands deep in my pockets, they trudged round the back of the building looking for last signs of a conflagration. And deep in my heart that night I could almost bring myself to hate them: these ratepayers, voters, fathers. Citizens of the world I longed and yet dreaded to enter. Back in Bentink Street the gallery doors were long closed. Not four hundred yards away my daughter fought her way towards the light. I hailed a cab and asked for Kensal Rise.

*****

The door edged open, leaving me fumbling for the light switch. As the pearly light stole into the lobby I turned round and my eye caught sight of the doormat. On it was a telegram with black edges, curling there helpless as a cry. I picked it up, slammed the door behind me and fingered at the thin paper. Reading the few short words, I walked through to the bedroom, took up the receiver by the bed and dialled a number in Cheam.

BOOK FOUR:

BELSHAZZAR'S FEAST

BOOK FOUR

My Dearest Benedict,

I am leaving this missive under the coverlet of the large bed in the master bedroom in the hope that you may discover it before the others. It's addressed solely to you: who else should I wish to communicate with now, anyhow?

It must be with a feeling of some relief that you find yourself entering for the last time the House of Clocks. Not that you've ever visited it very often, and God knows I've sensed the constraint you've always laboured under when here, struggling with your boredom and resentment under the lamplight. Do not feel badly about this: it's the case with every generation. I felt much the same when in the presence of my own father whom I don't think you will- remember. The living have always lived in terror of one another, though in time they learn perhaps to listen to the whispers of the dead. Perhaps you will even learn to listen to me now.

Whatever did you think of when you stared at your knuckles and listened to the clock tick, counting the hours until you were able to take your leave from this house of stagnation and heartache? For such it has been.

Oh, I know I've always endeavoured to keep it trim and shipshape. Never let it be said that I let you or myself down. I was never one to insist on my isolation, but when the dust settles on the bookcase and the ashes whimper in the grate, when the tea goes cold in the cup, what else has one but one's resolution to keep one from crying out? That and pride. Never underestimate pride, Benedict. It's what keeps one stirring morning after morning to face the frost, the disdain and the emptiness. You, I think, have your own share in full measure.

However can I begin to explain myself to you now, suspicious as you are of all that would trammel and restrain you? And yet I must try. There's a great shadow that seems to lie over all of us: the family, I mean. I don't know how much you've suspected, or how much the pall that has fallen between us of late is due to anything Claud or Rosie may have told you. I hope that in time you may discover the full truth, and have indeed already taken steps to that end. Meanwhile I must speak of matters which in life I found it difficult to discuss - when did we two ever discuss anything? - but which always seemed obscurely to rankle in the background. It concerns Rosie's child. You cannot but be aware that your aunt had a daughter whom the family in conference thought it wisest to have adopted. I don't know what other impressions you may have gleaned. Perhaps you think that Rosie's brothers forced her to forgo the girl and ruined her life in consequence. In our defence I will say two things.

You are a creature of another generation. You do not

recognise the strength of the prejudices which bound ours. I do not speak of my own prejudice or of Claud's - certainly not of Rosie's herself. I speak of the ostracism meted out in those far-off days to those who, it was felt, had fallen by the way. When I say we believe she would be blighted for ever, I do not speak in metaphor. There are few fates more lasting or more destructive than that of the fatherless. You may have learned something of that anguish from your friend Andria. Did you not tell me she herself was orphaned?

Yet for all that I wrestled to let her keep the girl. I argued with Claud for hour after hour, but he would not listen. I knew, after all, what it was like to hold one's own child in one's arms. I had held you. But to the fatherless the privilege and curse of parenthood carries little meaning. I will be truthful: I always thought it was your own lack of offspring that turned you against me or at least made it so difficult for you to understand. Perhaps you will feel differently now, and perhaps when you see the light in your own child's eyes you may learn something of what has always afflicted and blest,

Your Loving Father.

P.S. Ben, there is another favour I must ask of you, as much perhaps for your own sake as for mine, though perhaps if the truth were known for all of us. I am not one for the grand gesture, unless you consider this letter to be one. But there is one last act of homage I would like you, like us, to make. Do you remember the laurel near the south wall of our little plot in Finchley? I hope you may have learned to remember it with fondness, as you used to play under it on summer evenings when you were a boy.

In her last illness your mother used to lean on my arm as we went round the herbaceous borders: she loved that Finchley garden, small as it was, and she loved that tree. It was, I know, her fancy she might like a sprig of it on her grave, but of course I could never get round to it, what with one thing or another, these last few years. But I did manage to transplant a bit to the garden here: you will find quite a fair tree of it growing near the green house.

When you've laid me to rest, there's just one thing I would require of you. Take a cutting of the old laurel, and plant it where she wanted. It'll cheer her through the cold nights, and she'll have a little bit of England in her rest. I think of her now lying alone in Middelharnis, so far from us all, so alone, though she's with her own people.

Do you remember the Dutch rose she planted in Finchley? Somehow it was a keepsake, a reminder of home. Exile, was it? I don't know, but she kept a lot back, and I never broached the subject. There was always a part of her that missed the Netherlands. You haven't been back there for so long, Ben, though you did so love it as a boy. Would it hurt you too much to go back, and do this one thing? I am not a demonstrative man, so perhaps you can perform this one small act for me. Somehow it's more your style.

Forgive me, I will never forget you.

There was an initial sense of blankness followed by strong resentment. How dare he depart at such a moment and in so painstakingly private a manner? What right had he moreover to so extraordinary a store of eloquence who in life had seldom passed beyond cliché, proverbial piles of wisdom endlessly repeated? Having chosen his time - for only thus could I make sense of the uncouth movements of destiny - why had he not prepared me better, rather than imperceptibly sliding out of life after fabricating this appeal, so exquisitely lunging, from the grave? There was no countenancing his death as having participated in anything as slipshod as mere coincidence. Everything in my father's mortal life had been planned, as I recognised with a new and sickening awareness moving among the dust-free surfaces of the now ownerless rooms, journals neatly stacked, pipes in serried ranks, clocks still ticking like the tumultuous after throes of life. A neighbour had discovered him when calling with a local news sheet, had rung at the pinewood door, failed to elicit a response, had taken alarm, broken the lock and found him by the fireside, his head sagging against his cardigan, *The Law Society Gazette* slipping from his still-warm fingers. It was she who had sent the cable, and the following morning she met me at the gate and murmured a few sentences of commiseration before leaving me to face the great empty house and my own sensations.

Did I experience sorrow, contrition, the twisting

innards of remorse? I had too much to do: contact the undertakers, phone the firm for which once he'd worked, drop a note to Rose. Idly I leafed through the address book next to the phone. There under "R" I discovered the number of Dad's local parish priest, down as "Father J. O'Rourke". I dialled the number and got one of those new-fangled answering machines. There was a curt message delivered in a voice in which the flat vowels of Middle England were superimposed on a soft substratum of Dublin Irish. Father O'Rourke was telling me he was not available "at this time", but if I cared to leave my contact number, he would get in touch just as soon as he could. I gave him the number in Kensal Rise, put down the phone and sat for a while in thought.

People misconstrue the topography of grieving. The soul has too many layers, more than the mind can contemplate. If I discerned in myself any awareness of error, any dishonesty revealed, it was like a blunder which time and conscious skill had covered over: faint, the mere *pentimento* of grief. As I moved around the stern and lifeless rooms, busying myself with papers, directories, files, the objects of the household did not accuse, nor blend into some vivid phantasmagoria of guilt. Rather did each seem to define itself in a fresh clarity or vivid aureole of light. Few things are so real as the detritus of disaster, or in this case cast-off husk of one guttering, quilted existence. Set free from a context of proprietorship, the facts of use and expense, the very furniture assumed a new objectivity and a new threatening calm.

I spent much of the afternoon trying to contact Claud. His exact whereabouts since I had abandoned him on the pavement next to Christina were unknown to me, but I was familiar with the name of the guest house that served as his London *pied-à-terre*, and, phoning, elicited a tortuous answer. He'd booked in two days previously, had left first thing that morning saying that he was paying a professional visit out of town, but might soon be back. Planning any kind of family gathering was not going to be simple. There were the people at Father's church, but he was not so well established there as he had been in Finchley, and the priest would not promise to call until the following morning. A simple service would have to be organised, a gravestone designed and paid for. Naturally, there was no question of cremation. Not for father a trundling along smooth conveyors, mechanised consolation of a crematorium organ electronically wailing. Father would go down to a literal grave with his sinews intact. He would exact his appropriate rites of death, and he would exact them in full measure.

No definite news had emerged from Gower Street. Throughout the day I kept up a volley of phone calls, meeting only with unsatisfactory, evasive answers. Andria's pains had ceased before midnight, commenced briefly again in the small hours and had since subsided to show no signs of revival. This was to be no easy birth; her body seemed determined to demand its fill of uncertainty and discomfort. They did not seem inclined to induce a delivery, but still would not let her leave. I could only wait by the phone side, full of trepidation and still unclear about my feelings concerning this event or the cause of my sojourn in Cheam. Whatever the incoming news, it was clear I would have to spend that night in Surrey.

Sleeping in the guest room, beneath those starched and perfumed covers, I had a dream of unusual poignancy and vividness. We were on the roof of Hampton Court Palace, looking down beyond the great East Front towards Long Water and the ornate, spacious gardens. Father had often taken me there during my infancy: I remembered the endless corridors of the maze, flowerbeds that seemed to stretch on for ever. Not the immaculate topiary of trees did we circumnavigate now, however, but the immense square chimney stacks, feeling our way round uncharted reaches of gable and window. Step by furtive step we crept, along the sloping tiles from South Wing to East Wing, from William's Wing to Mary's, and every inch of the way his eyes were blindfolded and helpless, his hands trusting and reaching out before him. He was dressed in an old wool dressing gown and slippers: not one of the spring weight Jaeger dressing gowns he reserved for milder months, finally bequeathing them to me to wear with evening nonchalance until one fine careless movement rent the thin silk for ever (latterly Andria too had grown peculiarly fond of these castoffs, purloining them for months before the material lay in ribbons around her hips). It was not father's Paisley-clad form that memory served up now nonetheless, but the chunky huddled shape of winter months, exposed to the keen Autumn air as I steered him between the tall brick columns of the chimneys. The evening grew colder, and the light began to fade. South westwards towards the river a mackerel sky had given place to silvery twilight. Soon the palace gates would be closed, the lawns and borders deserted. Inch by blundering inch blindly he followed me, blindly leading him on.

*****

If I was to become a father, it was not to be with either ease or grace. A further call to the hospital that morning extracted the information that Andria been released. No ambulance this time: they had simply put her in a taxi and told her to come back when the waters had broken. There was no sign of this being imminent, and, since everything seemed normal in most respects, they still seemed reluctant to induce. When I got back to Kensal Rise that evening, I discovered her sitting on the settee looking tired and sad, with a cup of coffee in front of her. As I entered, she gave a brief smile, mirthless and thin. I gave her a hug, then asked her whether the ambulance had brought her. No, she said, Jocelyn had kindly dropped her off. He had apparently just left. Then she took a swig from her mug and winced.

"Cold."

"What?"

"The coffee. Cold."

I moved through into the bedroom and opened the Art Deco monstrosity that served for our wardrobe. I unbuttoned my trench coat from top to bottom, released my right arm from the sleeve and said, "So nothing as yet?"

"Does it look like it?"

I released the other arm and folded the coat very carefully over my right arm. Then I rummaged through the metal shoulders along the rack inside the wardrobe - the sort of shoulders you get from the dry cleaners - and finding none vacant, removed an obsolete waistcoat and repositioned it on another shoulder beneath an equally obsolescent jacket. Then I put my trench coat on the vacated shoulders, swung the wardrobe door to, and found that it would not close. I put my back against it and started to shove. The wardrobe wobbled slightly on its legs.

"So how long do they expect it to be?"

No answer. I opened the wardrobe door, took out the coat and tried again. The wardrobe gave a wheeze like a barrel organ at its last gasp. I opened the door again and considered stripping the contents article by article. Then I sat down on the bed and said, "Dad died."

She said, "I know. You left a note. Come here."

"I'm sitting on the bed."

"Come here."

"I'm sitting on the bed."

"Well, bring the bed then."

I walked into the hallway and peered through the gap between the living room door and the frame. Andria sat there like a Dutch genre painting bisected by hinges.

"What did they do?"

"They put me on this bed thing."

"Well, one would have expected that."

I moved through into the living room. She gave another weak smile. "It was a very special bed."

"And?"

"It tipped up in all sorts of directions."

"Well?"

"There were two nurses on duty. They chuckled a lot."

"So?"

"I missed you."

I sat down on the chair opposite her. The springs sank beneath me, almost touching the floor. I looked across at her, and our two gazes met like two buttons on a string. The string held tight. I looked away.

"Poor Andria."

"Poor Ben. Come here"

I moved across and sat next to her on the settee. We had not sat like this for weeks. She reached across and very lightly, without looking, moved the fingers of her right hand down the light blue denim material of my left shirt sleeve. (There was a plain platinum ring on the ring finger of this hand; I had never asked her where she had got it.) She waited until her index finger reached the fold just beneath the elbow where I had turned up the cuff, and then collapsed sideways against me.

"Poor Ben."

"Yes."

Then, very gently and with a solicitous slowness, she undid the front of my shirt, and put her right hand flat against my chest. I winced slightly in pleasure-pain: there was limited heating in the room and her fingers had an electric chill. I removed her hand, placed it between my own, and warmed it with a rotating figure-of-eight movement between my palms. I let her hand fall against my lap and, turning her face towards me, cupped her chin in my right hand and kissed her full on the mouth. She tasted slightly salty, saltier at least than I remembered. (It is one of the constant surprises of a long relationship, one's constant rediscovery of such things.) When I withdrew my tongue, she leant against me again, then stood up and replaced the plate rack, picked up the electric kettle and filled it at the hot tap. As she did so, I told her a bit about Dad's letters, mentioning the laurel tree but omitting everything about the legacy, Rosie's baby and such. I walked over to the peeling mirror over above the sink, took a toothpick from a mug, and started scraping at the space between my top left canine and the adjacent molar. A consolatory simmering started to my right.

Then she said, "Oh, by the way, a priest called. I put his details on the notepad on your desk. He said could you possibly meet him next Thursday. I wrote down the time and address."

I consulted the pad and called the number she had scribbled down. I got the identical answering machine with the identical accent, and said I would be there.

Then she called, "Ben?"

The kettle started spluttering. I turned off the switch, put one and half teaspoons of instant coffee into each of two mugs, poured some milk into each mug and filled them with water from the kettle. The coffee was very pale: I should have poured the milk last.

"Ben?"

I put two heaped teaspoonfuls of granulated sugar into the mug on the right and two pips of saccharine into the mug on the left. Then I carried them through and, without spilling them, put them down on the table.

"The cutting," she said.

"What?"

"The laurel tree. Is it still there?"

"Of course it is."

"You must, you know." She lifted the blue mug to her lips, sipped, and looked away.

"You must"

"Yes," I said. "I know. I know."

"Go and plant that laurel, Ben. You must."

*****

Early next morning I caught a bus to Waterloo, and all along Ladbroke Grove found myself scanning the faces of my fellow passengers for signs of distress. So all-consuming is the fact of bereavement, so obliterating of all lesser concerns, it comes to seem intolerable to the sufferer that others should share neither his awareness nor his plight. Envy of the non-afflicted seizes one, together with a sort of low and passive contempt. It is as if, having seen beyond the backdrop of this performance of the living, one is entitled to call a halt, bring down the curtain. One is not; I was not.

As soon as I got back to Cheam, I knew things were not going to be easy. Echardt was, I knew, sole executor of the estate, but that, it dawned on me as I stood among the dust-covered lumber, would not lift the burden. Like it or not, I was responsible for this: the grandfather clock, the pipe rack, the back numbers of the *Law Society Gazette*: everything. It seemed to have a sour justice, even a pertinence: do prisoners inherit the onus for their gaols? How much of it all would accrue to me was, of course, something yet to be determined. I had no idea how the tragi-comic farrago of the will would end. To me now it was all matter of fraying bric-à-brac, curtains, tables, chairs, things I hated and loved, things to be got rid of, things to be dispensed. It was the landscape of my childhood: it was everything, and it was nothing.

I made a pitiful attempt to sort things out, and then, as the March light failed beyond the fake mullion windows, collapsed and inanely and for the first time in months switched on the television. Once more, it seemed, I was condemned to stay the night. There were some tins of soup in the kitchen cupboard. I warmed myself a tin of asparagus soup (cooking has never been my forte) and sat down in front of the set mindlessly watching quiz programmes until, looking down, I discovered that the soup had grown cold. I tried to pour it down the sink, but then, remembering some oft-repeated warning of Andria's about blocked drains, tipped it into one of the Law Society Gazettes and placed it in the bin. Then I tried to watch an arts programme that should have been of immense interest to me, but halfway through it realised I hadn't taken in a word. So I switched off all the lights and dragged myself upstairs to the guest room, lay down in my clothes and was soon fast asleep.

That night, I dreamed of Hampton Court again.

At eleven o'clock on Thursday morning, I made my way to the address that Andria had noted down on the pad. The presbytery turned out to be a modest and semi-detached Mock Tudor house halfway down a side street. There was an old bicycle propped up against the garden fence, with one of its wheels missing. The grass had not been cut for some time. The front curtains were still closed. I gazed up at the top storey, where the curtains were also shut, then rang the two-tone doorbell. There was a shuffling pause followed by the barking of a dog. The door edged open, and I found myself looking up at a tall figure clad in a long, black cassock. There was a plated silver cross handing around Father O'Rourke's neck. He looked down and me and said, "Ben."

I took one step backwards and said, "Jake?"

*****

"I got pretty ill a year or two after leaving college. I was living with a bird called Mo at the time; she looked after me when I felt seedy, fed me, brought me books.

One morning I sent her down to the library at St Pancras to fetch a copy of that nihilist masterwork *Waiting for Godot*. I had seen a production of it before and felt it would mesh in with my mood. I was feeling pretty fed up with everything at the time having dropped out of art college. I could see no clear way head, and thought my pessimism needed feeding. I scribbled down the title on a piece of paper which Mo lost. She must have got muddled up because when she got back she was carrying in her shopping bag something called *Waiting on God*. It's by this French chick called Simone Weil who became a bit of a heroine to me, a bit of a leading light. She was brilliant, brilliant in a way that I'm not, read the Bible in Greek, taught philosophy in various secondary schools, then worked in a Renault factory for a while so as to get the feel of ordinary life. During the war she came to England to help with the French government in exile. De Gaulle thought she was mad, which I suppose she was, but in a very special way. She wanted to be parachuted back into France to help with the Resistance, but they told her she was unfit being as blind as a bat, and besides, as she was Jewish it would have gone hard with her if she'd have been arrested. She went on hunger strike out of solidarity with people in the camps, and her writing was only published after her death. There was one passage in the book that really grabbed me. It's where she says I have the germ of all possible crimes, or nearly all, within me. We are surrounded by evil things: she was, I am. These things, she says, horrified her, but they did not surprise her because she felt the potential of them within herself, even as they filled her with disgust. I read that and I thought, 'that's me'. She says somewhere else that if she were ever surrounded by a fanatical group singing Nazi songs over and over again, she is afraid that she might turn into a Nazi out of pure gregariousness. That, she says, is a very great weakness, but that's who I am. That struck home as well. Evil is real; it's inside you and needs fighting. It's out in the world and needs fighting. Then one day I was dragging on this joint and I just thought, 'What the Fuck?' I mean, '*what* the *fuck*?' And one thing led to another. Does all of this surprise you?"

"Erm, not really. Not a lot. I mean, pretty gob-smacked actually. I mean you as a priest. Does that mean you actually hear confessions and things?"

"And things."

"Masses and stuff?"

"Celebrating masses and stuff. I'm on in half an hour as it happens. If you happen to want to…?"

"No, thanks, I'd much rather not."

Jake took a swig of Nescafé and winced.

"Ah well, mate. I heard you had an exhibition?"

"Yes, that's right."

"Pictures of women and things."

"Yes, pictures of women and things. Christina amongst them, as it happens."

"Christina?"

"Christina Echardt. She was with us in Foundation if you recall. Then she went to Oxford."

"Ah yes, I think I remember. Wasn't she a sculptress? Barbara Hepworth and things."

"Not that I am aware. Lives in Pimlico nowadays, you know. Down by the river."

"In Pimlico? Well, well."

"Yes, in Dolphin Square. It's that big red-brick development full of the weirdest people. Spies and things. All of the Houses are named after admirals. She's in Grenville."

"Well I never. Grenville did you say?'

"Yes, its's got these big windows looking South towards the Thames. With those steel frames they used to have in mansions blocks of the thirties and forties. I did a big painting of her there. It was in my show. Did it against the window. Painted her, that is. We had about two hours of day before sunset. Trouble is the light kept on changing minute by minute. You have to be careful about that, you know. The quality of the light is essential, I find."

"I can well imagine. So impressive. Well done, Ben old man. But now I really have to get ready and togged up as it were for Mass."

"Gosh. You mean chasubles, copes and stuff?"

"All that clobber. A Mrs Martin starches my surplices. Devoted to the BVM and the parish. Salt of the earth. Does the flowers too. Well, nice to catch up. See you at the Requiem."

"Quite. Quite. *Ciao* and all that!"

*****

Tuesday was the day fixed for the funeral. There was to be a said Requiem in the church with a couple of hymns followed by a brief liturgy of committal at the graveside. Andria had left a message at the reception desk of Claud's hotel, and a faint, wavering phone call inter-dispersed with many peeps the evening before informed us of Rosie's intended bus journey from Maida Vale. When we arrived at the church they were standing together in the very back pew: Claud in his raincoat hanging appealingly at the back, Rose in a black serge suit according ill with the rampant rouge she felt obliged to administer for the occasion - and looking in opposite directions. The church was brick-built and ugly, in twenties pseudo-Perpendicular. It was also, at least at the outset, virtually empty, though appearances were somewhat improved two-thirds of the way through by the discreet arrival in a side-aisle of a gentleman I eventually placed as the man-in-the dove grey suit from the gallery, now clad in elegant pinstripe.

Employing all of his tiger charm, Jake delivered a six-minute homily expounding the Catholic doctrine of immortality but without mentioning Purgatory or Hell, which by the mid-1980s already seemed to be on the way out. To my surprise he smuggled in an anecdote about Dad having withheld my pocket money one Saturday after I'd spilt blackcurrant jam on a rug. I'd said nothing about this at the Presbytery the previous week, so I could only assume that, despite all appearances, he must have been listening to me all those years ago when we used to eat together in the student snack bar. Taken in what I was saying and retained it. This surprised me because, as far as I was concerned, back then his attitude had been one of barely disguised demotic disdain. Perhaps, after all, there had been depths.

As we entered the churchyard the party was augmented by two morose-seeming parishioners who looked as if they made such attendance a habit, preparation perhaps for their own imminent demise. They held back when the procession reached the graveside. I had not attended a burial since my mother's, but now, as the unfamiliar English words proceeded, nudging unforgettably the Latin which lay beneath, I found myself closing my eyes and, half-opening them again, imagined each of these figures - Rosie, Claud, Andria, Echardt - whom I had never before seen in one company - appear to join hands in some kind of macabre but joyful dance, implicitly confirming what in actuality each seemed so reluctant to concede, the sharp frail communion of their flesh. The illusion can only have lasted for three seconds, but as it did so, above and beyond their gay but solemn rotation, in the sun-blest space above the grave plot, frisked and revelled, like a Raphael cherub, the chortling form of a girl child.

There was no formal reception, or anything resembling a wake. Nescafé in the clergy house sufficed, with Jake and the lady I took to be Mrs Martin dispensing sugar, milk and unobtrusive words of condolence. After that, for much of the time, I chatted to Rosie while Jake appeared to be deep in conversation with the pin-striped man. Then the pin-striped man came up to us. Rose looked a bit flustered at his approach, but I left them chatting together and had a word with Claud. Twenty minutes later I stood at the doorstep consulting the train timetable, and felt a tap at my shoulder. Turning round I saw the man I now recognised as Claud's employer. He nodded slightly before shaking me by the hand, his skin soft and glossy as an art brochure, and said: "You'll be in touch about the other matter?"

"Sorry. Of course," I was obliged to retort, unsure where to put my eyes.

"It's not of pressing importance of course. But the offer still stands if you want it. Think it over, will you?" and then added, "While we're about it, there's a couple of other matters we might discuss. Your father and I were very close at one time. Give my secretary a ring when you've a moment. I'm pretty tied up for a week or two. Perhaps later in the summer?" He handed me a card which read, "Echardt & Sons, The Poultry."

*****

"Run, man!" yelled Jocelyn. "For Christ's sake run!"

It was entirely typical of him to turn up at such a moment. Three hours earlier, I'd been quietly absorbed before the mirror, then Jocelyn swept in with Andria large on his arm, and now, of all things, a crisis.

It was now I remembered he'd said he'd be over from Camberwell that weekend. He'd been coming round as promised and met Andria at the bus stop. She was returning from the clinic where they'd told her nothing was imminent, and now this. Our telephone was naturally out of order in retribution for two quarters' unpaid bills. I was yet to receive a cheque from the Gallery, and Andria did not rise to anything as magnificent as Maternity Leave. Why in God's name hadn't they detained her in Gower Street?

Once out into Peploe Road, I picked up my heels and ran, Jocelyn's face staring out at me fiercely from the upstairs window. So little time. It was then with a surge of rising panic I saw a lorry of juggernautical proportions negotiate the bend at the top of the street, where it remained firmly stuck, the insignia 'mother's Pride' staring reproachfully out at me. The driver's face was scowling despairingly from the cab, his vehicle firmly lodged between me and the phone kiosks. The engine revved, the driver sulked. I ranted and raved.

There was a Methodist Church on the other side, newly converted to Sikhism. Pulled by the spectacle, two drunks were loitering at the entrance, the smaller of the two supporting the larger, an Irishman, from falling. As I stood there fuming and irrelevantly consulting my watch, the taller swayed backwards and issued his verdict: "Wanker!"

Then his companion collapsed, depositing him on the pavement, narrowly missing the neighbourhood cat who'd been licking at his boots.

From the alcove above the temple door, some kind of God was louring at me mystically. The lorry was now firmly jammed: there was no way I could squeeze round her. I thought of taking another route, but paralysis had suddenly seized me. The minutes leaked by; four past six, five past. The cat miaowed. On the kerb, beside his stricken vehicle, the driver was scratching his ears.

He was still standing there consulting his driver's manual when suddenly my paralysis deserted me and I discovered a detour through some houses, only to find the kiosks either *hors de combat* or occupied. Banging at the door was useless. Through the glass loomed squashed yobbo faces, safety pin noses, Cherokee hair. What was I to do?

By the time I contacted the hospital, I'd made a tour of the district. I cantered back to the flat; Mother's Pride was still stuck. I rushed up the pathway, loped up the stairs, to find Jocelyn wiping his hands, and in the kitchen sink a bawling stranger called Titania.

*****

"As for Mr Henry, he suffers from one supreme handicap: an inability to lose himself. He is torn between two subjects: both women; but both are alike set in aspic, congealed as it were by his own precious self-regard. Finally, all of his work is self-directed. Judging from his contribution to this exhibition, he has much still to learn, in life perhaps as much as in art."

The verdict of the critics, enunciated so pointedly in July, fell about my head like so much redundant thunder. So they called me self-absorbed. To one who had laboured for months at the portrayal of two women so different in shape and *ton*, so dissimilar in the very cast of their mind, as Andria and Christina, the revelation that he had all along been stuck within the lineaments of his own skin caused less the intended irritation than an initial mood of compensatory hilarity. In struggling with those studies of Andria's vertebrae hour after hour, in wrestling with the enigma of Christina, had I then been doing no more than endlessly painting myself?

For days after the close of the exhibition, which had remained open for its full course solely due to Doig's reputation I went round in an ostensible swagger of contempt and bogus self-confidence, based on very little at all. So they had praised Doig to the skies and thrown me scraps of sanctimonious advice. What more did it mean but that he was established in their esteem, and I a relative greenhorn? True, every one of his pictures had sold, whereas virtually all of mine would have to be returned by van to Kensal Rise, but even here there had been something of a reprieve. The day before the close I received a note from the gallery director saying that five of my works, including the large portrait of Christina, had been purchased at one fell swoop by the same anonymous benefactor who had helped finance my share in the show. The news helped to buoy up my spirits, though I would have been pleased to have known a bit more.

Yet, however strong my outer resolve, it was days before I troubled to take up as much as a crayon. For years, painting and drawing had been lifeblood to me. As others fill in crosswords, go on jogs, or frantically practise the 'cello, so every morning without fail I had picked up my sketch pad and, flexing my fingers over the surface in a little agony of preparation, had embarked on those series of sketches, some little more than doodles, that I had hoped might one day lead to something greater. But now as Andria and I attended to our daughter in the cramped spaces of our flat, never once did it occur to me to lift a pencil. To be frank, I had no time. Ideas drifted vaguely through my mind, little clouds of intuition; yet the determination to give them concrete shape, to hear once more the scratch of charcoal on paper, the bristly crunching of brush on canvass or board, seemed temporarily to have departed. It was only during the third month of such passivity, when Andria and Titania had gone for a check-up at the clinic, and the hours seemed to stretch out before me, that I compromised with my inner torpor and, swinging my legs off the divan where I had sprawled since mid-morning in lethargic contemplation of the ceiling, slouched over towards the apple-green chest of drawers, and taking the oval mirror down from its customary position, moving it across precariously to my worktable. I then straddled one of a set of stripped pine chairs looking at it. For minutes I squatted there without moving and stared into that mildewed pond - cleaning was not one of our household habits - in the depths of which, beyond the murk and dust, sat a personage called I.

And so they called me self-absorbed: the critics, Christina. What, as I leant against the back of the stripped pine chair, did I see? A man of thirty-two summers, hair straggly and indeterminate red-to-mousy, parted to the left and bleached towards brow. Lips full and carmine from too much booze. Eyes shifty and grey flecked with brown, inclined on occasion to part company. Right eye: direct and acquisitive; left cowardly, prevaricating, quizzical. Nose long and pointed, tilted slightly towards the tip. Ear-flaps fleshy, rest of orifice hidden by hair. Crown of head swathed in a black felt beret Andria had given me to disguise incipient bald patch. Skin white to tawny, freckled in patches and pock-marked on cheeks. Teeth indifferent and much-filled, gums decidedly swollen. Expression mobile but inclined to pout, especially when absorbed in - what? - itself. Was this a fit object for adoration let alone a portrait?

I had attempted to paint myself on previous occasions. Indeed, during periods when sitters proved hard to come by, self-portraiture had been something of a stand-by. But as I studied myself in the mirror that afternoon, taking in each crease and crenelation of skin, each shelf of bone and moulding of the flesh, it was in no mood of idleness or observation of some time-worn rite, but in earnestness. A beret Andria had given me, a size too big, drooped slightly toward the back; around my neck, the open flaps of an Indian muslin shirt were just visible above the furry ring of my pullover. I took up my sketch pad, licked a piece of charcoal and started tentatively copying the padded half-moon of my jaw.

*****

Dolphin Square, 14th August, 1985.

Andria (if I may call you that?)

Forgive me for barging in on your life like this, especially after so momentous a life event. Ben told me all about it. Well done! And congratulations on naming her after the Fairy Queen. What an achievement.

I suppose you might say that none this is any concern of mine, and you might of course be right. You will guess who I am: my name's Christina. We met briefly at the private viewing before you fainted (so glad it was alright in the end, though). I'm the somewhat unwilling subject of one of Ben's pictures. Rather idiosyncratic, I thought, and maybe a bit out of place in that show, but it was the treatment on which he insisted. He didn't sell much I gather; I just hope the whole experience was a bit of a boost for him. He could do with a little *succès d'estime*, though you would probably say that he could do with some money. *Faute de mieux*, notoriety will do, and he seems to have got a little of that. Have you seen the papers?

The real point, as I see it, is this: he neglects his opportunities. I suppose he will have told you that my dad knew his for ages; they were even bosom pals of a somewhat taciturn variety. They even seem to have had some kind of unspoken agreement between themselves, though quite what about I was never quite clear. The fact is this: now Ben's dad's gone, Father wants to help him. And the tragic waste is: Ben simply won't be helped. Dad tried to land him some job in the firm months ago, but he did nothing about it. Absolutely nothing, so of course it went to somebody else. In the world of commerce one can't as they say simply hang about, especially nowadays. Why should one?

Ben's such a sweet boy, but he simply seems to have no will power, or if he has it's hidden beneath so many layers of lethargy, pride and cultivated resentment that only someone who knew him intimately could ever reach it. That's why I'm writing to you, really. If anybody could goad him into taking up his opportunities, you could. I know you must me terribly preoccupied at the moment but do think about it. Dad's making noises about wanting to see him. When he talks like that unprompted, there's sure to be something serious afoot; I know the signs.

Apparently, Dad had a word with him after the funeral, but he has done nothing about it. Not a sod as yet. Could you just try your best to make sure that he doesn't mess this one up? Could you? Ben thinks I'm as hard as nails, you know, but I do have feelings, and even if I hadn't it's a crying shame to have to watch somebody ruining their chances out of pure, voluntary paralysis. I don't need a reply to this screed, but just in case you'd like to get in touch I've slipped my address and telephone number in with this letter.

The best of luck gain, and once again, apologies for my presumption.

Christina Echardt.

*****

"I had that dream again."

"Uhuh?" Andria turned over to face the wall. "Look, Ben, I'm really tired. Is that her crying again?"

An hour or so later I said, "I had that dream."

"Which dream?"

Andria was right of course. There are few things which are of less interest to others than the nocturnal workings of one's mind. They are like the workings of the digestive system, of absorbing fascination to the person within the body that produces them, of none to other persons. But, later in the day, she said, "I never dream nowadays. Haven't the time."

"Perhaps you just don't remember."

"I wish I could, I really do. We all need a Hampton Court, you know."

That evening I dreamed of it again.

Hampton Court was what my father with his Jerome K. Jerome vocabulary always called a "treat". It always seemed to me an egregiously complicated treat, rather like a sixteen decker ice cream. To begin with you had to take the bus to Westminster Pier. You then had to board a boat, one of those long low ones with tarpaulins, or else a proper steamboat. The last time we did it (and it happened about once a year) there was even a paddle steamer. The boat took you downstream, beneath the flying arches of Hammersmith Bridge, then on through Putney and Richmond, where if you were lucky you ate lunch. This was packed, and eaten under the tarpaulin, often sheltering from the wind, since amongst his other characteristics Hamish possessed an unfailing instinct for inclement weather. You ploughed past Kingston, and then there was a place where the river narrowed. Henry the Eighth came this way *en route* for the palace, and there was some story about an extra channel having been dug to protect him from the inquisitive eyes of drinkers in the pub on the opposite bank. Then there was an island, and then looking to our left we saw the tall palace chimneys - the chimneys of my dream - through the trees.

You got off at a low jetty where mother always needed helping. Then you walked across the road bridge, turned right up the long drive until you found yourself facing the Tudor West side of the palace, Henry's side. I think that one of my very earliest memories must have been of staring up at one of the unicorns on the Moat Bridge and asking Hamish to explain the coats of arms. I was about four then, I suppose, and very keen on knights. Was there any armour? "Yes," he said, "in the King's Guard Chamber", so then we went through the outer Gate House, and through the Base Court where with all his delight in technicalities father would explain the Great Clock, with its hours, days, and months. Then on through Anne Boleyn's gateway into the spacious inner courts with their fountains plashing endlessly amid cool stonework, all the long night and day.

What happened next depended on whether you were visiting the palace or the gardens. In earlier years, the palace was a blur. What I do remember was the maze, where in time-honoured style we got lost. The grounds to my eager young feet seemed to be endless. We used to play hide and seek around the cherished topiary of the trees. These were officially out of bounds, but the delinquency of it seemed delightful at such times as father's instinctive puritanism, his concern for law and order, unaccountably relaxed.

Out of all those earliest visits, those before the age of ten, I retain one very distinct memory. It was one of the very rare occasions on which we actually got lost. We had been visiting the Great Vine in its house by the south wing, beneath the watchful windows of the King's Quarters, and had intended to find our way back to the fountain garden and thence to the river. Instead we found ourselves wandering southwards down a pathway which led to an enclosure we had not yet visited, in the corner of which stood as square building announced by its notice board as the Banqueting House. The place was closed, but through the long windows one glimpsed a panelled interior within and paintings which had all the ornateness of those in the palace itself. One set of windows overlooked the river over a low iron railing which was, however, at this point impassable.

The whole enclosure had a delicious and quite unexpected privacy about it. My father stopped and took his bearings from the plan, then folded it up and put it inside the deep pocket of his waterproof. Then he looked up, surveyed the enclosure and the raised terrace leading to the banqueting house itself, which had all the quaintness and sequestered charm of a Gazebo, sniffed and said, "Good place for a tryst."

I did not know what a tryst was. I dimly suppose now that I thought it some variety of plant, something that might twine up the walls. My mother smiled one of her remote smiles, and we all just stood there, listening to the silence, the wind through the trees. There was a pause while we attended to the hush and the insistent rustling beneath it, before Father added, "Best by night. Best by night", and then we passed on.

When we got back home, I looked "tryst" up in the dictionary. Had my parents ever had such things? It seemed unlikely.

Trysts or not, Hampton Court seemed invariably to bring out a sentimental strain in my parents. It was during one of those later visits, when I was eleven or perhaps twelve, that I first began to understand something of the peculiar topography of their marriage. If I close my eyes now, I can re-create the moment almost exactly. We were in the Queen's Drawing Room in the centre of the East Front, from where the long windows look down on the garden with its trio of paths radiating towards a semi-circle of trees, beyond which the vista opens towards the receding distances of Long Water. It must have been part of my folk memory - because I cannot recall having been told of it - that the procession of Queen's apartments along this side of the palace was no accident. The Queen had chosen the east side. Not for the garden I am sure, and not for the Baroque splendour of the scene, but for what one could see albeit faintly in the background: the grey recession of Long Water. The foliage beyond I was informed - though I had not yet been there - was Home Park. It was in this room that the Queen had stood on cold February afternoons, her gaze drawn by that long truncated canal, the end of which, hidden in the mists lingering over the park, suggested as no other sight could, the level flats and narrow waterways of Holland.

On the afternoon in question Father had led me away from the window towards the far wall decorated by Verrio in a later reign to represent Queen Anne receiving homage from the four quarters of the earth. We had just turned round to inspect the adjoining wall, where Anne's husband is seen surveying the British fleet, when my eye was caught by the figure of my mother staring down at the Fountain Garden and Long Water beyond. Her head was done up in a scarf, her arms were hugging her sides. Even as I looked, she leant back against the wall of the window alcove and tilted her head back against the wood panelling. Beyond her the vista was clear as far as the garden gates, beyond which it was occluded by the March fog drifting over the canal and then the trees of the park. To my left, Father was explaining the lay-out of the fleet - the masts, the port-holes, My Lord Admiral's uniform. My mother just stayed there, before Wren's long widow, gazing.

It was then that I remembered some ten minutes earlier walking up the long sweep of the King's Staircase with its allegory of the Caesars to enter the King's Guard Chamber and, with the military enthusiasms of boyhood still alert within me, gasping slightly at the spectacle of Yeomen's armoury spread out against the north wall. Men are children too, and father was no exception. In the inventory which followed I registered two facts: that there were about 3,000 items up there, and that there existed a particular item of weaponry, in which Hamish seemed to take special delight, called a halberd. But I also registered something else, the force of which did not strike me until later.

Father put his pipe back in his mouth and dribbled slightly over the metallic density and palpable, the thing-ness of it all. As we drifted through into the King's apartments, we had to our right the enclosed spaces of the private gardens; the deep sunken Pond Garden behind its gates and, between its high brick walls, the bleaker beds of the Privy Garden. It was not until we had turned northwards into the Queen's apartments that I understood the personal significance of all of this: the armour, the stolidity, the enclosed private spaces of the King's Rooms; the long stretches, the mist-filled vistas of the Queen's.

Long Water had been constructed in the reign of Charles II but, in planning the refurbishment of the palace with Wren, Mary had insisted on overlooking it. And there was another thing: the separation of the two suites, a communal isolation, a mutually negotiated privacy. I would not at the age of eleven have appreciated more than a tiny fraction of the meaning, but in later years whenever I re-visited the palace, with Andria or else by myself, I recognised in the layout of its rooms something of the substantial mystery of their marriage.

*****

Kensal Rise, October 10th 1985

Christina,

Look, I know you said I needn't reply to your letter, but it was a godsend, and yes, albeit belatedly, I must. Apologies for the delay. Changing nappies, mostly. (Ben does help, or at least he tries, though mostly his mind seems to be elsewhere.)

You are so right about him of course. Does anybody in the world understand him? I've been beating my brains out at the sheer enigma of Ben for years without success. Then suddenly, out of the blue comes a letter from someone who has an inkling, or at least seems to understand the parameters of the problem.

When I tremblingly read your sentences - not in the least presumptuous - about the riddle, malaise and pure incomprehensible bog that is Ben, I simply clapped my hands for joy. Something leaped at my bosom I say, and it wasn't just this other being whose body has so unaccountably joined my own. Even if it was, thank the lord, for even now she has been granted some premature insight to appreciate the length, breadth and depth of the problem.

Yes, you're right, Ben's clueless. Not intellectually clueless, though all of his ideas have always been of a rather crack-brained idiosyncratic variety. But if such a thing exists as real, *bona fide*, ethical cluelessness, why he's got it. Ben is like this: if you hauled him up on a ledge five hundred feet above the ground and told him that his salvation lay in stepping to the right - not only his salvation but his wealth, his peace, his self-respect - he'd step to the left without a moment's thought and damn himself for ever.

What's to be done? I don't know. I raised the question of the job and he ignored it saying he was "nature's freelance". It's one of his phrases and quite apropos if you happen to be Francis Bacon or somebody, but the fact is that Ben's not anything like Francis Bacon (except in a certain convoluted, self-conscious weirdness). He's not even, if you will excuse the expression, a very good artist. He is just what he is, himself, *sui generis* almost, as if he were his own breathing, crawling self-justification.

I will try my best I really will, though quite what it will amount to I don't know, having long ago exhausted all expedients. In the meantime, do you mind if we keep in touch? You see I'm stuck in the flat all day, and things do get bottled up. Ben and I have always belonged to quite different worlds. Nobody that I know knows him, and it would be just such a relief to be able to talk or even write to somebody about him, though it might be preferable if he doesn't know. He's manically suspicious and is bound to dream up some bizarre and irrelevant conspiracy. He's exasperating, mysterious, and I do love him so. I will write again when I can, though Lord knows there's little enough opportunity at the moment. I can only write this because Ben's friend Jocelyn, a former teacher who seems to have taken pity on us all, has taken them all out for a walk.

Yours gratefully, Andria.

*****

Dolphin Square, November 23rd, 1985

Dear Andria,

How nice to hear from you. Yes, let's keep in touch by whatever means you like. You've got your plate full at the moment, but whenever the mood takes you, or when things are bit easier, do not hesitate to contact me. I work during the day now, but evenings are free. You can always phone, or else write. It's no good expecting things to be easy; I can't supply answers. But there is a provisional answer, which I suppose we must try. It is this.

There is one thing which divides Benedict from both of us, and this is his beliefs. You don't share them and neither do I (I used to, but that's a different matter, as the priests will tell you firmly enough). If they had a go at Benedict (which he will never let them: he hasn't been to Mass in years, has he?) they would also have to tell him, I'm afraid, that he has reconstructed Catholicism out of his own sick fancy, made a graven image of it stolen from his own disease. That may be a ponderous way of putting it, but what I mean is this.

I think that Benedict labours under one illusion: that his state of artistic and personal confusion conforms to a variety of Grace. It does not. He once, in a fit of drunkenness or honest abstraction or both, described himself to me as a sort of Antinomian Catholic. That's a very cumbersome description which only somebody of his degree of intellectual arrogance would aspire to, but what it seems to mean is this: that is you love God, or try to, then God and the Church will let you off all the rules and forgive you for even the most callous perfidy, provided you say you're sorry.

I don't know whether this casuistry has got a rag of theological respectability with which to hide its shame. If it has, so much the better, but it strikes me that even if it is valid, Benedict has re-interpreted it, matching it ineptly to his own circumstances. For love he has substituted art (or rather his sense of himself as an artist, which I am just bright enough to see does not quite amount to quite the same thing). He is a sort of artistic trier, and takes his trying for good faith, and because he is an artist of sorts, he takes it for granted that God loves him. So he can get away with the most appalling things, trample over everybody's feelings, including his own, and somehow there will always be a let-out clause, somehow the hand of absolution will always be held aloft, and the people rise and sing.

You can play on this. I first met him fifteen years ago when we were both students in Kingston Art College (it was before I went to Oxford, where he did not follow me, but I remember it as if it were yesterday). He set his cap at me, thinking me grand, remote, stylish, upper-class, what-have-you (all of these stereotypes existing in his mind, of course. In reality his station in life is, and always has been, just about equal to my own). He was rather a pathetic, gangling young man, very kind, pimply and inept, a sort of moral and social greenhorn. In any case, I had a boyfriend at the time called Jake O' Rourke. Funny thing is he's a priest now, would you believe it? He actually called round the other day. Got my address somehow or other. Hasn't changed a bit, apart from the cassock. Sorry to digress.

But I do remember Ben at the time, and remember my reactions to him too - a mulch of maternal feelings mixed with self-contempt for feeling that way, combined with a very real recognition that any reciprocation could only be false and disastrous, hurt him as much as me. So I let him down as kindly as I could, and then all these years later he turns up at my door with some lame excuse. It all started again, at least in his mind, but this time I could see he was stronger. He had you, I suppose. For weeks he seemed to be in some kind of trance (he thought it was a Satanic trance I think, but then as you say there's no interpreting his mind). I played along a bit, tried to re-assure him of my regard (for at some level, even if it's not the level one would prefer, one does respect him), but I could see it was no good, see it increasingly, so I tried once more to cool it, but the cooler I got, the warmer did he. (I think he enjoys being abused. I think he enjoys the pain. The pain seemed to feed his portrait of me for the exhibition, not that I could understand it at all, not that anybody can. Poor Ben. Did you see the reviews?)

Dear, dear Andria, how are we going to cope? And how, what's more, are we going to help dear Ben? I'd love to see you and discuss all of this, but is it quite the time? You must concentrate on one thing now. Please give Titania a hug from me and tell her, "Welcome".

Yours gratefully,

Christina.

*****

The door gave way with a rattle. The offices of Lawrence Echardt Ltd were housed at the top of a very long spiral staircase that had somehow got incorporated into a modern ten-storey building above the roaring traffic of The Poultry. As I made my way through the early December streets, my mind was full of a sense of foreboding mingled with futility. It was several months since Echardt's summons, and even now I could not see the point of it. This was not a part of London I knew well, redolent as it always seemed of august and dapper gentlemen rushing to appointments in board rooms or select downstairs wine bars. It was not that I had ever despised finance. It was simply that its rituals were alien to me, representing a side of the world's affairs with which others, father notably, habitually concerned themselves, but from which I seemed for some reason exempt.

I primed the secretary as to the reason for my visit and was asked to wait behind a glass-topped table loaded with glossy magazines which turned out on inspection to be back numbers of the Sotheby's Catalogue. Before my eyes swept miniatures, ormolu pieces and jade: numbered, classified and priced. I was being wafted on six figure carpets when the receptionist said, "He'll see you now," and led me to Echardt's office.

I had not known quite what to expect. Though I'd seen the man twice now, at the gallery and the church, these brief impressions were overlaid with a composite picture compiled from father's conversation. I think I still imagined something Dickensian: a blend of Gradgrind and Dombey: someone immensely tall in sombre, well-cut garments - a frock coat would not have been inappropriate - white sideburns wispy below ears, a voice deeply resonant with power and quiet understanding, an expression of mingled severity and gentleness.

But when I stepped onto the Persian carpet all I could see was the desk, an antique Chippendale with many drawers and a glass paper-weight holding down blue-coloured forms. Then a grey-suited form detached itself from the curtains, and I recognised the man Claud had been haranguing that evening: slender, the shoulders erect, eyes crabbed beneath the folds of skin, and, over everything, that air of modest, almost tremulous withdrawal, a tiredness and sadness like creased and fading Vellum. Could this be Christina's father? But then something about the mouth betrayed him and the way that he indicated the swivel chair between us and said, "Do please take a seat. I haven't an immense amount of time."

As I lowered myself into the chair, the atmosphere seemed so much that of a Victorian set piece - a Tissot perhaps - that I imagined a fob-watch snap. On the mantelpiece, above an aging radiator, stood a full- faced photograph of Christina, her expression subdued and oddly like her father's. Walking forwards towards the desk, and feeling for a brass bell-knob on his side, he said, "I assume you'd like some coffee?" There was an awkward silence before he resumed, "I really am most terribly grieved about your father. And so glad we had a chance to meet at the funeral. It's been a very long time."

After the secretary had come with the cups and departed, he handed me mine and said, "About the position we offered you. Have I impression you were less than frantically keen?"

"More or less."

"All to the good. It's just as well to be honest." He stirred his coffee, replaced the spoon with equitable precision, then looked up and said, "Now to other matters. How much do you know about the connection between our two families?"

"Very little. Dad was always dropping obscure hints. He was always talking about you."

"He spoke of you too. He was very fond of you, you know, fonder than you perhaps may have appreciated." The similarity to Claud's parting homily caused me to lower my cup.

"And your uncle never discussed the subject?"

"No. At least, not at all explicitly."

"You know of course that he has worked for us now for a great many years. In a station well below his capacity I might add. There are some temperaments …" His voice trailed off into a smog of suggestion. "But I dare say you know something of that yourself …" ("… of that yourself," Christina repeated beneath the glass, "… of that yourself.")

"You can scarcely be aware how much pleasure it gave your father to know that you and my daughter had met at last. You may have thought the fact had passed him by. Let me assure you, it did not. It is not my business to inquire where things stand between you, or indeed if you are still on speaking terms. The fact remains that I owe it to you to tell you the truth. I wonder if, in speaking to you of her, your father ever intimated that Christina was not my wife's child?' A sort of gloomy inexorability seemed to surround the question.

"No," I replied. "I had no idea."

He looked me straight in the eyes and asked, "Does the information surprise you?"

I looked across to Christina for guidance. "No," I said. "Should it affect me in some way?"

Echardt leant backwards slightly and said, "I rather gathered from the terms of your father's will that it might afford you at least some concern." He had his daughter's habit of returning questions to their owner. "I'm surprised your father gave you no inkling."

"He did seem anxious … well, he was always urging me to introduce myself to Christina. We met once, briefly, when at college."

"And your father never gave any indication as to the source of his desire."

"None at all. I'm afraid I always thought it a little mad."

Echardt then stood up and walked back to the window where he remained ruefully surveying the traffic as it wound its way towards Cheapside. There was another long pause before he continued. "Before his death, your father extracted a promise from me which in deference to our long-standing friendship I will honour. I'd prefer you told nobody else of this. And especially not Christina. Do you understand?"

"Christina herself knows nothing?"

"No, nothing. Christina is your aunt's child."

In the far distance I could hear the traffic droning on toward Ludgate Hill and the West End. It formed a soothing background to Echardt's voice as, its consonants dry and a little clipped, the vowels liquid with contrition, it asked, "Does that shock you at all?"

"No, but I don't quite see how it's possible."

"You knew of course that Rosie had a child?"

"Well yes."

"Then you must hear me out. I'll be as brief as I can. Towards the end of the war I was living for a short time in Highgate. There were still hostilities with Japan, but my unit had exhausted its function and I was on a kind of short-call commission while in the meantime I tried to build things up again here. It was not an easy period. Things were in very short supply, and during the war the art market of course had been completely moribund. I was terribly alone. I was married at the time, but my wife had sustained injuries in the Blitz, and was partly hospitalised. When they released her, she was living in a nursing home for a short time near the Angel. I used to go and see her three times a week. She needed constant attention."

As he spoke, Echardt had his back to me. Had I intervened I might have saved us both unnecessary embarrassment, but something in his manner restrained me. It is extraordinary how unkindly the blemished can treat one another.

"I'd known your father since shortly before the war. We were both members of the Society of Vincent de Paul. On Maundy Thursday that year I went to the Oratory to attend the *Tenebrae*. You know the office, of course. The darkness, the plainsong, *Pange Lingua*. When they stripped the altars it seemed to be the end of everything. Afterwards during the vigil I caught sight of your aunt's face in the candlelight from a side chapel; she was praying next to your father. Afterwards, on our way out, your father introduced us. She had not long moved into her basement in Maida Vale. There was a liaison of a sort that went on, I suppose, for the better part of eight years: dreadful years for me, sickness, disruption, shortages, confusion everywhere beneath that silly euphoria. Your aunt never complained about her position. I do believe that she too had been badly shaken in her way. We did everything we could to keep things from my wife. In my heart of hearts I believe that I did nothing deliberately to hurt her. I still believe that at her death she suspected nothing."

"Then why ..." I began. In all fairness I should not have stopped him. It takes one sinner to pick another's sores.

"My wife and I could have no children of our own. The nature of her affliction made the very thought of childbearing impossible. The arrival of a lovechild placed me in a considerable quandary. Fond as I was of your aunt, deeply though I pitied her, I could not let her ruin my marriage. We went over the possibilities together 'til the small hours night after night: your father, myself, Claud. It was inconceivable that I should leave my wife, whom in any case your father held in deep affection. It was equally impossible that your aunt should undertake to raise a child unaided in her straitened circumstances. The accommodation we reached - not without your father's considerable reluctance I might add - was that after a decent interval we should arrange for my wife and myself to adopt the child anonymously through a Catholic Adoption Society, who were not, needless to say, apprised of the circumstances. Your father was a trustee of one such society, and the arrangements did not prove difficult. Your aunt was told just so much and no more. To this day she believes her child was given to strangers."

"Do you mean to tell me Rosie has no idea?"

His face was turned half towards me: "Do you think that if we'd have taken her into our confidence she could have borne to have kept away? In view of the circumstances I had long since broken off all contact."

"And still, neither of them knows?"

"When my wife was still alive it seemed kindest not to raise the question. Christina was fourteen when she died. Afterwards it would have been foolish to rock her confidence with a revelation which could achieve absolutely nothing. She is in any case my child."

He then turned round and faced me, the ordeal of contrition over.

"I suppose you're wondering where I stand with Rosie. After my wife's death I did make overtures, but they were repulsed at the time and I haven't thought to disturb matters since. I think in a way she'd be glad to forget the past, though like all of us she's … When I spoke to her briefly after the Requiem Mass the week before last it was the first time in years. I think you see she's really in love with the man I *was*, little though he deserved it." A smile suffused the weary face. "I suppose you'll want to go away and sleep on all this now. Gradually bit by bit, we must all learn to forgive one another, I suppose - God willing."

In an appalled silence there seemed no fit reply.

*****

"Do you mean to tell me that you're cousins?"

"Well, that's what the man said."

"How creepy!"

Andria was packing clothes in the apple-greed chest of draws which suddenly didn't seem big enough. From the moment of the birth we had been inundated with cast-offs, mostly from perfect strangers. The whole of human existence had become pathetically and endearingly scaled down: there were knitted caps with bobbles, knitted tops and trousers, little bibs and tuckers, miniscule mittens, miniscule drawers, baby socks and shoes, and lot of things in assorted sizes called baby-grows. Then there were lilliputian sheets, lilliputian pillows - all a ghastly a shade of yellow - and thousand upon thousand of miscellaneous dummies.

We had spent much of the last few months in a state of parental absorption, much like bereavement in its secluding effect, but with this unexpected and welcome compensatory glow. For weeks we had been staring down at an empty Moses basket acquired by me in a fit of uncharacteristic preparedness at a jumble sale and now, unaccountably, there was somebody in it.

There was also a division of labour. Nappy-changing, after my first few cack-handed attempts, I left to Andria. To me accrued the Bottles. For reasons of her own Andria had decided to bottle feed, ignoring all fashionable advice and sticking to what she thought of as sensible. You could not, she said, breast feed while reading Petronius. I did not comment on the practicality of this, since bottle feeding seemed to be not much better. But in the meantime I acquired after a manner of speaking new and unseemly skills, the most important one of which was the Preparation of the Feed.

The procedure was this: the bottles were plastic with teats on them. You were supposed to sterilise the lot in boiling water (bottles and teats), then boil some more water and fill them, six at a time. After that, you let the water cool and when it was lukewarm - not before - you very carefully spooned in several plastic spoonfuls of dried milk. This was the textbook version; mine was different. In my method, you swilled the bottles under the warm tap, then you spooned in the milk so that it lay at the bottom of each bottle like the cone at the bottom of an egg-timer, and then you poured in the dried milk and stirred it in. You did this with the door closed so that Andria would not notice, while talking in a loud voice about the difficulty of the supposed procedure. Then, when one of the bottles was cool, you handed it out to Andria.

She took it in her right hand and said, "But how come you never knew?"

"It was all hushed up years ago. They had Christina adopted, telling Mrs Echardt nothing about the birth to save her pain. They told Rosie that she was going to strangers. The strangers were the Echardts."

"Very pious, I'm sure. And all to save Mrs Echardt pain?"

"I suppose. And Echardt embarrassment."

Andria picked Titania up from the Moses basket and plonked her on her knee. She gave me an imbecilic smile, and then Andria placed the teat firmly between her gums. A sucking noise ensued, less like the lapping of water than the eructations of a superannuated iron.

"What about Rosie's pain, I'd like to know."

"Well, we know about all Rosie's pain."

"And Christina's pain?"

I looked down at my recumbent daughter and winked. Her lips made a loop like that on a Roman mask, and then carried on sucking. Every so often she took these operatic minor breaths.

"I never knew Christina felt any pain."

"Honestly!"

Later, when we were sitting round the table eating a take-away and Titania was temporarily asleep, she took the opportunity to ask: "So what are you going to do about it?"

I bit on a spare-rib and said, "Not a lot."

"You can't do nothing."

"Nothing," I said, "is precisely what I am expected to do. At least according to Echardt."

"And Echardt's word is law?"

"Echardt's shame is law."

She wiped her fingers in a paper napkin while staring across at me reproachfully. "Benedict, grow up."

There was a wail from the bedroom. "Well I'm older than her, anyway".

Andria stood up and moved towards the bedroom saying, "Sometimes."

Conversation lapsed during the next feed. I dithered around with my sketch book, and then took a brief look at a paperback guide to Wills (the complexities of Dad's state were still intermittently worrying me). When we were tucked up in bed with Titania snuffling in the basket beside us, I brushed her lips briefly with mine and said, "Moody."

"Well, one gets like that."

"I suppose so." (In another paperback, I had learned something of post-natal blues). "Anything I can do?"

"Yes."

We made love, for the first time in months. I went gently, but she seemed to feel no pain. Afterwards she turned over towards me and said, "You don't think she might prefer to know?"

"Who?"

"Christina."

It was not a question I could answer with any certainty. I tried to sound knowing and important as I said, "According to Echardt, it's best to leave things as they are."

"Why?"

"Mrs Echardt was her mother. At least that is what she was led to believe. It's a memory she holds dear."

"And?"

"It would be a pity to spoil it, wouldn't it? When you've grown up in the bosom of a happy family, and one half tragically disappears, the last thing you want to learn is that the cherished missing half was an illusion."

"Still…"

She lay on her back looking up at the ceiling. There were tiny stretch marks along the rim of her pelvis. Her voice was dreamy as she said, "She's got the opposite problem from me, hasn't she? I don't know who I am, and she thinks she knows who she is, but it's all a gigantic error."

"Yes, I suppose you're right."

She got up and put on a nightdress. As she was lowering it over her shoulders, she said, "Do you know what? If I was her, I would prefer to know."

"I'll think about it."

She got into bed. "You don't have to do what Echardt says, do you?"

"Of course not."

Several minutes afterwards when I thought her fast asleep, she spoke out of the darkness, in the sleepiest of voices: "Tell her, Ben."

*****

Dolphin Square, January 10th 1986.

Dear Andria,

Excuse me for writing again, but how is the baby? I did ask Ben when we last talked on the phone, but he's terribly vague about some things, and all he seems to think about is his 'work'. I'm surprised he's got time for work. But I suppose he makes time for it, so long as it's not at your expense.

Yes, I know, you've a thousand things to think about, and sorry even to trouble you. If I ever gave birth to a child, which at this rate I doubt, I think I'd feel sort of mysteriously *enthroned*. It is the supreme and divine privilege, at least that's what Father O'Rourke says, not that he knows anything about it, from either end. After all, it's not something one can ever know about unless one has done it. That's why hearing about somebody else makes one feel so humble. I want to share in all of your feelings, but can't because I simply don't *know*. There are so many things that I don't know, even some quite basic things; sometimes, I confess, I get quite overwhelmed with this sense of my own ignorance.

Forgive these futile flutterings, but once again well done and bless you. And you will make sure that Benedict helps and things won't you? Sometimes he's such a futile worm.

Yours adoringly,
Christina.

*****

Kensal Rise, February 14, 1986.

Dear Christina,

Thanks for your recent note. Yes, she is lovely. I do value your understanding, and your sympathy and everything. And of course we must meet, but at the moment I am trapped by a sort of duty and a sort of loveliness. Ben's being helpful … well, quite.

He goes off rambling sometimes, down to Surrey to sort out this probate and things. Why does everything happen all at once, after years and years of nothing? If you see him, do keep an eye on him. All this responsibility is, I fear, proving something of a strain.

Yours frantically,

Andria.

*****

"It's wind."

"She's smiling at me."

"I tell you, it's wind."

Titania was looking up at a nappy sack which was swaying two feet away from her unfocused eyes. The sack was being wielded by Jocelyn who'd been spending weekends with us on and off since Christmas, having seemingly taken pity on our – or more accurately on my – helplessness. He was company for Andria, and I can't say I objected to his presence much. The solitude of his grey-walled flat having at last got to him, he occupied our tiny spare room on these occasions, casting the occasional critical eye over my attempts at self-portraiture. Mercifully, he spared me his comments on these, except to call my palette unconscionably dark, and the references to Rembrandt too marked. "Sombre," he remarked one afternoon as he stood behind me. "Sober harmonies, like an organ piece by Franck." Jocelyn has always indulged a weakness for these synaesthetic allusions.

With Jocelyn thus in attendance, and Andria harassed but vigilant, I got on with my work. I'd started again on the self-portrait, but after six or seven such attempts switched my attention to my daughter whose liveliness of feature proved more rewarding by the hour. With her bow-shaped tonsure and persistent grin she managed to look at the same time absurdly young and almost gaga. When the resemblances to Father in my sketches grew too suggestive, I endeavoured to combine the two of them, ending with a wizened homunculus who stared out of me from the sketch pad with a sort of precocious senile knowledge. Then I broke it down into phases and started a sequence from the cradle to the grave. Titania evolved into Benedict who turned slowly - horror of horrors - into his own father.

A few days later, Dad's solicitor phoned while Andria was out and confirmed that the terms of the will were indeed as I had expected. He was not sure about the legality of the clause concerning Christina, but he would check. That afternoon I boarded the train to Cheam and, all the way down those dim suburban cuttings worried about The Problem. I had already reached one or two decisions, or rather, as I sat drawing, the decisions had settled themselves somewhere at the base of my brain. There was no point in telling Andria about the terms of the will. I had no idea how valid it was, and in any case saw no point in worrying her with prospects or contingencies that could only cause her anxiety. She had never asked questions about the estate, being far too preoccupied with Titania, and in any case considering this my province. Nor could I confide in Christina without raising issues I preferred, at least temporarily, to leave fallow. Had all this perplexity been part of

Dad's intention? I felt like the victim of a plot who - was powerless to disclose his dilemma, a plot moreover whose principal conspirators seemed perversely to have vanished.

Half of me, of course, wanted to forget about the whole thing. Father, Claud, Christina - something within me wished them all with the devil. This was not, however, within the realm of the possible. I was stuck with the consequences of the crime, if crime it was. I was also stuck with a history written not extraneously around me, but physically within. A man cannot forget who he is. If the hours I had spent poring over my face in the glass, the hours I had spent before my daughter, were telling me anything at all, they were telling me this: that I possessed a name and an ancestry. Whence sprung the pugnacious line of this jaw? With whose assurance shone these eyes? Whose was the swagger of this mouth; whose lines of doubt crept around the moulding of this brow? My father had departed, but he had gone leaving messages, and the messages were inscribed in the very creasing of my cheeks. A family is a state of the body.

And then, ever and anon, I struggled with the questions of motive. Echardt's confession had shaken me, not for its content so much as for what it had revealed of the deviousness of Father's mind. If the pact of silence between Echardt and Father had been principally of Echardt's making, its disclosure so soon after Father's death could only, I was sure, have been part of the bargain. Why, after disguising the truth for so long, had

Hamish gone to such lengths to impart the truth of Christina's origins?

My first reaction had been to wonder at the need for pretence. Yet, thinking over the question during the ensuing days, I began to discern the weird logic of his discretion. What Father had been striving to do was to save her, to save both of us: her from the clutches of familial anonymity, me from the consequences of a drifting existence which in his eyes could only spell disaster. To have informed me of the real state of affairs any earlier would have been to lend my developing relationship with Christina a sense of coercion, and by so doing to have set me at loggerheads with his wishes. To have told Christina would have been to disturb the fragile hold on tranquillity she possessed, to plunge her for no reason into a maelstrom of self-doubting. Pointing me in her direction, merging us, implicitly joining our hands - these had been his means finally to gather her in.

A nagging thought persisted. Had the conspiracy of silence extended any wider? Had it extended, for example, to Claud? When my uncle first sent me after that chimera of perfection he called Christina, no ulterior motive had entered my mind. Idealisation, after all, was his pabulum. The most I had felt was pity for one held is futile bondage to a supposed sublime. But had he, all along, been implicated in some quite different way? Did the moment of tension between Echardt and himself I had witnessed at the gallery betoken some guilty pact of which I was even now unaware? There were two possibilities: either my uncle knew everything, or else he knew nothing. If, as Hamish had suggested in his letter, it was to Claud's prejudices that he had finally succumbed, had his contrivance of sending me off in search of Christina been his way of joining by tender contrivance what his earlier obduracy had set apart?

When, months earlier, the content of Father's will had come to my attention, they had assumed in my eyes the aspect of preposterous. But now that he was dead, they were more sinister, and the problems posed more pressing. The thought of conforming to the conditions of the will, and thus winning for myself a precarious inheritance never for a moment entered my head. But was there not some way, even a symbolic way, in which I could be true to Father's wishes? Not literally of course. How, without causing more devastation than I dared contemplate, could I possibly marry Christina? But look deeper. Was that, in the obscure recesses of his mind, what Father had really wanted? What he had wished for surely was plain: a settling of old sores, a healing. And in our own way, without observing the letter of his commands, could we not indeed prove faithful?

It was while sorting through the papers in March that I came across a tattered and dog-eared Guide to Hampton Court, issued by the Ministry of Works in 1952. It was several nights since I had suffered that dream, but this discovery seemed at least fortuitous. Then I remembered what Andria had said in bed several nights before about the necessity of disillusioning Christina, and determined at once on an expedient. I would obey my summons, enact Father's tryst. I would meet Christina in the principality of my childhood and see where events, or perhaps the presiding spirit of my father, led me.

Five minutes later, I was on the phone.

"Christina."

"Ben."

"Look, are you free next Thursday?"

"Not during the day, no. Why?"

"I want to see you. Something important."

"I'm not really free 'til Easter now. Bit tied up. I'm taking spiritual instruction you know."

"Golly. I mean, from a priest?"

"Yes, from a priest. He's set me these exercises. Quite time-consuming as it happens."

"Golly. I mean, Ignatius Loyola and things?"

"Ignatius Loyola and things."

"Gosh."

I let this sink in.

"Whips and scourges and things?"

"Not that extreme. What about Easter Monday?"

"If you like, but it will have to be latish."

"Dinner?"

"Where?"

"Hampton Court."

There was a puzzled pause on the other end before she said in quite another tone, "Why there?"

"I can't explain. I'll tell you when I see you. Do you know a place called the Mitre? It's by the bridge. You can get a train from Waterloo. It's a stone's throw from the station. Look, Christina, believe me, it's important…"

*****

Day by day as work on my own self-portrait progressed, I brought myself to consider the self-portraits of my Master. It must have been on the second or third of our visits to the National Gallery that Claud first introduced me to Rembrandt. At this stage, our sessions had assumed rather the character of lessons in art history. What I recall particularly is, on a dull September afternoon, being taken round to a quarter of the gallery still strange to me and being introduced to a Man in a Blue Sleeve. He looked unconscionably sure of himself - quite offensively cocky I thought at the time - and was apparently painted by somebody called Titian. Then I was led in virtual silence back a few rooms to another wall where a different man, thirty-four years of age it seemed though he looked to me fifty, stared out at me with an arrogance and haughtiness almost equally offensive, and, what is more, in the same position, though the sleeve this time was dark brown. Claud had then talked about something called "influence".

I wasn't all that interested in "influence". In fact, I'm not sure at this stage if I even knew quite what it meant. But I was interested in the signature. I remember squatting down on the cold parquet floor to look at it: *Rembrandt f.1640*. For months afterwards I tried to adapt my handwriting to his, going to immense pains to imitate the looped form of the R. Perhaps I had understood "influence" after all. In any case, that was apparently enough for one day. On the next occasion I was taken to an adjoining room and shown an old man in a russet coat who seemed to have absolutely no connection with the first, so unused was I to construe the continuity of twenty-six summers behind the hoary mask of sixty. In fact he looked rather like Dad. His lips were pursed in much the same way (did he too wear dentures?), his hair was greying, and he looked lost. What is more he held his hands together as if to warm the fingers (Father had poor circulation, and already on January days his fingertips were blue). Claud then said, this is also Rembrandt.

To be frank, it did not seem possible. What had happened to the swaggering grandee in the other room? He looked frightened, and his nerve seemed to have failed him. This was all the more confusing because Claud then proceeded to talk about something called "courage", the very last quality the portrait seemed to display. Not physical courage I was told, but moral courage, the courage to face up to "the depredations of time". Depredations, which I'd had to check up in the dictionary, seemed about right: "Rembrandt van Rijn" looked washed up, finished. It was years before I got to know the grotesque self-travesty in Cologne, skin the colour of putty, cheeks like old wind bags, carriage stooped beneath a homely scarf, eyes staring out with all the obscenity of senile vacuity.

I was in my twenty-sixth year then, and Claud's word came back to me: "courage". How much courage was needed to paint that picture with trembling hand, to avow the shrivelling of the blossom of youth (the self-conscious swagger of the Florence portrait) into a veritable death's head. *Sic transit gloria mundi* I allowed, but how could he bring himself, I had learned to inquire, so manfully to shoulder the scythe?

But at sixteen and a half such sophisticated wisdom was, I fear, beyond me. Was Claud trying to tell me something? Catholic as we both were, a certain Celtic Calvinism seemed to pervade these occasions, as if art's lessons were life's also. Was he using the paintings to preach, or was he, as I choose to see it now, more likely just warning me?

There was one painting by Rembrandt of 1635 which definitely partook of the nature of a warning. It hung in the same room as the earlier of the two portraits, and it was called *Belshazzar's Feast*. It was based on an episode from the Biblical Book of Daniel. The King of Babylon was dining with his wives and concubines, one of whom had just spilled the wine. She had spilled it because Belshazzar had risen from the table as if with a bad case of heartburn, though in fact he was staring behind him toward a disembodied hand framed in a white cloud which was writing a message backwards. The message was incomprehensible, but I took Claud's word for it that the letters were Hebrew. They apparently read *Mene, Mene, Tekel, Upharsin*, and meant: "Thou hast been tried in the balance and found wanting." Twice we finished our visits with this picture. It seemed to hold some special significance for him. Had Claud himself been tried in the balance? Had I?

In the intervening years other portraits had crossed my path most, not all, of which I discovered for myself. Two in Vienna I remember particularly: the working painter, hands on hips (Kenwood House, a mere bus ride from my student lodgings, had another such with palette and easel), and that premonition of self-doubt, *Self-portrait in a Wide-Brimmed Beret:* the eyes tightly defensive around the vulnerable ridge of the nose, the mouth slack and dejected. In Edinburgh he seemed buttoned up against the cold, his hat snug over his ears, the lips taut and determined. I confess it was Claud who had pointed me in the direction of this one; it was Claud also who, on the occasion of my parents' silver wedding, bequeathed a reproduction of the Berlin portrait which over the years I had by dint of constant study I suppose come to know better than any other: a man of twenty-eight, a married man in the fullness of health, the beret (surely the identical garment as appears in the Florence portrait, painted the very same year) pulled firmly against the crown of the head, the darling of fortune, the husband of Saskia, Titus's omniscient father.

Then, in the third week of March, six months after the birth of our daughter, a gift arrived by post. It came wrapped in stout brown paper bearing the postmark

'Engelfield Green'. It was Andria who answered the door, skimpily clad in the last of father's frayed dressing gowns, already showing a hapless window at the side. I threw the parcel down on the Japanese bedspread and tore away many layers of wrapping, each one thinner than the last, revealing at length a fine reproduction of *Belshazzar's Feast*. On an enclosed slip of paper curled the address of some guest house near Windsor, beneath which in Claud's inimitable calligraphy were inscribed the words "Study for a Feast of Fools?"

I looked up at Andria.

"Whatever does he mean?" I murmured. Outside, in the guttering beyond the windowpane, chaffinches were nesting.

*****

I made last minute preparations for that Easter Monday night. It was now March 31st, Easter Sunday, and I'd been to Mass in the morning. (Easter was one of the few feasts I then observed.) My plan was to travel down to Cheam that evening, spend the night there and the following morning doing some more clearing up in the house, then take the train down to Hampton Court late in the afternoon. For months, apart from the funeral, I'd slopped around in sweaters, cords and casual shoes, but as the evening of that ambiguous assignation approached, I found myself thinking quite uncharacteristically of what I might actually wear. Did it, could it, possibly mean that much? At one level I had committed myself to something like a game of hazard; at another it was a celebration or some sort of feast, at which for once in my life I'd elected to play the host. And the guests: well, I had invited Christina to dinner, that much was clear. But was it her, and her alone, that I had invited? At times as I prefigured her sitting there in the plush surroundings of the Mitre, a whole troupe of ghosts seemed to file behind her back and one by one to take their places at the table. One sat in the chair beside her, lifted her hand and placed it in mine. The ghost wore the face of my father.

And then I remembered - for it had not occurred to me at the time - why of all places I had suggested the Mitre. My mind went back fifteen years to a pimply, adenoidal lad who had squatted in a suit too tight for him drinking soup while the talk drifted on to property values and esoteric questions of taxation. Later, light-headed and more than a little bored, he had sat self-consciously sipping a liqueur which appeared to have been named after him, while somebody in pin-stripe paid halting compliments to his parents. Presents lay around the table: silver plated forks amid tissue wrapping; a miniature pendulum clock whose gold pillared front seemed equally plated, and flowers with prosaic inscriptions. The voice rose and fell amid insincere guffaws, cheroot smoke wafted in the pearl lamplight, the waiters came and went, the last with a reckoning which he inconspicuously handed to Echardt. From where he sat slightly to the left of the orator - whose public speaking seemed more than proverbially unaccustomed - Echardt rose slightly on his thin haunches, placing his hand discreetly within his jacket as he did so. Noticing the movement, my father made a gesture with his own hand towards the equivalent vicinity, the offertory intention of which was smartly gainsaid by a motion from Echardt's. We went out into the February air, smoke trains cavorting in the chill. Another anniversary, another duty done.

But was it a trick of memory, or was it sober truth, that as the couples made their way to their waiting vehicles on that long-lost February night, and felicitations and apologies pervaded the air, the woman on whose arm Echardt stepped from the lofty portico of the hotel was in fact my aunt Rosie? Boredom distorts the recollection of that evening, wishful thinking came after it, but the conjunction was not impossible, nor in that innocent time, when adult relationships were taken as part of the given structure of the world, did it behove me - or perhaps even occur to me - to ask questions. If so, it must have been the only time I saw them together in the same company before my father's funeral.

It can only have been a sense of similar momentousness which caused me on the morning of my dinner date to don a pensioned off suit of mine I found hanging in the bedroom of Dad's house. When my Bohemian alter persona considered this eccentric piece of behaviour, I told it I would be seeing Christina, but I wanted first of all to call on Dad's lawyers. This was true enough, but it was not for the solicitor that the suit was intended. In any case, when I phoned the lawyer's offices in Sutton there was no answer. It was only then that I recalled that it was a public holiday, so their offices would be closed. Eight hours later, I sat in the Mitre, holding Christina's hand in mine.

The place had changed a good deal. I last remembered it in the era of serviettes in rings, when lit by suspended oak chandeliers and panelled in the sort of light stained wainscoting then associated with the Tudor style but inseparable in my mind with the dining rooms of respectable department stores of the second rank. Wimbledon stores must all have had such dining rooms, as had our local emporium in Finchley. Somehow the whole ensemble had contrived to suggest less a banqueting hall than the venue of a tea dance such as I supposed my father to have attended in his remote youth. This time the panels were darker, the lights recessed. The napkins were extraordinary concoctions in pink, the flambée tray gleamed, execrable muzak oozed on a continuous tape. The food was poorer, and the menu lavishly written in language supposedly productive of salivation, but in practise of mirth. We had laughed a good deal over the description of the rather ordinary Dover sole over whose bones Echardt's daughter now sat smiling as I told her about Claud's gift, and its elusive message. "Meet for a Feast of Fools, it said."

"Well, Ben, it is All Fool's Day."

"So it is. So it is. Sometimes, I must confess, I do feel like a fool."

"Sometimes, you look like one. But it's well after

Midday. Too late for tricks now. In any case, Ben dear, would I ever make a fool out of you?"

I was not sure how to respond to this remark, but then she said, "Ben, your eyes are closing."

"I've been up since six."

"Hardly your style."

"No, hardly."

If we held one thing in common, Christina and I, beyond the supposed but to her unknown bonds of our flesh, it was the kind of minimal Englishness which permits discretion on matters of moment. My Dutch relatives would, I am sure, have sized up the needs of the situation immediately and solemnly have declared their intentions. But this was no part of my design nor, I was pleased to note, did the mood of the evening yet require it.

"So why so early?"

"There is something about an empty house that makes it seem fuller than a full one. That's not very clear is it? Well, perhaps it's not supposed to be. The place is kind of filled with absence. You feel obliged to get up because there is nobody to invite you to breakfast."

"Except yourself."

"Not even me. The toaster's broken. And coffee's hardly breakfast. Well, it is in Kensal Rise, but in Cheam the rules are parental. I actually went out yesterday and bought myself some bacon."

"Bacon?"

"Yes, bacon. And then I had toast."

"I thought you said the toaster…"

"I did it by the fire. You know, sort of holding it…"

We ordered our sweets and, while they came, she nibbled at the carcass of a roll and asked, "What are you doing in Cheam exactly?"

"Tidying things. Well, as best I can…"

"Much to tidy?"

"Books, furniture, journals. Sometimes I just want to gather the whole lot and tip it all in some builder's skip conveniently placed in the garden."

"Is there one?"

"Oh no, not in Cheam. It's the sort of place were workmen do their tasks quietly and then flit away unseen. Lower orders. Sometimes I feel like one of them myself."

"Poor Ben."

I released her hand, leant back in my chair, and felt the atmosphere tauten.

"Much legal stuff?"

"No. Yes. Well, quite a lot, and most of it well out of my ken. All to do with probate law. As you say, not my style…"

"Poor Ben. You will have to become responsible."

"Me. Responsible?" I raised my hands in what I hoped was a gesture of becoming helplessness.

"You can't make that gesture for ever."

I examined my hands. "No," I said and lowered them. "I can't."

"Surely there's only you. I should have thought it quite straightforward, except for the house of course, and you can put that in the hands of agents."

"Well, it's less straightforward than I expected. There's my aunt, for a start. She must get something. The will indicates a proportion, but it's not clear what of. The total amount of the legacy depends on lots of sub-clauses I don't even pretend to understand. I do wish they'd turn off this music." Romantic slush was swilling round the dining room, invading auditory and other nerves. Muted strings had just simulated ecstasy for the fourteenth time since the hors-d'oeuvre. I called a waiter and politely protested. I was told the other patrons appreciated it, and that in any case it was only the best variety of muzak. I let it pass and miserably picked at my mousse. When this paroxysm had subsided, Christina asked, "Wouldn't your father's solicitor help you? He's sure to have had one."

"Oh yes, he had one in Sutton. I meant to see them this afternoon, then I remembered that it's a Bank Holiday. Look, Christina, do you mind if we continue this conversation outside?"

I paid the bill hurriedly, then we left. We crossed the road to the steps by the bridge and clattered down to the deserted riverbank. To our left lay the palace shrouded in gloom; to our right pleasure launches bobbed beneath tarpaulins. The water made a swish against the jetty; the whole width of the river was under one immense shadow fitfully lit by moonlight. Where the moonlight hit moving water, little highlights danced and shone. I took Christina's arm. As we paced the bank in perfect consort she asked: "Well, did you go and see my father?"

"Oh that. He just wanted to express his condolences. Nothing serious."

Silence, shadows, inscrutable swans. "I saw your reviews," she added nonchalantly, after an interval.

"Were they all that dreadful?"

"Pretty dire."

"It wasn't a complete disaster, you know. Someone bought five pictures."

"Yes I know. It was Dad. He's put two of them up at home, including the portrait of me."

"Honestly?" It was hard not to sound crest-fallen.

"Yes, I'm afraid so."

A vague plashing was heard in the darkness. "But why on earth?"

"Helping the struggling painter, that sort of thing. He seems to feel responsible for you in a strange kind of way."

"It's not as if we were related or anything."

"I think that in Pater's eyes we are. You should hear him going on about you sometimes, almost as if he'd promised to look after you. Society for the Protected of Benighted Benedicts, that sort of thing. It's part of his Edwardian code of honour to aid lost causes. I'm sure he's got the impression you're just the weeniest bit helpless."

"Whatever can have given him that impression?"

"Things my dad must have told him. Me too probably."

I halted our progress and looked over the Tijou railings to our left. We had drawn level with the Banqueting

House, the gables of which were just visible beyond the trees. I stepped back out of the moonlight towards the railings, so that we were in a little coverlet made by the branches. We stood listening to the silence and the slight soughing of the wind.

"Good place for a tryst," I said softly and kissed her gently on the forehead. Her skin was cold, and lightly scented with musk. Then I drew apart from her and said "So you've been discussing me behind my back? A few months ago you didn't even know my name properly. You called me Henry."

"Did I now?"

"Yes, you got me quite the wrong way round."

"Dear Benedict," she said invisibly, "you're ever so believing. Henry just seemed to suit you somehow. Like a steam engine. Plucky and indomitable. One of life's gallant failures."

"Thanks."

"Well, I did say gallant."

I took a few steps back towards the river and looked across the railings at the palace, the roof and chimneys of which were irradiated by a faint of aureole of light. The wind was growing stronger now, and there was a crackling amid the branches.

"I don't know why you agreed to come this evening," I said, "if that's your attitude".

"I just thought you might be a bit down, that's all. In the doldrums, that sort of thing. There's a Florence Nightingale in all of us."

"I'm glad I'm such a deserving cause."

"It's not so much that you're deserving. In fact, I'm not so sure you deserve anything very much. You just seem to get prior attention, like a relative in need."

I suppressed the reply which suggested itself and instead asked, "Are you implying I need you?"

"Well you must, I suppose. Otherwise, why am I here?"

"Oh, don't worry," I said. "I'll manage."

"Fighting Temeraire?"

"Fighting Temeraire. But scarcely to my last berth. I'm a long way off the scrapyards."

"Bloody but unbowed?"

"Look Christina. I've got to tell you something."

"Do we have to? Perhaps it's something I already know."

"I don't think you do. I'll just tell you and then, if you like, you can tow me off into that sunset over there."

We were looking northwards towards the palace, which was surrounded by its nimbus of light. "That's not a sunset," she said. "It's not even the West."

"Well, whatever is it then?"

From left to right, across the whole span of the horizon, the sky was lit by an orange glow. At first I thought it might be luminosity from the streetlights, but the colour was wrong, nor could it be a trick of the moonlight. I took several paces back towards the riverbank, then stood on my toes, attempting to peer over the lime trees of the nearer gardens towards the south front, the chimneys of which were now obscenely and unnaturally visible, illuminated by some shifting phantasmagoria of light. My second thought was that unbeknown to us a *son et lumière* performance was in progress, of the sort in which the National Trust and other bodies entrusted with the care of ancient monuments delighted. But the season was wrong, and in any case the palace grounds seemed resolutely shut. My third thought was to scale the railings, difficult at this point, but I managed by placing my left foot in Christina's cupped hands to get a purchase on the top, which was speared but manageable. Then I half sat, half squatted on the top of the railings immediately behind the Banqueting House and looked north.

The whole length of the roof of the King's Wing, from just above the presence chambers in the west to the vicinity of the King's bedchamber in the east, was pyrotechnically alive. Shards of flame were billowing across it eastwards in the direction of the wind, inter-dispersed with sparks performing a kind of maenad dance in the darkness. The crackling we had had heard a few minutes previously was nothing to do with the trees under which we stood. It was the muted cacophony of a conflagration, the intensity of which could be sensed even at this distance, some three hundred yards from the palace.

"Quick. It's the King's Rooms," I said, and with one almighty bound leapt over the railings and landed in the moist vegetation on the other side.

"What on earth?"

"Come on!"

I cupped my own hands between two of the nearer

railings and, with what seemed like preternatural swiftness, Christina jumped over to join me. I took her hand, and we raced up the avenue of lime-trees to the right of the Privy Garden. Then, when we reached the gravelled walkway underneath the King's Front, I let go of her hand, and walked forwards by myself.

Most of the two upper floors of the central recessed section of the King's Wing was burning quite steadily. From where I stood the skewering flames formed a frieze against the darkness, twisting up from the balustrade of the top storey like the fringe along a brazier, or the flames of Blake's own Hell. Even from down here, the heat was very strong. There was a thud as a beam fell in, a yell like a bell tone, a tinkling of fallen glass.

"Whatever can have happened?" Christina called, her voice hammered out by the din.

"Hard to tell. Some damn fool idiot did it my accident, I expect. People live in the upper storeys. Old people."

"God!"

Whatever the cause, it had been going on for some time. We were very far from alone. Two fire-engines were parked near the vine house ineptly spouting foam, and there were others to our right. In between, the paths beneath the burning section were a cacophony of gesture. Figures blundered past, lit eerily by the glare. A footfall echoed in the darkness behind me. A hand on my shoulder: "Get out of the way, son. Unless you'd like to help."

I stood there undecided as a padded rectangle was

thrust into my hands which jerked up to receive it. Something nudged me in the ribs, the edge jagged through the wrapping. Christina came up, her perfume brackish in the heat.

"What are they doing?"

"Saving the pictures. Look, put this over there."

I handed her the bundle, shrouded like a Crucifix in Holy Week.

"Where?"

"Over there for now."

There was a stack of bundles by the wrought iron latch gate of the Pond Garden. From above, light squibs fitfully lit up the parterres. Christina took the burden from me, the coarse canvas slipping through my fingers as it went. Then she humped it over and dropped it crudely on the top of the growing pile. Then she came back.

"Anymore?"

"Oh, there's plenty more. Most of the masterpieces were in the King's Rooms." I stared upwards. "Were".

To our right a human chain had formed, just in front of the Vine House. The great exposed bed accommodating the roots of the vine was a mill of people shouting. They were handing out bundles from a gate at the centre of the south wing, while the larger pieces - unwieldly squares some twenty feet wide - were being manhandled crudely through the gate, up the path and into the Vine House, the door of which lay ajar.

Each picture needed three or four men to carry it. A fireman was guiding them, as if they were traffic.

"Grab this one!" said someone in my right ear. I staggered over to the wrought iron gate with the bundle and placed it as carefully as I could on top of the growing pile. Then I went back for more. The bundles were arriving in a continual stream now. There was a sort of exhilaration mixed up in the panic. I craned my neck to look once more at the upper floor where the fiercest part of the inferno could now be observed through the oval windows, like some internal vision of torment, Armageddon trapped. Shapes writhed in the furnace, iron rods, pipes, silhouettes as in a Javanese puppet show. I stepped back the better to see and a face passed me in the gloom, half perceived, the body in the shadow, the features luridly lit up.

"Lay hold of that," a low voice said. "Guard it well." I took the proffered parcel, staggering beneath the weight of it, and felt against my cheek a sudden whiplash of wind.

I wanted to thank him, so I looked across and saw his face loom briefly towards me, distorted like a face in a fairground mirror, gaze intently and depart. Then he stumbled off by the low wall of the sunken garden, hogging the dwarf hedge, snaking amid the crowd. Above his shoulder he carried another load having, I can only assume, fetched two from the palace, the lesser of which he had given to me. That remaining was heavy enough for two men, and he lumbered under it as if under a cross - not a major martyr, but outer acolyte at a Crucifixion, St Joseph of Arimathea in a minor master, some martyrology in a provincial Bavarian gallery. I stared after him, my eyeballs flinching from the searing heat.

"Claud!" I yelled - it had been seconds before I found my voice.

"Claud!" The tall figure turned round - had I been mistaken? The features grew sterner, hortative. I heard, as if lip-reading from an immense distance, the words, "Save them. Save the pictures", the voice that spoke them thinned out by the wind. A phrase vortexed up through the darkness, from some deeper region of my mind: "*Domine, serva nos*", and then I saw him no longer.

"Yes," I said subduedly, more to myself that to him, and then bumped backwards into Christina.

"How many can they have saved?"

"I don't know. All, most. Except for the panelling. I don't give much of a chance for all that Grinling Gibbons."

Lime wood burns. I recalled my father, on a lambent day in March, taking me aside by the panelling in the Presence Chamber, and tracing its shapes in the heated air with one gloved finger - tendrils, pomegranates, twined couplings of fruit. Father liked such wooden fruit, safe like still lives. Fruit was useful. "Now that's something I do appreciate," he'd said to my mother, who was admiring an architectural fantasy by Jacques Rousseau over one of the doors. Had I handed that Rousseau out? No fantasies for Father. Fruit you could put a price on. Of what use now? Gibbons was carbon, Gibbons was charred.

"Look, I can't take any more," Christina said. "Can we go back nearer the river?"

We stepped back out of the glare into pitch darkness, shielded by the long west wall of the Privy Garden, where the avenue of limes led off southwards towards the river. To the back of us were the glassy slopes down which I'd tobogganed as a child, under the watchful eye of Hamish. Christina was close to me now, sweat mixing with her perfume. I turned my face toward her to see a little rill of sweat coursing down her neck, soaked up by her fur collar.

"Sad."

"Yes."

"They'll restore it."

Consolation is like gruel. "Ever read Ruskin on restorations? Anyway it will take millions of pounds, and years."

A crash was heard above us, and looking back I could see that a whole section of the upper structure had given away, like a tooth that falls out suddenly, incontrovertibly. My cheek felt wet, and suddenly I realised that there were tears in my eyes.

I had not cried, I think, since they kicked me out of the Slade.

"That's my childhood up there," I said, and unaccountably my chin was moving.

I fumbled in the pockets of my cords, looking for something to mop it up. "And guess who I saw - well, I think so?"

Christina did not answer. She was standing several feet

away, staring up at the ruination of the palace, her hands in the pockets of her flared, black coat. Then she turned her face to me. She was smiling now, a pale smile of sorrow.

"There is nothing one can say is there?" she said after a moment. "About any of it, I mean. Nothing one can say, ever?"

"No." I had to shout it out to make myself heard over the distance and the shindy beyond her. "Nothing."

"Ben," she asked, her voice softened and inquisitive. "What were you about to tell me? Before this happened, I mean."

"Oh that. That wasn't anything important."

She looked at me fixedly for maybe three seconds and then she lowered her eyes. She had not got her answer, and thinking back over the whole experiment of the evening, I could not help wondering whether I had got mine. But one thing I did discover. Christina turned away, and as she did so I saw once more what I had known and lost, what had made it all perversely worthwhile, all that muddle and hurt pride. All that heartache. Her tall figure was a graceful silhouette. Across the paleness of her neck, her hair swept down in one voluptuous curve. Women wear their beauty like costumes: most beautiful when, momentarily, they forget what they are wearing.

Clamour. Footfalls. Scorching. The roof fell in.

"No, nothing important really."

BOOK FIVE:

THE JUDGEMENT OF PARIS

BOOK FIVE

Events moved pretty quickly after that. Ten days after the Hampton Court fire, I called at the solicitor's offices in Sutton half-an-hour earlier than my appointed time and sat in the sparsely furnished waiting room glancing at the newspapers. *The Daily Telegraph* carried an interview with Doig. He was looking smug in the accompanying photo, leaning with his left elbow on his desk, ogling at the camera and sporting striped braces. His replies to the questions put to him by the paper's arts correspondent, however, hinted at problems. "Life sometimes brings you up short," he was quoted as saying at one point. "Life can sometimes be tough."

I wasn't quite sure what Doig had meant by this, so I turned to the previous Saturday's *Surrey Comet*. It had a double-page spread featuring back-and-white photos of the gutted palace. "Some members of the public," it reported, "helped to remove precious artefacts, including paintings, from the stricken building."

When I was admitted to see the lawyer, I was told that the provisions of Father's will were all valid, unless it could be proved that the fulfilment of his wishes was contrary to law, or else to what the lawyer euphemistically termed "public policy".

"A whitewash term, Mr Henry, and not one on which the law books offer much guidance. We are in the realm of legal precedent, you understand, not of statute. I am not an expert in this particular branch of law, but these difficulties do sometimes arise. The best I can say at the moment is this: that if the literal enactment of the testator's conditions can be demonstrated as leading inevitably to actual and palpable suffering, or to the deprivation of clearly enunciated rights, the court might feel moved to discount them."

I did not know what all this meant, and neither I suspect did he. It was the sort of language my father used when cornered. I pressed the man a bit harder than was customary with me, upon which he mentioned the "desired cohesion of families, and the rights of unborn children." This seemed like a chink of light, so I told him what he apparently did not know, and explained about Andria and Titania. He looked, I remember, less shocked than intrigued, promised to consult an expert in probate law, then issued me out of his office, shaking my hand in the passage with, I thought, unnecessary firmness.

On the way back in the train I got to thinking about Doig. What had he meant by the hints of discouragement in that newspaper interview? Up until then, I had not had the faintest inkling of his dark side. Naively, I suppose, I had always taken him for a shameless extrovert, what in the vocabulary of a later generation came to be known as an "arsehole". Perhaps, I thought for the first time, the impression of him that I had carried with me for over fifteen years was something of an oversimplification. Was his exuberance and boastfulness a recoil from inner doubts? The point about Doig was that he was a deeply disarming and perplexing creature: a generous bully. Perhaps it was inevitable that, somewhere along the line, the bullyboy attitude, and the basic humility entailed by his occasional fits of generosity, should come apart.

I have been pondering this question quite a bit lately, and with particular persistence since Doig's early death at which, as I have said already, I rejoiced when it happened. In fact, when I heard of it on the radio in the year 2011, I jumped bodily in the air. It is now clear to me that at such moments I was simply remembering one half of him. There must, I think, have been sadder undercurrents all along, or what subsequently happened would be inexplicable. I often think about this, and in search of an answer yesterday I dipped for the first time in many years into Jocelyn's biography of him. Turning to the relevant chapter, "Success and Faltering", I was gratified to read that in his account of our – or should I say Doig's - exhibition, he does actually get round to mentioning me, but somewhat in the light of a younger artist whom Doig had once magnanimously encouraged but who, so the implication runs, had not since quite fulfilled his potential.

True enough. But towards the end of that chapter, Jocelyn does indicate a gradual darkening of Doig's mood in the later 1980s. This is not in itself surprising, but in view of the personal distance between the two men at which I have hinted, and which in his book Jocelyn is careful to disguise, I am a little surprised that he had picked it up the signs so early. Had Christina perhaps conveyed to him something of Doig's changing mood? I really must ask Jocelyn the next time we meet. This is more seldom than it might be, owing to Andria's increasingly possessive attitude since her sixties. It is a wonder, I sometimes think, that she allows him out at all, even to meet me.

Back then, however, she did seem a lot less clinging. So that when, a few days after my visit to the solicitor's, I again broached the question of Father's commission and asked whether she and Titania could come to Holland with me, she replied, "Look, I need time and space. I'm working on the thesis still, and then there's this paper about Terence. It's difficult as it is, what with the demands of dear Titania and everything."

There was then an awkward pause. To break the silence, I called, "Andria?"

"Yes, beloved?"

"I did what you said."

"Uh, huh?"

"I saw Christina."

"When?"

"Last week. After I'd been down to Cheam."

"Well, did you tell her? About Rosie and everything?"

"Yes. The lot."

"Where?"

"By the river. We met for an early dinner."

"And …"

"Hampton Court burned down."

I had just entered the flat. Outside it was a luminous day, the sort of spring day when even the dustbins shine, when the grottiest parts of London look verdant, the parks like Paradise. For the first time in months I had no topcoat to remove. But back inside, I seemed to have stepped back several weeks. Winterly Andria peered at me over her studying glasses. "Yes, I'd heard actually."

"Only the King's Rooms, mind you. The rest of the palace seems to be intact."

"What were you doing in Hampton Court?"

"It seemed a convenient place to meet. Halfway between Cheam and Pimlico. Well, nearer to Cheam."

"So you told her everything? About her being your cousin and so on?"

"Yes, everything."

"Gospel? Cross your heart?"

"Cross my heart."

"Well, at least it cleared the air."

"I thought so."

"Oh Ben, Ben. I believe you're growing up."

Our daughter was sleeping in her new cot. As she slept, Andria tinkered with her work. She had, she said, almost finished a draft of two chapters. The thesis was entitled "Columella and the Later Traditions of Bucolic Writing in Rome, together with Certain Remarks on the Georgics of Virgil." She had phoned her supervisor who had expressed certain doubts about the "certain remarks." Could she not remove them? Andria contemplated the comparative merits of the doubts and of the remarks. It seemed finally as if the doubts would win. In the meantime she fed Titania out of a bottle every four hours and had taken to nagging me intermittently about Holland.

"But Ben, you must do what your dad asked. It's only reasonable."

"I can't go to Middelharnis now. Not until the estate's been settled."

"Oh that. That'll take months. Go now. It's spring."

I glanced at Titania in her basket. "But I don't want to go alone. How will you two manage?"

"Oh, we'll cope. Jocelyn will help us. Jocelyn will always help us."

"Good old Jocelyn."

Yes, solicitous as ever, Jocelyn the True, Jocelyn the Just, Jocelyn would help. With Jocelyn the remarks would always win over the doubts. He still called round every morning, and during my absences in Cheam it had been oftener.

"Still," I said, "I would hate to leave you both."

*****

A couple of days later I was about to make arrangements for my journey when the phone went again and, after several breathy seconds, a wavering female voice with a marked Irish lilt asked, "Excuse me. Is this a Mr Henry?"

"Speaking?"

There was another breath-filled pause.

"I'm sorry to phone you at this hour." (It was four o'clock in the afternoon.) "The truth is I didn't know who else to contact. It's about one of our guests…"

They had found my contact details in a threadbare wallet stuffed into the back pocket of his neatly folded trousers on the back of a bedside chair. I had always assumed Claud to be ancient. In fact, he was only seventy-two, which by today's standards seems young. He'd gone in the night, and had been found cold in the bed – I can scarcely say "his" bed - when they entered the room to give it a weekly clean. He had not been down to breakfast for a couple of days, and they'd assumed he was resting, or out. The landlady seemed upset: he'd been staying there on and off for years. "Such a gentleman," she said. "A real old-style gent … And so regular in his habits … We are not quite sure what to do with his things…"

"Is there much?"

"Well, there's coats in the wardrobe, and other clothes in the sideboard. Shoes of course. A battered leather suitcase. The main thing is that there's this bundle under the bed…"

"Bundle?"

"Yes, he's brought it along before. Wrapped in an old blanket and done up with twine. We've no idea what it is … If you could come and see. There's also a letter, quite separate, in a brown paper envelope."

"Not straightaway, I'm afraid."

"Yes, but soon. We don't want to seem ungracious, but we need the room."

There was a lump in my throat, so I just said, "Not today, but yes, very soon." People die in packs, they say. More poignantly they queue at the traffic lights, mournfully yet expectantly, like London buses. The number six queued thus, and so in distant, tube-less Camberwell, did the Number three. For Claud, I thought, the lights had stalled at amber for what seemed like years now. In the early summer of 1986, the lights had eventually turned green. Except that, in the case of human mortality, green of course means red.

In the absence of wife or offspring, I was - I soon realised - the next of kin. There were a number of practical steps that needed to be taken, as I was well aware after Father's recent decease. I gave the landlady permission to contact a local undertaker in Kilburn, and said I'd pay, not knowing quite how. After that, I wasn't sure how to proceed, so on an impulse I phoned Jake. My uncle deserved a decent, Catholic send off, and he was unlikely to have had a parish priest of his own. I got the usual answer machine and left a message. Early the following morning Jake got back to me and said that he'd be performing some errands in the middle of town that day, and could I meet him about lunchtime in the Church of Saint Anselm and Cecilia on Kingsway, just down from Holborn tube. It seemed to be convenient for both of us since it's on both the Central and the Piccadilly lines. When I called back to confirm the arrangement, Jake said he'd be sitting in the nave at quarter past one, just after midday mass.

I got to Kingsway early and sat for twenty minutes in the Shakespeare Head pub sipping at a tomato juice with plenty of Worcester Sauce. Then at ten past one I sauntered down the road to the church. It has a broad and welcoming façade in a sort of garish neo-Byzantine style. People, mostly middle-aged women, were leaving after Mass. At the entrance I nearly bumped into a tramp who was begging apologetically at the door (beggars were more of a rarity in London in those days). He was dressed in a grubby mac, had a somewhat furtive air, and at first sight I mistook him for Claud. "Of course," I immediately thought, "it can't be…" It was the second of the phantom resemblances that were to afflict me for some years. The first had been by the Thames when we were clearing paintings during the Hampton Court fire, but there were to be several others of varying degrees of vividness. I'll tell you about them as we come to them. Even nowadays I can be arrested in mid-stride when walking down a high street and am momentarily convinced my late uncle is approaching me along the opposite pavement. It can be disconcerting at times. On this occasion I gave the man two twenty pence coins and wished him Good Day for the departed's sake. He thanked me with a touching old world courtesy that struck at the heart.

If the entrance to the church is Baroque, the interior is pleasantly plain. There were one or two figurines of saints in the side-chapels of course, and the flicker and scent of candles in the semi-gloom. As you approach the main altar it grows brighter, and the sanctuary and the wide arch to the chancel are stark white. Jake was sitting in the third row of pews from the front reading a paperback of a book by Tielhard de Chardin. It was called *The Phenomenon of Man*. He looked up and gave me a brief, comradely smile. (As a student, if I remember right, he'd usually scowled. Then he moved up and made room for me along the seat.) There was an embarrassed silence for a little while before he asked me if I'd been there previously. Once, I said, after attending an event at Saint Martin's. I couldn't think what to say next, so I remarked, "Odd mixture of saints. Saint Anselm, Saint Cecilia. Cecilia's music, but the other one…"

"Oh, I can do that. Archbishop of Canterbury under the Normans. Cured William Rufus of his sickness. Invented the Ontological Proof for the Existence of God. That's about all I know…"

"Ontological Proof?"

"Well, I'll put it to you as it was put to me as a trainee priest. God is by definition perfect. Existence is an attribute of perfection because, without it, perfection wouldn't be really perfect. Right? So if God is really perfect, he must exist."

It sounded so neat and yet so unconvincing I was a bit stuck for a reply. But I thought for a little and then said, "Isn't there a flaw in that argument somewhere?"

"Tell me."

"Well imagine a perfectly beautiful woman. She wouldn't be perfect in her beauty unless she existed.

Therefore this beautiful woman would have to exist…"

"Perhaps she does. And perhaps you could paint her."

"Perhaps she does." I replied deliberately. "And perhaps I did." We seemed unexpectedly to have come to the point, so I continued, "I knew a man who thought like that. He was my uncle…"

"The one who's just died. You were telling me about him. Didn't I once catch sight of him?"

"At my father's funeral, yes. He was standing near the back."

"Ben, tell me about him."

I had this sudden idea. "I can do better than that," I said, "I can show you. Are you doing anything for the next hour?

"Well, the printers down the street are running off our parish magazine. I said I'd collect them by three."

"Well then, let's walk."

From Kingsway to Trafalgar Square, it's about a fifteen minute's stroll, brushing past L.S.E. types on the way to the Aldwych, and businessmen and shoppers along the Strand. As I accompanied Jake's more loping stride, I told him as much about Claud and his various oddnesses as it seemed necessary for him to know, including a bit about his background, and the relationship with my father which I'd always found so mysterious. As for his unearthly commission of the previous year, I relayed that in the most general of terms. Naturally I did not mention the Echardts for fear of opening old wounds. In my carefully edited account, Claud had laboured under an obsession with some unnamed girl, whom he'd asked me to paint. No harm there. All the same, we were skirting the crowded steps of Saint Martin's-in-the-Fields when it struck me that this had been a slightly rash move. But we'd gone too far, both physically and psychologically, to turn back.

There was no Sainsbury Wing in those days. You entered the newly scrubbed façade of the main Gallery building immediately off the square, by one of two broad flights of steps. We sidled past tourists consulting their cameras (today they'd have been scouring their phones). Nobody searched bags back then, so we were soon ascending the principal interior staircase towards the Early Italians, then sidling through the thronged outer rooms. At Piero della Francesca we turned right as I carefully guided him towards Holbein and the painting of Christina of Denmark in the room beyond. It seemed an appropriate spot in which to talk of Claud and his obsession.

There were one or two people standing in front of us. "Is this the girl?" Jake asked when they'd moved off.

"Yes. Do you know the painting?"

"Not a lot. Tell me."

"Henry the Eighth commissioned it because he was maybe interested in marrying the girl. So Holbein produced this rather idealised version of reality. It didn't work out."

"And so?"

"Claud wanted me to make a similarly flattering portrait of this other girl."

"And did you?"

"Not quite. You see, I'd known her before, and I knew she wasn't quite what she seemed."

There was, of course, nothing to connect the image on the canvas with our Christina, apart from the name, so he asked, "Meaning?"

"She was someone I'd fancied in the past. A friend encouraged me. I thought that she was interested too, but she went and fucked the friend."

"The bastard."

"Quite."

We both looked at the painting for a while. Jake seemed to be taking her in.

"And so what did you paint?" he inquired at last.

"Oh, something a bit more ordinary."

"Not what you were asked for?"

"No."

"Why not?"

"That would have been dishonest. You see, there's no such thing as perfection."

He thought for a while before saying slowly, "But I don't quite follow your logic. There are different ways of being real. One is to paint what a camera might see. Common-or-garden realism, you might call it. The other is to paint with understanding and vision. That might even be closer to the truth. At least, sometimes."

"I didn't think I was up to that."

"Why not?"

"It would be like painting what wasn't there."

"Not where?"

I painted straight at the Holbein: "There."

He looked at me with a quizzical expression I recalled of old. "But, Ben, it is there. It's there on condition that you see it. Or your uncle sees it. Or someone sees it."

"Sees what?"

"Sees perfection. Sees Beauty, sees Truth, whatever."

"But that's the whole point, Jake. Don't you get it? It wasn't true. It isn't true. That girl had hurt me. My friend, I thought, had betrayed and misled me. Almost I hated them."

"And do you still?"

I swallowed hard. "Sometimes."

His face now wore a haunted and devious look it had sometimes displayed when we had talked things over in Knight's Park during our Foundation year. Then he spoke in measured tones. "I'd say, Ben old man, that perfection is always there when and if you see it. And you can always see it. Suppose you stare at a tramp and see an angel. Aren't you peering through to what he or she might become?"

"You mean you convert them into someone else?"

"Isn't that what conversion means? What do you think it might mean?"

I was feeling scandalised, and not a little wrathful. "Distortion, then?" I yelled, and one or two gallery visitors briefly turned round.

"No," he replied with infuriating softness. "Not distortion. Vision. You see what God sees. God so loved the world, etc."

I had a flashing mental image of the Claud-like figure at the door of the church.

"Jake, that's nonsense and you know it."

"But it's what we do. It's what I do. Why ever else would I walk around dressed like this?"

Then Jake looked at his Seiko wristwatch. "Time to go. We haven't really discussed the requiem mass and things. Did you say your uncle died in Kilburn? I can borrow a church from a friend. They are not short of Irish folk in Kilburn. Some of my best friends live there. And some of my best enemies too. Do you carry a diary?"

As it happened, I'd brought my Collins pocket one, so we both scribbled in a date and time: provisionally the morning of the last Saturday in April, the twenty-sixth, in about ten days' time. He would have to check with his colleague to be sure that the church would be available. It would mean postponing my visit to Holland for another few days, but then I'd be free. Once we had put our diaries away, Jake had to leave to retrieve his magazines, so I accompanied him as far as the first floor landing. Awkwardly shaking hands, I told him I would phone to confirm the arrangements. He clomped down the stairwell and was soon lost in the crowds.

I felt, as you can well imagine, not a little wound up by this interview. I had also an hour or two to spare, since I'd told the landlady in Claud's digs that I would call round about seven. So, instead of following Jake out of the Gallery, I performed a tardy homage to the dead. I retraced my steps through the double swing doors and turned right towards the Flemish collection. Soon I was in the room devoted to Rubens and sat down on the

cushioned bench in front of his *The Judgement of Paris.*
On several occasions Claud and I had sat thus, intrigued
and not a little puzzled by the allegorical canvas before
us. It was a work that had seemed to preoccupy my
uncle, and also to trouble him. For several minutes that
day I stared at the floor, lost in thought as I attempted to
make sense of Jake's homily about Truth and Beauty.
Making no sense of it all, I lifted my eyes and
concentrated on the painting before me.

There it hung in all its puttied fleshiness. White: how
Rubens must have loved the paleness of northern skin,
found satisfaction in its dimmer tones. The whole of a
man's work: an apology for alabaster. Plaster saints: I
remembered Rosie on plaster saints, but the three ladies
disporting themselves before the seated Paris were no
saints, only too anxious for the earthbound regard of
Paris. Choose.

You will remember the composition. There to the right
is Hera or Juno, matronly and perturbed, her hair swept
backwards from the forehead. To the left stands Athene
or Minerva, her back to the onlooker, her right hand
sweeping out towards a group of shepherds to her left.
Beyond them a jade river leads toward a future
intermittently perceived. Athene has her face towards it:
she is the only one whose eyes are not directly turned to
Paris. It is her the cherubs indicate in a *sotto in su* group
suspended on a cloud at top of the picture, their fingers
pointing to her: Athene, Queen of the Air. Choose.

Paris is in a trance. Ignoring Zeus's Queen, ignoring
the Queen of the Air, he has eyes for one alone,

bestowing the coronet upon Aphrodite, her vermilion cloak parted to reveal peerless breasts; ample, dimpled thighs. Choose. And Paris has chosen: beauty, disorder, death. Iphigenia whimpering in Aulis, the dagger at her throat, Hector in the dust, the towers of Troy keeling. Sorrow, degradation, ruin: Paris had chosen them all.

Or had he? The painting conspires with the male myth according to which it is we who decide, we who do the choosing: of our womenfolk, and of the future. Yet, sitting there that distant afternoon, I could not help but suspect Rubens had been hinting at the very opposite: it was the three goddesses were doing the selecting, feeding Paris's egotism by pretending the power of selection is his. Certainly, it was the women who appeared to me to be the strong ones.

So who, I then got to thinking, was being judged after all: was it Paris, or the women? It all hung on the preposition, didn't it? Did the painting show a judgement *by* Paris, or the judgement *of* Paris? In the painting he looks weak, feckless, hounded by desire. If it all goes wrong, it is he who will be judged. I rose to my feet and made for the exit.

It had turned into quite a bright afternoon and, as I emerged from the building onto the dais at the head of the outer stairs, I was momentarily dazzled by the sunlight. For about half a minute I stood there overlooking Trafalgar Square, Nelson's column, the fountains, the pigeons, and the empty fourth plinth. Then, resolving to make for the underground, I swivelled to my right. I was about to descend the steps when I caught sight of a couple coming up towards me, arm in arm. They were engrossed in conversation, the man evidently somewhat older than the woman, and both were elegantly dressed. At first they did not see me, but then the man looked up, and both of them stopped. At this point I myself looked more closely. The woman was Christina, and the man was Doig.

None of us knew what to say. For perhaps five seconds they stood arrested on their lower step. Then they came up and joined me and we all went into a balletic pantomime of exaggeratedly polite gestures accompanied by conversational clichés.

"Well I never!" said Doig.

"Small world!" said I.

Doig bowed from the waist. I bowed from the waist. Christina smiled.

"Whatever are you doing here?" I asked.

"Come to see some pictures, Mmm?" he replied.

"Original that," I remarked.

"Quite," quoth Doig. He was, I now noticed, unshaven.

"You've met Christina," he perceptively observed. "Of course, you would have done. She was at your launch."

"So were you," I retorted. Doig laughed and bowed again. I laughed and bowed again. Christina stifled a smirk.

"Well," I said, "I won't detain you."

For a third time I bowed. Christina smiled, and looked sideways. "Thanks," said Doig. "I wish you a very good afternoon."

They dived into the building, heads lowered. Christina had not said a word.

*****

I spent the next two hours in the Chandos pub at the corner of Saint Martin's Lane. This time, I was drinking whisky. At about six, I lurched to my feet and, forgetting about the tube, made for my usual number six bus which I boarded at Charing Cross, alighting at Kilburn Lane. It was rush hour and, by the time I reached the guest house, I was ten minutes late. I was also slightly dizzy with drink. The landlady met me in the hall, which smelt of over-boiled cabbage; she was in something of a hurry, since they were cooking supper. They had already cleared Claud's room and packed his clothes into black plastic bags. I told her that she could send them to a local charity shop, giving her ten pounds for her trouble. Then I asked her about the mysterious "bundle" which she had stowed away in a cupboard under the stairs. It was wrapped in coarse plaid cloth and tied roughly with what looked like old fishing tackle. Inside was a dingy canvas of around nineteen inches by sixteen, held in a very dilapidated gilt frame loosening at the corners. With it, and tied to the picture with string, was a scruffy white square of card on which was written, in Claud's unmistakeable copperplate, "To Whom It May Concern." Beneath that was one sentence in the same hand that read, "I would like my nephew Benedict to have this."

Then I looked at the canvas. It showed an elderly tonsured monk or friar on his knees sniffing ecstatically at a length of dun-coloured fabric. His habit was brown, so I gathered that he was a Franciscan. His eyes were closed in fervent devotion, and there was an expression of rapt dedication on his face. Above him danced two cherubs, and there was an unexplained female figure held in a luminous cloud to their left. It left me nonplussed. Early Renaissance was what I guessed, possible Italian, though of course it might have been an example of much later pastiche. It could also have been a copy, or even a fake. Beyond that I had no idea. The obvious solution was to apply to Jocelyn for his opinion. With that end in view, I packed it up again, thanked the landlady, and left. I had quite forgotten to ask her for the separate letter in a brown envelope she had mentioned on the telephone and she, in the midst of her domestic chores, had neglected to give it me.

Back at the flat, I showed the mysterious canvas to Jocelyn, who by now had almost taken up residence in our flat, relieving the pressure on Andria and bonding satisfyingly with Titania. He suggested we seek further advice and volunteered to ferry the questionable bequest along to Christie's for an official valuation in a few days' time, when he had a moment. Naturally, I fell in with this plan.

*****

There are two Roman Catholic churches in Kilburn. Jake had agreed to "borrow" the Immaculate Heart of Mary, off the Kilburn Park Road. It is quite a noble-looking edifice with white pilasters on the façade. We had agreed to hold the service at eleven o'clock, once the congregation for the nine o'clock mass had dispersed. As a matter of fact, they did not disperse completely. As Jake had observed, Kilburn is not short of Irish, and quite a number frequented that church, especially at weekends. Elderly females predominated, of course, of the kind that will attend anything rather than return to their lonely homes. So we had a ready-made nucleus. I had somehow persuaded Andria to come along whilst ever-faithful Jocelyn attended to Ti. Jake had worked his devilish charm, so we even had an organist of minimal skill. And there was a contralto singer as well, who warbled a Gregorian hymn of which the parish seemed to be especially fond:

Alma Redemptoris Mater, quae pervia coeli
Porta manes, et stella maris, succurre cadenti,
Surgere qui curat populo: tu quae genuisti,
Natura mirante, tuum sanctum Genitorem,
Virgo prius ac posterius, Gabrielis ab ore
Sumens illud Ave, peccatorum miserere.

Andria helpfully translated this for me. It was a desert island of Latin amid a bleak North Sea of modern-sounding English. Jake read a homily that he had evidently prepared with some care. It was not customary, he said, for the Church to dwell on the personal attributes of the departed, but on this occasion he was making an exception. This took me by surprise, since he had hardly met Claud, but he went on to generalise on the basis of our conversation in the gallery. My uncle had not been a fashionable figure (well, I could have told him that). He had led a solitary life, dedicated to an unfashionable occupation of dwindling relevance. What had kept him going was an unselfish love of art, on which he maintained the defiantly unmodish attitude that all art offers us an image of perfection, potentially of the Divine. His commitment to this old fashioned view had got him nowhere in worldly terms. There were even those who might have seen him as some variety of Holy Fool. If so, it was they who were the fools. Claud's vision was consonant with that of the saints. He had been right; it was the world that was wrong. Then we sang "Thine Be the Glory" and were soon outside in mild Spring sunshine.

We had arranged for a simple reception back at the flat: sandwiches made with Mother's Pride bread, crisps, soft drinks or tea. We were serenaded throughout by a very vocal Titania. Jocelyn poured the tea, while Andria slumped. Jake came for half an hour and then left to prepare for the evening mass at Cheam. Once he had gone, Jocelyn took me aside and told me that Doig had phoned whilst we were out and asked to come round. He was still in London after consulting his doctor in Harley Street and seemed to want to chat. Did I know whether Doig was in trouble? Did I know that he was ill? No, I said, you know Doig better than I do. I felt like adding, "And I don't even like the bloke." Fortunately, I held my tongue.

The last of the guests took their leave, and then the doorbell went. Andria answered it and showed a still unshaven Doig into our rather cramped living room. He was looking, I thought, terrible. We offered him tea, but he seemed to prefer a glass of brandy, which luckily we could supply. After swilling it back, he asked if he could speak to Jocelyn alone. Andria said they could use our bedroom (we only had the one, where Titania slept in the corner). They went through and I could hear subdued voices through the door as Andria and I saw to Ti.

Twenty minutes later, they came through, and Doig thanked Andria and left. We were silent for several minutes after that. Even Ti was relatively silent. Then Andria went into the kitchen, and I asked Jocelyn what was up. He seemed unwilling to talk at first, and then he asked me if I had recently seen Christina. I told him I had not seen her since she and Doig had almost bumped into me outside the National Gallery ten days previously, and that I had not spoken to her, or been alone with her, since the Hampton Court fire at the beginning of the month. Jocelyn displayed little reaction to this information, but when I mentioned the casual meeting outside the gallery, he nodded and went quiet. What had he meant by these questions, I inquired? "Oh, nothing," he replied, and that was it. At least, it is all that I remember. I was, as I recall, far more concerned as to how I was going to pay the not inconsiderable undertakers' bill.

It had been weeks since my last visit to Rosie. I had, of course, seen her briefly at the funeral and more frequently in the mind's eye, in which her image increasingly, though incongruously, combined with Echardt's. But some time I knew I must go and see her in the flesh, renewing the old familiarity, attempting to stitch into it the weave of new discoveries. The Rosie of old, the pure, the immaculate had gone. Is not such innocence always a mental fabrication of our making? Perhaps. People revise themselves the more we know them: the closer in flesh they are, the more difficult the reassessment.

Nonetheless, betwixt my dashes down to Surrey, I found time to call round on one afternoon of unseasonable heat, and knock once more at the subterranean door amid the familiar milk bottles. It was with mixed feelings that I saw the light bloom on the other side of that frosted door pane. Rosie always kept the curtains well closed, even in the sultriest of weathers, and today was no exception, nor was the kiss she gave me on entering with its mingled bouquet of perfume and decay, nor the fumbling along the corridor crammed with bric-à-brac which every month seemed to pile higher.

She had she said been visiting an Arundel acquaintance who occupied a little house by the castle, in the garden of which they had sat discussing Our Lady of Salette. Her friend was a tertiary, and much versed in matters theological. They had argued about Aquinas. How wide my aunt's acquaintance with Catholic circles, or indeed Catholic thought, in general had ever been, I had never been able to gauge. On only one or two occasions since the inception of my regular visits had she ever given me cause to revise my opinion of her as the most determined recluse: revisions, moreover, no sooner formulated than suppressed, so adamant was I to preserve my impression of Rosie as some kind of latter day Julian of Norwich. Was this role perhaps reserved for my eyes alone? Once more we sat in her shaded rooms, the great heat outside firmly excluded, talking.

Had the confidences I had received from Echardt a few days previously altered my views? It all belonged in so legendary past it seemed hardly to matter. I was quite convinced that long ago the carnal fires had subsumed themselves into the eternal. There was the sense of her loss of course, but that had always been with me. Loss had so long seemed an essential aspect of Rosie's character, that now I knew in the last resort she had rejected her lover I could even see her condition as something chosen, and the more sacrosanct for that. It was difficult if not impossible this late in the day to connect her presence with Echardt's. The photograph stood where it always had, on top of the open piano. Comparing the erect little figure with the gentleman with whom not a fortnight previously I had been in conference almost as if of the Confessional, I noted how skilfully the photographer had flattered his subject, intended as the result had in all probability been for Rosie's eyes and her eyes only. It was clearly a studio portrait, made long before the days of platform booths. The pose was taken sideways from the waist up and angled so as to exaggerate the subject's stature. The officer's uniform was chunky about the shoulders, the hair close-cropped but more luxuriant than of late. There was an austerity about the expression, a noble lassitude which reflected one aspect of the Echardt to whom I had spoken so recently and to whose shameful admissions I had been privy. "She is in love with the man I was." Rosie had remembered what she wished, and the photo was her failsafe.

It was with Father, however, that her thoughts lay now. His death had clearly touched her deeply, and, much though we both resisted dwelling on a subject which lay uppermost in both our minds that afternoon, inevitably the moment arrived when, after the tea and biscuits, after the evasions and irrelevancies, we both fell silent for a minute before, looking up beyond the parrot's cage to where the banished sunshine dabbled the curtains, she said:

"I wonder what your dad's up to now? Gone to consult with his Maker, I dare say."

Quando Judex est Venturus, intoned Philophilus, taking up the refrain, though imagination failed to supply an adequate picture of Dad quaking before a judgement seat. I could only think of him making representations before some celestial stipendiary magistrate, bleakly bored among the files, blotting paper and seals.

"They'll be through with him by now," continued Rosie, "or else somebody will pay. Hamish wouldn't stand waiting around. I can't see him biding his time 'til Judgement Day. If there's one thing you could say about your father, he knew his own mind."

Tuba mirum spargens sonum.

Father had certainly got his way in most things, though, as had recently emerged, his will was of no overbearing order. Had he finally triumphed over me? It was time that I mentioned Titania.

"And how's your young lady?" she asked, saving me the trouble, and at last the truth was out. "Titania, did you call her? Queen of the Fairies, is she? How lovely to have a daughter of your own."

Unconsciously our two pairs of eyes had drifted across towards that other photograph in its silver frame above the now dormant gas fire. How odd I had looked at it as soon as I had arrived: the look direct, the hands folded together, the dress in a ruck round the thighs.

"I don't even know who she went to, you know," said Rosie. "They wouldn't say."

"But the picture ..."

"Arrived in the post anonymously three years after she was born. It's my only clue really as to what she grew up looking like, then or now."

"But I still don't understand, Rosie. What had you to lose?"

"My independence. My dignity. This little flat and all its quietness. Hours browsing through those old journals without let or hindrance, though I suppose that came later. Finally, we become what our choices make us. Also I was quite a popular young woman in those days, believe it or not. Suitors were ten a penny, though they've all vanished long since. Wouldn't want them now anyway. You don't get a second chance. Don't neglect yours, Benedict."

Voca me cum benedictis.

She looked up at the bird-cage, its satin cloth now dappled in sunlight.

"I've been teaching him the Latin office. The Ordinary and snatches of the Missa Pro Defunctis. Rather solemn I dare say, but it comforts me somehow. What a pity your father couldn't have been buried with the Latin rites. How he'd have adored it."

Her eyes wandered back in search of mine.

"Don't judge us too harshly, Benedict," she put in, simply.

"I don't see how I can, Aunt," I said, standing up now with my hands deep in my pockets. "I'm no better myself and that's the truth of it."

"You don't think you're quite equal to being a father, do you?"

Pater noster, Pater noster.

"Don't worry, you'll manage," she said. "You're a lot stronger than you think."

She looked over toward Christina's photograph once more, and then said brightly, "What a pity you could never meet *my* daughter."

*****

Darling Christina,

Excuse me for troubling you again, but would you mind keeping an eye on Benedict? He is full of this trip to Holland, which he seems to want to do by sea from Harwich to the Hook. I could manage this bit alright, and Jocelyn could look after Ti (he's had enough practice after all), but Ben tells me he's then going on down south to the island of Middelharnis to plant a laurel on his mother's grave. His dad put this as a kind of codicil in a letter he wrote to Ben just before his death, and it's had the most drastic effect on him, though of course he likes to pretend that it hasn't (but, as you yourself note, he's just like that).

Also, he's full of an old obsession with a picture by this seventeenth-century Dutch painter Hobbema showing an avenue leading into the town, and he seems to want to depict the scene as it is now in his own crazy style. This is likely to be time-consuming task, knowing just how slowly he works. Besides, it's sure to be the most private of occasions and I just hate to intrude. I know this may be cowardly of me but I never knew his mother, and this private mythology is a bit beyond me. I just wondered whether, as you seem to have become sort of honorary family, it might be more in your line. Besides, I need all the time I can gather to work on this dratted thesis, let alone looking after Ti. If I leave her with Jocelyn for too long, he might just go off his head. My only fear is that Ben may go off his, and hang himself on the nearest windmill or something.

Would you be a dear, and just sort of nanny him through the ordeal? Hold his hand a bit? It won't be difficult. You could always pretend it's some kind of liaison or something: he's frightfully susceptible to that sort of thing, being very insecure of his power over women. He'd be far too frightened to make a move of course: the thing is to appeal to his mind. He's far more likely just to collapse in your arms and weep (he does this, quite regularly). Think about it, would you, and let me know? I must go now: Titania has wet her thingies.

Yours in haste, Andria.

*****

Dear Andria,

I'm afraid there's no chance. Of course, I understand about Titania and I understand about Jocelyn, and I understand - or think I understand - about Ben. What you describe sounds to me like the sort of private rite which nobody could possibly understand except the celebrant, and while I can't claim to be able to plumb these particular mysteries, under ordinary circumstances I'd gladly attend and make sure the principal agent comes to no harm. But there are a couple of complicating circumstances right now. First, I've got involved with this middle-aged, married artist who is going through some sort of mid-life crisis and has left his wife, who's called Lettuce. Well, I mean, who wouldn't leave someone called Lettuce? I would. Even so, I tried to provide a shoulder to cry on, but then inevitably he fell in love with me. Now he seems to be going off his head with thwarted desire and is threatening to kill himself or something. To be quite honest, I'd do anything to be rid of him, and I keep on suggesting little trips he might take to get him out of the way. Thus far, he has just clung. Which is what, I assume, Lettuce did.

Second, and partly as a result, I've been going through a bit of a spiritual crisis myself and have been taking advice from an ever so sweet Catholic priest who has given me these exercises to do based on Ignatius Loyola. They have done much for my peace of mind, and I won't be able to concentrate on them if I take time off. So altogether you'll forgive me if I decline.

As for dear Ben, my impression is that he's trapped inside his skull. Well, we all are really, but Ben is especially trapped inside his. He's ever so sensitive about some things, but for the remainder of the time he seems to suffer from a sort of social myopia. In fact, it's worse that: often he seems not to perceive what is going on around him and, if he does, appears to misinterpret it. There are even occasions when he doesn't appear to notice an emerging situation when it's staring him right in the face. As for hanging himself from a windmill, I doubt if he'd be capable of tying the knot.

Love, my darling, Christina.

*****

April 11th, 1986

Dear Mr Henry,

Further to our conversations on April 8th, I have been giving some serious thought to the provisions of your late father's will. As you may be aware, the lion's share of the legacy is left in trust to your child, with the provision that should you decide to marry the party specified, two-thirds of it are to revert to you.

The case is thus a complicated one but, as it stands, my preliminary thoughts are these. The stipulations in the document are highly unusual; they are also exceptionally unambiguous. In such circumstances the law will almost certainly insist that they be respected. I am therefore minded to proceed to set up the trust in favour of your daughter along the lines stipulated. In that case, the balance of the estate – about a third of the whole – will revert to you.

Having said which, I have yet to consult an expert in probate law. I hope to do so next week and will communicate to you the substance of the advice I receive. My expectation, however, is that my opinion will be confirmed. Should you, of course, choose to abide by the condition stated in the clause to which I have a drawn your attention in respect of marriage to the party specified and the adoption by you both of your child, the whole of the estate will then pass to you as sole beneficiary.

Yours faithfully,

Roger Pebloe, LL.B (Hons).

*****

Dear Christina,

You'll think me silly, and you'll think me absurd, and you'll think I've had too much Vodka, but will you marry me? When I saw you on Easter Monday in front of that ruined palace with the hair tumbling down your back and the memories of thirty years falling down across my distracted brow like so many wisps of cinder, I decided you were the bravest, the most beautiful, the finest, the most reckless and understanding being on which my eyes had ever – well - clapped. I love you, I adore you, I worship the very ground on which you stand. I know you'll think this is wanton, I know you'll think I'm a fool, but what can I do: victim of my poor, heedless heart that I am? O mea culpa, mea maxima culpa and all that kinky plainsong.

What a handsome couple we would make.

Yours distractedly, Benedict.

P.S. Excuse the scrawl. Am in Cheam and have just discovered the cellar.

*****

Dear Ben,

No. Whatever can you be thinking of? Just No.

Yours as ever,

Christina.

Dear Andria,

Has Ben taken leave of his senses? He has just written asking me to marry him. Sort him out, will you? Bereavement is a condition that none of us envy, but surely even condolences have their limits. I have one distraught artist on my hands as it is.

Yours candidly,

Christina.

*****

April 19th, 1986.

Dear Mr Henry,

Following my letter of last week, I have now had an opportunity to consult a specialist in probate law, who has been kind enough to vouchsafe his professional opinion. Contrary to what I said in my last letter, the case is, I am afraid, somewhat more complicated than we at first thought.

As you may realise, binding conditions attached to an estate are rare but they are far from unprecedented. The administration of your father's will should in fact be comparatively plain sailing. However, in this instance the law would need to balance the wishes of the testator with the rights of your child's natural mother. If you did decide to fulfil the condition laid down by the testator, the case would therefore indisputably go to law, and this might be expensive (might in fact, in the manner of these things, swallow up the very legacy such action was designed to secure).

It is, of course, impossible to predict precisely how a court will react in any given instance, but the gist of the matter seems to be this. The clause concerned states that two-thirds of the estate are to revert to you should you choose to marry the named party and, having done so, to bring your child (now daughter) up within that union. Such a marriage would perforce have two consequences. Firstly, it would stand in the way of your marrying the child's mother, and thus obviate any possibility that you might legitimise the child. The court would in all probability take the view that this would be a de facto encouragement to irregularity, and what I believe our grandparents used to refer to as "loose living". Secondly, and more trenchantly, it would deprive the mother of her legal rights.

If precedent is anything to go by, the court may well decide to disregard the relevant clause. I stress that one cannot be absolutely sure of the outcome, and that shifting social mores might conceivably sway the court. They might for example take the view that illegitimacy is so common nowadays that precedent could safely be set aside, or at least modified. This, in my colleague's view, is possible but scarcely likely. Attitudes have changed somewhat since I was a young man, but I scarcely think that we have yet become so debauched as to see the upbringing of a child within the bosom of a legitimate family as a matter of light concern. And, even if society at large has elected to take the other view, the law, which in such matters normally lags behind social custom, is almost certain to take the traditional line. In any case, the rights of the child's mother are likely to prove binding.

In that case the almost certain outcome would be that the principal stipulation of the will would stand, and the money be placed in trust for your child until such time as he comes of age. I await your further instructions.

Yours faithfully,

Roger Pebloe, LL.B (Hons).

*****

Dear Christina,

Did I by any chance send you a letter last week requesting your hand in marriage? I can't be sure of the exact order of the events, but I do have a hazy impression that something of that sort may have occurred. It has been a somewhat stressful period what with one thing and another and stress, as the doctors say, will come out in the oddest of ways.

If so, I crave your indulgence. Pour on me all the scorn of the Gods.

Yours apologetically,

Ben.

*****

Dear Andria,
Will you marry me?
Ben.

*****

Dear Ben,
No, of course not,
Yours,
Andria.
P.S. Whatever can have got into you?

*****

Dear Christina,
It's alright. He asked me to marry him too. He does have these weird turns sometimes, and grief both for his father and now his uncle seems to have exacerbated his habitual mild insanity to a state of definitive dementia. I expect it will pass through the acute stage to the merely chronic in a very few weeks, but until that time I think it best if we encourage him to go away for a while. Should we prompt him to expedite this welcome trip to Holland, do you think? Sorry about the other distraught artist. Perhaps we can get rid of them both at the same time? It would give both of us a break.
Yours affectionately,
Andria.

*****

Beyond the stern the wake spread out in a great widening trough which threatened to engulf the horizon. In the maelstrom behind the funnel, six or seven gulls performed their drunken dance in the cross-winds while, against the rail or hidden behind heaps of tarpaulin, groups of intrepid peered back toward Harwich and the Stour.

Once Felixstowe and Harwich had fallen far to our rear, and the waters of the estuary had been replaced by the churning, foam-dense stretches of the open sea, there seemed little point in staying on deck. I paced once or twice around the base of the funnel, being careful to avoid stacks of deckchairs which here and there lay scattered in our path, and then, shuddering, I made went below. It would be many hours before the Hook hove into sight. There was little sense of an excursion in me now; what pulled me on was a memory. Descending the heaving staircase I negotiated the corridors past rows of shops and made for the First Class Bar. My ticket was in one of the most modest of price-ranges, but rock music exuded raucously from the Second Class Lounge, and the restaurants were packed. One kind of indolence breeding another, I was only too happy to find a little peace among the elderly and well-to-do. I had my pad of paper with me, thinking to capture a few marine impressions from the scenic window, so I purchased a double whisky and moved over to the ingle-nook where, lulled by the movement of the engines, I sat staring out at the grey stretches of the North Sea. Cleft by the ferry's momentum, the waves were swirling in a shroud of white: eastward, towards Rotterdam, the grey-edged clouds were brightening.

The coach from Rotterdam to Middelharnis takes just over an hour, and leaves every twenty minutes. I'd already booked a room at Der Oude Bank hotel in Middelharnis, giving Andria their contact details in case she wanted to contact me. Once we'd docked and gone through passport and customs, I hopped on board the bus which got me to the island by the early evening. I checked in at the hotel and went in search of dinner which I found at the Brasserie 't Vingerling near the harbour. I ate the veggie option on the menu, truffle risotto. It was modest is price and delicious. After a restful night I breakfasted on ham, cheese, croissants and plenty of good, strong coffee. Then, donning the lightest of spring jackets, I set off in search of the grave.

The graveyard lay in the northeast corner of the isle of Goeree, about half a mile south of the Haringvliet, and not three miles from where my grandparents once had their abode. Since Hobbema's time they had filled in the channel between the island and the coastal polders, so it was no longer strictly insular, even if folklore had it so. To my mother it was always a haunted island place. She had spent about eight years of her childhood here, though the family had drifted away, and in later years her parents had moved up country to Utrecht. It was to Utrecht that our annual Dutch forays were made with stopovers in Amsterdam, but once every few years my mother would insist on coming down here to where her roots lay. It was years before roots as such became fashionable. For her they were never a cause or a banner, but more humbly, just a fact. Quite simply, this is where her heart lay. In later years she must have spent virtually all of her time in towns, not out of preference, but out of the necessities of marriage, out of that which the world exacts from us, the gruesomeness of compromise. Compromise is an ugly word, and my father's life was full of it. It is the law of life: to comfortably, dryly and moderately construct, bit by bit, that which we have it in ourselves to construct. Building is a humble, even at times humiliating, art, and my father was expert at it. Latterly he had built his paradise too, in Cheam.

For a Dutch graveyard it was an oddly neglected place. The Dutch have a national vice called tidiness. It is the one aspect of the country that I find truly appalling. The streets are spotless, the trains run on time. In Schiphol Airport, through which I had once the misfortune to pass, the platforms of the railway station gleam. If you watch a Dutch barmaid at work, she rinses and meticulously stacks glasses by the hundred while gossiping energetically to her friends. I once spent three quarters of an hour watching some workmen in Groningen cobbling a street; they did it almost as I watched, smoking, chatting. It was as effortless as breathing, this instinct for order, this predilection for pure work.

That, however, was in the far North of Holland. South of Rotterdam things start imperceptibly to fray. The nearer one gets to the Latin lands, the great Romantic wound, the weeping boil of the world, the more the niceties slacken. This too was recognizably Holland, but a Holland whose pristine waters seemed to have mixed themselves with some Lethe of forgetfulness.

I stumbled through the long grass and found myself in the densest part of the undergrowth. I had to hack away the before coming across the plainest of upright tablets, bearing the simple inscription, *Hic Jacet Neeltgen Henry (1916-72), Uxor Carissima Jacomi Henrici. Ecce Ancilla Domini.* There was a low upright gravestone under some elms at the back, with a simple black and white photograph behind lichened glass.

I remembered this photograph from the old days at Finchley. In North London it had stood in an oval silver frame on the mantelpiece; I think my mother was especially fond of it. There is a moment when the hope, or perhaps the illusions, of youth finally depart. One moment you are in the light, looking ahead, the next you are in this tunnel that goes on for ever. The backward glance takes but a moment; it was this moment the photograph had caught. As she looked out at me through the dust and slime of fourteen winters, she seemed to peer across the murk and achievement of the later years, the years that had made me, the years that she had lost. Behold the handmaid of the Lord.

There was a breeze blowing off the sea to the windward side. Here, however, I was protected and almost warm. I slowly loosened the buttons of my overcoat. The yew trees above me were still bare. I looked across to a single cypress standing beside the memorial chapel, put the map back in my pocket and said, almost to myself, "Good place for a tryst."

A flutter overhead announced an aerial commotion: a flock of swallows was arriving from the south. The recent months had been temperate on the whole, though we were still several years before the mild winters of the late eighties. I put down my duffel bag on the side of an adjoining grave, loosened the cord, and foraged within. I had packed the cutting in a jam-jar with water to keep the root fresh; the top of the jam-jar was sealed with silver foil. I removed several sheets of newspaper from the top of the bag, and then took hold of the trowel. I levered the jam-jar out of the bag and stood up.

In my right hand I held the trowel, and in my left the jam-jar. There was a momentary comedy as I got my right and left confused, but then I knelt down and found a convenient place to the right of the gravestone, where I rammed in the trowel. The soil was dank and smelly after the winter, but soft enough to dig. I humped up two trowelfuls, piling the earth to one side.

I swivelled round on my right knee and took the jam-jar between my hands like an offering, the glass hard and chilly between my palms. Very gently I unwrapped the silver foil from around the neck of the jar, creating a little crinkling sound in the stillness. Then I picked out the cutting, and let the drips fall on the earth. I placed the sprig in the hole with the long stem facing downwards. I held the cutting in my left hand and gently lowered it into the earth. Then I firmed the soul round the cutting with the pointed toe of my shoe.

I stood and admired my handiwork. The cutting was

slightly crooked in the earth, but I hoped against hoping that it would take. I had done what I promised; I had wiped the slate clean.

"Well, you've done your duty, I suppose," said my mother.

"Yes," I said. "Sometimes I do."

I knelt down on one knee by the graveside, and for the second time within recent memory I started, very softly, to cry.

The way back lay by the cypress at the corner of the church.

As I strolled onwards, I could hear my mother ask, "Have you done everything you wanted?"

"Not quite," I said. "There's a place I want to visit."

"Hobbema?"

"Yes."

"The avenue?"

"Oh, yes."

"It's not still there is it?"

"I'm afraid so."

Then I heard Andria's voice say, "Not those sodding trees…"

*****

The poplars were inevitably stouter, and the church had lost its spire. No ships lay at anchor out in the sound; instead, to my left, towards Grevelingen, the drone of traffic was faintly audible. Perhaps there were one or two more houses. The sheds and drying stalls of

Hobbema's day had been converted into pitch-roofed villas, their solar panels glistening in the early evening sun. The rutted track was now a tarmacked road, though at this hour almost deserted save for one growing dot, a lone walker on the outer limits of visibility. Three months earlier the canals on either side would have laboured under ice. Now springtime had released them, their faintly brackish surfaces reflecting the coeruleum blue of the sky. The poplars reached up in their irregular, wavy lines, gnarled now and in placed stooping, yet still nodding deferentially to one another, still keeping neighbourly discourse against the scything backdrop of the wind. It was growing sharp and cold as the evening drew in, and above the solar panels to my right two layers of stratus cloud tapered off into thin wisps of grey. Way above the trees, against the uppermost layer of cloud, a flock of swallows cavorted, winged as a memory, migrating north.

The speck on the roadway was now a man.

Despite the cold and the relative lateness of the hour, the rituals of courtesy went on. Signs of social activity were discernible in the distant hamlet while, to the right of the road, close to the nearest of the pitch-roofed houses, two women stood talking. The woman to the left had recently donned a suede jacket. Perhaps mindful of the stratus cloud above, her companion held a light mackintosh slung over the crook of one arm. In a smallholding to the right of us a solitary enthusiast was plying his secateurs. Opposite him, on the other side of the road, children's voices rose from behind a beech copse and then died away, buffeted out of earshot by the persistence of the wind.

The walker on the roadway was clearly visible now, clad in a broad-rimmed hat, his shoulders weighed down by what looked like a fishing rod, his sturdy buff coat swaying rhythmically in orchestration with his stride. Seven, Eight. Slowly into the twilight the bells of the ancient church let out their carillon.

Over by the houses the gossipers had departed, taking their coats and their gossip with them. The smallholder had packed away his tools and was making his way homewards. Now every door within sight was closed in preparation for dusk, though through the envious evening the living room of each house was clearly visible, each with its own bright aureole of light.

The walker on the road strode onwards purposefully, like his archetype in Hobbema.

The bells tinkled across the polders, across the village, out into the enclosed waters of Harengvliet. As it told the hour, its pitch rose and fell, a faint metallic tinge caressing each note.

I was sure of it now. The walker on the road was Claud. The notes of the carillon died. Between the fields, between the dipping lines of poplars, strode the unbidden guest.

The walker on the road had raised his hand. Above the spireless church, its carillon resounding in its after-hum, the flock of swallows had banked out to sea. Over the nearest of the dwellings the stratus cloud, greyer now, released a light patter of rain. Caught by an abrupt convulsion, the avenue of poplars shivered and then lunged. Phantom or embodiment, through the forgiving light, the figure lumbered on.

I looked again. The fishing rod was an easel; the walker on the road was Doig.

At first, I thought we would break into that balletic-cum-conversational routine we had performed outside the Gallery. Instead, Doig said, "Aren't you cold, man? You're wearing practically nothing." This seemed a fairly daft remark, seeing as it was a fairly balmy evening in May. So I called out, "Why aren't you in London?"

He had drawn level with me now, his face still unshaven, his dress unkempt, his eyes wide and staring. He said, "Why aren't you in London?"

I explained about my mother, the laurel tree and the need to re-create Hobbema. When I got to the end of my garbled account, Doig said, "Yes, your friend Christina told me all about that. She said you'd be here. She told me to come and fetch you. Correction: she said I should come and keep you company. I think she wanted me out of the way. I've run away from my wife."

"What's your wife called?"

"Lettuce. Well, Laetitia as it happens. Actually, at the moment I have nowhere to live, old boy. Care for a few days in Amsterdam, mmm?"

*****

Such a visit was not in my general plan, but it was a

chance to share my city: a city of waterways, a city dredged from destruction, a city on stilts. A city seemingly made for Spring with its window boxes sprouting flowers, its tree-lined banks, its light and shade, every inch of every canal telling a different tale to every waking hour, this endless parade of shade against water, this neighbourliness, this frankness, and above all, the friendliness of it all: bicycles, barges, anarchist students, men of affairs and intellectuals sitting in groups over half-pints of beer or glasses of thick yellow *advocaat*. Each interior an invitation to quietness, caresses, familiarity or talk. Stepping over the cobblestone bridges, avoiding the hurtling bicycles, my memory seemed to colonize each shop and street corner, each cloud and tree. I had depicted these sights in my mind a hundred times and often too on paper, decorating drawings irrelevantly with gables, house-fronts, half-recalled glimpses of an irretrievable past.

Doig, though, seemed incapable of perceiving much except, principally, his own disquiet. We took single rooms on two different floors of a mid-range hotel, a converted warehouse close to Dam Square on Gravenstraat. Doig insisted on it, and the reason for his choice became rapidly obvious on the first evening, since it lay just round the corner from what he loudly declared to be his favourite bar in the world, Wynand Fockink. The name, that of the seventeenth-century founder, sounds innocuous in Dutch but, when pronounced inaccurately in English, it appeared to appeal to my friend's – must I call him friend? –

facetious sense of humour. So we went round there at six, by which time, Doig announced we had already missed four hours' decent drinking.

The proeflokaal or tasting room lay about halfway down a narrow lane called Pijlsteeg behind mullioned windows with a green sign outside, clearly visible from the square. The bar itself is narrow but long, and painted mustard yellow. It is lined with shelves bearing antique – or faux antique – jars, and bottles of various designs. The chief feature, however, is a long wooden bar top behind which are displayed the entire range of some fifty house liqueurs. Mercifully they serve draft beer as well, and to this I restricted myself for the first hour so – the place shuts at nine. Doig, on the other hand, instantly declared that by closing time he intended to sample the entire gamut of the establishment's famous gins.

Wynand Fockink, you must realise, is a gregarious space, but it is also a traditional watering hole governed by a strict protocol. Draft beer is conveniently pulled into half-pint glasses. With the plentiful gins and liqueurs it is quite otherwise. These are served in tiny, fluted vessels of a distinctive waisted shape, filled to the brim. In order to avoid spilling any of the precious liquid, the convention is for customers to bow or genuflect before the bar-top and take their first sip hands free, without lifting the glass. There is something both bohemian and at the same time ceremonious about this act, something abandoned and at the same time pseudo-ecclesiastical, as if one is paying homage to the spirits of drinking, or in the case of the gins to the drinking of spirits.

Doig's first choice was *Oude Jenever*, which looked and, he assured me, tasted suitably venerable. Despite his growing stoutness, he more or less managed his initial feat of ritualistic obeisance without slipping or slurping. He then went on to the friskier-sounding *Vijf Jenever,* with which his poise in its preliminary imbibing was less assured. By the time he had ordered a glass of *Junge Jenever*, he was having to steady himself by placing his hands to either side of him along the bar top. The barman did not fail to notice this symptom of inebriation. Nor did I; besides, I was still on my first glass of beer. Doig had also got into a vigorous argument with a local artist, to annoy whom or – more significantly I suspect - to annoy me, he was maintaining the heretical opinion that Rembrandt was the most overrated painter in human history, and that the whole Dutch school, of which I was so fond, was based on a fraud. "Chocolate box art, Hmmm," he called it, fit only for jigsaw puzzles and dishcloths. This oration was not going down too well. In order to distract him, I tapped him on the shoulder and put a question that I had longing to ask for the last few hours. "And how was Christina?" I inquired. "Apart from kicking you out, that is?"

There was silence, disturbed only by the hum of conversation around us. Doig stroked his unshaven chin and demurred. At first, I was convinced that he had not heard my question, drowned as it probably had been by the din in the bar. He swilled down the last few drops of *Junge Jenever*, placed his slender glass on the bar top, gestured to the barman and, fumbling with his wallet, ordered a glass of *Superior Jenever*. As the man poured it, Doig carefully observed the virtuoso movement of his wrist. Then he paid and turned back to me.

I repeated my dangerous inquiry: "And how is Christina?"

Doig turned back towards the bar, lowered his chin and attempted to sip. He was now visibly staggering, his feet awkwardly splayed. He noisily took in a few drops, wiped his lips and raised himself unsteadily to his feet.

"As well as can be expected," he said. "Under the circumstances, Hmmm?"

I finished off my beer with a toss of the head and said, "*What* circumstances?"

Doig raised his glass to his lips and took a second sip of his superior gin. "Hmmm," he said, "not bad."

"What circumstances?"

"Well, the spiritual exercises and all."

"Yes?"

"Well, Ben, I don't know what you feel about religion. Were you not raised a Catholic?"

"Yes." I was in no mood to deny.

"In my view," drawled Doig, "and it is only my view, your friend Christina is a little too thick with this Catholic priest."

"Oh yes?"

"I don't know why, and I never like to pry, but it's a little odd, because his parish is miles away, somewhere down in Surrey."

I put down my empty tumbler, turned to the bar and motioned to the shelves of house liqueurs at the back. I ordered a glass of *Hansje in de Kelder*. Then I carefully lowered my head and took the ritualistic first sip.

"On to the liqueurs are we now, Ben?"

"Yes, do you fancy one?"

"Hmmm. I don't mind if I do."

He swilled down the last few drops of his *Superior Jenever*, turned back to the bar, and ordered a glass of *Bruidstanen*. After I'd paid and he'd sampled it and risen to his feet, I found the courage to continue. "In Surrey, you say. Might that be somewhere like Cheam?"

"Hmmm. It might." He enlarged his eyes and took another sip. "Care for another one, would you?"

Doig then bought me a glass of *Volmaakt Geluk*. He got himself a glass of *Boswandeling*. Looking into the distance, over the heads of the other drinkers, he remarked, "I would say from the appearances of things, and I am only a visitor and guest, that this priest from Cheam is wine-and-fucking her on a regular basis. Mind you, it is not for me to judge."

That was the last thing we said on the subject. My mind, in any case, was in a whirl, and I did not know what to think, did not know even now whether Doig was simply trying to humiliate me, or just playing games. At five to nine I managed to extricate him and guide his wandering footsteps out into the open air of the street. I felt a deep need to breathe. Pretending not to hear his belched suggestion that we take a tour of the Red Light

District along Oudezijds Achterburgwal, I attempted to steer Doig towards the hotel. We had not eaten all evening, but he did not seem to mind. Instead he suggested we take a stroll around the neighbourhood. When we reached Keizersgracht, I only just dissuaded him from relieving himself gushingly into the canal. As we made our uncertain way back along Gravenstraat, I inquired, "Doig, is your wife really called Lettuce?"

The following morning, I got up at seven and took a solitary walk to clear my head. For several minutes, from say a quarter past seven to a twenty minutes past, I stood on the bank of the Keizersgracht staring into the smooth surface of the water. Back came my face, intent and mysterious, puckering its brow in a frenzy of concentration and supressed anger. Then a glass-topped motor launch swirled past and swept on towards one of the bridges. My face broke into shattered segments which rocked back and forth and then gradually reassembled. It was a visage intolerant of distraction, its presence disturbed by the passage of the launch. Then gradually the eddy settled, and back came that old look of absorption, the eyes straining forward and round in their sockets, the pupils large and distended by an effort of control. The previous night, was it Doig that had spoken, or the gin?

We had just about thirty-six hours left in Amsterdam, and I was determined to alter Doig's jaundiced estimate of the place. That afternoon we were returning after lunch at one of the Indonesian restaurants along Bloemgracht. We had reached the West Bank of

Prinsengracht when a sudden unexpected downpour sent us scuttling through the raindrops to shelter in the cool reaches of the Westerkerk. Around us the nave rose like a forest of Northern pine, in whose uppermost branches the day broke through in patches of filtered luminosity, drawing the eye up from the ice-cold flagstones of the floor, beneath which the great of Amsterdam slumbered, with Rembrandt interred in the darkness beyond them. Later that afternoon I showed him the Agtercaemer on the floor beneath the workroom in Rembrandt's house. Around the walls hung drypoints and etchings. Among them was one entitled *The Walking Frame*. It was an immaculate seated nude and in the background, so lightly done the eye had difficulty picking her out, was a woman bent over a knee-high wooden pen, inside which a child clung and pawed its feet. Inside the pen, Titus, Rembrandt's little son, was learning to walk. At that moment, I felt a sudden, and unfamiliar, longing for home.

We reserved the last morning for the Rijksmuseum. On our family visits to Amsterdam it had always been in the nature of a flying stop. My father had a limited appreciation of painting for its own sake, any my mother had visited the gallery so often on her own compulsory outings from Utrecht that to have lingered over the exhibits would have been for a variety of self-imposed torture. I suppose I must have been there first aged around six, because the paintings were still a good foot above my head. By the time my eyes drew level with the base of the pictures, my attitudes - thanks to Claud - had been transformed. I liked the Early Italian triptychs because they reminded me of altar pieces, and I still recall kneeling down on the parquet floor one chill winter morning to inspect an angel's foot. The foot was remarkable enough, but I mainly remember the flannel edges of my pants rubbing against the exposed skin of my thigh. Did the infant Rembrandt have such trouble, I wondered, scuttling around the backstreets of Leiden?

What felicity my mother's people possessed with interiors! Here the corridors led between fluted white arches hung with chandeliers, and each had its right and inevitable climax, each led like a flawless argument to one great painting: a conclusion awaited and proposed. So my mother had arranged her kitchen at Finchley, brass pans gleaming against immaculate white walls, the table a scrubbed island of beige in the tiled sea of the floor; in the living room too, and in every honeyed cell of the house: objects, paintings, chairs, each in its own penumbra of light, impressing the infant eye with its proportion, its this-ness, temporal yet in the transforming memory suspended in time. So this greatest of galleries was orchestrated, drawing one scrupulously and inevitably toward one great canvas. As Doig and I wandered down the central aisle that Thursday morning, between side-galleries leading off like chapels, we gradually became aware of a concentration towards the far end, the source of which was not evident until, emerging at the chancel of this matchless cathedral, we sighted *The Night Watch* at the far end.

But first came the guild portraits, dozens of them: Thomas de Keyser's *Company of Captain Allaert Cloeck and Lieutenant Lucas Jacobsz*, Bartholemeus van der Helst's *Civic Guard to Celebrate the Peace of Wesphalia*, all that masculine grandeur, all those bland, self-satisfied faces. Behind me I could sense Doig growing restless. They were all like school photos, he said, like his leaving photo from Repton School in 1959. When we got to a characteristic montage by Franz Hals, he could stand it no longer, and shouted for all he was worth, "Not more fucking ruffs!"

But then we reached *The Night Watch*. Who, in that sanctified hush, with the blanched light falling from above across Frans Banninck Cocq's goodly beard, could possibly resist it? There they strode, fleshly, in the raucous grandeur of their sins: polishing their rifles, clashing pipes, laughing. Who in this sublunary sphere would wish their humanity to be portrayed better, or worse, than this? You have been weighed in the balances and found wanting. But it was Rembrandt who paid the cost, his reputation, his prosperity in pieces. Observe how perilous it is to portray men as they are.

We stood looking at it for perhaps seven minutes before Doig said, "You know they rejected it. The Night Guard commissioned it, and then they turned it down. We think of Rembrandt as a success. In life he was a failure, Mmm? What was he facing in the end, eh? The loss of friends, disorder, ruin. Whatever else it is that one risks. He'd diced it all on one great canvas, and lost. Former students used to pick him up by the canal side, buy him a mug of warm grog and press a few coins into his palm. No wonder he looks amused in some of the self-portraits, Mmm? It could just be that, in the end, the truth turned out to be the funniest thing in the world. And no wonder. Look at that picture. He has not painted a company, or even a group. The weapons are all pointing in different directions. There is no discipline anywhere, Mmm? That's why it's so much better than all those others. Art is not commemoration; art is disturbance."

"Is that why you are a good artist: because you are disturbed?"

Doig gave me a peculiar hard look. "I am not a good artist. I am a successful artist. It is not the same thing."

I was staring at the floor. "I am neither good, nor successful," I said.

Foolishly I thought Doig was about to contradict me. Instead, he remarked ruefully, "It is better to be like that than to believe you are genuinely accomplished because others make a fuss of you. A celebrity is," – he clicked his fingers in mid-air - "nothing."

"Is that what you think you are: nothing?"

He did not reply.

In his biography, Jocelyn reports this conversation. The trouble is that he'd picked up accounts of it from both of us, and our versions differed. This is what he wrote:

> In the May of 1986, Evans travelled to Holland, where he met up with Benedict Henry, the artist with whom he had shared an exhibition in

Bentink Street the previous April. He was in a depressed state of mind, and had recently walked out on his second wife. [There is no reference to Christina in Jocelyn's account.] He had not been sleeping well, and his normally modest intake of alcohol had increased to an extent that was worrying both to himself and to his friends. One Saturday they visited the Rijksmuseum in Amsterdam, where, faced with the masterpieces of the Golden Age of Dutch art, he at first took umbrage in an aggressive attitude towards the representational painting of the seventeenth century, which he claimed was worthless, before experiencing a severe and almost certainly unjustified crisis of confidence and re-directing the note of severe criticism against himself.

I have a hunch that the phrase "and almost certainly unjustified" was added at a late stage, probably at Andria's suggestion. It is the "almost" that stands out. Manifestly in this passage, Jocelyn's profound and instinctive conservatism – or more precisely his tendency to react against received opinion – is emerging for all to see. The tone there comes perilously close to his repeated conversational gambit that "Doig's art has less to do with art seen than with the art scene," though of course here he is putting it more subtly. What he wants his readers to believe is that, all along and deep down, Doig had shared his own low estimate of his work, and that his nervous collapse of that year originated in an acknowledgement, an underlying recognition, of his own professional deficiency. Jocelyn even seems to be suggesting – or am I reading things into his words with the benefit of personal knowledge? - that Doig had left his wife because he was an inferior artist and human being, or maybe that he was an inferior artist and human being because he left his wife. Whichever way round that observation is put, it is a pretty damning verdict. What came to annoy Jocelyn subsequently was his belief that the biography was well received, and sold well, on the strength of its meretricious candour. In his view, this meant that he had become a successful author on the basis of writing a bad – that is to say an egregiously uncharitable – book. Which, in his eyes, made him guilty of a literary equivalent of Doig's artistic chicanery, or maybe of his personal self-delusion. Hoist with his own petard, you might say.

*****

Of course, all of this came out several years afterwards. I breathed not a word of it on my return to London two days later. I'd left Doig in Amsterdam where, as he told me at almost the last moment, they were displaying a few of his early canvases in the Hermitage Museum in the South of the city. Clearly this had been an additional reason for his visit, though he had been slow to impart the information: had he wanted to get in his dig about Christina and Jake first?

Anyway, clearly, he would spend the remainder of his stay basking in a certain amount of public admiration, which would do his diminished self-esteem some good. So I left him brooding at the hotel, and took the ferry back to Harwich.

All the same way in the boat, I could not help speculating about Doig's reactions over the last few days, which appeared to me to have consisted of a mass of contradictions. For instance, while we were drinking in Wynand Fockink he had attacked Rembrandt's reputation; standing in the Rijksmuseum, on the other hand, he had defended his transcendent genius. Superficially, there was an explanation; in Wynand Fockink his remarks had been fuelled by strong gin; in the gallery he had been sober. But it had been whilst downing the contents of last-but-one of those slender glasses of near-lethal *jenever* that he had dropped his noxious hint about the relationship between Christina and Jake. Did that mean I could safely disregard what he had said?

Even if I could disregard his poisoned remarks, why I now wondered should it so disturb me? What, after all, was Christina to me now? Had she not been toying with us all, playing with us all emotionally, all along? Whatever else had that shemozzle at Dolphin Square been all about? Why had she got me to pose for her, and then posed herself? Why had she seemingly led Doig on, and then abruptly dropped him? Wasn't she just heartless after all? And yet...

When I got back to Kensal Rise, Jocelyn was tending Titania with tender care, and Andria was still getting on with her thesis. There was one major change, though. When I arrived Titania was sleeping and Andria was up a stepladder in the drawing room, while Jocelyn held a pot of paint and handed her brushes. The walls were slowly being covered in grey. I thought nothing of this at the time, since change is always welcome and the previous colour had been a dingy sort of magnolia. They were halfway down one wall when Andria suddenly remarked, "Oh by the way, we got a plaintive phone call from a woman called Laetitia."

"Laetitia?"

"Yes," inserted Jocelyn, "except that she signed herself off as 'Don't-Call-Me-Lettuce'."

I thought for a while. "But that's the name of Doig Evans's old wife. The one he's run away from."

"Well," said Andria, dipping a brush into the pot of grey paint, "she sounded quite young to us."

"Yes," concurred Jocelyn. "And angry and upset and all that. Quite a handful, I'd say. Said she was really missing him."

Andria corrected him. "Actually, that's not true. She said she was quite glad to see the back of him. All the same, she needs to have it out with him first."

I thought for a while. "You know, I bumped into Doig in Holland. He's got some of his paintings on show at the Hermitage."

"Yes, we know," remarked Andria.

"Yes," agreed Jocelyn. "We know about that already."

"How so?

"Oh," Andria replied absentmindedly whilst dabbing at a corner with her paint brush, "Laetitia told us."

"Lettuce told you?"

"Quite," confirmed Jocelyn. "Lettuce-leaf he called her apparently."

Andria was surveying her handiwork. 'Far from wilting, I'd say. Says she's coming down here soonish."

"Down where?"

"Down to London," Jocelyn informed me.

"When? When?"

"Oh, we don't know," he retorted vaguely, helping Andria down from the stepladder. "Sometime. Actually next Friday. We said she could stay here."

*****

She stood buxomly in the doorway as if rooted and inquired, "Is somebody called Jocelyn living at this address?"

Jocelyn was finishing applying white gloss to a skirting board in the kitchen. He called through with, "Yes, that's me."

"I'm Laetitia Evans."

She was not in the least as we expected. Nor, it has to be said, did she much resemble a lettuce leaf. She was on the tall side: around 5 ft 8 ins, broad-shouldered and florid. She was also exuberantly beautiful in what I would classify as a characteristically Mediterranean fashion: long, dark hair, greying now but then a luscious raven, large and penetrating brown eyes, high eyebrows that had no need of a pencil (they do now), slightly pouting lips adorned with vampish Red Velvet lipstick, generously-shaped breasts. Think of Doña Isabel de Porcel as depicted by Goya. Think of a crimson bougainvillea bush in garish subtropical bloom. Laetitia was (and is) full in figure with, as was obvious as she stood in the doorway that distant morning, long, shapely legs. It was instantly clear what had attracted Doig to her in the first place.

It didn't it take us long to work out what had driven him away. Two emotions, in my calculation, were likely to have caused Doig Evans to flee from his spouse: boredom, or fear. Well, Laetitia was decidedly not boring, nor would I have called her exactly frightening. The adjective that springs to mind is formidable. Laetitita Evans was quite some lady, and no push-over for anyone.

We sat her down in the living room, where the furniture had just been replaced. Small talk appeared not to be her style. She was also aware we wanted to know where she was from, what she was, what she was doing there, and what the current state of affairs was with Doig or, as she called him "Dear Doig, or Doig the Dire". And she was at pains to dispute his account of the rift. "Left me, did he?" She blew smoke through both nostrils - back then Letty smoked cheroots - and added, "Well, I never. Wonders will never cease. Is that what he told you? Well, well." She took another puff. "The rat!"

Her accent was singsong and northern: Liverpool was

my first guess with my then ignorance of everything beyond the Trent (in fact she was raised in Salford, where her father ran a chippy). Somewhat taken aback by this volubility, Jocelyn and Andria had withdrawn to the half-decorated kitchen where they were consulting with one another while making us coffee. They were well within ear-shot. She asked in her nasal up-and-down voice, more to me than to anyone else, "What do you think of Doig the Dire's paintings then?"

"Um. Alright," I said. "I exhibited with him last year."

"Oh, so you're this Ben, are you? He quite admires your work, you know. We even have one of your thingies in the bedroom. Right on, if you ask me. Restful. But what do you reckon on his?"

"Interesting. Interesting. Certainly well received."

She blew cheroot smoke and stared into mid-air. "Experimental, isn't it? Emperor's New Clothes, I'd say, Emperor's New Clothes. Did he mention our daughter?"

"No. Not at all. Not in the least. What's she called?"

"Bella. She's our only child. Bella's sixteen."

Andria had brought through the coffee cups and asked Letty if she took milk.

"No thanks. Black. Plenty of sugar, please."

Jocelyn was standing above us, watching Andria pour. He asked, "Do she and Doig get on? I mean, do they communicate?"

This elicited a subdued explosion, followed by a snort. "Communicate? Communicate? He's been on the phone to her all hours, pestering her about school. Tells her she must concentrate on her art. Tells her to do her art homework."

"Sounds alright to me," observed Jocelyn lamely. "I always did mine."

"Ah," said Laetitia, "alright for you then, wasn't it? Do you by any chance possess an ash tray?"

Jocelyn handed her a glass one. The air was thick with smoke. Laetitia took a sip of her coffee and remarked, "Ah, but there's a little problem, you see."

"So?" said Jocelyn.

"Bella wants to do Chemistry instead. She wants to work in a Chemists."

I found this transition difficult to fathom and felt a need to clarify. "I'm not sure I follow," I said, and then added pedantically, "Chemists don't study Chemistry precisely."

"Well, what's the point of them then?"

"You see, they're not actually Chemists in your sense of the term. They're Pharmacists. They study Pharmacy".

Laetitia took another long draught of her coffee. "Well, whatever. The fact is Bella doesn't want to study art. She's not the artistic type. Closer to the autistic spectrum, if you ask my opinion. They're quite different, you know. My Bella doesn't relish being bullied. She was sick to the gills with his nagging. She wanted her dad to leave, and finally so did I. Bella doesn't want to be an artist. She wants to be Prime Minister. Bella wants to be Mrs Thatcher."

This remark caused general bewilderment, so she

added for our benefit, "Mrs Thatcher studied Chemistry."

Nobody reacted to this well-known fact, so she slowly added, "Mrs Thatcher is the Prime Minister."

*****

At this point, it behoves me to say a little about the way in which Letty is portrayed by Jocelyn in his biography of Doig. I am in quite a decent position to shed light on this matter, seeing as I was present on the very first occasion on which Jocelyn and Letty met. What he says about her in his book is, of course, inevitable coloured by hindsight. He had obviously interviewed both of the principal parties as to the causes of their breakup, and in his account of it he strives valiantly to be fair to be both of them, whilst hiding his own residual, and not insubstantial, animosity towards Doig. But his description of Letty herself also conveys something of his - and maybe our - first impressions when she first entered our lives immediately after her rift with Doig. Here is what Jocelyn has to say about her background:

> Doig was immediately struck by Laetitia Attipoe's appearance. Her father was from Togo (formerly French Togoland) on the coast of West Africa, a former German territory mandated to France by the League of Nations as part of the 1919 post war settlement. By the

1950s it was coming up to Independence. Her father, who was determined to be a chef, had quit his hometown and made a beeline for Paris, then got himself a job in a hotel in central Manchester where he met and married Laetitia's Maltese mother, who was training to be a nurse. They moved to Salford where, two years later, little Laetitia was born.

Jocelyn then forsakes his factual-seeming manner, and drops into journalese:

Laetitia seemed to him to be perfect material for a model. She was stunningly attractive, of exotically mixed birth, and eye-catchingly dressed. She was tall and lissom, and had a face etched with character. She had started studying at a technical college in the city, but her parents were in no position to supplement her grant, so that she was quite short of money and glad of a model's fees. Several portraits resulted, in a manner which Evans was soon to abandon. After their marriage she ceased to sit for him. A daughter, Isabella, was born, but soon afterwards strains began to appear in the relationship. For several years Evans commuted southwards on a weekly basis to teach at the Camberwell School of Art. As his reputation grew on the back of his maturing expressionist style, he spent longer and longer periods away from home, and the fissures in the marriage grew ever wider.

To which I should add that, from the moment she entered our flat in Kensal Rise, there existed between Jocelyn and Letty an undeniable understanding. They were opposites of course, but opposites frequently attract. Jocelyn has always epitomised for me the zenith of aesthetic refinement, and "refined" is not an adjective I would ever apply to Letty. She stood up to him, and she had limited patience with his digressions. He seemed to relish this treatment in an obscure masochistic way. To put it bluntly, he appreciated her cheek. Mostly, though, he enjoyed her ability to see right through Doig, both as artist and as human being. Both these ranges of negative insight were of considerable use to him when he came to write his book.

What is even more significant is that from the off Jocelyn appeared to discern in Laetitia a solution to several interconnected personal problems: the problem of Doig for a start, the problem of me, and, lastly and in his eyes conclusively, the problem of Andria and himself.

On that occasion, Laetitia stayed for three days. After an initial standoff, she seemed to get on well with Andria, largely on the basis of proving to be an excellent confidante on matters maternal, about which she had very decided opinions. As she repeatedly assured us, she knew all about little girls. As soon as she set eyes on Titania, Letty behaved like a person in love, and was immediately promoted to the position of courtesy aunt. While she and Andria were thus engaged one afternoon, Jocelyn and I took the six bus into the West End. It was now three weeks since he had dropped off Claud's bequest at Christie's, and they'd been in correspondence several times since. A difference of opinion had emerged, not helped by the painting's very peculiar provenance. Giles Farnaby, the in-house expert, was used to assessing items originating from great country houses, or at least from established families. He was even used to pronouncing on artefacts that had been auctioned anonymously in the past, or which had arrived on his desk after a complex history across several countries or continents. Lurking under the bed of single room in a rundown boarding house in Kilburn fell into none of these familiar categories, and he wished to know more. Whilst I was abroad, Jocelyn had been unable to quiz me as to whether, from my familiarity with Claud's movements, I was in a position to shed further light on the matter. I could now confidently inform him that I was not.

Negotiations were not assisted by the fact that Jocelyn and Farnaby came from different professional worlds, and regarded one another with a certain degree of mutual suspicion. Jocelyn was an art historian with wide and eclectic interests; he was not, however, a specialist in the Early Italians and was quite conscious of this fact. He nonetheless possessed a seemly pride in his calling and was inclined to regard Farnaby as a grubby-pawed commercial puppet only to be trusted on questions involving the market. Farnaby for his part had started off by deferring to Jocelyn's academic credentials. It soon became obvious to him, however, that when it came to the minutiae of attribution, my friend was lost. It had thus been agreed that Farnaby should consult a man at the Courtauld Institute, then in Woburn Square, and to communicate that personage's more reliable opinion to us at four o' clock this Tuesday afternoon, at which hour we entered Christie's impressive premises in King Street, St James and asked to see him.

Farnaby clattered down the stairs looking brisk and a little disdainful, then asked us into his office, where his manner lightened up. The magus at the Courtauld, it appeared, had been helpful but ultimately undecided. His verdict concerning Claud's painting was, firstly, that it badly needed cleaning. Peering through the murk and varnish, however, he had thought that he could discern a likeness to the handiwork of Ruggiero da Belluno (1321-1388), an obscure artist of the fourteenth century better known as a teacher than as a painter, whose own devotional pictures, however, were not to be despised. Whether this was an authentic, if minor, Belluno, or whether it was merely a product of his workshop or school, he could not tell. However, from the nature of the subject matter, and especially from the expression of voluptuous ecstasy on the face of the central figure - that is of the kneeling friar - the known work to which it bore the closest resemblance was *Saint Bonaventure Worshipping the Unwashed Loincloth of Saint Clare*, last listed in the catalogue of a sale in

Munich in 1924 as a bona fide Belluno, but since lost sight of.

Farnaby stopped speaking and looked at Jocelyn. Then Jocelyn looked at me, and I looked at Farnaby before saying, "Well?" This got Farnaby talking again. On the whole he advised caution, with much wagging of the head. The attribution that he had just adumbrated for us, he went on to declare, was to a large extent uncertain, but was bound to arouse interest. Bearing this in mind, if we wished to put the canvas up for auction with them, he would suggest a reserve of £30,000. If it fetched that price or higher, we would be the fortunate recipients of what in 1986 was a tidy sum. If, on the other hand, the doubts surrounding its attribution led to a lower sequence of bids, we could always buy the thing in, and take it away with us. It was for us to decide.

We begged for time to ponder, took our leave and fell into the Chequers Tavern in Duke Street. It is a long and narrow bar well patronised by businessmen and civil servants from nearby offices, and by staff and readers from the London Library round the corner in St James's Square. By now it was ten past five and fast filling up. Jocelyn ordered, as I tried to find a seat. I failed to do so, so we had to stand. The hubbub was considerable, and we had to shout to be heard. "I suppose we sell, eh?" was my opening gambit. Jocelyn took a swig at his Forster's lager and said, "It's your painting, young Ben."

*****

When we got back to Kensal Rise, Bella was bouncing Titania on one wool-encased knee. She'd arrived without warning an hour previously after taking the bus from St Pancras, where she'd stumbled with far too much luggage from the 5.15 train from Macclesfield. Laetitia immediately introduced us, but there had been no need for me to be told that this was Doig and Letty's ebullient daughter. She had medium-length chestnut hair done up at the back in an elastic-band-secured bun, puffy cheeks and her mother's arched eyebrows and insolent mouth. She wore green tights and louche sandals, currently unlatched. Her turquoise, look-at-me nylon top was embossed with a pattern of open-mouthed kisses, crimson as Laetitia's lip-stick. Manifestly, she intended to stay: wherever else would she go? On the table beside her, BBC Radio 4 was loudly delivering the seven o'clock news. A ferry carrying 600 passengers had capsized in Bangladesh. The Americans had staged another nuclear test in Nevada. In Russia, the population was still attempting to cope with the fall-out from Chernobyl. Bella's very own idol Margaret Thatcher was on a state visit to Israel. "I admire her," cooed our latest guest obediently, and gave my daughter one further bounce. "We really admire her don't we, sweet?" Titania didn't look too sure.

"Well, what did Christie's say then?" inquired Andria from the kitchen, where she was frying what sounded like chops.

"They weren't entirely sure," I said. "It might just be

by an obscure early Italian called Ruggiero da Belluno."

"Balloon-o," Titania echoed delightedly, "Balloon-o."

"So?"

"Reserve price 30,000, they reckon. If we care to sell it, that is."

"Oh sell," went Andria, appearing hands on hips in the connecting doorway. "Just sell."

She was on her way back to the chops, and then re-appeared. "Oh by the way, the landlady from Kilburn called again. You left a letter behind. From Claud, I think. Sell it, Ben, just sell."

*****

The letter arrived in the post the following day. The envelope was crumpled with a second class stamp but no postmark, so he'd obviously drafted the text with the intention of sending it, then changed his mind, but kept it just the same. Inside, the letter was written in his habitual neat copperplate, and dated Thursday, May 23rd of the previous year, so he must have written it a couple of days after the exhibition, then lost his nerve. It said:

Dear Ben,

This is just a note to say how deeply I was touched by the invitation to your show the other evening. I am loath to comment, since I've always regarded myself as an amateur in the true sense, which is as much as to say a true lover of art. Permit me to say at the outset, however, that I am quite sure that you possess a hundred times the natural talent of that other fellow, fuss though they may have made of him. His stuff is not my cup of tea, I fear to say. Nor my mug of cocoa either. Very blinkered of me, I'm sure, but then I was always in the rear guard of fashion, alas. Or maybe not alas.

Naturally I was pleased to see that the organisers had devoted a whole wall to our little folly. I am convinced that it deserves it, though the result is not quite what I expected, or initially had in mind. I also recognise your tribute to our second favourite Dutchman (and, yes, I am sticking to De Hooch, whatever you and the *soi-disant* experts say). To be frank, though, you made the young lady look ordinary. Of course, I preferred her reading to her hoovering - as an old bachelor I suppose I would - but to me she didn't look exactly exalted in either posture. I don't necessarily intend this as a criticism: you obviously wished her to look real, in circumstances and a setting that were equally real, or should we call them "realistic"? Forgive the inverted commas, but I never did attend a course in what they call "art appreciation". Which may mean that I am an uneducated clot, or may also mean that I have preserved my tastes and convictions intact.

The question, I suppose, remains as to the true meaning of the "real". Is ordinary the same as real? I can recognise the skill and honesty of your handiwork, while being true to my opinion, maybe my illusion, that my Christina - call it my vision of Christina - is the true and only one. I shall retain that vision, or that prejudice, until I die, which may not be all that long now. I need to die happy, swathed in my dreams. They are mostly what have sustained me throughout my solitary, but not unsatisfactory existence. Perhaps you will come round to my view, some day or other.

These are the ramblings of an elderly man, but they are genuine and they are sincere. I am not a trained philosopher, and my inclinations must appear to you to be naïve. I remain, however, under all conditions, and through all the chances and changes of this weary life,

Your affectionate uncle, Claud.

I had got up late that morning and devoured this tardy missive whilst dawdling over breakfast. There seemed to be no requirement of confidentially, so my first thought was that I should show it to Andria. But she was out already, doing some research in the Senate House library. So I showed it to Laetitia instead, curious as to what her reaction might be. Laetitia read it with painful slowness while munching on her cornflakes, sniffed, and then remarked, "Poor sod. No wonder he never married." Then she handed it to Bella who read it much more quickly between mouthfuls of Marmite-smothered toast. Bella handed it back to me with a terse, "Well, it stands out a mile, doesn't it? Your uncle was really gay." That epithet was not, as I recall, part of my personal vocabulary at that period, but the recent AIDS epidemic had brought it into currency, and it was already part of Bella's. I had no firm objection to her opinion, either now or then, much as I think it wrong (and much as I objected to – and still very much object to – Bella's partiality for Marmite). When Andria got home, we showed the letter to her. Her response was that it was all "unutterably sad". I did not entirely agree with her on this point. And in recollection, I am still forced to disagree with Andria's diagnosis of my late uncle's state of mind. If Claud was ever sad, then that sadness was part of a much larger picture.

*****

This partiality of Bella's for Marmite was to become something of a source of contention with several of us, both then and more recently. At one time I fancied she might be suffering from some sort of eating disorder – a disorder that I went as far as labelling "Marmitis" – until, that is, Andria disabused me of this suspicion by telling me that she knew a thing or two about eating disorders, having been mildly anorexic in her teens, and that Bella's strange and childlike partiality for this noxious nursery food was nothing more than a protest against growing up launched by a hypersensitive, abrupt, but otherwise healthy adolescent girl. My disapproval, she went on to imply, demonstrated nothing more than my fundamental ignorance of average female metabolism. Even so, I spared no effort thereafter to diversify Bella's diet. I had very little effect. Even while studying for her part-time B.Pharm at King's, which required a demanding bus journey to the Strand and back every day, she insisted that every morning her mother pack her Marmite sandwiches for lunch, painstakingly cutting and spreading them before wrapping them in silver foil and placing them in a name-tagged Tupperware container. In the face of my continuing disapprobation, I must say that Laetitia exercised a commendable amount of tolerance over this. Titania, I gather, despite being a lot more adventurous in her own culinary propensities, has been every bit as understanding in this respect.

Not so Doig. When, a few days after myself, he arrived back from Amsterdam, we were inundated with telephone calls for several days, calls in which he demanded to speak to his daughter. At first Bella would not be drawn, taking umbrage in the loo. Then bit by bit she was coaxed out as far as standing by the phone receiving messages that were conveyed to her through a mediator, that is through Jocelyn or myself. At length a compromise was reached. She was, she declared, ready to meet her father provided that it was in the presence of someone else, more precisely of one of us. Whereupon Doig proposed a pub, but of course Bella was only sixteen. Then he suggested a hotel like the Dorchester, where he would pay for lunch (the proceeds of those lucrative sales were still rolling in). Naturally, Bella found everything about this arrangement far too intimidating, including, predictably, the menu. It was Andria who made the breakthrough. She had read in the *Sunday Times* that, in the face of middle-aged public demand, a retro branch of the once popular Lyons' Corner House had opened on a corner of the Strand close to Trafalgar Square. It was on a convenient bus route – the trusty six again - advertised itself with photos of cute waitresses who wore black uniforms, white aprons and cute-looking caps, was altogether very unthreatening, and served a cream tea every afternoon from three. This tea included sandwiches, one or two of which, as a brief phone call confirmed, might be prepared with a thin layer of Marmite. I would go along and hold my nose whilst Doig interviewed, browbeat, and probably cross-examined Bella.

We set out one afternoon in June in the middle of a summer thunder-storm. Bella was wearing a green anorak, and I was wearing my usual trench coat. It was about ten past four when we arrived, after sloshing through muddy water in the gutter at the corner of Northumberland Avenue. When we entered the tearoom, Doig was sitting in a corner reading the *Burlington Magazine.* There were two plastic carrier bags by his seat. He had saved us two chairs. He ordered two cream teas to be shared between us. Bella refused the tea, so Doig opened the conversation by inquiring with laboured curiosity, "Darling, what do you drink nowadays?"

"Nothing."

"Nothing? You used to like Tizer."

"Tizer!" Bella's eyes enlarged, and an expression of mixed disgust and contempt convulsed her face.

"Oh gosh. Then Lucozade, Mmm? You always enjoyed a glass of Lucozade."

Bella mimicked being sick and said, "Yuck!"

At this point I saw fit to intervene. "She drinks Coca

Cola, sir. She drinks Coke."

"Well, then…" Doig fished out of the first carrier bag a white cardboard box. At the front of it was a clear cellophane window through which four slender, tapered glasses could be descried with the words *Wynand Fockink* inscribed around each in antique, curvaceous lettering.

"What are those?" asked Bella apprehensively.

"A set of drinking glasses, my dear."

"I can see that. But what are they for?"

Doig looked a bit nonplussed at this inquiry. "For drinking out of, Mmm?"

Bella was now looking across to me with an air of complicitous pity. I chipped in with, "I'm not sure you could get a lot of Coke into one of those, sir." At which Bella started to laugh.

I thought it might be a shrewd idea to change the subject, so asked, "How was the Hermitage, sir?"

"Oh, hospitable, sycophantic, full of arts journalists." Doig wrinkled his nose and turned his attention once more relentlessly towards his daughter, who was looking more and more as if she wanted to flee. "Done much painting recently, dear?"

Bella was inspecting the tablecloth. "No, Dad. I don't *do* painting."

Doig looked at a loss. And then he looked rather sad. Defeated, almost. He tried again. "Well then, drawing. You used to be pretty keen on that."

"No, Dad. I don't study art anymore. What's the whole point of it all anyway? It doesn't cure. Artists just think

404

about themselves."

Doig had now unpacked the box of matching glasses. He detached one of the four and showed it to his daughter, amorously fingering its elegant waist-line. Then he handed it across to her. "Isn't that pretty?" he asked.

Bella looked doubtful. She inspected the glass ruefully, murmuring, "Suppose."

Doig thought he'd try another tack. He asked with affected brightness, "Do you remember, when you were a little girl, I used to tell you stories?"

Bella nodded perfunctorily. There was a far-away look in her eyes. Then she puckered her brow. She turned the glass round and round, held it up to the light, then held its upper rim against her right eye, surveying a family of customers at the neighbouring table through the refraction of its concave lip. She wrinkled her brow again and murmured, "Yes?" more in interrogation than in agreement.

"Well," suggested Doig, a little desperately, "stories cure people sometimes. A lot of paintings tell stories."

"Mum told me stories too," said Bella grimly. "Hers were a lot better."

There was a longish pause, during which Bella reached out and took a sandwich from the cake stand. She opened it and inspected the filling, which was of honey roast ham. She put the sandwich back.

"When are you going back home?" her father asked her.

"Oh," Bella said. "I'm not sure we're going back

there." She selected a different sandwich.

At which, Doig stopped trying. He reached for his other carrier bag and lifted out a taller box which opened to reveal a stout bottle of *Oude Jenever*. He turned to me. "Something for you, dear boy. Ever heard of a gin tea?" He unscrewed the top and poured generous slugs of spirit into two *Lyons' Corner House* teacups as Bella regarded him with ill-disguised disdain. Out of the corner of my eye, I noticed the approach of waitress with black uniform, starched apron and regulation peaked cap.

*****

Unsurprisingly Bella was rather stirred up by this interview, so afterwards I steered her across a drizzly Trafalgar Square and towards the Gallery, which she was reluctant to enter at first. But there was about an hour to go before closing, so I eventually persuaded her through the double doors at the head of the inner staircase, and past the Italian Primitives. The summer tourist season was getting under way, and many of the rooms were more than a little crowded. For perhaps twenty minutes we walked up and down past the milling multitudes, with Bella largely staring at the door. When she stopped and I with her, I noticed we were opposite Rubens's *The Judgement of Paris.*

Bella's initial comment was that the three goddesses were "gross". Then she said that they were "obnoxious". Then she sat down. After which I too sat down and took her hand. "Your dad's got a point, you know," I said, gallantly taking Doig's part.

"I hate him. Mum hates him."

"I know you both hate him. But he's still got a point."

"So paintings tell stories? Ones that are good for us?"

"Potentially, yes. What does *this* painting show us?"

"Three fat ladies, and a man with beady eyes. Oh yes, and a chap holding an apple."

"What's the man with the beady eyes doing?"

"Leering at the ladies."

"Why?"

"Men do that. They do it on the bus. All the time."

"Does that worry you?"

"Not especially, but I think its's rather sad."

"Perhaps this man is sad."

"He looks really pleased with himself to me."

"Apparently, he's trying to choose between the ladies."

"I don't think so. Maybe..." She paused for a moment. "Maybe they are choosing him. Or not."

So I told her all about Paris and the three goddesses. Told her that Pallas Athene meant wisdom and knowledge, that Juno meant a certain regal quality and an albeit difficult wifedom, that Aphrodite meant the allurements of desire. Told her about his going off with Aphrodite who was standing in the middle, and then about the Trojan war.

At the end she said, "Serve him right. Perhaps he should have chosen one of the other two." Then she bucked up, reached out, and clasped my other hand between hers and said quite simply, "You're ever such a sweet man. Why don't you marry my mum?"

*****

I did, as it happens. But that was a couple of years afterwards, following Doig's and Laetitia's divorce. And thirty years or so before Doig died of an aneurism in Aberdeen.

I had long since twigged as to another reality I should have recognised for ages. When in that smoky bar in Amsterdam Doig had spoken maliciously about the hypocritical liaison between Christina and my friend-cum-foe Father Jake O' Rourke, he had delivered nothing more or less than the truth. Jake had evidently broken down Christina Echardt's defences one more, and as it happens, conclusive, time. Manifestly (should I not have known all along?) the new Jake in this respect was very like the old Jake, though his technique may have been different. Bearing in mind my conversation with Bella in the Gallery, however, perhaps the syntax of these revelations should run the other way round. Should I not have said that, after some hesitant meditation upon my un-Doig-like characteristics, my tender care and sorely tried toleration of her daughter, Laetitia came round to the idea of marrying me? Should I not also have stated that, in emphatic if deferred appreciation of his morally duplicitous charms, Christina ultimately came round the idea of devoting her life to Jake? Maybe I should also add, of moving with him to a three-bedroom flat in Tite Street, Chelsea?

All of these developments feature in the concluding chapter of Jocelyn's biography of Doig, but obliquely so, and principally as a backdrop to his subject's last, pessimistic phase, his so-called "Brown Period", his decline, descent, and abrupt decease.

In that account, I myself feature but tangentially. All I am trying to do here is to fill out the events for the sake my godson Claud, who has expressed a certain amount of courteous, and possibly insincere, interest in the elusive personality of his near-namesake. My uncle, naturally, does not feature in this account at all. For obvious reasons, Jocelyn devotes far more attention to his own marriage to Andria and adoption of his step-daughter Titania, two occurrences the near inevitability of which was another factor I should have faced up to for some time. In the acknowledgements section of his book, I am glad to say, Jocelyn does thank me for my help, and for the many conversations with me he recorded (the recordings are now held in the British Library Sound Archive). He also mentions Christina's contribution towards the project, though in the text I notice he draws on her recollections with well-judged caution, selectivity and tact. He ends the acknowledgements with a grateful nod towards Titania's services as a typist, and her half-brother Claud's much-needed advice on the occasions of which their computer played tricks, as computers are wont to do.

About one fact alone do I beg to demure. In an

indulgent parenthesis to the penultimate sentence to this section Jocelyn insists that Titania's half-brother owes his Christian name principally to his father's long-standing admiration for the mythological paintings of Claude Lorrain, on whose *Seaport With The Embarkation of Saint Ursula* the author had published a number of academic papers. But Jocelyn is far from the only man who has revered that picture. Only I perhaps know, and Claud the Younger himself certainly suspects, that the pillow talk in the matrimonial bedroom had for some time featured Andria's speculations over the peculiar relationship I struck up once-upon-a-time with my bachelor uncle, his quaint obsession with the woman who is now Jake's wife, and the bizarre commission which set off some of the above events. Perhaps Jocelyn has buried that auditory debt, and naturally prefers his own explanation.

Persuaded by Christina, Jake has long ago quit the priesthood and made something of a name for himself as a freelance expert on spirituality, latterly and infamously in the media. Jocelyn and I are more than a little sceptical about this area of interest, over which Christina herself has latterly demonstrated a marked enthusiasm. In an unguarded moment Jocelyn once remarked to me that when a man starts using terms like Spirituality, it is a sure sign that he has gone to the bad, and that when a woman starts using it, it normally means she is having an adulterous affair (though I cannot vouch for the relevance of the latter cynical observation in Christina's case). Jocelyn dropped this bombshell after we had watched together an especially nauseating episode of Jake's TV series *Faith and Paint*. With an unfortunate effect on Jake's burgeoning professional ego, this series was widely broadcast on both sides of the Atlantic and led to a sequel entitled *The Shock of the Nous,* in which, displaying to some advantage both his widening religious affinities and his sun-tanned complexion, Jake is shewn disporting himself in locations as remote and exotic as Istanbul and Jaipur. (To be fair to him, during an episode about William Morris, he appears in Oxford in the rain.) Wherever he is, though, and however hot it is, Jake is shown wearing his trademark black frockcoat, matching black silk trousers and high leather boots. He wears his greying locks very long and looks like a cross between Franz Liszt and Svengali.

He now exists in a glittering social zone more or less beyond my reach, though I am pleased to record that he has not quite dropped me. We receive an annual Christmas card signed by both of them (most of these, in what must be a nod to Christina and my mutual past, bear the unmistakeable imprint of the Foot and Mouth Painting Society). I got a birthday card for my sixtieth, and once, when he was filming a profile of *Stanley Spencer and the Realm of the Spirit* at the Tate Britain, there was even an invitation to join him off set for a late afternoon drink at the Morpeth Arms down the road in Pimlico. He arrived in full filming gear, black frock coat and all, and talked a lot about Spenser and Sex before asking me how we both were. Bella had just won the

Pharmacist of the Year Award, so I was able to boast about that before he suddenly broke in with, "Of course, you know this neighbourhood well."

Dolphin Square lies just along Millbank from the pub, so of course I said, "Yes, I do."

There was a meaningful silence, and then he said, "You never really understood Christina, did you?"

"Well, I painted her alright."

"True, and her dad bought the result. We've got it hanging in the hallway at Tite Street. I think Christina's fond of it, and maybe of you too. Actually at the moment she's re-reading *The Sea, The Sea*. Bit long-winded, she says. But it's full of reaching out towards the Ineffable…"

Ineffable was one of the buzz words from his latest series. We'd had *Titian and the Ineffable*, largely filmed at the Prado, and *Tiepolo and the Ineffable*, featuring sublime ceilings in Venice and Milan. *Spenser and the Ineffable* would surely have to be shot at Bookham in Surrey, a bit humble for Jake.

"What didn't I understand?"

"Her ordinariness, her sublimity. Which are largely the same thing."

"Mystic Insight?" This was another term culled from a recent series of his (the last but one, on *The Pinnacle of the Soul*).

"I think you will find," he said, with a telegenic sweep of his locks, "that all along you were painting the inside of your own mind."

"I was required to paint an ideal. I did not think that

Christina was ideal. Nor do I. Do you?"

"The trouble with you, Ben," he said, putting down his glass, "is that you think the real and the ideal are different things. They are not."

"The trouble about you, Jake," I should have said but did not, "Is that you've traded on the ideal, turning it into real estate." I just stopped myself in time.

After Jake left to continue with his busy social life (he and Christina were entertaining Lord and Lady Melvyn Bragg to dinner that evening) I ordered myself another drink and retired to an upstairs bar. Nowadays, this semi-private space is known as the Spying Room, because it has a direct view across the river towards MI6, but it is also furnished with a few mirrors, so it is quite a good location in which to spy upon oneself. My no-doubt inebriated cogitations were as follows. My uncle Claud had thought that Perfection existed; therefore, that Christina (or rather his vision of Christina) existed even though, as I was well aware, this person (or this version of this person) did not. So I had painted two faces of the real Christina instead, disappointed Claud (whom from now on, to distinguish him from Andria and Jocelyn's son, I must call Claud the Elder), but kept faith with myself.

The Jake I had known as a very young man had poured scorn on Perfection and had set out to destroy it. In the process, he rapidly discovered, he was destroying himself. He then had a convulsive change of heart, re-invented Perfection, and called it God. (This was the stage at which, in that pseudo-baroque church off

Kingsway, he had defended for my sake the Ontological Proof.) But then the real Christina reappeared in his life and got in the way. So he ditched God and married Christina, and both of them re-located the perfect ideal, which he re-labelled The Spirit and put on the telly. A very shrewd move, as Jocelyn would doubtless have said.

As for myself, I had long lost sight of Perfection, whether in the alert and intelligent shape of Andria, or in the seductively erotic form I had intermittently glimpsed in Christina. I had placed my bet and, once Doig had got rid of her, had opted for a headstrong, bossy, at times crochety, but decidedly sexy and, as I was fast discovering, loving shrew. Faced with the Goddesses of wisdom and ecstasy, I had rejected, or been rejected by both, and cast my lot with the troublesome and earthy Juno, who possessed the indubitable advantage, in my opinion – though not in Claud's or Jake's senses - of being thoroughly and reassuringly real. That evening, as the Morpeth Arms filled up with early evening drinkers, I went home to her, glad of my choice.

*****

Home, I should clarify, is Camberwell. Once it was clear that Andria and Jocelyn would marry, he moved properly into our flat, and I moved into his: lock, stock, Laetitia, Bella and all. When the money from the sale of the Belluno Veneration came through (exceeding

Farnaby's expectations, it fetched £53,000), I was able to purchase the lease, and later to extend it. We have lived here ever since.

Andria and Jocelyn, incidentally, honeymooned on the island of Andros, of which she knew from an early comedy by Terence and he from a painting by Titian, now in the Prado, in which the Andrians are depicted as everlastingly sozzled on wine, freely flowing from every inland stream. (The island, I gather, proved something of a disappointment in this respect.) It was quite some time before I was free to wed Laetitia but, once her divorce came through, we tied the knot at Camberwell Registry Office with Jocelyn as best man, with Bella as a rather butch bridesmaid, and Jake and Christina as honoured guests. We took our honeymoon on the honeyed isle of Malta, where my new wife still has family in Villeta.

The flat in Kensal Rise is still painted grey. Indeed, it has been re-done in ever paler shades each five years or so. Once Titania came into her inheritance from her paternal grandfather, she was able to loan Jocelyn and Andria a lump sum towards its purchase and, what with Jocelyn's pension and Andria's part-time teaching, they seem to live quite comfortably, thank you. Our walls, in stark contrast, are no longer grey, since Laetitia insists on Sunflower Yellow. Above the mantelpiece hangs a copy of the Belluno Veneration (the Hammershois have all been shifted to Kensal Rise, where they appear very much to advantage). Our Belluno is a fake, of course, a botched pastiche by some early twentieth-century fraudster, though neither Laetitia nor I can tell the difference (even if Jocelyn on his occasional visits makes a point of visibly wincing). With less discerning guests, we pretend that it is the original (now in a private collection in Derby) and spin extravagant fables linking my late uncle with espionage rings in Eastern Europe and drug cartels in Bogota. Nothing that we fabricate in our wildest dreams comes anywhere near the sheer strangeness of the truth.

Perhaps the only person who appreciates the resonance of several of these events is Jocelyn and Andria's son. I am not sure whose idea it was to make me his godparent. Perhaps it was Jocelyn's idea. There has never been much tension between us and, despite his stepping into my shoes with respect to Andria, I am happy to say I have always rather liked the guy, and he has always looked with a kindly eye on the affairs of a former pupil who in certain respects must appear something of a disappointment. Or perhaps Andria suggested it, since we remain on affectionate, if occasionally exasperated, terms. Claud's godmother, incidentally, is Christina. I am not sure how seriously she takes her duties, but there are lots of reasons why I should undertake mine with slightly more than the customary sense of responsibility. First, Claud is Titania's brother. Secondly, he is the child of two of my oldest friends. These factors in themselves would have secured my interest in the boy. They were given a decisive boost, however, when Claud's termly reports from the Manor School began to comment favourably on his aptitude for art, and more especially for representational painting. He has done facial portraits of both of his parents and his sister (the results hang in their hallway). When he painted my likeness (the effect, I fear, was far from flattering), I rewarded him with a full set of Windsor and Newton oil paints encased in a bamboo box. It was the least I could do. But I also thought that we should keep in touch personally, so every few months we arrange to meet in the National Gallery in Trafalgar Square, and each time we select one picture we would like to concentrate on. It is a quaint and perhaps silly custom, but it gives me considerable satisfaction, and it does not seem to irritate him too much (or, if it does, he is much too polite to say so). On the first occasion, we arranged to meet in front of Hobbema's *The Avenue, Middelharnis* (now hanging in the Saintsbury Wing) which I have known for a long time, and which was familiar to him from its many reproductions (I'd even given him a jigsaw puzzle that featured it one Christmas). But then we did the rounds: Botticelli's *Adoration of the Kings,* Canaletto's *The Feast Day of Saint Roch,* Tiepolo's *The Banquet of Cleopatra,* Velázquez's *The Toilet of Venus,* Titian's *Bacchus and Ariadne.*

This rewarding ritual has kept us going for some years now. Whatever the painting, however, the protocol is the same. As soon as we meet in front of the elected canvas, I insist on absolute silence, for at least ten minutes. Initially I had the feeling that young Claud found this enforced requirement something of a strain. On the first two or three occasions he kept on looking at his wristwatch, and during the next few of these vigils he was prone to interrupt, which I found pretty annoying. Interrupting someone who is speaking can be frankly intolerable, but interrupting someone who is not speaking is sometimes far, far, worse. But then, slowly, he began to assimilate the point.

So, what was – what is – the point? In my mind, I was trying to provide my godson with something that nobody else would give him. At home, of course, Jocelyn in full chatterbox mode would fill him in on the background to these various works of European art. Well, Jocelyn is an art historian, and has written several very good books, his biography of Doig among them. If, seeking for an alternative, Claud was unwise or vulgar enough to tune in to one of Jake's television programmes, then he would see a narcissistic individual in cute leather boots preening himself in front of a painting kept in some distant gallery which could only be reached by air, with all expenses paid and a decent fee for himself and a camera crew he is pretending is not there.

Jocelyn, you see, knows *about* art, and Jake knows – or thinks he knows – about the *significance* of art. I know about neither of these things. As far as I am concerned, the only way to approach one of these masterpieces is to lose yourself in it. The losing of the self is part of the point, and the fittest tribute, therefor, is silence. You can always talk afterwards, and usually we do. In the meantime, you are privy to something akin to contemplation, a variety of personal renunciation which redeems the rest of life. Nowadays I attend church less and less often, so I am forced to search for substitutes. If, in my capacity as godparent, I have failed to introduce young Claud to God, I reassure myself with the thought that at least I have introduced him to Titian. For my own part, I have come believe that these sessions in the gallery are the closest I will ever get the Divine. If that is true, then I am lot closer to Jake than I like to think.

I am not quite sure how young Claud regards his ageing godfather. Probably as a harmless eccentric, an elderly relative who has to be humoured for the sake of family peace. Once or twice, when turning away from the picture chosen for the occasion, I fancy I have caught on his face a look of mild embarrassment. If so, I do not mind. Maybe, in times to come, he will recall these meetings with fondness, gratitude and, one hopes, with forgiveness. If so, it is something else I will have handed down.

As for myself, life treats me well. To my surprise, I found after a while that I rather enjoyed living with two bossy women. A possible explanation for this may be found in a theory I sometimes air in company that members of my family are irresistibly drawn towards strength. I have been giving a lot more thought to this idea recently, even more so since, after a lengthy period of co-habitation and a welcome change in the law, Titania married Bella. They got hitched in the splendid surroundings of Hampton Court Palace, now licensed for weddings, and afterwards Young Claud, who was

Best Man, made an impressive and insolent speech in which he compared the newlyweds to Botticelli's *Venus and Mars*. After the reception, Laetitia and I walked the length of the Privy Garden, restored since the fire of April, 1986 to its seventeenth-century Dutch symmetries, just as William III would have known them. Past the ornamental statues we went, past Ceres and Bacchus, past Vulcan, past Apollo and Marsyas, past Apollo gazing at the Sun. As we approached the double Tijou screens that divide the garden from the river, we too gazed up at the western sky, savouring the dying embers of the day, the scents of evening, the ever-changing, ever-melting quality of the light.

A NOTE ON THE PAINTINGS

The Midwife Taking Leave of the Girl from Andros is the first of four scenes from Terence's comedy *Andria* depicted by the Danish artist Nicolai Abildgaard (1743-1809). It is held in the Statens Museum for Kunst in Copenhagen and was on loan to the National Gallery in London for "Danish Painting: The Golden Age", the inaugural exhibition in the Gallery's new Sunley Room, from September 5 to November 20, 1984.

Christina of Denmark, Duchess of Milan, 1538 by Hans Holbein the Younger (1497/8-1543), *The Avenue at Middelharnis*, 1689 by Meindert Hobbema (1638-1709), *Belshazzar's Feast* (circa 1636-8) by Rembrandt (1606-1669), and *The Judgement of Paris*, probably 1632-500 by Peter Paul Rubens (1577-1640) are all © The National Gallery, London. All four are in the National Gallery's permanent collections, though now hanging in different positions or rooms from those they occupied at the period when the novel is set.

The interiors of the Dutch artist Pieter Jansenns Elinga (1623–1682) were until comparatively recently misattributed to his mentor Pieter de Hooch (1629-1684). His *Interior with Painter, Woman Reading, and Maid Sweeping*, reproduced on the cover, is held in the Städelelsches Kunsinstitut und Städische Galerie in

Frankfurt.

The work of Vilhelm Hammershøi (1883-1916) was, at the period this novel is set, comparatively neglected. He was the subject of the solo exhibition "Vilhelm Hammershøi: The Poetry of Silence" at the Royal Academy of Arts in London from June 28 to September 7, 2008, the catalogue for which, entitled Hammershøi, was co-authored by Felix Krämer, Naoki Sato and Anne-Birgitte Fonsmark (ISBN 978-1-905711-19-1). Hammershøi was a great admirer of Elinga.

These are historical artists. Other characters in this novel are purely imaginary, and any resemblance to persons living or dead is purely coincidental.

BV - #0084 - 240521 - C5 - 197/132/24 - PB - 9781912964758 - Matt Lamination